# Memories of an Ash Covered Sky

# Memories of an Ash Covered Sky

Fire Destroys Everything—Except the Past

Mike Walters

Self Reliant Press, LLC

Copyright © 2025 by Mike Walters

All Rights Reserved

Book Design by Mike Walters and 100 Covers

www.MikeWaltersNovels.com

This book is dedicated to
my mom, and to every mother and father
with the strength to open their arms
when their children return home.

# Author's Note

While inspired in part by real places and events, *Memories of an Ash Covered Sky* is a work of fiction. All characters, dialogue, and narrative elements are products of the author's imagination. Any resemblance to actual persons, living or deceased, is purely coincidental.

I've taken creative liberties with various aspects of law enforcement, aerial and ground-based firefighting, and local government response. Though I conducted extensive research and consulted with professionals in the region, my goal was never strict factual accuracy. This story is grounded in emotional truth, character depth, and narrative flow—not procedural precision.

Out of deep respect for the real men and women who serve our communities with bravery and integrity, I chose to change the names of all fire districts, police departments, and public agencies referenced in the novel. If any detail in the story diverges from real-life operations or protocol, it is entirely the product of fiction—not a reflection of the incredible work performed by first responders in Southern Oregon and beyond.

The work these men and women did during the Almeda Fire was beyond reproach. Their courage, coordination, and tireless commitment in the face of overwhelming devastation saved lives and gave hope when it was needed most.

To the firefighters, law enforcement officers, and emergency personnel who put their lives on the line every day—thank you. Your service, dedication, and sacrifice are appreciated more than you can imagine.

—Mike Walters

"Family should be the place where you can be your most complete self. Where you're accepted and appreciated, seen and valued, even in moments of disagreement."
— Oprah Winfrey

# Thoughts

Fire reflects the quiet devastation that can fester within families, often unnoticed until it's too late. The unraveling begins with small sparks of resentment—misunderstandings, unspoken words, unmet expectations—that gradually grow and spread.

Just as flames strip the land bare, a lack of empathy erodes the core of family life. Warmth fades into cold indifference, turning loved ones into strangers. Trust becomes fragile, vulnerable to the smallest spark—a lie, betrayal, or broken promise—and suddenly, everything ignites.

Flames consume everything in their path, much like the absence of communication can hollow out a family. Strong connections fade into shallow interactions, leaving delicate fragments of healthy connectivity. Land will heal in time, but the wounds of fractured relationships can linger, if unaddressed, forever.

Destruction isn't just about losing possessions; it's about losing connection. Lack of communication exposes the slow erosion of relationships—falling apart not in one sudden blaze, but over years of neglect and silence, fueling the destruction of families.

In the deepest canyons of estrangement and destruction, a path home still exists. The clouds of anger and disappointment may obscure a parent's love—like dense fog in the night—but that love is never extinguished. Healing requires courage, vulnerability, and a shared willingness to mend the broken threads of the past. For a child, the journey back begins with an unwavering belief that they are welcome—that the door will always remain open.

Memories of An Ash Covered Sky

# Newfound Clarity

Sky Wilson trudged down an endless, urine-soaked street in Fog City, her senses dulled to the stench of concrete, waste, and rot. She didn't notice it anymore—not most days. But sometimes, her nose would wake up and slap her with the full weight of the filth she lived in.

She scanned the street, unsure where she'd crash tonight. Her eyes caught a ragged sign taped to a door beneath a flickering light. The door hung open, revealing a dreary staircase.

**There's Hope For the Planet,** the sign read, with smaller print below: **Masks encouraged.**

Sky let out a dry laugh. Hope? For this place?

She reached into her back pocket, pulled out a tattered photograph, and stared at it for a moment before shoving it back into her filthy jeans.

Twenty-five months and nineteen days on the street had made certain habits hardwired—scanning for threats, exits, opportunities.

Water dripped from the staircase above, the railing rusted and corroded by years of salty Pacific air.

A low hum floated from below.

She eyed the stairs. Maybe there was a corner she could hide in for the night—maybe longer if luck smiled on her. Luck. A cruel word. A liar.

She pulled her oily auburn hair into her collar, zipped her tattered black Patagonia jacket, and wiped the grime from her face with a rough hand. The jacket was a godsend—a gift from an aunt who'd found a better life in Sweden. Sky often thought about leaving too, but fear—and something like hope—kept her tethered. The staircase creaked beneath her boots as she

1

descended. At the bottom, a folding table sat against the wall. A box of blue surgical masks rested beside a crusted bottle of sanitizer.

She tugged out a foul-smelling handkerchief from under her shirt, sniffed, grimaced, and tossed it aside in favor of a clean mask. She rubbed sanitizer over her hands, then over her face, chasing dirt she could never quite scrub away.

"I thought the pandemic was over," she muttered.

A clipboard waited. She grabbed the pen.

**Name:** Sky Wilson

**Address:** The Streets

**Phone:** No Thanks

**Email:** AreYouFuckingJoking@Nowhere.com

Irritated, she dropped the pen. It hit the table with a dull thud. Eyes turned. She shrank, willing herself invisible. A beat. Then another. The stares faded.

Sky slipped into the last row, a creaky chair giving way beneath her. She counted the people in the room—twenty-one. She always counted. At eleven, her favorite number, she paused. A woman sat there, tired but alive. Sky wondered what her story was.

A tall man at the front gripped a battered podium, knuckles white, voice unsteady. The scruff on his face didn't match the uneven fire in his words.

Sky's old drama teacher would've torn him apart for faking it.

Her body ached. She shifted, trying to focus.

"Humans are the problem," he said. "The planet is at stake. The planet wants to eradicate us."

Sky smirked. "Eradicate us? What a dick."

She wasn't done with this planet. Not yet. She wanted more. A partner. A tiny home. A dog—maybe a cat. A kitchen where she could learn to bake sourdough. Quiet weekends by a lake.

The planet didn't need saving—it adapted, rolled with the punches, threw a few of its own, then went about its business, indifferent to the humans roaming its surface. People scrambled, tripped over themselves, clung to life, and tried to figure out how to do better next time..

His words kept coming, but she tuned them out. She felt the ocean chill creep in, rubbed her arms, squeezed her legs for warmth. Summer, but it didn't matter. *How in the hell can I feel cold in summer?*

She glanced around. Some in the room looked like her—lost, maybe homeless. She envied the speaker's conviction, even if it was bullshit. At least he seemed to believe in something.

She closed her eyes. No images, no escape. She struggled to dream at all anymore.

Blinking hard, she pulled the photograph again. Unfolded it. The crease cut between bodies—a sharp, painful line of separation.

She stared.

The distance between them felt like an ocean.

With sudden clarity, she knew—she wanted to close that distance.

Was she ready?

She didn't know.

Despite what she did.

Despite what she let happen.

She wanted to go home.

# Life-Altering Event

Pushing north over Talent, Oregon, southeast winds swept across the Siskiyou mountain range at twenty to twenty-five miles per hour. The small southwestern town rested under a dark star-filled sky, unaware that today would bring more than oppressive hot arid weather.

Murphy Wilson, chief of Talent-Phoenix Fire District, serving the communities of Ashland, Talent, and Phoenix, struggled with another sleepless night. His dry, burning eyes squinted at the Scrabble board on his phone. He fumbled through his pack for his reading glasses, finding only pens, business cards, charging cords, loose change, and what appeared to be granola crumbs.

After several minutes of frustration, he wiped the sweat from his brow and accidentally knocked something from his head. It clattered to the floor, sliding under his cot.

He chuckled when he realized—they were his glasses. Fishing them out, he brushed off a dust bunny.

Pleased they were intact, he popped his neck to relieve tension, wiped the lenses with his t-shirt, and rested the reading frames on his ears.

Staring back at his phone the word *Javelin* came to mind, bringing a surge of satisfaction. He dragged the tiles into place on the phone's screen, scoring eighty-three points. Satisfied with the win, he turned off the phone and stepped onto the fire station's rear patio.

Warm summer air greeted him as he debated whether to grab an acid reflux tablet or ignore the discomfort. He stared at the moon, then turned his gaze eastward toward Grizzly Peak. The mountain, named after Old Reelfoot, the last known grizzly bear in southern Oregon, loomed under the moonlight. Wilson thought of the dry conditions, recalling one of his favorite sounds; the crunch of twigs, leaves, and pine needles under his fast-rolling bicycle tires.

Smoke from Pacific Northwest fires blanketed the surrounding mountains, creating an eerie haze. Overnight, the wind shifted, bringing low air quality back into the valley. The moon, undeterred, tried to pierce through the smoky night and offer a flicker of comfort.

Rubbing his eyes, Wilson muttered, "I should've been a meteorologist." He returned inside to his cot; certain the sleeping condition shortened his life with every restless night.

Fire chiefs rarely sleep at the station—that's for the "sleepers," the ones who stay overnight. But Wilson, married to the job, kept a cot in his office and used it now and then. He wasn't sure if the sacrifice was worth it. His health was slipping, and the lack of real sleep was catching up with him.

When his girlfriend was away for work or visiting family, he preferred the station's noise and activity over an empty house filled with sad memories.

Mumbling about the need to exercise and eat better, he slipped off his black Crocs and aligned them under the bed, ensuring the position wouldn't slow him down in an emergency. Sinking onto the edge of the squeaky cot, he rested his head in his hands and forced deep breaths, grateful the Rogue Valley remained fire-free this season. Exhausted, Wilson made a firm decision about his future.

He thought of his home, a peaceful retreat nestled in the Siskiyou foothills near Talent, Oregon. Memories of playing in the fields and hiding in the barn flooded his mind. At fifty-three, he longed for the worry-free days of childhood. Retirement beckoned, but he considered if the timing ever felt right. Thirty-two years as a firefighter was enough. Right?

Chief Wilson shifted his thoughts to his unfinished Mercedes Sprinter van parked in the barn. He dreamt of completing the interior retrofit, loading his gravel bike and fishing gear, and escaping. The chief wondered if his partner, Sandi, would join him—likely with the condition of staying in a nearby hotel.

The relentless pressures of life pushed him toward change. The fear of a heart attack—like the one that claimed his father too soon—loomed over him. Thoughts of family led him to his estranged daughter. Where was she? Did she resent him? Hate him? He shuddered at the thought—if she was even alive.

He longed for reconciliation but doubted he deserved it. Love warred with the regret of his past mistakes as a parent. Shaking off the negativity, he turned his focus to what he could control.

For the third time this year, Wilson resolved to write a resignation letter—short and final. He lifted himself off the scratchy wool blanket. His eyes scanned the cold, sterile office, with its rough brick walls covered in cheap frames holding accolades and medals. Reaching for the Tylenol on the nightstand, he tried to recall when he last took a dose.

Overcome with exhaustion, he decided the letter could wait. Swallowing a couple of tablets, he set down the white plastic container and lay back. He told himself to relax and focus on meaningful sleep.

Drifting into a rare moment of relaxation, he imagined riding his gravel bike with Sandi through the Painted Hills of Eastern Oregon. The sweeping countryside and rolling roads brought a sense of calm. His body relaxed, thoughts of retirement filled him with quiet satisfaction, and his mind slipped into sleep.

Chief Wilson couldn't have imagined what the next day would bring—a life-altering event that would challenge him and change thousands of lives across the breathtaking valley he'd spent all his adult life protecting."

# Let Me Guess

Theodore Daley, Teddy to his friends and familiar acquaintances, pressed the accelerator of the modified golf cart's floor. Garden utensils shook and rattled behind him as the tires of the decade-old cart bounced over dilapidated, annoying speed bumps. He released his foot from the accelerator and slammed the brake pedal to the floor. The cart groaned as the brakes seized, but worn brake pads prevented the utility vehicle from screeching to a halt as he desired. The company would have to buy him a new cart at some point he reckoned. His plan was to run this one into the ground, then maybe, just maybe, they would purchase one of the new Carryall 700s from Club Cart he'd been Googling the past year. He wanted more hauling space, and fewer trips back and forth to the maintenance shed for increased efficiency. Which meant happier tenants. Happier tenants meant fewer complaints in Payne Creek Estates. How could ownership not understand this? His eight-year-old granddaughter, Emma, understood. Every time she spent a weekend with him while her mother went hiking on the PCT, she asked him.

"Grandpa, why don't you have a bigger cart? We keep having to go back and forth to the shed. If you had a bigger cart, you could save time." She always looked up at him with the clearest brown eyes Teddy's ever seen in a human being. Pigtails, usually with some pink scrunchies, pulled hair away from silken smooth skin and drew a smile from anyone, promising everything will be okay in the world.

Teddy would pat her on the head, smile back, and respond, "Correct, little one. I wish you were my boss. You would make sure I have everything needed to do the job properly. I know you would."

"I would, Grandpa." Emma, like a programmed robot, would turn her head, look straight ahead, and kick her feet, not yet able to touch the floor, back and forth in joy. "Sing 'Lemonade,' Grandpa."

Smiling, Teddy looked at the console above his head and touched an old yellow, torn, and peeling sticker with who knows how many germs hugging the edges. The sticker said LEMONADE, that's all—one word. There was no advertising on it that he could see. No dot com address requesting your time and attention. No phone number or name of a business. Only the word LEMONADE. Touching it made him hum and then break out in a tune he created on the fly one day with a giggling Emma nestled next to him on the cart's bench seat. The jingle started with, "Life may give you lemons, but that's okay. 'Cause you know why?"

"Why?" Emma shouted, every time. "'Cause, we're gonna make us some lemonade."

Moving on to work from thinking about Emma, Teddy thought the management company responsible for the overall community knew the situation in terms of maintenance needs but didn't care. Their sole aim—a bottom line. Nothing more.

In the past few days, Teddy had come to a final realization. Management wasn't holding off on buying a new cart—or any other much-needed maintenance supplies—out of admiration for his skills. No, it was because they were cheap. Over the years, he became so adept at fixing and patching things together, regardless of what he had or didn't have, that they saw no need to invest in better equipment.

He kept telling himself he'd let things fall apart to prove a point. But whenever something broke, he'd think, *Next time.* Then a homeowner would call about a problem, and he'd drive the cart over. Most would ask about Emma and offer him coffee or iced tea, depending on the season. Every time, he'd shake his head, curse himself, and fix the damn thing—like a turkey staring up at the rain.

Today, before he got in the golf cart, he grabbed his notepad from the seat next to him and flipped back to a section titled EMG. A list he had been begging management for; going on three years now.

1 - Repair the Security Gate (SAFETY Issue)
2 - Clear the SAFE space outside the fence (SAFETY Issue)
3 - Repair the perimeter sprinkler system (SAFETY Issue)
4 - Fix the plumbing and toilets in the clubhouse (HEALTH Issue)
5 - Fix the emergency exit in the clubhouse (SAFETY Issue)

Glancing over the words, he considered if he should add anything else. Wanting the list to be longer when the third-quarter property review comes up next week, he decided he would make another round through the grounds. He determined to go through the Priority page again and see if he could tweak an item or two and move it to the EMG page. The bigger the list, the better.

"Hi, Teddy. Thank you for coming over so quick."

Without looking up, Teddy recognized the voice. He set his notepad down on the seat. Clearing his throat, he straightened the baseball cap on his head and exited the cart wishing the resident were someone else.

"Let me guess, Mrs. Martin: the clubhouse toilet is plugged again?"

# Burned to the Ground

Chief Wilson moved around his cot unable to find a comfort zone. His nose recognized the familiar smell of coffee and the mild cooking smell of fireman scramble—two dozen eggs and whatever hadn't expired in the refrigerator, a station favorite. Rubbing his eyes awake, the chief hoped Staley had cooking duty this morning. His eggs were always worth the wait; no matter what he found in the refrigerator.

Voices echoed through the fire station, and music played in the maintenance bay. Staring at a dimly lit clock—07:00—and startled by the time, he rubbed his eyes and efforted to sit up. Looking at the clock again, which now showed 07:01—so, he wasn't dreaming. Unable to remember a time he slept this late—as an infant, most likely—the chief headed to the kitchen before breakfast got shut down.

Growing up on a small farm was fun but always challenging. His father always told him, "Sleeping is for city kids. The cows need to be fed and watered, the chickens need to be let out, and you need to make sure the porch is clean of snow or swept clear of pine needles"— depending on the time of year. "It isn't your mother's job, boy. It's yours."

Wilson grabbed his Crocs, still perfectly aligned under his bed where he'd left them that morning. Sliding them on, he walked to the station's dresser and pulled out a clean pair of his favorite briefs and a black flame-resistant t-shirt. After a quick shower, less than ten minutes later, he stood back at the dresser. He snagged a pair of jeans, slid them on, then grabbed his station-logoed shirt and buttoned it over his already sweat-damp tee.

Off to the kitchen, the chief considered taking the long way

11

and telling the maintenance team to turn down the music—but opted for coffee and leniency instead. The music irritated him on weekdays; he could never quite figure out why. He liked music. Hell, he loved it—certain kinds, anyhow. He hadn't missed a performance from The Brothers Reed in a couple of years. More than once, he caught himself humming one of his favorite songs of theirs, *Southern Oregonia*.

The COVID bullshit had hampered more than a few of their shows, but post-pandemic, he'd made it to the Roadhouse in Yreka twice in the past six weeks to catch them live.

Wilson pushed his way through the door; his fingers crossed, hoping to see Staley wielding a spatula. The chief's six-foot-five, two-hundred-twenty-five-pound frame filled the doorway. His steady confidence and positive energy changed the dynamic of

He stopped and took a quick inventory of the space. Several members of the team already chomped on breakfast. Looking into the kitchen, unable to see the cook, one firefighter, knowing what rolled around in the chief's head, belted out, "It's Staley, Chief. Good morning."

Chief Wilson smiled, nodded, and headed to the wall to grab his coffee cup. Turning his body, he held the large YETI mug under the spigot of the coffee urn and filled it with the black Guatemalan blend java juice ground fresh from Rogue Roasters—a station favorite. Wishing there was an iced coffee option in this summer heat, he appreciated any caffeine this morning, hot or cold.

Stepping to his left, he set the mug down on the closest table and said morning to the five team members already eating. Heading toward the grill, he couldn't help but notice a couple of face masks dangling from ears; all of them had their faces buried in breakfast.

The mask protocol, lifted in the station, did not keep some from donning the damn things out of habit.

The chief stood at the kitchen pass-through, happy to see the best cook in the station hard at work.

"Good morning, Staley. What's the word this morning?"

"Morning, Chief. Nothing special. Good ol' station eggs with pancakes."

"Do we have any of the real maple syrup left?"

"Yes, Johnson went to Costco yesterday. We have plenty. The Irish butter too. We are set for at least a week."

"Good to hear. How are you doing today? How's that new baby of yours? Stacey, right?"

Chief Wilson watched Staley beam as he slid a slotted spatula under a pancake and flipped it. The breakfast cake turned a rich golden brown, blueberries spread across every inch—a pattern so even, every bite promised berry-bursting flavor.

The chief thought about buying a food truck, hiring Staley, and sitting back while the money rolled in. The kid was a decent firefighter, but a better cook.

"Yes, Chief, it's Stacey, and she is fine, thank you. The wife is taking her to the doctor today. Six-month check-up. I can't believe it is six months already."

"Well, enjoy it, young man. The years will go by faster than you can imagine. Trust me. You will never regret a single moment you slow down and appreciate your time together. I don't have many regrets in life, but my devotion to the job over my family is a big one. No matter what I do now, those are times I can never get back."

Silence filled the space between the two. The chief reflected on years gone by and moments missed with his daughter. Awards lined his office shelves, but a kaleidoscope of memories with Sky became more challenging each day to pull from the recesses of his brain. In a trance, pangs of guilt pushed against conscience.

"Chief. Chief."

"Shit, sorry, Staley. Thanks."

The chief reached out and took the plate from the junior fireman.

"No worries, Chief. Is that going to be enough, or will you want another serving?"

The chief looked down at his plate and took in the pleasing sight of three large eggs, three beautiful strips of thick bacon, and three fluffy, blueberry pancakes—a large slab of butter already melting on top.

"I'll be okay, Staley. Thanks. Damnit, we need to get you a food truck."

"Say the word, Chief!" Staley replied with his typical response.

Chief Wilson moved toward his coffee and sat down with his team. Their plates all pushed aside, they bantered about the baseball playoffs, if the NFL could complete a whole season under the waning pandemic cloud, and what to make of baseball with their shortened season. The chief reached for Tabasco and shook the hot red vinegar over his eggs as if his life's existence depended on the amount he could add.

Listening, forming an opinion about the conversation and ability of the Dodgers to finish the job for once, he devoured his eggs. Pushing the pancakes to the center of his plate, he sliced the top of each cake back and forth, breaking the surface to allow better syrup absorption. Grabbing the plastic jug filled with New England tree nectar from the middle of the table, lifting one side of the stack with his fork, he poured a generous portion on the plate under the cakes. Lowering the stack, he then lifted the middle cake, covered it with more syrup, lowered the top cake, and added a finishing pour. Taking a drink of coffee, he set his cup down and stared at the pancakes, understanding an important juncture of pancake eating is patience. There could be no hot-sauce contamination and no egg-yolk bleeding into the syrup. He accomplished both feats this morning. Now, the maple syrup needed time to soak into the cakes. Each bite needed to achieve near full saturation of the golden cakes.

"What do you think, Chief?"

The chief looked up from his blueberry-laced cakes and responded without missing a beat. "The Dodgers—finally. They dominated all year long and have way too much talent."

Someone snickered. Chief Wilson, unsure who, took his first bite of pancake. A small bit of syrup dripped out of the corner of his mouth. His tongue, with deliberate reflex, slithered out like a snake and pulled the syrup back into his mouth.

"You realize they are down three to one to the Braves, right, Chief?"

Swallowing—the pancakes needed another minute or two to absorb the syrup—the chief took a drink of coffee and set his cup back down.

"Doesn't matter. It's their year. Karma. The Astros and Red Sox cheated them out of a title the last two years."

"The Braves are rolling, Chief. But unfortunately, Dodgers pitching and lack of timely hitting are letting them down, again, in the postseason. In typical Dodger fashion, they can't hit when then need it."

Chief Wilson took a second bite. Syrup squished out of the pancake, a blueberry burst inside his mouth, his tongue and mind relished the taste. Then, contemplating his response on why he thought this would be the Dodger's year, the station incident alarm blared through the building. The five young men sitting with him jumped up. The chief watched as one took a long final swig of his coffee. His cup landed hard on the table and splashed.

"Sorry, Chief."

"Don't worry about it. Go save a life."

Chief Wilson took another bite of pancake, and before swallowing, added a bite of bacon so all the flavors could combine in breakfast glory. The salty crunchiness of the bacon merged with the sweet syrup and flavor-filled blueberry to near perfection. Almost done, he wondered if there were any pancakes left. Staring down at a middle age slow-growing gut, he passed.

Distracted by the heat inside the station, the chief considered the day. Even with temps reaching the high nineties today, he loved the fact that in less than fifteen minutes, he could be on a protected bike path slicing his way through the Rogue Valley. He hoped to make time this afternoon for a quick twenty-five-mile ride on his gravel bike. Savoring his final bite of pancake with bacon, the chief pushed his plate away, leaned back in his chair, and savored the remainder of his coffee.

Hearing the engines roll out of the station, the chief took his dishes to the kitchen. Returning for several trips, he cleared the table and then cleaned the surface down with Clorox wipes. Satisfied the table was clean, the chief sat for a couple of minutes before heading to the dispatch room to start his day. Hoping today would be calm; he considered more coffee but instead washed his cup and hung it on the hook number one, marked CHIEF.

Heading toward the dispatch room, Chief Wilson couldn't help but notice the floor had too many scuff marks, and he could see dirt against the wall. Frustrated with the crew's failure to meet the station standards, he decided to dock points for whoever was on cleaning duty. He hated a dirty station and couldn't fathom why there was dirt in the crevice against the wall. This week presented itself with a lot of downtime, and the station should be spotless.

Pushing through the dispatch door, Chief Wilson saw the back of the station's primary dispatcher, Jane Wettle.

"Morning, Jane."

"Morning, Chief."

"What did you send the team on?"

"A home near the High School. Sounds like a flash fire in a kitchen. They are on scene already, and the homeowner all but had the fire out when they got there. They are going to stay on for a while and help with cleanup."

"When they get back, please tell them I said to clean the hallway. The floor is full of scuff marks and dirt."

"Will do, Chief."

Starting to pivot and walk out, the Chief stopped, considered the dispatcher for a moment, and reminded himself to ask her about her day. He prided himself on keeping a pulse on personal lives and knew there was no better way to build and maintain a team then by knowing about their lives. Showing them, he gave a damn.

"How are you doing, Wettle?"

"Okay, I guess. Bad dream last night, though. So, I'll be glad when we get through today."

"What kind of dream?" The chief asked, curious. Wettle's dreams seemed to mimic future events on at least two separate occasions. So, any time she cared to share one, everyone in the station paid attention. This morning was no exception. Watching Wettle, the chief sensed she held firm with an unusual reluctance to respond. Fighting patience during her delay, he stared at the middle-aged woman, who in another life, the chief could see himself asking out to dinner.

Nervous, Wettle looked up at the chief, and her alluring brown eyes—filled with trepidation, seemed to signal she didn't want to speak. The chief held firm, attentive, eyes locked in, waiting.

"I dreamed Ashland burned to the ground, Chief."

# Bilateral BK

Kaley rolled over, lifted her head off her disappointing flat pillow, and stared at the clock, which illuminated 4:23 in subdued red neon. Her mouth mimicked vulgar curse words in silence knowing that falling back asleep would not happen. It never does. Outside, wild sounds—cats, dogs, and rambunctious raccoons in trash cans—reverberated back and forth, pinging off the multitude of high-end manufactured homes. Dozens and dozens of houses lay, in a random order, inside the torn and mangled perimeter chain-link fence of Payne Creek Estates. Not where or what she envisioned after leaving college, Willamette University, with honors in humanities.

Family comes first, though, right? That's what her mother told her over and over until the age of seven when the drinking started. At least that's what she remembered. Hell, out of manipulation, the phrase reverberated through the air; whispered to her in the womb.

A loud, disgusting, guttural cough rang out from the opposite end of the house that her mother called home for the last twenty years. There wouldn't be another five, would there? Kaley hoped not, then rolled over, trying to avoid remnants of her guilt-infested mind.

*This happens every morning. Why do I think the way I do? Am I stuck, or can I get out of this train wreck? Do I even want out?" Whispering to the air in the room as if it would respond in some intelligent way, she considered reaching for her cell phone on the nightstand—another reflexive repetitive morning routine. Instead, Kaley stared over at the end of her bed at a bookstand lined with a dozen unread self-help books. Gifts from a couple of well-intentioned friends. Both—whole.* "Easy-fucking-life," *she mumbled.*

Today is going to be different.

Blah blah blah—her mind mocked the thought as it slid back into the reason she was here.

*Pain surged through her skull, crashing side to side like waves in a cracked shell. The heat still burned in her memory, the screams still echoed—relentless, terrifying, beyond words. And beneath it all, that sound—like ringing in her ears—that never stopped.*

*She remembered the yank of a hand in her hair, the pull on her left arm. The feel of hard-packed earth beneath her— dirt and gravel grinding into her back and partial bare ass. The sound it made was sickening, unforgettable. In her mind, it always came back louder—distorted by the smells and screams that crashed through time without mercy.*

*A voice yells, "Stay with me, Lattimore. Don't you fucking die, you pansy-ass piece of shit! I'll kill you myself, you beautiful human being. Do you hear me?"*

*Retching and fear precedes blackness.*
*Drifting.*
*Silence.*
*Peace.*
*Light.*
*Elation.*
*Knowledge.*

*Then—a jolting awareness explodes with excruciating pain.*

*A beep that seems familiar echoes as her eyes open. Blinking, she looks down at her right hand, wiggles her fingers, and turns her head to the side. There is a large glass window,*

19

*clean and inviting, lined with heavy beige curtains pushed aside. She stares outward, toward blue skies. White fluffy cumulus clouds hung, suspended like cotton from the rafters of a barn. Below the blue and white are incredible colors of nature—yellows, browns, shades of orange and brilliant greens as far as she can see. Kaley's mind reacts to her eyes' interpretations as if this were their first experience taking in the earth's beauty.*

Dragging a reluctant mind back to the present, Kaley rolled over in bed, adjusted her pillow, and slid her hands underneath in a futile attempt at dozing off for bonus sleep. Staring at a wall illuminated by pulsing internet router lights, she thought of coffee and the immediate pleasant response her body has when the dark liquid courses through her system. The only time she can muster any compassion and care toward her dying mother: during a caffeine or vodka, surge-induced love fest.

Recognizing the repetition and determined to break the routine, she sat up, threw the covers aside, and stared down at the nubs on both legs—just below her knees. *Bilateral BK*— a term she'd grown to despise thanks to the medical staff's constant, clinical repetition. It felt like a never-ending reminder of her frailty... and her supposed shortcomings as a future contributor to society.

Sad-induced moisture formed in the corners of her eyes. Refusing to let the tears break free, allowing anger to control self-pity, adrenaline surged through her mind as she reached for her prosthetic limbs.

# A Booth if That's Okay

Sky peeled her sore forearm off the sticky passenger door armrest in the nondescript minivan. She knew the uncomfortable feeling underneath flesh had nothing to do with circulation from restricted veins. Unfortunately, the mental toll on her psyche the past week caught her unprepared this morning. Sensing depression, she tried to will it away. For the planet's sake, she moaned. *Blah blah blah.* She struggled to focus on saving the round sphere the others in the van with her seem so passionate about.

More preoccupied with heading north toward the home she had abandoned years ago than with a planet that was doing just fine without her input, she once again found her fragile psyche jolted by reality. Whenever she sank too deep into thought, memories seized her—slamming her against an invisible wall, forcing her to confront the harsh truth in the mirror: the infuriating feeling that she was nothing more than white trash.

Taking her eyes off the vast unending fields surrounded by several mountain ranges of the Southern Oregon and Northern California landscape, she glanced at the driver, Steel. She chuckled at the stealth name the podium man picked for himself—Steel. Really? The last thing she thought of when looking at him was a piece of steel. Rubber, aluminum, but not steel. He had a certain appeal about him; she'd give him that. However, she wouldn't trust anyone who blamed others for the world's problems. She considered her childhood and, for a flicker of a moment, skirted guilty thoughts around the irony.

The man, all of a hundred and fifty pounds soaking wet, moved with the kind of desperate swagger that begged to be seen as more. A wiry frame, a waif really, but packed with misplaced confidence—bold, relentless, and, somehow, a strange unplaced magnetism.

Sky glanced out the passenger window and listened to the click click click of the turn signal as the van eased off Interstate five at Exit 773. She thought she saw an Yreka sign, miles back, near Weed. She wanted one of those damn "I Love Weed" t-shirts and wished they stopped to eat or pee there and not in the historic miner town.

Steel, pointing forward, shouted. Sky contemplated this, knowing shouting is unnecessary in a van carrying only four people, all of them silent the last thirty miles. What did he gain by shouting, she wondered. A sense of authority? What a douchebag.

"We are stopping at the Black Bear Diner here to eat. I recommend eating hearty. If all goes well, the next day and a half will be a long one. We will stand a lot and burn some calories for sure."

Sky snickered, his shouting slicing through her thoughts like static she couldn't tune out. Why did he always have to shout? And *hearty*—who even used that word anymore? There was no way she could get behind this guy, not emotionally anyway. And so far, she saw no reason to believe the man-made global warming nonsense he preached nonstop but never backed up with facts.

She couldn't put her finger on why. He loved the planet; hell, he claimed to worship it. His head seemed to be in the right place. She chalked her dislike of him to simple karma, two souls on different journeys who don't click. Or was it the man's lack of authenticity and continually blabbing a litany of garbage he read in a journal somewhere? She felt his words carried no sincere passion—a rich kid who lashed out for the sake of a tantrum to get attention. From whom or for what Sky didn't know, and she didn't want to know. She had a long list of her own issues.

Steel preached about planet survival—Sky longed for her own survival.

Having shed the American need for constant approval, she accepted that not everyone had to like each other—and that included her. She gave herself permission not to like certain people, which oddly made it easier to tolerate those she didn't care for. It relieved self-created pressure.

Steel, she snickered, was a prime example. She did not like him. Every moment in his presence grated against the very fiber of her being. But for now, he was a convenient nuisance, so she'd endure his overbearing and pathetic antics a little longer.

Thinking about her father's homemade breakfasts and realizing she was going to eat soon; Sky craved a thin crispy maple-syrup-drowned waffle as the van exited the freeway. After going through one traffic light in the small town they arrived at a diner guarded by a big chainsaw-carved wooden black bear. She picked her backpack up off the floor and giggled.

"What's so funny, Sky?" Steel challenged in tone as he turned the van key off.

Surprised with someone paying attention to her antics, Sky realized her snicker was louder than she intended. She responded without missing a beat.

"Nothing. I was thinking of a time as a kid when I almost lit a stack of hay on fire."

Sky looked at Steel—his stare sent a message that he didn't buy the bullshit she tried to sell.

So, Sky held her chin down a bit as if she was obedient and succumbing to his leadership. Then, in an unintended moment of memory reflection, she transported back in time to her childhood and something Laura taught her.

*"Sweety, when you get in a position where a man wants to let you know he is dominant—humor him. Lower your chin ever so slightly."*

*At this point, Laura grabbed her chin with rough but somehow delicate, shaking fingers and lowered it an inch.*

*"Now, raise your eyelids and pout your lips a touch."*

*Laura would display how to look demure by adequately showing the manifestation of submission herself. Sky never called her mom anything other than Laura; this was some weird rebellious transformation around the age of eight or nine for Sky. Her mother, Laura, found the rebellious streak and first-name-basis charming.*

*"They melt, thinking you are weaker and submissive. It's a man's world, sweety. We don't have to like it, and we don't, but we must learn how best to play in it—manipulate it to our advantage."*

Steel peeled his glare away with a slight grin. One born out of victory and satisfaction that Sky experienced dozens of times from men. Satisfied, she played the earth-loving neanderthal with the care and attention she gave the books in her backpack; she exited the van and popped the side door open for the other two to escape.

Steel stood at the front of the van, where the foursome gathered, and he waited for them all to look at him.

"You won't need your backpack, Sky," Steele commanded.

Sky fought not to roll her eyes and refused to lower her chin, staring straight at him. "How do you know, Steel? I am a woman. I always need my bag. Can we get on with this now?"

Watching Steele's jaw tighten, to Sky's morbid pleasure, she listened as he held his tongue in response to her before continuing.

"Remember, no names in here. Be polite, but not too nice. Focus on not bringing attention to ourselves. Sky, you sit with me. Rose and Acorn come in a few minutes after us and sit at another table. Order fast and eat faster, back in the van in forty-five minutes, max. If you aren't here, you'll be hitching."

What a dick, Sky thought. Like he'll leave someone behind knowing successful protests are all about numbers. All this guy can muster are three people to tag along with him. She wondered if he had plans to meet others in Medford on the way to Portland for his pathetic Earth-first mission. Maybe he'd told her—Sky assumed he had—but most of what he said never made it past her ears. She refused to let it.

Walking toward the front door, Steel grabbed her hand and squeezed. Repulsion reverberated through Sky's entire body. She ripped her hand away, and her fingers slithered out of his mealy, soft skin. Stopping, he glared at her. Without hesitation, she started to lower her chin but stopped.

"Look, we need to look like a couple."

Sky, pleased with the opportunity to rebut—countered. "No one will buy us as a couple. I am three inches taller than you and much prettier."

Reluctant toward her next action, Sky softened her eyes looking upward at Steel. Remembering Laura's expression, the last time she hit her for being a less-than-perfect child, Steel had the same repulsive look in his eyes. *Typical,* Sky thought. Lips locked tight; her mind wrestled with letting them open and releasing the smartass words she longed to set free.

*One more day* buzzed in her head as she took an unnoticeable deep breath through her nose before speaking.

"Steel, you said we don't want to attract attention to ourselves. If we walk in there holding hands, that will draw attention. If we walk in there like we don't give two shits about each other, no one will be the wiser."

The two locked eyes as silence hung between them like a slow-rolling Oregon coastal fog. Steel's vacant brown eyes attempted dominance: Sky's gaze remained steadfast and

25

determined. Her goal; control, through calculated manipulation.

"Come on then, you little bitch."

Sky, smiling inside, felt a warped sense of comfort by the familiar condescension of an adversary as she fell in step with Steel while they headed toward the front door.

She silently repeated, "One more day, one more day, one more day," as they stepped through the front door to the sound of a crying child, the clatter of dishes, and the smell of bacon grease, burnt coffee, and clothes steeped in agriculture, hard work, and sweat.

What a welcoming stench, Sky mumbled to herself as her stomach growled.

As the two stopped in the lobby by the Wait-To-Be-Seated sign, Sky bent a little at the waist and put her mouth close to Steel's ear and whispered, "If you ever grab my hand again, or touch me at all, I will destroy you."

"Hi, just the two of you?" a young tooth-stained server asked.

Steele, appearing paler than when they walked through the door, unable to speak, looked at Sky.

Sky turned her head toward the server, "Yes, please. A booth if that's okay and thank you."

# The Life of a Neanderthal

Chief Wilson, intrigued by Wettle's dream, headed to the back patio for a curiosity peek of the weather. Gazing north to south, he stared again at a haze-covered Grizzly Peak as he had done hours ago in the moonlight. Grateful he saw no significant smoke, only remnants of distant forest fires, he turned, picked up heavy feet, and headed back inside. Wondering what the rest of the day might bring, the chief sat down at his desk and brought his computer out of sleep. Pressing the keys to enter his password, he let the PC run a minute so the operating system could finish loading.

Satisfied, the laptop now ran at peak efficiency, he started Word and searched for resignation letter templates. Unable to find anything satisfactory, the chief searched Google and picked the first template on the list below the ads. A quick read of the mock letter satisfied him with the simplistic approach he desired. Downloading the template, the chief cut and pasted the text and tweaked it to fit his needs. Twenty minutes later, satisfied with the way his life-changing document read, he saved the file before printing.

Glancing across his office at the printer, a green light confirmed the Inkjet waited on a command from his computer. Hearing the firehouse bay doors open and the unmistakable beeping of fire rigs backing in, the chief selected print, and thirty seconds later he held his resignation letter. Giving it a quick read, seeing no typos, he signed the document and dated it September 8.

Deciding to head to the county office in another thirty minutes, hoping for an element of surprise so the county commissioners wouldn't have time to plan a rebuttal, Chief

27

Wilson decided not to phone ahead like usual.

Antsy and itching to get out of the station, he figured that if all three county commissioners were unavailable, he'd pivot and make an appointment for later. Jackson County, Oregon, operated under a three-member Board of Commissioners: the Chair, the Vice-Chair, and a third member. Technically, he reported to the board as a whole, but he preferred dealing with the commissioners directly—one-on-one conversations that would then make their way back to the board. He'd been handling things that way for years, and he wasn't about to change now.

But he wanted to talk to the Chair. Sure, any of them could accept the document, but he respected her the most. Her family grew up in the valley, like he did, and he trusted her judgment. The other two? Not so much.

Feeling teenage giddiness, and more relaxed than usual, the chief grabbed a full-sized envelope from a desk drawer and slid the letter inside. Pleased with his decision, relief swept through him, and he thought about calling his lady friend, Sandi, to give her the news. Knowing she'd get excited for a moment, then retreat into doubt, he hesitated, then made the call.

The retirement claim wasn't new for the chief. Twice, over the last year, after grueling stretches of political bullshit ricocheted around the granite halls of city hall, he'd start writing a letter and tell Sandi, "I am through! That's it!" However, today he printed the resignation letter; a first for him.

Single for years now, after a failed marriage, Chief Wilson considered the fire department both his wife and mistress, leaving no time for a healthy personal relationship. However, as he began considering retirement, his desire for a partner grew stronger.

Eighteen months ago, he met Sandi, a traveling nurse, at a county fundraiser, and she touched his heart in a way that

28

surprised him. Overnight, he found himself in a relationship; the first since his wife walked out. Longing to spend time with her, thoughts of the Fire Department took a backseat.

A self-sufficient woman, who embraced the single life for years, Sandi understood first-hand the importance and love of work too, which took pressure off him. They both cherished their time together but also embraced their opportunities for alone time.

A cyclist herself, earlier in the month she bought a hybrid bicycle used for light road riding, hard-packed trails, and gravel roads. Intrigued with the idea of a new-style bicycle and embracing time on gravel, he bought the same model as well, and the two now looked forward to riding on backcountry roads whenever they could get away together.

The chief pressed send on the phone screen and after the third ring heard, "Hello, handsome. How's life in the Rogue?"

Pleased with the greeting, he never tired of hearing Sandi's voice or her constant positive affection, he responded. "Hey there, beautiful. Well, the Rogue is still here. Not as cool a place though with you gone."

"Hah, you are so full of shit. But I love it. Don't stop."

"How are the folks?" the chief responded, knowing Sandi enjoyed her time in central Oregon with parents. Once a month on her extended time off week, she'd try to get to Bend and spend time with them. She'd either ski, hike or bike, depending on the time of year.

"They are good. Dad wants to know how the Sprinter van project is coming."

"Slow." The chief paused long enough to emphasize slow but quick enough so Sandi couldn't respond. "Hey, listen, about that. Guess what I did today?"

"Oh, I don't know. Your full of shit, so, did you install the composting toilet?"

"Funny. Nikki Glaser wanna-be."

The chief felt Sandi's impressive soul-filling smile on the other end of the line.

"I give. What?"

"Typed my resignation letter. I am getting ready now to drive over to City Hall and hand it in. I am done. I am full. Nothing left to prove."

Now he felt her doubt piercing through the cellular sound wave. Several seconds went by. The chief, uncomfortable with quiet space in conversations, bit his lip, channeling his inner Bill Clinton, and waited.

"Let me guess—another meeting with the bureaucrats and they got under your skin?"

The chief thought about Dan Akroyd and SNL before responding with, "Sandi, you ignorant slut." Laughter burst out on the other end of the phone.

"How long have you been waiting to fit that phrase into a conversation with such perfection?"

"Decades."

Both continued chuckling.

Sandi took the next leap in the conversation. "You're serious. Aren't you?"

"Yep, I have the letter in my hand and am leaving in a few to deliver it."

"Wow. Congrats. I guess it's my turn then. You know, it's funny, but I am going over retirement options with my folks right now. Trying to be smart about the decision. I didn't think part of the conversation would be about you retiring as well. I wondered if we could stay together with one of us retired, and the other wasn't. Now I'll have to shift my thoughts to wondering if we can stay together if we are both not working."

Sandi talked a lot about retiring. It seemed to the chief like a cathartic exercise for her. Playing along, the chief would ask her if she would be up for traveling together with their bikes in a decked-out cargo van. Sandi always responded with, "Will we be able to shower?"

"Of course, you goofball," he'd interject with affection. "I am not talking about being a burned-out hippie in a dilapidated cargo van. Haven't you ever seen vans that people trick out like RVs? Fantastic for road tripping and camping. A great alternative to a hotel. Personal and under the stars."

"Under the stars?" Sandi would question looking a bit dazed and confused. Chief Wilson would counter with, "Didn't you ever camp as a kid, Sandi?"

"Yes, we camped a lot. I was a kid; I didn't care if I showered or not. I'd go jump in the water and be good." Sandi would pause, the chief would stare and wonder if he and Sandi were right for each other. They seemed like it, but what did he know about a healthy personal relationship.

Sandi almost always finished her thought with, "I am not a kid anymore. I enjoy being clean."

"Thank heavens. I get it. You know there are all kinds of cool outdoor showers now. We can build one in the van if we want. Besides, we are not having sex if you aren't clean. Ain't happening."

"Yeah, right! Since when does that ever matter with you, you neanderthal?" Sandi would laugh and jab him in the chest.

Hearing the fire station personnel break out in laughter, he paused the conversation with Sandi and tried to listen. The laughter, a pleasant distraction, ricocheted through the building. Envious, he seemed unable to laugh himself, some mental block as if his soul ran out of laughter in a previous life. He felt like when he laughed, he sounded like a psycho with a sore throat and could not remember the last time he felt a genuine hearty throw-your-head-back laugh. He felt envy hearing joy burst outward from others. Who the hell can't laugh?

"Sandi, I need to get going. I wanted to share the news with you first. Be prepared for seeing a lot of me in the coming months." Both voices froze at the realistic thought of changed lives. How much did they care about each other? Do they want to be around each other more? "Shit," the chief mumbled to himself realizing he had not considered this thought, fully.

"Okay, sounds good and congrats. You know, one thing I love about you Murph Wilson—you don't mind if I go off and do my thing for a while. We will be great in retirement. I have my friends, and well, you have your right hand, so we'll be okay."

"Ha! Nikki Glaser again, you mean, nasty woman. Listen, tell your folks I said hi, and I look forward to them visiting soon. Tell them they better be at my retirement ceremony. It will be a spectacle, I am sure."

"Will do. And Murph, congrats. You are going to love your free time. I know it."

The line went silent. Heading out of his office, continuing thoughts of an actual retirement, and wondering if it could ease him into laughter, the chief moved toward the equipment bay with his resignation envelope in hand. His feet, as if stuck in deep wet smoldering ash, shuffled down the hall; memories stormed and swirled in his conscience.

The accumulation of stories over thirty years as a first responder went on and on. He wished he paid better attention in high school English and college—perhaps he could write a book about all his crazy situations. It seemed everyone wrote novels these days.

Reaching the station's central bay, the chief watched the crew moving around the engines, inspecting and prepping for the next call. He considered yelling out—asking if the maintenance records were up to date—but thought better of it. Nothing would've changed since his spot inspection two days ago.

Halfway down the hall, he reversed course. He had no real

desire to engage in dispatch's condescending busy talk. Instead, he spun around and made for his county vehicle. The realization that his earlier impulse to connect with the crew felt needy only added to his irritation.

He pushed through the glass door, and a blast of dry, stinging heat slapped his face. The southern wind bit at his skin, sharp and relentless, like needles. It clawed at the envelope in his hand, snapping at the edges, trying to tear it free. His grip tightened, knuckles white as he held on. He glanced at his watch, steady in his decision. Still, a flicker of doubt crept in—would the Chair be in her office? For a moment, he hoped she wasn't, though he didn't have the time—or the will—to unpack why.

Stopping at the side of his county-owned vehicle, the chief opened the door. Holding the handle, he stood for a moment staring—taking in the station's scene juxtaposed against the mountains' backdrop. Looking up and down at the side of the vehicle, aware for the first time he'd miss the decked-out Ford F-250 and he'd need to buy his own vehicle. The Sprinter van did not lend itself to daily driving. An SUV, perhaps or fix up his old pickup truck?

The last vehicle he drove regularly was a beat-up 1972 Chevy C10. It wasn't any old truck; it had belonged to his grandpa, who'd handed over the keys a week before he died. That truck carried more than his teenage dreams—it carried his grandpa's memory. Every weekend as a teen, he'd spend hours tinkering with it, hoping to keep it running for another week of school.

It was still around, tucked away in the barn. He considered trading it in months ago when he splurged on the Sprinter van. The thought of letting it go hadn't been easy. Parting with his grandpa's Chevy felt like closing the door on a piece of his past, and the sentimental value outweighed any blue-book price. But maybe it was time to move on, stop looking backward, and quit hanging onto old things that no longer served a purpose.

But when the dealer offered him less than the tires were worth, he couldn't go through with it. Instead, he parked the old Chevy in the deepest corner of the barn, where it still sat gathering dust.

He kept telling himself he'd restore it once he retired— bring it back to its former glory. Not that it ever had much glory when he was a kid. But it wasn't just about fixing up an old truck. It was about holding on to the last piece of his grandfather.

Climbing into the cab of the county rig, he shut the door and gripped the steering wheel with both hands. His chest felt clamped in a vise, each breath short and uneven. The corners of his eyes throbbed—hot, swollen. He gave his head a hard shake, like it might knock loose whatever was clawing at him from the inside. Damn emotions. No matter how much he wanted a break, they weren't letting up.

He started counting to fifty—something his grandfather had taught him years ago—and gradually, his breath steadied. When he finally exhaled fully, he turned the key and eased the rig out of the parking lot and onto Highway 99.

As he headed north toward the county office, he wondered how long he could hold off boredom once he retired. Cycling, fishing, maybe living like a damn Neanderthal? If that's what retirement took, he'd grab onto it like flies on caveman shit.

# A Craggy Pit

Kaley clamped the half-smoked cigarette between her chapped lips as she shoved her way out of the manufactured home. The door smacked against the frame with a hollow rattle and bounced back—once, twice, three times—before clanging to an almost closed position.

"Cheap-ass door." The words slipped out with the same bitterness she tasted every morning. She turned, gave the bent door a hard shove, and waited.

Click.

A small, satisfied smirk tugged at her mouth. It was a rare win. Most mornings, she had to ram the thing twice, maybe three times, before it stayed shut. She'd made a game of it by now. If that piece of crap door ever latched on the first try, she'd take it as a sign—swing by the mini-mart and buy herself a damn lotto ticket.

A dark, tormented part of her loved hearing the aluminum and wood strain against the force of her effort. Waiting for the predictable script to play out, she waited for her mother, reeking of Listerine and fresh-rain air fresheners, to yell from inside her bedroom, "Kaley, don't slam the door!"

Kaley raised her hand and flipped off her mother, the gesture sharp and deliberate. She snatched the slow-burning menthol from her mouth, ground it against the home's, stained siding until only ash and smear remained, and flicked the butt into the metal trash can.

She eyed the steps, her jaw tightening. They weren't steep, but they might as well have been a goddamn mountain. Bracing herself, she gripped the railing and maneuvered down, each awkward step a test of balance and grit. Her prosthetics pinched and rubbed, the effort leaving her breathing harder than she wanted to admit.

At the bottom, she dragged herself to the car and collapsed into the driver's seat, her hands trembling. Muttering under her breath about how death should've taken her in the Middle East, she sat there for a good five minutes, fists pounding the steering wheel until the pain in her knuckles dulled the ache in her chest.

Today's routine started like all the others. But the hot, gusting winds and air so dry it scraped her throat only made everything feel more off-kilter, like the world itself was trying to push her out of place.

Staring out the windshield, Kaley noticed a difference in the way she felt. Light bounced off clouds that looked like they were trying to escape. Throughout the sky, reflective colorful light, like thousands of mood rings from the seventies, hover. A sense of foreboding and an odd, pending, doom hung in the air. Staring with hope through the windshield, she watched with curiosity and wondered if this was how Midwesterners felt during tornado season—watching clouds gather in a rumbling mass as the earth crafted wind-driven chaos from scratch to unleash hell-on-earth.

The sun continued peeking, on a slow climb, behind mountains to the east, clouds peppered the horizon, and the sky turned a brilliant shade of earthly pink. Relaxing her grip on the steering wheel, she got herself in a comfortable position and buckled up. Turning the ignition, efforting to bring the vehicle to life, she listened to it sputter and jerk as if it had an acute case of lung congestion. Struggling to run, the car engine smoothed as it warmed, and she glanced at the tachometer as the idle settled on 900 RPMs. Reaching toward the dash, she turned the radio on and watched as the Android auto app connected with her phone. Staring at the phone's screen, she looked for a familiar app icon that a friend at work encouraged her to download and listen to. Some bullshit she downloaded weeks ago.

Kaley listened to one of the audio segments right after she downloaded the app, and when the woman speaking went on and on about being "the owners of our thoughts and controllers of our destinies," Kaley nearly threw her phone out the window. Something in her mind whispered: *Rest. Stay calm.* Like when she wore the uniform—her life had depended on how she reacted. She stopped the app, set the phone aside, and got back to work. But in the back of her mind, something stirred— a new, unfamiliar edge she didn't want to shake.

On the drive to work, Kaley reluctantly queued up her friend Mia's motivational guru again. She wasn't sure if it was the fiery morning sky, the nicotine rush, or her psyche skidding toward a craggy pit of permanent despair. Desperate for some kind of mental normalcy or even a hint of peaceful relief, she pleaded with her car's sound system, hoping Mia's damn app would deliver one or the other.

As she guided the vehicle down the road, trying to shove her mental discomfort aside, a soothing voice spilled through the speakers, assuring her that "the universe is what she makes it."

# A Pathetic Smirk

Sky took another bite of grease-soaked hash browns, the taste yanking her straight back to her childhood. It reminded her of the well-used grease her grandmother kept in the kitchen—a massive aluminum can of Crisco. Its cool, white, creamy paste seemed magical. Sky wondered if Crisco still came in those tubs.

Her grandma used that stuff for everything. Biscuits that were always light, fluffy, and delicious, whether smothered in sausage gravy, homemade blackberry jam, or plain butter. That pasty grease was also the secret to her grandma's legendary pie crusts and cakes—recipes so good the judges at the fair handed her blue ribbons every single year Sky could remember.

But it wasn't just for cooking. Sky once watched her grandma scoop a dollop of Crisco on her fingertip and smear it over a squeaky door hinge her grandfather always forgot to fix. The damn thing stopped creaking with one twist of the hinge, like magic.

Her grandpa had duct tape to fix everything; her grandma had Crisco. The thought made Sky smile on the inside.

Sky struggled to recall more about her grandmother. The old woman died when she was seven or eight, and most of the memories, outside of Crisco and cooking, disappeared from her mind like wind-driven fog.

Her last joyful memory with her grandfather—who died a year after her grandmother—was at the fair. They wandered through rows of animals, Sky wide-eyed at the massive cows and the snorting, funny-sounding pigs. She always longed to take home one of the big, fuzzy rabbits with sad eyes and a twitchy, puffy nose. Even better, a baby goat—mischievous, full of wild, endless energy. *Why couldn't they stay small?*

Sky sipped her coffee, the bitter warmth coating her tongue as her thoughts churned. She forked the last bite of pancake—syrup-soaked and sticky with the mingled sweetness of maple and pecan—and let it melt in her mouth.

She didn't want to leave. The restaurant buzzed with the low hum of clinking dishes, murmured conversations, and occasional bursts of laughter. Comfort wrapped around her like a heavy blanket, the kind she hadn't felt in too long. Her chest tightened, eyes prickling with a heat she didn't want to acknowledge.

What went wrong in her life? How did a human veer so far off the path? Or was this her path? She didn't want to believe anyone's path would take them to cold, urine-soaked streets, days without food, weeks without a shower—then end up in a room of angry rich whiners wanting to save a planet that didn't need saving. Or perhaps their ideas were nothing more than an attempt at getting back at successful parents who didn't fit their idea of what a human should do with their life? What was all this for?

To Save The Planet. Right?

Sky's eyes locked on Steel as he crammed another pepper-coated bite of egg into his mouth. Bright orange beads of yolk clung to his three-day-old stubble—his sorry excuse for a man's goatee. Disgust twisted her gut, but it unraveled fast, dissolving into something heavier.

Sadness.

Empathy.

The sensation rose up like a shadow she couldn't shake. When was the last time she felt that? Maybe it was the satisfaction of a full belly, the hunger silenced for a while. Or maybe her ever-present anger had crawled off somewhere to sulk, hiding deep in the recesses of her mind.

She half-heartedly tried to dredge it back up, craving the raw heat of its comfort, but it slipped through her fingers like dry sand. Weird. Anger had always been her go-to. As dependable as a scorching day in the desert. Always there, always ready.

But now, its absence left her feeling exposed. Hollow. Hell, maybe the emptiness—just maybe—was making room for something else.

Scanning the restaurant for the restrooms, she calculated an unexpected move. Their server appeared to be in route with the bill. Steel wiped yolk off his plate with a piece of margarine-soaked rye. Sky stood, tossed her pack over her shoulder, remembering Steel's voice at the van, "If you aren't here, you'll be left behind."

"Where are you going?" Looking up at a standing Sky, mouth full of the last bit of bread and yolk, Steel's eyes scanned the nearby tables.

"The toilet. I'll be right back, okay?" Sky replied in a surprising, kind, and thoughtful tone. Wondering what entity jumped into her mind and body, she felt a rush or peaceful surge of calm wash through her body.

Steel's eyes and brow relaxed, but his lips scrunched together with a force reminiscent of a car being crushed into a junkyard brick of metal and steel. He nodded, giving reluctant approval. "Hurry, we leave in five minutes."

"Not to worry, Steel. Saving the planet, and the people on it, is important to me."

With her latest lie, Sky spun away and brushed against the arriving server. Then, walking by the rest of the group at a nearby table, she made her way past the register, staring at a sign and door leading to the restrooms. Pulling a sticky door handle, she peered inside the door and noticed signs for Men and Women.

"Damnit, no back door," she mumbled.

Her heart sank, but she refused to waver. Instead, she turned and made her way back toward the register—and, with trepidation, the front door. People stared. Moving with slow and deliberate intent, wanting to be invisible, she wondered if it was the grime on her skin or the stench of body odor that made them recoil.

At the register, she glanced back at their table. Steele was locked in a pathetic, animated argument with the server, demanding a discount—even though every scrap of food had vanished from their plates. Sky had emptied every small, white plastic container onto her four thin slices of wheat toast. A pile of non-recyclable plastic sat in front of her, foil lids peeled back, not a speck of jelly left. *Why is everything wrapped in plastic?* She didn't have the answer, and didn't care to dwell on it—not now. Her eyes swept across the other tables. The rest of the group, like Steele, were giving their servers hell. *What is it with these entitled assholes?*

Without hesitation, Sky slid out the front door, looked left toward the freeway, and then south across the street at a busy gas station with illuminated neon signs selling liquor. Moving her head west toward hills covered in pine, juniper, rock and dirt, she eased her way toward the van. She looked over her shoulder at a family of five with loud and cheerful children. The mother looked exhausted, but the father's face glowed. He looked happy, which seemed odd to her with the mother out of sorts.

Nervous of being discovered, staring back at the gas station, she wondered if she could convince someone in the parking lot for a ride. Or perhaps she should hide, wait for the planet savers to leave, then figure out a next step. Looking down at her less-than-welcoming appearance, she stared back at the van, contemplating giving up and crawling back inside the grease-soaked diner to embrace her life of disillusionment and pain.

High off the ground with oversized tires and wheels, a dark-colored pickup slowed in front of her. Sky noticed an Oregon license plate on the front as the diesel engine rumbled to a stop between the restaurant and her. The passenger window lowered, a young guy about her age leaned over and, with a deep voice, asks, "You, okay? You need a ride somewhere?"

Sky liked the energy coming off the pickup and the tone of the guy's voice. He sounded genuine, caring even. But hell, what did she know about genuine and caring anymore? Life on the streets had twisted her view of kindness, left it dirty and warped.

"Yeah. My group left me here."

"Well, I am not going far. Heading home to Rogue River if you are interested. I could get you that far."

"Sorry, but I smell. Long story."

"Well, we can leave the windows down."

Sky watched the young man smile. Handsome with bright eyes and a kind grin, could she trust him? She peered over the bed of the pickup toward the front door of the restaurant. No enemy activity yet. The pickup looked clean and didn't appear to carry a serial-killer vibe.

*Besides, didn't rapists and killers always drive beat-up old sedans or nasty-looking vans with no windows?* Sky pulled at the pickup door handle, threw her backpack on the floor then yanked herself up into the cab slamming the door behind her. Then with an instant awareness of her smell, she smiled, "I am going to leave the window down a bit. Sorry, but I need a shower. We were camping, and I haven't bathed in a week."

*At first, pleased with her quick, impromptu lie, a twinge of guilt washed over her. Damn, guilt ruins things, she thought. And lying was no way to start a relationship. Relationship?*

Laughing, her mind spiraled with confusion.

"Don't worry about it. My turn to say sorry and hang on. I am in a bit of a hurry. I make deliveries once or twice a week down here from Rogue River for my uncle. Today I am running a bit late."

Welcoming the height of the pickup truck and the high-back seats, she lowered herself in the seat. The pickup surged forward, then stopped at the traffic light heading toward the freeway and a hopeful escape. Sky looked out the back of the tinted window, noticing her group standing next to the van. Their faces looked bewildered as they scrambled, looking around the parking lot. They were searching for her. She thought her heart should race, but it felt calm and steady. As her hopeful hero guided the pickup toward the freeway, she turned around and stared eastward, out the passenger window, toward a towering picturesque and unmistakable snow-capped Mt. Shasta.

Heading toward southern Oregon and potential reclamation, Sky watched the driver turn the radio down and glance at her before turning the pickup onto the freeway.

"I get the sense you are running from someone. Do you want to talk about it or leave it alone? We have about forty minutes of drive time."

Sky smiled and thought "leave it alone" sounded perfect. Instead of saying as much, her mouth seemed incapable of moving, she grinned a pathetic smirk and nodded.

# Kiss My Ass

Chief Wilson eased his vehicle into a reserved parking spot at City Hall. Opening the door, he closed it halfway when he realized the resignation letter was still sitting on the seat. Pulling the door back open, the chief grabbed the envelope and then slammed the door shut behind him. Nodding to several people who acknowledged his presence heading up the front steps, the anticipation of his near-final decision excited him and seemed to have a grip on his tongue.

Moving through the main lobby door, the chief glanced at the shiny floor and, for a moment, wondered if the floor back at the station was getting the attention he requested.

With no issues at security, Chief Wilson smiled at the guards and quickened his pace toward the commissioner's office before changing his mind. Noticing the lettering on the door as he opened it and stepped inside, he wondered for a fraction of a second if he should run for one of the three county commissioner positions. Chuckling at the ludicrous thought, he let the door close behind him.

"Good morning, Judy."

"Good morning, Chief; what brings you down here this morning? Are you retiring again?"

Irritation flickered through the chief's mind, but his previous indecisiveness warranted the comment.

*Bitch* was his initial thought, but he said, "Yes, you smartass," instead.

"Oh, sorry, Chief. I was joking—you know me."

"Well, I have earned your doubt. No worries. Bad on me for being so wishy-washy. Is the Chair in? Or one of the other two commissioners?"

"No, they are all in Salem for the day and won't be back until tomorrow afternoon."

There was an element of disappointment, conflicted with relief, in the chief's facial expression. He felt the muscles in his face sag and saw from Judy's reaction that along with the tight lines on his forehead, his expression didn't go unnoticed.

"Do you want to make an appointment for tomorrow? I could also get this to the board."

Chief Wilson thought about the request for a moment. Then, glancing down at the folder in his hand, he considered her question. Afraid he'd change his mind again, he took a step closer to Judy, sitting at her desk, and stuck out the folder for her to take.

"No. You know I prefer dealing with the commissioners and I am certain the Chair will get in touch with me once she sees this."

Judy reached up and took the folder from the chief. Knowing the chief over the years and sensing what may be in the folder, she was the one with a surprised facial expression now.

"Oh, what is this, Chief?"

"My resignation letter. Please let the Chair know I am happy to meet with her when she can make time."

With that, the chief felt his imaginary tormenting monkey slink off his back and hit the floor, running.

He typed letters up before, signed them, told Judy over the phone countless times what he was doing, but he never went through with it. Until today.

Relishing the rush of intense energy pulsing through his body, the chief had a sudden urge to go for a long mountain biking ride through the trails at Mt. of the Rogue.

Grinning, pleased with himself, he let the impulse pass and for a moment watched a speechless Judy squeeze the folder wondering if it was real. Expecting a verbal reaction, the chief, not wanting any further discussion, turned and left the room.

Exiting the office, he felt as though he had glimpsed a monkey, fresh off his back, running, at the end of the hall, away from him. Then, smiling at himself as he walked out of the building, the chief pictured himself flipping off the monkey and mumbled the words under his breath: "Kiss my ass."

# Guts

Sitting in silence, save a low hum of music oozing through the pickup's bass-filled speakers, Sky stared eastward. There was a familiar howl of wind slamming against the vehicle as it entered and swirled inside the cab. Glancing at the driver, she attempted to smile; a half-hearted grin was all she could muster. Her mouth felt awkward with a lack of verbal commitment. Searching for something to say, she turned her head and felt the wind push against her face.

"My name is Bill. Bill Tyree Johnstone. My friends and family call me Billy. Some people call me B.T., and a few others call me B.J., which, for obvious reasons, isn't my favorite."

Sitting in an awkward state of uncertainty, Sky wanted to speak—to form words and get them out into the air—but her mouth felt stuck in pasty-thick mud, the kind that clings to your boots and won't let go without a stick. Her lips stayed sealed, and her tongue sat frozen, like a diving board bolted to the concrete edge of a backyard pool.

The pickup moved up a long hill as the driver switched lanes and eased the vehicle around a slow-moving truck. Sky felt helpless and weird; words were never hard for her to create. Her father used to say she could keep a room full of monks entertained all day, if necessary, she talked so much. Feeling an intense pull toward her father and reconciliation, longing for the security a parent is supposed to provide, she figured the feelings manifested because she headed toward Oregon. *Yes, that must be it.*

"Well, are you going to say anything? I am not a serial killer or rapist. You looked sad and desperate. You are the first hitcher I have ever picked up. Please don't make me regret it."

47

Sky turned her head and shoulders, words stumbled out of her mouth like a fumbled football bouncing around waiting to be recovered.

"I'm Sky. My name's Sky. I am heading home to Oregon. I'm Sky."

Mortified, embarrassed, and angry at herself, Sky turned her head away and thought, *What in the hell? Why does this guy have me on my heels?* She felt a strange sense that the tables turned on her in some unexpected way in terms of being in control of the interaction.

"Are you retarded? Or, am I supposed to say mentally challenged?"

Feeling a cool stream of acceptance and empathy rush through the cab of the pickup, Sky relaxed. Turning her head toward Billy, staring at him, she liked the sound of the name Billy. He smiled, she smiled, and they both burst into laughter.

"I am sorry, Billy. My name is Sky Wilson. I haven't been camping. I kind of ran away from home a few years ago and am heading back. The closer I get, the more nervous and uptight I get. And no, I am not retarded, but I am a dumbass."

Now Billy took a turn, sitting in silence. Sky figured he didn't know what to say. *But, of course, most people didn't when she mentioned she was a runaway.*

"Don't worry; I'm over eighteen. I promise if we get stopped by the police, I won't scream that you abducted me."

Sky hoped for a laugh, but Billy's face flushed instead. His pale skin—Irish or maybe Scottish, she guessed—made every reaction painfully visible. *Great.* He probably regretted picking her up. *Damnit,* this wasn't what she intended.

The two sat in silence as the pickup sped up Anderson Pass, undulating and ongoing climbs before Interstate 5 peaked at the Siskiyou Pass. In all her glory and grandeur, one of the Cascades crown jewels, the fourteen-thousand-foot Mt. Shasta loomed in the rearview. Mt McLoughlin, another picturesque peak to the northeast, made her appearance from time to time between the breaks in the landscape as southern Oregon drew closer by the second.

"Cat got your tongue?"

"Shit, sorry. A little freaked out about the runaway thing, I guess?"

"You can drop me off if you want; I understand," Sky replied, hoping her words fell on deaf ears.

"Nah, that's okay. I appreciate you being upfront with me." More silence hung until Billy asked, "What's it like being on the run?"

"Being on the run?" Sky laughed and responded, "I am not a convict on the lam!"

"Well shit, I don't know what to call it. What's it like being uh… on your own? It can't be easy."

"Easy is the last thing it is that's for sure." Sky hesitated, deep in thought, as the last couple of years replayed in her head like an award-winning Jared Cruce documentary: gritty, touching, and real.

"Where is home? Ashland?"

"No, Talent. My dad has a big house and acreage in the foothills. He's been the fire department chief for quite a while."

"Talent is nice. More affordable than Ashland, for sure."

"I never liked it," Sky responded. Her mind focused on her dislike of Talent. It wasn't about the town. Shuffling her thoughts, she knew the disdain was more about dissatisfaction with her life when she lived there. Too many parental fights before her mother walked out, never to return. And a dad who worked more than he was home; he loved the fire station more than being around her she often told herself. Another lie.

Her eyes swelled. She fought back emotions; they subsided. She looked left out of the front windshield and recognized the unremarkable top of Mt. Ashland, save for the giant soccer ball sitting on it. At least, that is what it looked like to her as a child. She knew it was for weather or radar or something technical. Regardless, the mountain without it had no character—unlike McLoughlin or Shasta. It did have a historic ski resort and nestled up against the Pacific Crest Trail, but beyond that it was a round mound of forgettable elevation.

The mountain resurrected memories of childhood and learning to ski with her father. He was so patient; he stayed with her and all the inexperienced skiers the whole day on the easy lift. Her dad never once got mad or frustrated; one of the few times she appreciated him the way a father should be.

"I graduated from SOU last year and stayed put in Rogue River. Working construction with my uncle for now to pay the bills. I am not sure what to do next."

Sky considered Billy's last response and wondered if she would have liked college.

"I would have liked to have tried college," Sky said in a quiet, reflective tone before finishing her thought with, "Did you like SOU?"

"College was fun for sure. I loved it. I didn't want to leave and have to face reality." Billy let the comment hang as he pressed the turn signal and switched lanes. Safely back in the slow lane he continued, "So why can't you go to college? Do you have your GED?"

Sky considered the last question. She wasn't sure how much she wanted Billy to know about her. But her education and aspirations seemed harmless enough, so she plowed forward.

"I have my high school diploma. I graduated when I was sixteen."

"Damn," Billy blurted, clearly impressed. "That's exceptional."

Sky smiled; her ego soaked up the unintended praise from her rescuer.

"I couldn't stand high school and wanted out as quick as possible. So, I graduated early and left."

"That takes guts," Billy said as he accelerated the pickup around a slow-moving truck. To Sky's dismay, the traffic ahead thickened, forcing them into a single, crawling lane through construction.

"Not so sure about that," she said softly. "The older I get, the more I realize it wasn't guts—it was fear. Fear of staying, fear of being stuck."

*And fear of becoming like my mother,* Sky thought. *Bitter, disconnected, always one wrong word away from exploding.* That fear had gripped her tighter than she ever admitted. Leaving had felt like escape—like survival. But now, looking back, it felt more like abandonment.

She lowered her chin, eyes fixed on her lap. Sadness tightened in her chest as the full weight of what she'd missed came rushing in. Not just the solid roof and loving protection of her father's home, but the rest of it too—the life of a normal teenager. Proms, late-night talks with friends, track meets, football games, parties she pretended not to care about but secretly wanted to be invited to. She hadn't just left a house—she'd left a chapter of life behind she couldn't get back.

# Number 1, Window 3

Seventeen minutes of commuting behind her, Kaley parked, then sat for another fifteen minutes in her car, listening to a soothing voice. Checking her wristwatch as the voice paused on the phone app, Kaley, not wanting to be late, stopped the app, turned the phone to silent and got out of her car. Heading toward the rear trunk, she stopped short, deciding to leave her wheelchair behind today. A whimsical, smartass voice registered in her head that she won't need it today—she is strong enough and her legs won't hurt. Pushing aside cartoonish thoughts of bullshit, the remainder of her legs always hurt, she relented and focused on being *calm* heading for the hospital's entrance.

Making her way through the hallways, her lower torso felt unfamiliar. She had done this same routine the last several years, almost daily, and her mind always returned pain from what remained of her legs. A new awareness of a life of possibilities swirled around her, rattling her confidence. For the first time she could remember, she didn't think about being a double amputee. She didn't feel bone-deep pain. Several times she looked down as she walked, wondering if her legs were still there. Focusing on controlled breathing, she replayed in her mind the words the woman spoke from her phone.

"Life decisions are choices. Misery is a choice. Pain is a choice. Joy is a choice. Satisfaction is a choice. How we react to everything that goes on in our life is a choice. How do you want to live: controlling your choices and how you think, or feeling trapped like a puppet?"

Minutes later, Kaley sat at her workstation staring at a bubble-bouncing screen saver. She couldn't remember how she got there or when she sat down. A pleasant vibration bounced around inside her ears, and she focused to isolate the reason behind the noise.

"GOOD MORNING, Kaley. EARTH to Kaley. Are you okay?"

Kaley shook her head and turned toward the noise. Her workmate, Mia, stood next to her, snapping long, slender, fingers inches from her face.

"Ha. Shit. Sorry, Mia. I listened this morning to that app you told me to download and I guess I kind of spaced out thinking about it."

"Well, it's about time, Kaley. She's amazing, isn't she? I listen to that app every morning when I am getting ready for work and then while I am driving here. She will change your life for the better."

As Mia kept talking, Kaley feigned listening and started organizing her desk, bringing the PC out of sleep mode and making sure there were enough pens in the small stainless cup etched with the hospital's logo.

"I know you do, Mia. You have told me every morning for the past month."

Mia smiled, sat down, and casually pulled her hair back, working it through a scrunchie. Kaley watched closely as she formed a perfect ponytail, the orange band a striking accent against her rich auburn hair. As a young girl, Kaley had always wanted hair that color. Even now, she found herself mesmerized by its warmth and depth. "Well, remember, listen to her..."

Kaley interrupted Mia and finished her sentence for her. "Every day for at least two weeks to give her a chance. It will change your life."

"I know, I know, I know, Mia. Shit, girl! You don't need to remind me." Kaley couldn't help but respond.

Mia's facial reaction showed hurt or confusion. Kaley didn't feel like diving into the why and what, or discussing Mia's mood further, so she looked away.

Both women busied themselves as they sat in silence. Kaley looked at the clock and realized that seven minutes needed to tick by before she pulled the shade up on her customer service window and started registering patients. She longed to get back in her car and drive around the Rogue Valley listening to what she hoped to be a life-changing podcast. This morning, her mind and body responded with a positive oomph to the words from her car stereo. She knew it had something to do with listening to the woman and her soothing confidence and voice. Life couldn't be this easy though, right? Choosing to feel better about oneself and things going on around her—no way shit is that simple.

Kaley reflected, for what felt like the thousandth time, on her life and the choices she'd made. *No regrets*—that was her go-to line, something she told people often. But she didn't live it. Not really.

Her mind worked differently. It clung to a deeply buried bitterness she kept trying to ignore. She knew something had to change. But the struggle—that was the constant.

Beyond the Army's half-hearted attempts at rewiring her with counselor-speak, she had no idea what to do about it. Not in any way that felt practical. Or real.

Her desire to become a lawyer, one with an impressive communications degree from the prestigious Willamette University, went up in literal flames the god-forsaken moment the damn IED erupted. Years of life after the military found her floundering around from job to job finally landing her at a "bullshit" hospital job she despised. She lived with her medicine-dependent, drunk-ass mother. She hadn't been on a meaningful date since the Army fucked her over, spent no time with friends, and grew tired of her best weekend moments, which include a battery-operated piece of handheld plastic. The hospital job paid her bills and kept her fed, but joy in her life didn't exist, at all.

This morning, with the simple act of listening to a woman's voice during a podcast, Kaley's mind pulled her toward transformation—like she could break from the shackles of despair and do something with her life.

Looking up at the clock, Kaley watched the secondhand tick down the final ten seconds to 0800. She raised the blind, revealing a lobby full of the usual morning crowd—patients waiting to check in for appointments, evaluations, and scheduled tests.

Beating Mia to the punch for perhaps the first time, Kaley smiled as a quiet pulse of satisfaction moved through her chest. She pressed the button on her console, and the LED sign above the front desk flickered to life: "Number 1 – Window 3."

A man stood up, checked the screen, and made his way toward her window. Kaley sat a little taller, ready to start the day—on her terms, for once.

# That's What I Want

Listening to the noisy four-by-four pickup tires grinding as they rotated in snail-paced construction traffic, Sky took her thoughts and escaped into quietness. Continuing to search for purpose and direction, she stared out the window unaware of the countless pines and growing elevation of the Siskiyous. She tried to focus on individual orange cones as they moved by, but her eyes couldn't lock onto one long enough to see them with clarity. Much like her life the last few years, speeding along with no sense of purpose.

Frustration pulled her mind away from the cones toward the day's possibilities, which spun in her brain like a fast-moving merry-go-round. Unable to embrace commitment toward a definitive goal, or any sensible plan of action, she thought of a soldier marching. One foot in front of another. "keep going," she mumbled.

The little girl in her wanted to reconnect with her father. The young woman in her fought the fear of paternal rejection. Thinking about her mother—wondering if she was even alive—sad thoughts about missed family opportunities swirled through her mind. It was ironic. Her father, as far as she could recall, had never once rejected her. But her mother had walked out on the family and never returned. So why did she believe her father might?

Sky concentrated on the final memory of her mother, seared deep into her mind like charred grill lines on a thick midwestern steak.

*Her mother, wearing one of her second-hand sundresses, paced around the living room. Sky sat at the kitchen table eating a bowl of Corn Flakes, covered in pure white sugar and bathed in milk. A knock at the front door propelled her mother toward the entrance with a suitcase in hand.*

*When she opened the door, a lithe, peculiar man stood there—cigarette dangling from weather-chapped lips, his red face traced with tiny spider veins of blue under the skin. He hesitated, glancing toward Sky, then pushed open the screen door and extended his hand, as if inviting her mother to step into another life.*

*Laura reached for the man's hand, then paused. She set the suitcase down and turned toward Sky.*

*Sky felt an unwelcome sensation as her eyes began to swell and moisten—triggered by a painful, unresolved childhood memory. Road noise distracted her for a moment as the sound of the pickup tires softened. Clear of the final orange cone, scarred with black streaks of rubber, Billy's pickup eased back to normal freeway speed.*

*Sky's mind pulled her back to corn flakes; her mother faded in and out of memory.*

*The suitcase teetered, looked like it might fall—then, as if by magnetic magic, remained upright. Her mother stared at her while she chomped on cereal. To Sky, her mother's eyes seemed vacant and dark, like tiny black holes on either side of her nose. They didn't just look—they consumed.*

In the present, inside the heat of the pickup truck, Sky's neck bristled as the memory gripped her.

*That childhood morning carried a strange chill—unusual in their typically cozy home. It whispered across the back of her neck. Setting aside the spooky feeling, young Sky took another bite of cereal and caught a faint whiff of cigarette smoke drifting in from the man at the door.*

*She didn't like him. Thin and frail, he looked like someone who had already taken too much from the world. He moved through their home like he belonged there—too comfortable, too confident. Too aggressive.*

*Her mother said something unintelligible.*

*"You… be… goo… Sky…"*

*Sky stared, fascinated, as Laura reached for the man's hand. His eyes darted around like he was waiting to be caught. Sky looked down at her bowl, the milk sweetened and tainted with the last of the corn flakes. She was disappointed the comforting meal was nearly over.*

*"What's for dinner tonight, Mom? Can we have tacos again?"*

*She scooped the last of the sugary milk with her spoon, pausing before it reached her lips. The milk sloshed, spilling over the side and splattering into the bowl. And then—her mother picked up the suitcase, took the man's hand, and walked out the front door. It stayed ajar.*

*Sky didn't worry. Of course, her mother would come back to close it. Maybe she just forgot. She reminded herself to ask for five dollars for the school fair. It was going to be so much fun. She'd wear pants—no smart girl wore a dress to a fair. The boys would have an unfair advantage in jeans. She wasn't about to let that happen.*

*Still thinking about her outfit, she lifted the bowl to her mouth and slurped the last few drops. Wiping her lips with the back of her hand, she pushed her chair back, stood up, and carried the bowl to the sink. The loud clang echoed as she set it down. She peered into the deep, food-stained ceramic, expecting to see broken glass—but the bowl had survived. The spoon rattled inside and finally stilled.*

*Sky looked out the window above the sink, hoping to see a deer. Or at least a gray squirrel with its big, bouncing tail. She loved how they moved like joy itself. But all she saw was the fountain. The water barely gurgled—another thing her dad needed to clean.*

*She turned and stared at the still-open door.*

*Why hadn't her mom come back to close it?*

*Why had she stuttered before walking outside with that man?*

*Sky walked toward the door, thinking she should open it all the way and look outside. But she stopped short—scared. Scared of what she might see… or not see. Her hand hovered, then pulled back toward her chest.*

*With the sudden energy only a child can summon, she spun and raced upstairs to get dressed. Her mother must be outside, waiting with the strange man to drive her to school.*

*That suitcase. Those vacant eyes. They confused her.*

*But even in that moment, Sky didn't imagine the truth.*

*She had no idea she'd never see her mother again.*

"We should get to Ashland in another fifteen minutes. Where do you want me to drop you off? Is there somewhere else you need to go? I can take you as far as Grants Pass if you need me to, but I don't have enough time to go any further than that today. I live in Rogue River, not sure if I mentioned that or not." Billy's fast-paced voice rang loud in Sky's ears, returning her mind to the dense musty air of the pickup's dank cab.

Sky didn't know what to say. Nervous, she reached up to wipe her eyes.

"You, okay? You got quiet. It seems like you were somewhere else."

"I am fine, thanks. Memories flooding back—some shit I need to deal with. I hoped they were behind me and I wouldn't have to come to terms with any of them. You know, happy to bury my head in the proverbial sand."

"Join the club. I can't believe the shit that pops into my head sometimes."

Sky thought Billy replied in a sweet and empathetic tone.

"I saw a sign for a rest area a ways back. Could you drop

me off there, please? I will hang out there until I can figure out what I want to do."

"You sure? I don't mind driving you somewhere."

Sky thought Billy replied with odd eagerness.

"No, thank you. I have some shit to figure out. The rest area is fine." Sky wondered about free coffee. Her bones, still chilled from months on the San Fran streets, established a new level of discomfort the last couple of weeks. She struggled to imagine if they would ever warm.

"Okay. It's a new rest area with a welcome center and other amenities. At least I think there is. I only see it from the freeway when I drive by. I have never needed to stop there. From the freeway, it looks nice."

Sky didn't respond. Instead, she stared at the window and continued to reflect on her life. What could she do? What should she do?

Sitting in silence, tired of being cold and hungry, she realized she wanted little more than to feel calm. Tired of sleepless stress and unwavering doubt, she couldn't remember the last time she slept in a bed. Her back felt forever out of place from cold, soul-draining piss-stained concrete. Her mind wrestled daily with meaning and purpose. Did anything matter? She wanted to believe something mattered.

She looked at Billy. "Please drop me off at the rest area. I'll figure my shit out there."

"Okay. If that's what you want."

Sensing disappointment in Billy's response, Sky replied in a dull matter-of-fact tone, "Yes, that's what I want."

Turning her head, she stared out the passenger window again. She didn't want Billy to see her face as another tear slid down the side of her right cheek. Sky mumbled the words, "I want to go home."

# Side to Side

Teddy eased the cart to a stop beside the maintenance shed in the back northeastern corner of the manufactured home park. He sat for a moment, staring east at the sky. The wind churned through the treetops—oak, pine, and spruce bending under its push. He tried to recall what the weather lady had said that morning as he got ready for work. Probably more dry heat. The air had been parched for months, no rain since spring.

Curious about global warming and the earth's ever-changing climate, Teddy went to the public library and checked out three books on the topic. But two chapters into each, frustration set in. Every one of them dove headfirst into political gobbledygook. He didn't want lectures about how humanity was ruining the planet—he wanted the science: the hows and whys behind the weather and climate.

In Teddy's mind, it was simple. Humans had a responsibility to be good stewards of the earth—to fix mistakes when they found them and stay vigilant about doing better, especially with things like plastics and waste. But once politics got involved, real concern seemed to get buried beneath arguments about who's right and who's winning.

"Okay, Ted. Snap out of it and get to work. You can't go sandbagging it all day long now," Teddy says out loud, as if the break in silence might motivate him.

He walked to the front of the shed and deposited the plastic cup into the trash can. He reminded himself to take the cans out later this evening for tomorrow's curbside pickup. Looking at his list, he headed to the property entrance to tinker, yet again, with the frustrating security gate.

61

Sliding back into the cart, he turned the wheel and pressed the accelerator pedal. Three minutes later, he parked in front of the security gate's main panel. Getting out of the cart, he went to the rear, and lifting a toolbox lid, grabbed a number-two Phillips screwdriver and a voltmeter. A dark-blue Prius pulled up, slowed, and the driver lowered their window while coming to a quiet stop.

"Good Morning, Teddy," squeaked the voice from inside the car.

Teddy smelled a sickening scent wafting from inside the car. There were at least thirty different tree shaped air fresheners hanging from a dozen spots inside the vehicle.

Everyone around the park knew Ms. June Pearl was a hoarder and lacked any modicum of cleanliness. Whenever the woman had a maintenance issue, dread coursed through Teddy's skin. Her house smelled like soiled newspaper and wet magazines with an overpowering smell of decades of smoking. Air fresheners, new and old alike, littered the floors, shelving, and countertops. Anywhere two inches of free space went unclaimed, the woman placed a plastic air freshener. There were stacks and stacks of them. Each stack a rainbow of colors.

*Thank god for COVID*, he'd tell himself every time he'd enter her home. He'd get in and out as quick as possible. Even though COVID seemed to morph into nothing more than the flu, Teddy would still wear a mask, and he knew Ms. Pearl took offense. He didn't give a shit; her home belonged in a massive Petrie dish.

Ms. Pearl, more than a few times, said to other park residents that Teddy was rude to her, but none of them put any mind to it, knowing the woman all too well.

Teddy thought the woman was one long nap away from dropping a burning cigarette on the floor while she slept, burning down the entire development. He asked the park owners to have her cited, but no one could come up with a legitimate reason. Stupidity wasn't against the law. At least not yet, even though Teddy thought it should be.

"Hello, Ms. Pearl."

Teddy wanted to say more than hello, but this woman frustrated him. She'd said several bad, and untrue, things about him in the last couple of years, and he felt he didn't owe her any syrupy kindness, a standard hello would suffice.

"Are you still tinkering with this gate, Teddy? You've been going at it for months. Why don't you pay someone who knows what they are doing to fix it?"

The question hung in the air. The words, at Teddy's pleasure, wafted away into nothingness.

"Teddy, I am talking to you. Are you going to answer me?"

Another resident's car pulled up behind Ms. Pearl. Teddy smiled, knowing the mean and nasty hoarding woman would now have to move on.

"There is another car in back of you, Ms. Pearl. Have a nice day."

Ms. Pearl mumbled "stupid asshole" loud enough for Teddy to hear as the window of her car closed, cutting off the pungent odor of fake scents and all-too-real body odor. He couldn't remember being more thankful for anything so simple as another car pulling up, forcing Ms. Pearl on her way.

Teddy didn't recognize the car, or the man driving, but with over one hundred homes in the park and people coming and going monthly, he couldn't know everyone.

He nodded as they drove by and then looked down at the schematics and troubleshooting instructions he printed out at home. After months of searching, he found the exact model of the decade-old security gate and remote activation pad. He felt better today about making progress on the damn thing. The entire development depended on it functioning. Perhaps, once

63

he got the gate fixed and proved yet again his value to the community, he'd get that raise he wanted.

Teddy took the access panel off the gate's security panel. Setting the screws on top of the panel box, he took his stainless Leatherman from his back pocket. Looking at the photo diagrams, he compared the wiring on the panel to the image he stared at on paper. Both showed eight wires. Next, he compared the colors of the wires, and they also matched. Flipping the piece of paper over, hoping the staple was strong enough, he read troubleshooting information about the gate opening and closing in an intermittent fashion.

He knew the power to the panel and gate was good, because he checked it at least half a dozen times in the last six weeks. He checked it again, in case senility crept up on him. Next, he isolated the control wire and performed a polarity check with the activation button released and engaged.

Checking each way in the paved entryway to the park, with no cars coming or going, he pressed the button and watched as the gate started to swing close before stopping halfway. Teddy cursed, jiggled the wires, and then watched as the gate swung back open, coming to a full-open and stopped position against the concrete privacy wall.

"Shit," Teddy said out loud. He considered screaming and then throwing the multimeter onto the highway, hoping a truck would run over it. However, calmer nerves took over. Tossing the electronic device into the back of the maintenance cart, he scrunched diagram papers up in a ball and tossed them in back as well. Grabbing the screws from the top of the security panel, he reinstalled the access panel making sure all the screws were tight. He slid his Leatherman back in its sheath, pleased with the sound of the button snapping the cover shut.

Contemplating whether to climb into the maintenance cart, Teddy hesitated. Gripping the plastic-handled screwdriver tightly in his dirty hand, he faced the panel. He glanced around again, checking for witnesses. Convinced he was alone, he raised his left hand and slammed the back of the tool down onto the security panel.

A loud click echoed. Teddy stared in disbelief as the gate, frozen in place just seconds earlier, lurched forward and swung closed.

He frowned, lowered his head, and shook it slowly. Typical.

Muttering a curse under his breath, he stood there, unsure what to do next—until a car rolled up. As if mocking him, the gate's sensor worked perfectly, and it opened without hesitation. The driver gave him a polite nod as they passed.

Teddy stood with his mouth agape, then glanced at the panel, contemplating whether it might just be easier to leave the damn gate open for good.

# Sadness and Anger

Sky walked out of the sterile, brick, welcome center, relished the southern Oregon scenery, put the earth-harmful Styrofoam cup of coffee to her lips, took a big sip, and remembered she hated tepid coffee. On the streets for months, she hadn't forgotten what a good cup of coffee tasted like and what she held in her hand didn't qualify. However, free trumped quality, and the senior woman who served it to her couldn't have been nicer, so she feigned gratitude. Sky thought the woman lived in her memories but she struggled to place her.

In no mood to chat, Sky stepped outside after spending a few minutes staring at a faded poster of Crater Lake National Park—the nation's fourth national park, established in 1902, as the sign reminded her—along with snapshots of other far-flung corners of Oregon.

*A memory surfaced—her mother and father taking her to the caldera as a child. She remembered standing at the edge of a trail, gazing down into the deep, endless blue below. The steep slope leading to the water fascinated her. Her young mind didn't register fear, only curiosity. So, she dropped to her butt and began scooting toward the edge, wondering what it would feel like to slide all the way down.*

*Her mother screamed—sharp and panicked, the kind of sound that could crack glass. But that was all. Just the scream. It was her father who lunged, grabbed the back of her jacket, and yanked her to safety. He didn't say much, just knelt beside her, holding her hand tight in his for the rest of the day. He didn't let go until they were all buckled into the car and driving back down the highway toward home.*

Now, so many years later, Sky thought about that grip—

firm, protective, steady. A wordless message: You're safe. I've got you.

But what lingered even more was the absence of her mother's touch. Sky remembered the scream, yes, but nothing else. No hand on her back, no arms wrapping her up after the danger passed. Just the sound. Loud. Distant. Like scared for the sake of being scared—not out of worry—but out of raw fear.

As a child, she didn't understand why her mother had yelled instead of rushing to pull her close. Back then, she thought maybe screaming was just what moms did when they were scared. But now, older, wiser, and more wounded, she saw it differently. That lack of reach—that distance—started long before she realized.

Her father had held her hand. Her mother never reached out.

Finding an isolated picnic table, Sky perched herself on top, placed her feet on the connected bench, and dropped her pack next to her on the plastic surface. Waiting for the inevitable, she sipped at the coffee and looked across the parking lot toward the southeast. Grizzly Peak, looking like what she thought the Scottish Highland might be like, stood stoic, still covered in green with old-growth forest at the higher elevations. The grass in the foothills shimmered a golden color of wheat. Sharp, chiseled rock formations jutted out across the landscape due east of the visitor center. She loved the landscape in southern Oregon as a child, and years later, nothing changed with her perception.

South of her, she made out another childhood memory: Pilot Rock.

*Sky reflected on hiking one time with a childhood friend and her family at Pilot Rock. The trail wasn't difficult, but climbing the final fifty feet took some shimmying and hand-gripping of rocks to reach the summit formation. To the dismay* of the childhood friend's mother, Sky went against the controlling women's wishes. Later, Sky lied to her parents, claiming she didn't hear the mother tell the girls not to climb the final stretch because of the "treachery for little girls."

Her friend waited below while the father climbed up and plopped down next to Sky on the hard rocky surface. She remembered this as the first time an adult, other than her father, treated her with dignity. Several feet away, her friend's father winked at her while they both searched over the vastness of the land. Without looking at her, he told her, "I am glad you came up. It is beautiful up here. It's a waste to come this far and not experience the beauty up here. I keep telling my wife, but she always huffs, rolls her eyes and stays below. Her loss, right? Anyway, it is one of my favorite places to hang out. I let my thoughts wander. I think about nothing but the beauty of the land."

Thinking the wink beget a simple, tacit, approval, Sky smiled looking across the few remaining miles of southern Oregon toward northern California. Considering what he meant by the land, she loved the let my thoughts wander phrase he used.

She often let her thoughts wander. But she never thought about the land before. Sky focused on how pretty and peaceful nature seemed to her and liked the idea of thinking about the land and counting on it to be stationary and reliable. The hills and mountains never changed, save the seasons and weather. The trees remained steadfast, falling when high winds howled and an occasional drought or nasty beetle she read about in fourth grade, occurred. The lakes filled and receded, the rivers never ceased to pulse with unrelenting power, deer were plentiful; the doe got pregnant, birthed spot-covered babies, and the bucks grew and shed horns as often as the changing of the leaves.

Letting her thoughts meander around in her youthful mind,

68

*Sky dreamed of being a majestic bald eagle soaring down the Klamath River, wondering if she sailed over the land below and found her mother what might happen. She reasoned with an eagle's amazing eyesight she should be able to find her mom. Would her father miss her when she was gone? Her mind raced with wishful thoughts about getting unconditional parental love from her mother. She had it from her father but for some reason it didn't count.*

*Hearing her friend's mother raising her voice below, the father stood, smiled a magnificent smile, reached over and patted Sky on the back, and said, "Okay, let's go before we escalate the level of trouble were in."*

*Sky, liking the idea that he included himself in the getting in trouble portion, popped up and headed back down the rock, sliding the final twenty feet on her butt. Receiving a litany of words she refused to acknowledge from the waiting mother, Sky took it in stride, hoping her father wouldn't get too mad when the sad woman made it clear that Sky was a belligerent child.*

*Watching the way her father looked at her, she wanted him to care, which made matters worse. She couldn't figure out what she did wrong and why he wouldn't spend any genuine time with her and talk with her. If a conversation of any substance started, his phone seemed to ring as if on cue. He'd claim he needed to head to work or that a "special" meeting came up. An old soul at a young age, Sky surmised that both her parents left her, even if one of them still happened to be present.*

Not understanding if her memories soothed her, or reminded her of robbed youth, Sky stood and walked away to deposit her Styrofoam cup in a large plastic-lined trash can. She knew the contents were destined to end up at the dump, piled with tons of other crap the earth could never absorb. Did it matter? She didn't know, but she also felt a responsibility to be smart with waste. Plastic angered her, but what could she do about it besides harbor depressing anger?

Returning to the bench, she looked around the parking lot and saw the inevitable van approaching. Knowing Steel, piloting the white behemoth, would hunt for her and be furious at her insolence, she wondered why she abandoned the idea of running and waiting to be found; she braced herself for the verbal litany of hope-for-the-planet garbage destined to spew from Steel's mouth. Why in the hell she stuck around for this shit escaped her?

Reaching down, Sky picked up her backpack and slid it over her shoulder as the white van parked by the sidewalk a good fifty feet from the table she claimed as hers. Standing, she walked toward the van as the occupants sat motionless inside, staring as if black clad agents were about to swoop from every hiding point and descend on the van with a resounding vengeance. Her knees ached and wobbled, step after step.

Thinking she wouldn't make it to the van, weak legs somehow carried her the requisite steps. As she arrived at the passenger door, she pulled the handle and swung the door open. Seeing the angry face of Steel, she considered climbing inside but recoiled, then bent over and vomited.

A tear fell with the last of the coffee that refused to stay in her stomach. Sky wiped her mouth with the back of her left hand and stared inside the van. Not understanding a word of what poured from the mouth of a screaming Steel, she searched for pleasant childhood memories. Thinking about what life might be like if her mother stayed, she welcomed then encouraged the swell of sadness and anger building inside her.

# How Can I Help

Several hours into her day, moving through the motions more reflexively than ever, Kaley's mind kept circling back to the voice she'd heard during her morning commute. Something about it left her feeling hopeful—rejuvenated. Her heart pulsed smoother, steadier, beating with a vigor she hadn't felt since her military days. *Invincibility* came to mind... followed closely by *youthful naivety*.

The previous patient she assisted and checked in, a mid-fifties male who she could tell loved misery and feeling sorry for himself, didn't even get her down. After processing his paperwork, she sent him on his way to a colonoscopy; glancing to her right, she saw Mia sitting unoccupied staring at the window and smiled.

"How are you doing, Mia? I can't believe how much better I feel today."

Mia returned a smile and responded, "I am so happy for you, Kaley."

A short pause followed. Neither wanted the rare and joyful moment to end. Mia, taking short breaths, appeared anxious and uptight to Kaley.

"Is something wrong, Mia?"

"No, thinking about the fire."

Kaley stared at the busy waiting area. Knowing she needed to buzz in the next patient to process, she instead pivoted toward Mia.

"What fire? What are you talking about?"

"My previous patient said a fire started in Ashland and is burning toward Talent and a few homes and businesses already burned."

Kaley, trying to process the thought of a fire flashed to the Middle East and her final deployment. A tingle coursed through ghost feet that were no longer part of her body.

"We haven't been at work that long, Mia. How is that possible? Fires are in the woods, not in towns." Kaley's mind flashed back to the Camp Fire and the near destruction of Paradise, California, in recent years, then realized how ridiculous her statement sounded once the words left her mouth.

"Your joking, right, Kaley?" Mia responded.

"I know. Stupid. Forget I said it."

Kaley looked up at the clock then back at Mia. "I am going to the breakroom and see if there is any news on the TV, okay?"

Kaley watched Mia glance up at the clock, then returned her stare before responding. "Okay, but hurry back and let me know what you find out. Glad I live in White City."

Kaley flipped her sign around to signify her window and station as CLOSED then got up to amble down the hall. Within minutes she stood around a small television that hung on the wall in the employee break room. At least half a dozen people stared at the screen listening to one of the local new stations.

Kaley listened for a few minutes and thought she understood that the fire departments controlled the blaze—at least according to the news station. She wondered if her mother got out of bed yet. She contemplated calling her but knew how pissed off she'd get if the phone woke her up from sleeping.

Ambling away from the front of the TV and the hushed whispers of those still watching, Kaley moved over to the refrigerator and opened the door. Looking inside, she saw her last Summer Edition Red Bull energy drink, so she grabbed it and closed the door. Reaching for a solo cup off the back of the counter, she filled it with ice from the refrigerator door.

Pouring the sugar-filled liquid into the cup, anticipation filled her mind knowing the energy surge the addictive drink would provide. Tossing the empty can in the recycle bin, she made her way back down the hall to her workstation. Sitting down she switched her CLOSED sign to AVAILABLE, pressed the button to let the receptionist know she returned, and prepared to help someone else make their way back into the bowels of the hospital.

Mia finished up with a customer and addressed Kaley. "Well?"

Kaley, seeing a patient heading toward her window already, responded to Mia without hesitation.

"No big deal. It sounds like a fire started in Ashland. It's burning up portions of Bear Creek, but reports say the fire department contained it and it is under control."

Mia nodded and greeted the next person. Kaley turned to face the thick plastic screen that separated her from the patients. A woman approached, alone, her face carrying a sadness deeper than anyone Kaley had seen in a long time.

"Yes, ma'am. How can I help you today?"

# This Is Bad

As Chief Wilson drove the back roads home, he rolled down the driver's window, letting the hot air swirl through the pickup cab. It was as if, by letting the air in, he could somehow sniff out the trouble that seemed to be lurking beyond the horizon. The stifling summer heat carried a heavy sense of dread for what might come.

But for now, the pine-scented air and the familiar melody playing on the radio eased his nerves. The chief pressed a button on the steering wheel to turn up the volume, the soothing tune cutting through his unease. He considered asking Google who sang the melodic tune but dismissed the thought. It wasn't worth his time. He'd forget anyway.

Contemplating the song's lyrics, the chief returned thoughts to his current mood. He couldn't pinpoint why his spirits seemed to soar. He wondered if a simple resignation letter provided a noticeable boost in spirits.

Considering the day, the oppressive heat, his looming resignation, and the uncertainty of what the day might bring, the tune playing on the radio grated on his nerves. It had too strong of a beat with garbled, unrecognizable lyrics, and the two-way radio only added to the noise. Still, he half-listened, knowing that if anything critical happened, he'd receive a direct call. With a sigh, he lowered the volume of the obnoxious music until it was nothing more than a faint whisper from the speakers. As if on cue, his two-way radio squawked.

"Chief to dispatch, over. Come in, Chief, over. Chief, come in."

Grabbing the mic off the console, he replied. "Dang, Jane. Relax. Give me a second to grab the handset off the dash, okay?"

"Sorry, Chief. Heads up. I dispatched a call out near Bear Creek in Ashland a minute ago. Sounds like a fire is burning in a meadow near the creek."

"Shit, why the hell didn't I hear the call over the radio?" the chief blurted out loud, not expecting an answer from the young dispatcher.

"I don't know, Chief."

The chief, not wanting to engage in a back-and-forth verbal melee, cut Jane off.

"No response is necessary. Give me the location with the latest information."

The dispatcher responded without haste. "The wastewater treatment facility off Oak Street. It is near the dog park, but access is from Oak Street, Chief. Are you familiar with the area?"

The chief checked the side-view mirrors, rearview as well, reached over, and flipped a switch on the dashboard. The siren and lights activated with immediate intense clarity. Processing the situation, and the location, the chief responded, "I'm familiar with the area. I'll be there in ten minutes. Keep me updated!"

"Roger, Chief. Last known information: a fire that may have gotten away from a homeless person. No confirmation of this, though. I'll check in and get back with you ASAP. Over."

The chief didn't respond as he steered the county fire vehicle onto Interstate 5. He brought the speed of the vehicle up to seventy-five miles per hour as the traffic, in a choreographed fashion, moved to the right. As he passed a tree-surrounded rest stop on the west side of the interstate, he glanced upward and watched the tops of the trees sway and bend in what newscasts would soon call "unseasonably high winds." Cursing, he heard his county radio howl.

"Come in, Chief. Dispatch with an update on the Ashland fire. Over."

Pressing the mic button, the chief responded. "Go ahead."

No confirmation on the origination, Chief, but the report is that it's bad and growing worse by the second. Winds from the east are pulsing 40-50 through the valley and

pushing the fire hard. Helos are in route from the airport. Over."

"Roger, remind them there is plenty of water in Hastings Reservoir if they forgot. They don't need to waste time going to Emigrant Lake. The county has full rights to the water."

"I'll remind them, Chief. Over."

"I am almost on site. Thank you."

"Your welcome, Chief. Good luck!"

Exiting the freeway at the first Ashland exit heading south, the chief almost broadsided a white van. The driver didn't hear or see the red vehicle. Or, like so many drivers, acted like his vehicle was an exception to the law. Blood pressure spiking, adrenaline rushing, the chief yelled, "Shit," pounded the steering wheel, and sped around the vehicle. The guy behind the wheel turned his head as the chief passed, avoiding eye contact. The chief wanted to let the redneck realize he was in the wrong. A woman, however, sitting in the passenger seat looked and stared daggers at him as if it were his fault they had to use their damn brakes.

Fighting the temptation to call the police and give the car's license plate, he returned his eyes to the pavement in front of him and reclaimed his composure. Looking east, he stared at light-colored smoke billowing up from the valley floor as the winds pushed it to the west.

Glancing to the south, flames pierced through smoke, which now dominated the valley sky. A police vehicle approaching his rearview mirror projected lights in circles of red, blue, and white. Heavy smoke rose and billowed like a midwestern tornado and violently blew across the freeway. He contemplated having the Oregon State Police shut down the interstate but waited until he received a status update.

Wondering where the hell the helos were, he thought about the dryness of southern Oregon and wondered if retirement might provide the familiar intensity he felt right now. Every inch of his body tingled as adrenaline rushed through pulsing veins.

Exiting off Oak Street and the entrance to the waste treatment plant, the chief guided the vehicle to a stop. Jumping out, he donned his fire-resistant jacket and put on the chief's white helmet. Searching the scene for the on-scene crew, he pivoted and peered southwest toward the Siskiyou mountain range. His mind visualized the wind, understanding it left California and the Shasta valley gaining momentum. The chief knew from years of experience that hot air often pushed up the southern side of the Siskiyou Range, buffeting Southern Oregon and Northern California.

The southern air mixed with cool air swirling around the summit, then rolled down the northern face of Mt. Ashland before reconstituting with more hot air in the Rogue Valley. The atmospheric weather today: a perfect storm causing worrisome consternation. Thinking of the recent Paradise fire, concern filled the chief's thoughts for anyone in the way of the flames' path if the crew didn't control the blaze within minutes. The low-pressure zone of the valley he called home his entire life pushed and pulled the wind with a ferociousness that made him contemplate The Big Burn—considered the most devastating forest fire ever to torch lands in the United States.

"Chief! Chief!"

Chief Wilson pivoted and stared at the ash-covered shoulders from one of his crew, in a light jog, coming toward him. The intense face, streaked with soot, somehow accented the desperation in blue eyes that looked hesitant and foreboding. As the individual got closer, he noticed the county's second-in-command, Assistant Fire Chief Lindsay Paducah, his right hand for the last several years.

Out of breath from the smoke, Paducah stopped short of Chief Wilson and wasted no time in her first report of the fire.

"Chief, this is bad."

# Get In The Van

Sky stood rigid outside the open door of the van, keenly aware of the people emerging from the welcome center and those sitting in parked cars, their eyes locked on her. People pulled off the freeway into a rest area for a couple of reasons. Rest, sure, but mainly because their bodies needed to eliminate liquid or solids. What they didn't expect was to encounter a screaming woman shattering the mundane rhythm of their pit stop. But the strength of her voice, packed into such a small frame and laced with obstinate determination, seemed to demand an audience.

"Steel, you are an absolute, ego-driven asshole. You don't believe half of the shit you espouse. Fake comes to mind when I think of you."

Sky looked into eyes unable to hide chiseled anger.

"Get in the van right now Sky or so help me god." Steel, looking shell-shocked, tried to maintain a modicum of authority considering the audience.

A street-toughened Sky wasted no time in responding. "Or what? You'll hit me? Try it, motherfucker. Try it. I am begging you. Why don't you slither that scrawny pasty-white ass out of the van. Come over here and try to hit me."

As Sky remained steadfast in her stance outside the passenger door of the van, she glanced in the back seat. The other two in the protest party looked shocked. Their eyes pleaded for the shouting to end. Neither had the courage to back her up, though, as their eyes darted toward Steel, looking for approval and an end to the uncomfortable loud charade.

Sky looked at the floorboard of the van in front of the passenger seat and contemplated climbing inside. The fight and determination in her wouldn't allow it. Her feet, glued to the warming asphalt, backed away. The backpack slung over her shoulders seemed heavier than her body could support. The weight of the dirty canvas pulled her shoulders down toward her torso, and her legs felt as though they were sinking into the earth. Still, her feet propelled her backward as words flew out of her mouth.

"Go to your little protest with your pathetic signs, Steel! What a joke, Steel? I bet your real name is Myron or Darryl. No way your parents looked at you and thought, this kid is Steel." Sky swallowed searching for more courageous oxygen. "Stay the hell away from me!"

As freeway-resting onlookers watched, one large man with an impressive cowboy hat walked toward the van. Steele lowered his voice and pleaded with Sky.

"Sky, sorry, I know I am a prick sometimes. Hop in the van. I promise to be different."

"Ha!" Sky, marveling at the lie, threw her head back, and laughed.

"At least have the conviction, and balls, if you are going to be a prick, to be a confident one, Myron." Sky's legs steadied, anchored by her street-toughened feet on the pavement. Her back and shoulders straightened, and the backpack lightened, feeling like a comforting pillow. She smiled, realizing how the realization of adrenaline flooding her body strengthened her.

The cowboy made his way to the front of the van. Sky stared at him with a defiant look of confidence she couldn't remember ever feeling.

"You okay, ma'am? Is this man-boy being a nuisance?"

Sky tilted her head back and chuckled. "I am fine, pardner. Mind your own god-damned business!"

The surprised and dejected cowboy shook his head as he walked back toward the restrooms.

Steele leaned across the passenger seat. His arm and

hand strained through the distance to reach for the door handle. Finding enough vinyl to grip, he pulled the door shut and eased the van backward out of the parking spot. Moving forward through the lot, heading toward the freeway on-ramp, he kept his head staring straight ahead, finding no courage to look Sky in the eyes as he pulled away.

Sky laughed, flipped off the van, and turned to find a crowd of onlookers staring at her. Unsure how to react and still amped up from the interaction with Steel, her mind responded with less than admirable, angry adrenaline. Wanting to unleash a mother-taught verbal tirade of expletives, she focused on keeping it clean, hoping to emphasize her thoughts, not nasty words.

"WHAT ARE YOU ALL LOOKING AT? MIND YOUR OWN BUSINESS!"

Sky turned and walked toward the freeway and the rest area exit, muttering under her breath.

"Pathetic protest signs. Like they will fucking accomplish anything."

# Idiots

Teddy moved the cart away from the security panel and front gate of the housing development, steering it toward the maintenance shop. In the distance, he spotted smoke rising in the direction of Ashland and wondered what the hell was burning.

It was far too dry for anyone to be burning trash—and besides, it was illegal this time of year.

His mind spun through the possibilities: a house fire? Maybe a car overheating and catching fire? Or more likely, another dumb-ass trucker flying down the Siskiyou Pass like they were Mario F'ing Andretti—only to have their brakes give out and the whole rig go up in flames. He'd read about it plenty of times and even watched it firsthand over a year ago while sipping a beer at the local brewery that sat just off the freeway at the base of the mountain.

He thought about searching his phone for the video he took with his daughter. It showed a sapsucker trucker sitting on the side of the road. The poor schlub placed his head in his hands as his truck, engulfed in flames, tires exploding, burned before his eyes.

Teddy pulled the cart up in front of the maintenance shop, walked inside, and listened to see if the radio—always tuned to the local public broadcasting station—was playing any news about the smoke. Checking his watch, seeing it half-past eleven, he knew that *Here & Now* played. The food portion of the two-hour broadcast was his favorite. Culture was okay, finance was boring, and the technology portion useless. They never once talked about security gate panel technology, and he knew how to operate his cell phone, so...

The radio squawked—it sounded like the podcast-duo talked finance, so Teddy tuned out catching every other sentence.

Glancing out the window facing eastward, he saw the smoke in the sky and curiosity engaged his mind. He figured if it were important, Jefferson Public Radio would make an announcement. He also received alerts on his cell phone from the Watch Fire app, so he wasn't too worried.

"Yes, John, interest rates are going to rise. It's inevitable. So, if you are about to retire, meet with your financial advisor and ..." the radio continued to blare.

Teddy headed to the workbench and eyed the disassembled Weed Eater. He'd fixed the damn thing at least a dozen times over the past couple of years. What he really needed was a new one, but the park's owners had a budgeting philosophy of making a nickel work overtime—and he was the nickel, and he knew it. Unless he wanted to pull weeds by hand, he'd have to fix it again.

Picking up a screwdriver, he turned the screw of the choke back and forth a few times. Teddy grabbed the remaining pieces laid in a precise order on the bench, and with the help of the screwdriver and wrench, piece by piece he put the ten-year-old yard implement back together.

Staring around, his eyes found what they looked for as they locked in on a plastic two-gallon gas can. He wondered if the red jug had fuel in it. If not, did he have any two-stroke oil to mix with new gas? Teddy put the last screw in place for the pull-cord cover and set the screwdriver in its proper slot on the back wall of the workbench. Walking over to the gas can, he picked it up and moved it back-and-forth. Hearing no liquid slosh back and forth, he stared at his wristwatch and considered whether he should grab a burger and fries at Pump House today after he bought gas.

"We repeat," the radio crackled, and the word repeat got Teddy's attention. "There appears to be a small grass fire near the water treatment plant in North Ashland. Fire crews are on scene and there are helicopters in the sky dousing the fire. We will update you with new information as it comes in. Okay, sorry about that John, you mentioned the impact of warming on our local communities..."

*Global warming, my ass,* Teddy thought to himself. Cooling, warming, hot, cold, humid, not humid—duh. It wasn't because of humans. We are along for the ride assholes.

Heading for his pickup, Teddy looked around to see if anyone was in earshot, then said out loud, "I need a beer. Manmade global warming; please. Idiots."

# First

Chief Wilson arrived at ground zero expecting to see chaos. His thirty-plus years of firefighting taught him to expect and embrace the unexpected. Staring at the flames in the meadow while standing by the assistant chief, Paducah, it surprised him to see how the grass fire appeared to be no different from a controlled burn. How the smoke billowed through the valley and the wind-propelled fire had him thinking about fifteen-foot flames raging across open fields. Instead, creeping fire, pushed by the wind, danced across the meadow as firefighters tried to direct its path.

"Doesn't look like much here, Chief, but what we can't see is the fire is already pounding its way up the creek toward Talent."

At the north of the fire flowed Bear Creek. One of the plethora of feeder creeks that kept the wild and famous Rogue River flowing.

Decades of poor vegetation management surrounding the creek provided explosive fuel and a dangerous path toward several small towns and a larger city, Medford. Wilson listened as the chatter over the two-way painted a dreary picture of potential destruction.

As the wind with its invisible power pushed the destruction northward, firefighting choppers dangling overhead came and went—taking turns filling their fire-dousing buckets in small reservoir in the middle of the meadow. The chief wondered about the reservoir's depth and how much water it held and what would remain after they extinguished the fire. He made a mental note to feed his curiosity and take a drive by and investigate once the fire petered out.

Returning his full attention to the process, his resignation less than two hours ago an afterthought, he started providing orders to Paducah.

"Okay, I just made it through Exit 19, North Ashland. Head over there and see if

the Comfort Inn will be our best command post option. I like the high ground there and the easy access to I5 and 99."

"How do we handle resources, Chief? It is already an issue."

"Too soon to tell, Paducah. I'll burn up the phone now with anyone and everyone. We cannot let this thing burn like a wildland fire. If we don't shut the door on the fire, the Rogue Valley towns will suffer in a horrific way. I'll make requests for more support."

Paducah took a glove off and wiped her forehead with the back of the hand. Streaks of sweaty soot surrounded the area where her facemask sat.

"Oh, and Paducah get on the phone, lock down the mobilization team, and make sure the mobile command post is in route to you. When you arrive at the parking lot if you don't think the location is right, call me ASAP. Understood?"

"Roger that, Chief."

"One last thing, Paducah: Did I hear the fire is tagged, Almeda?"

"Yes, Chief. The closest street where the damn thing started."

"Unbelievable. What a way to spend one of my final days on the job."

Paducah, who had started moving toward her vehicle, stopped. Turning, she hesitated a second with what looked like a perplexed facial expression toward the chief.

"What's that, Chief?"

Chief Wilson realizing he popped the lid on a can of beans, one he intended to keep close to the vest until the moment of his choosing, pivoted his response.

"Nothing, Paducah. Lamenting how long a day this is heading toward. So many people are going to be affected. A real shame."

Satisfied, he answered Paducah, he dismissed her by staring at his cell phone.

Glancing up after a couple of seconds, Wilson watched as a fleet-footed Paducah resumed her jog toward her county vehicle. She climbed in and sped away with lights and sirens blaring.

Chief Wilson reengaged his phone and started making calls. After hanging up with the senior battalion chief in charge of positioning the county command post, he redirected attention to the US Forest Service. He needed to make sure the firefighting air tankers were on standby at Medford International Airport.

He wondered what the Forest Service would say. Requesting their help in a densely populated area wasn't typical, and he couldn't recall it ever happening in Oregon before.

Skimming through the phone's contacts, he found who he searched for—Dale Carson, the aerial fire operations commander in southern Oregon. He and Dale met over a decade ago while doing controlled-burn training in the Ashland Watershed. They considered their relationship professional friends.

The line rang two times when a voice on the other end of the line picked up.

"This is Dale. Can I help you?"

"Hey Dale. Wilson here. You got a minute?"

"Of course. Your ears are burning huh? I figured you'd call soon. Sounds like you got a potential mess on your hands. What can I do for you?"

Chief Wilson chuckled inside about burning ears before responding with, "It's bad but early. I am calling because we need your tankers in the air. First, are they available? And if so, what's the normal protocol for residential areas? I have never made an air tanker request before."

A lengthy pause on the line, Chief Wilson knew that a preoccupied Dale tried to handle more than one conversation.

"Sorry about that, Chief. Chaos in our office right now, as you can imagine. Your counterpart, Housey in District 3, is on the phone with my office right now as well. One tanker is on standby at MFR—waiting on a go from us. A lead plane is in the air right now getting data before we proceed. The other tanker is fighting the Obenchain fire."

"Fantastic. What do you need from me?"

"Nothing more than this phone call. Consider this District 5 official request for air-tanker support. Is the command post in place yet?"

"Working on that now—within the half hour."

"Okay. Have your post call our office when they finish setting up. By then I should have a better understanding of priorities. From a quick glance at the map, without aerial intel, I presume your needs are going to override anything else at the moment."

"Roger that. Not sure about highway traffic. I am going to call the state police and see about getting I5 shut down. With Bear Creek running next to the interstate from Ashland to Central Point and the direction the winds are pushing the fire puts I5 in the direct line of trouble. I can't imagine it's okay for tankers dropping retardant on traffic."

"Ha-ha. Not good. No. I just got off the phone with the Oregon Department of Transportation, and they are working with the state police already on shutting down the freeway. Starting with the southbound lanes for now. We can pivot and close both directions if necessary."

"Okay. Thank you, Dale. I'll give an update as soon as possible. If you need to reach me, please call my cell phone. Radio traffic is chaotic and clogged."

"Roger that, Chief. Go save our homes and businesses."

With that statement, the phone went silent. Unphased by the sudden end to the conversation, chief Wilson pressed *677 for the highway patrol. After one ring, someone picked up and answered with a smooth and fluid salutation.

"Oregon State Police. May I help you?"

"Yes, this is Chief Wilson of Talent-Phoenix Fire District and current incident commander of the Almeda Fire. Can I speak with someone about I5 exit and on-ramp closures? Can you connect me?"

The voice on the other end of the line followed a brief pause with, "Yes, Chief. Please stand by. I'll put you in touch with ODOT."

Chief Wilson held the phone tight to his ear, slowly turning in a full circle with methodical precision. Fascinated but not surprised by the chaos unfolding so quickly, he tried to recall a time when he witnessed the start of something so ripe with devastating consequences. His memory came up empty.

"Ryland Steen, assistant director for operations. Can I help you?"

Chief Wilson, surprised by the voice, struggled to come up with a similar fire over the years. Gathering himself, he responded.

"Yes. Thanks, Steen." Chief Wilson thought the name and voice sounded familiar, but he couldn't place either.

"This is Chief Wilson, Talent-Phoenix Fire District and current incident commander of the Almeda Fire. I want to prep a shutdown of a few I5 exits and on-ramps. The Almeda fire is escalating, and air strikes are eminent along the interstate. Fire crews need unabated use of the freeway. Also, the air tankers will skirt the freeway with retardant drops. We can't add to our problems with traffic incidents. Can you help with this?"

"Hey, Chief. Yes, I can. Not sure you remember, but we met at the ODOT fire conference last year."

Chief Wilson scanned his memory, and in a matter of seconds placed the name and the face. He remembered Steen treated him like a rock star at the conference earlier in the year making him feel uncomfortable with ridiculous attention. Ryland Steen went on and on about how his grandfather who died firefighting taught him about respect and admiration for the profession. The chief wanted to ask the guy why he hadn't gone into the profession himself but didn't want to take the time for a long-winded answer. So, he let the question go.

"Ahh, yes, Ryland. Nice to hear your voice. I'd love to chat, but under the circumstances this is not the time to catch up."

"Understood, Chief. We have all the approvals in place for when your team makes the call. No need to call us back. Call the OSP and let them know what to shut down and when. Does this work for you?"

Chief Wilson appreciated the man's candor and professionalism. Worry abated that Steen would go on and on with a useless conversation.

"Excellent, and thanks. Next time you are in Talent, stop at the station, and I'll show you around. Thanks, again." Chief Wilson regretted his offer, until he remembered his resignation letter sitting on the commissioner's desk, which meant he'd be hiking, biking, or fishing, not working at the station.

"Thanks, Chief, I'll do that, and please stop this darn fire. Most of us have family and friends in Talent and Phoenix."

Radio noise screeching and unending, the chief ended the call first.

# His Mind Searched

Chief Wilson sat for a moment in the county vehicle at the new command post. To the southeast, the wind surged off the Siskiyou Mountains, howling through the treetops. He opened the door, climbed out, and slammed it shut behind him before heading toward the command trailer. Inside, the usual chaos echoed off the metal walls. He listened for a couple of minutes, then, not liking what he heard, cut everyone off mid-sentence.

"Listen, people: this fire will not put itself out. And all of us yelling and screaming at each other slows our responses which is unacceptable. Calm down, get your heads together, and focus on your jobs. We got this."

The mood in the trailer changed in an instant. Tension eased, voices steadied, and pointless chatter stopped. Leadership provided necessary clarity when wielded, and Chief Wilson's authoritative, confident demeanor excelled when tensions were at their worst.

Satisfied with the reaction of the team, the chief reflected on his retirement announcement a couple of hours ago. Focusing on the state of reality, he stretched his aching lower back by raising his elbows up and twisting back and forth in a slow motion.

"Okay, Paducah. Give me the skinny." The chief directed the conversation to the station's battalion chief, Kylee Paducah, his rising star and third generation firefighter. The chief knew her grandfather and father, worked with both of them off and on over the years. The Paducah family, through years of dedication and sacrifice, made the county a better place to live.

Paducah rose from her chair at the end of the command

post. The entire post housed all the latest technology. Monitors hung from the walls and all contained live shots from the fires, the surrounding area, and satellite and weather imagery. The chief was not a fan of the command post and the feeling of isolation it produced. Firefighters loath feeling trapped. He wanted to be in the thick of it, not stuck inside metal walls.

The chief typically put someone else in charge of the command post. Today, however, he thought about handling it himself. In the next couple of minutes, he'd have to decide to stay put and get Paducah out in the field or leave her to take control of the post and head out himself. He considered another option: let the people inside the post do their jobs and both he and Paducah stay in the field. This wasn't a typical fire they were going to fight, and they both needed to be involved on the ground. He considered the options with the care of a seasoned chief.

Paducah bathed in her intensity, arrived from the end of the post and looked at the chief. At five feet ten inches tall, she didn't need to look far. Her solid frame, near perfect athletic posture, and confident demeanor commanded authority. This firefighter grew into a consummate pro, like her father and grandfather before her.

"It isn't good, Chief, and it's getting worse by the minute. Hell, second."

"Okay. Specifics please."

"We estimate the burn at forty-five minutes. We think it started near the water treatment plant."

"How?" The chief wasted no time asking.

"Not sure. Vagrant fire that got away? Arson?" Paducah's last word trailed off as she looked away and stared at a monitor.

"Okay. We'll figure that out later. What are we looking at right now? Wind, direction the fire is traveling, how fast, evacuation prep, etc.?"

Moving away from the chief, Paducah headed back toward a chair at the other end of the post, where she picked up several pieces of paper from the noisy dot matrix printer. She returned to the chief in seconds. Flipping through the pages, she started rattling off information.

"Looks like the fire started about 1100 hours. Winds are gusting at 35 from the southeast and increasing. We estimate ten acres burned already. Spot fires keep popping up with the damn wind, of course, both south and east of Bear Creek. So far there's one significant spot fire north of the freeway."

Paducah pointed to a monitor, and the chief's head, as if a puppet on a string, turned to see where she directed his attention.

"I requested crews here, here, and here. The wind is forcing our positions right now, and right now there aren't enough bodies to gain control. Two helos are in the air with Bambi buckets. I called the Oregon National Guard, and they are on standby if we want another helo in the air." Paducah paused, took a swig from the cup she grabbed off the table—what the chief presumed was cold coffee—then continued.

"Local crews from Ashland, Talent, and Medford are on scene. Grants Pass, Central Point, Eagle Point, and Klamath Falls are on the way. A hotshot crew from FarNorCal is in route. I am thinking we may want to insert them in the foothills north of Talent. There is a shitload of homes in the woods there, as you know."

Chief Wilson contemplated the scenario as he wondered about the third-generation property in those woods he called home, considering if it would even exist in twenty-four hours.

"And last, Chief, we should shut down I5 south of Medford and north of Hilt, and close all exits on and off I5 at Ashland, Talent, and Phoenix. We need unfettered access to these routes. The weather forecast predicts more wind throughout the day and into the evening. If we don't get control of this within forty-five minutes, Chief, we will lose a lot of buildings and potential life. Which begs the question: what about evacuations?"

Chief Wilson looked around for something to drink, saw a counter with a dozen or so bottled waters, and grabbed one. Removing the lid, he contemplated all the information Paducah provided, took a swig, and then screwed the cap back on.

"Okay, Paducah, excellent information, as always. First, what's the rotation time of the two helos? I assume they're getting water at Hastings Reservoir?"

"Just a couple of minutes right now, Chief, and yes." Paducah wasted no time in replying. "One bit of luck, Chief: the reservoir is close."

"Okay, keep the Guard helo on standby. We risk too much air traffic with such a short turnaround time and narrow drop zones. Unless we pull water from north of Talent somewhere."

The chief paused for a moment, thinking about ponds and reservoirs before finishing with, "We can assess in another fifteen minutes. By the way, what is the thought of Medford International air traffic?"

"Shit, Chief. I didn't even consider them."

Paducah turned from the chief and barked an order to one of the command post dispatchers. "David, call MFR and ask them to assess the smoke situation and visibility right now. They will need to assess a potential closure, so let them know who to call for status updates. We might need to shut down all incoming air traffic unless MFR can direct everything from the north."

"Thanks," the chief responded before continuing. What is the projected path of the fire, right now, based on the current conditions?"

Paducah walked a couple of steps closer to one monitor that held a detailed satellite map of the communities and

94

landscape surrounding the fire. The chief followed.

"It looks like it's tracking west along Bear Creek. Like I mentioned, there are a few hotspots from the wind in some unorthodox areas." She pointed north, across the freeway, and farther west toward the town of Phoenix. "Talent is in immediate danger, and the Butler Creek area between North Ashland and Talent. At the rate of burning, unless the helos get control in tandem with the boots on the ground, part of Talent, at least, will burn within the hour."

Paducah paused, swallowed hard—the chief thought she held back deeper emotions—and finished with, "We already have a few structures on fire in North Ashland. I think I already said, but to reiterate the Butler Creek area is next. Do you know how many manufactured and mobile home parks there are between North Ashland and South Medford, Chief?"

Chief Wilson, knowing Paducah's question to be rhetorical, didn't respond. His mind counted all the mobile home parks and the thousands of homes that spread throughout the small Southern Oregon communities. *What a day to retire,* he thought.

"What is the meteorologist saying about the winds, Paducah? Direction? Any intel about the winds shifting and putting Ashland in jeopardy?"

"I asked that very question, Chief, and they told me it is unlikely the winds will change any time within twenty-four hours. The easterly trade winds will continue for the next thirty-six to forty-eight hours."

"Okay, good. That's something, at least. If we know what to expect we can make calculated decisions. Get the dispatchers on the phones right now with the Jackson County Sheriff, and all the local municipality police departments in Talent and Phoenix. Evacuate Talent city limits, now. Place those south of Foss and Rapp roads on standby along with

Phoenix. I am going to call the commissioner's office, and the Oregon Department of Transportation, and request they shut down all exits and on-ramps between Ashland and South Medford."

Chief Wilson stepped out of the narrow, crowded command post and looked across the parking lot of the local hotel they'd chosen as their battleground eyes. Staring west at the rising smoke, he thought about jumping in his vehicle to race home and check on the property. But there was nothing he could do now—nothing worth risking it for—just a few clothes and some old photos. With any luck—his kind of luck—the wind would hold steady, and the fire would track north of his family's land.

He sighed, wondering now about the resignation, feeling as though this were some final test from the universe he needed to endure before he moved on with his life. His timing from where he sat right now looked like shit.

Pressing the number five on his cell phone, his mind searched for the proper words he'd need to request shutting down the interstate.

# Ore-Ida of Course

Waiting with the patience of a cheetah while sitting at an outside table staring eastward at rising and thickening smoke, Teddy nursed his favorite IPA. Unable to remember if he asked for the burger well-done, he considered getting up and asking the staff behind the counter but decided against it. He knew he asked for it bordering on charred—he always did. That wasn't something he'd forget. Kind of like him exiting the door after leaving home, then sitting in his car in the driveway wondering if he remembered locking the door.

Taking another swig of beer, he didn't know if his lack of recollection came from an advancing age, paranoia, or an obsessive disorder.

Giving a head nod to someone a few tables away, the only other person to join him in the local eatery so far today, Teddy rose and pushed his chair back before walking over to the condiment rack. Grabbing a couple of empty paper cups, he filled each with mustard, the bright yellow kind with no seeds or impurities to detract from the rich smoothness of an untainted pure and hearty mustard-seed cream. After filling up four small paper containers, thinking it would not be enough for his burger and the tater tots, he balanced them in his hands and returned to his table.

Setting the containers of creamy goodness down, he turned his attention to his beer, wondering if he had enough left to finish his meal. His routine was precise: three bites of burger, then a drink. The beer's flavor was a necessary complement to the grass-fed beef, and through significant research, Teddy had determined that three bites provided the perfect ratio.

As for the tater tots? Years of experience had taught him

he could eat those anytime without disrupting the balance between the burger and the adult beverage.

Swatting at a fly circling the rim of his glass, Teddy sat down and straightened his chair for a direct view of the rising smoke to the southeast. Reaching for the cafeteria-style transparent plastic cup of water, he wondered how in the hell the fire started and how long it would take fire crews to put it out. This time of the year, with the grass brown and most vegetation crispy, it would take longer than usual, but the local fire crews were great with isolated brush fires.

There wasn't any dark black smoke, so it must not be a structure of any kind. Probably a dumbass vagrant building a fire near Bear Creek when they shouldn't. Lazy-ass people needed to muster up some responsibility and work like everyone else. They made the surrounding communities look like shit, and he hated it. He knew countless numbers of them over the years and almost all said the same thing: "I don't want no one telling me what to do. I can live life as I see fit when homeless. Fuck the man." The few who didn't, who were in a tough spot, he rooted for, and he offered day jobs over the years to help them out.

Rousing him from negativity and judgmental darkness, the four-inch square piece of rigid plastic buzzed and vibrated on his table. He watched as one of the waiting staff headed his way with his tray.

Arriving at his table, the server smiled, placed his plate with the burger and tots on the table in front of him and said, "Well done like you always ask for, sir. I see you got your mustard. Do you need anything else?"

Teddy smiled, appreciated the fact she remembered him and how he liked his burger, and said, "No thank you. I appreciate you asking."

The young woman picked up the still buzzing notification puck and walked away. Teddy blurted out, "Do you know what is up with the fire, young lady?"

In a human-conditioned reflexive manner, the woman stopped, stared into the sky, and replied, "From what we have heard, it is a grass fire near Ashland. Not sure how it started, but one of our cooks has an uncle who is a volunteer firefighter, and he said from the color of the smoke it is natural fuel. I guess grass or wood. I don't understand, but it sounds like from what they are saying, it shouldn't be much."

Teddy nodded, paying attention to the cooked condition of his burger, then her words, after taking his first bite. The cooked meat was dark, no red or visible blood, which pleased him. Swallowing bite number one, fifteen more to go, he responded.

"Okay, this is good news. The last thing we need with these winds and dry conditions is a doggone fire burning out of control."

"I know, right?" The woman continued walking away, and in an obvious effort that showed anxiousness to proceed with her day, retreated toward the kitchen.

Teddy dipped a tater tot halfway into one of the mustard containers. Satisfied that his fingers had coated the golden potato treat adequately with mustard, he popped it into his mouth and closed his eyes for a moment, savoring the taste as it hit the back of his tongue. Then he washed the flavors down with the dwindling beer, which left him feeling a twinge of consternation.

Halfway through his burger, making quick work of the tater tots as well, Teddy couldn't relax. Traffic out front of the restaurant, feet away from the outdoor seating, seemed busier than normal. Several patrons entered, then left, taking food to go, and Teddy found himself alone again with one other guy, several tables away. Not one to chitchat with strangers, Teddy couldn't resist reaching out to the guy as he searched for normalcy in what looked to be shaping up as an abnormal day in the only town in America called Talent.

"What do you think? Serious fire or a bum heating a can of hash?" Teddy projected his voice toward the stranger.

The stranger looked up, then around, and realizing from Teddy's stare the question was meant for him, responded.

"I can't imagine anyone foolish enough to burn right now. It must be a structure fire or something. Sounds like there are choppers in the sky, even though I haven't seen them."

Between another bite of burger and a delicious mustard-doused, golden-brown potato puck, Teddy watched the stranger stand, throw his trash in a can, then exit the outdoor seating area without saying a word. The guy climbed into a beat-up old Subaru with California plates. Teddy figured the guy would retreat across Oregon's southern border to the land of snobs, high taxes, and gas prices, unless he was heading into Medford to do some tax-free shopping.

Wondering about the sexuality of the Subaru driver, Teddy returned his attention to his meal. He made quick work of what remained of the burger, then swirled the final tater tot inside the paper container no longer brimming with mustard. Unhappy with what little mustard remained, he popped the potato treat into his mouth, telling himself to get an additional container next time. Four is never enough.

Wadding up the paper left on his tray, he made a ball and placed it inside the red plastic container that minutes ago was filled with food. Picking up his drink, he tilted his head back and finished the locally brewed IPA.

Looking around and seeing no one within hearing distance, Teddy let out a satisfying burp. Standing, he deposited the food container in the closest can and placed his beer glass in the gray plastic wash bin. Heading toward his vehicle parked curbside, he stopped, gripped the door handle, and looked skyward at the incredible smoke billow like a massive mushroom cloud's slow crawl toward space. Thinking about the lack of mustard on his last bite of tater tot and how it all but ruined his perception of the entire meal, he thought the tot, as a side dish, should get more love.

Climbing into his pickup, he wondered if he should stop and get something for dinner. He couldn't fathom why he made summer chili yesterday. The dish made no sense when the temps hit northward of eighty-five. Not to him anyhow. He wouldn't eat it again tonight, and the cold-weather dish would do fine in the freezer until fall.

Buckling up, he peered through the front windshield and took another look at the unavoidable plume of smoke, which, taking over the valley skies, seemed to increase by the minute. He decided to forgo getting gas for the weed eater today, he'd do it tomorrow.

Irritation coursed through his mind as he put the pickup in drive, deciding to take another look at the troublesome security gate. The damn thing was a constant challenge to his mechanical skills, a stubborn problem that threatened his sense of competence.

# Got It, Chief

When Chief Wilson called the commissioners' office, the secretary quickly reminded him all three commissioners were in Salem for the day and wouldn't be back until tomorrow. She didn't mention his resignation letter, and he wasn't about to bring it up. Instead, he got off the phone as fast as he could, avoiding any lengthy conversation. There were bigger problems to deal with right now than his future employment.

Being reminded that all the commissioners were away, the chief considered his options. He had the Chair's cell phone and figured he should try and call.

Scrolling through his contacts, he found the number and called. It went straight to voicemail. He might catch hell for this later, but he was confident he'd stirred up enough attention during the first state-of-the-fire conference call. Even without the commissioners, their office—along with the Department of Transportation, the statehouse, and all the other key players— was paying attention. They'd already shut down the southbound section of State Highway 99. The commissioners had to know by now, and he'd probably get a call from them sometime today.

Interstate 5, though? That was a different beast. As the main north-south corridor between Southern Oregon and Northern California for a hundred miles, it wouldn't be shut down unless things got way out of control. Just how much more "out of control" did it need to get, he wondered. And he sure as hell hoped he wouldn't have to find out.

Stepping back inside the command post and out of the day's already hot sun with temps climbing upward from ninety, the chief asked for a bottled water.

Someone—he didn't know who, probably a young intern from the county building, handed him a plastic bottle of spring water. He unscrewed the top and wondered where the water really came from. The cynic in him thought it came from a garden hose or tank in the back of a warehouse. He didn't care. Wet and cool, the water quenched his deep thirst and took him back a decade in his thoughts.

*"I'm trying to be resourceful, like you taught me, Daddy."* His daughter, Alya, which means Sky in Arabic—replied as he towered over her near the campsite's water spigot.

His wife came up with the name, claiming it meant Sky. "Sky? Are we hippies now?" he'd asked her right before their only child was born.

He'd relented, figuring it made no difference in the end. But he'd decided right then he'd call her Sky, never Alya. How the hell was he even supposed to pronounce that?

Her grandparents—god rest their souls—her friends, her teachers, everyone called her Sky. No one ever seemed to pronounce **Alya** the same way twice. The name rolled around awkwardly, a clumsy foreign word in their mouths. Sky made sense and it stuck.

His wife hated it. He could see it every time someone called their daughter Sky, her lips pressing into a thin, irritated line. She even threatened to change the name, but the thought of slogging through paperwork and sacrificing her wine-soaked afternoons put a stop to that real quick.

Eventually, even she gave in, calling her Sky like everyone else. A small, petty victory he'd savored for years. Unhealthy? Sure. But what was worse? His childish satisfaction or the slow-motion train wreck of a divorce their daughter had to endure.

How he ended up marrying Sky's mother still perplexed him. He never understood her fascination with Arab culture. In

103

hindsight, he thought she praised the Middle East to be a thorn in his side. Watching young men and women come home, fucked up from tours in the sand made him loathe the place.

Chuckling at the irony, he thought about Sky and wondered where she was. Europe, with her aunt? Packing along the PCT? In Medford perhaps all these years? He didn't think so but knew stranger things happened. He missed her and agonized about not knowing where she roamed. He wondered if he'd ever see her again.

"I am getting your dumb water, Daddy."

He didn't understand why the word dumb, coming from his child's mouth, cut so deep. Made him feel worthless. What the hell had he done to earn so much resentment from the women in his life?

His wife? That made sense. Or at least he thought it did. They'd married out of desperation—not to be alone. But the joke was on him because he'd never felt lonelier than he did during their marriage.

Funny, looking back. They didn't even like each other. They seemed to love one another in some dark, twisted way, but being in the same room for long was a recipe for disaster. Therapy might've explained the mess, but that was a winding road neither of them had the desire to travel.

His daughter though? Why? He made certain she had what she needed—a roof, food, clothes, the necessities. Why his beautiful little girl called him stupid frustrated him. It must be the words of his ex, ricocheting through their home for several of Sky's formative years. He didn't know if he should be angry or sad. A bit of both coursed through his veins.

Wondering where the ex lived, he pushed the feelings down, but he struggled to bury them. Michigan, he last heard, but she loved being a vagabond and could be anywhere. Even dead. The woman relished her problems with repressed anger. A family trait, she claimed. He never met her parents. She said they died in an automobile accident, but he never confirmed it. For all he knew they lived in the same small southern Oregon town. He considered searching for them early in the marriage, as if that might somehow shed light on his wife and their relationship. Every time he pulled up in front of the private investigator's office, though, he'd get a welcomed alert from the fire-station dispatch.

"Okay, Sky, but hurry. I want to break camp and get home. Your school starts next week, and we need to make sure are all ready to go."

"Chief." Paducah stood within a foot of the chief, but he didn't respond.

"Um, Chief. Chief!" Paducah raised her voice a couple of octaves trying not to yell.

"Shit, sorry, Paducah. Processing information about the fire," the chief lied. He knew better than to tell a co-worker his mind floundered in a deep personal rut of wonder.

"Should I stay here, or get in the field chief?"

Not wanting to be stuck in the command post, Chief Wilson hesitated for a moment. He made his mind up, but his mouth fought to hold on to the words. Paducah needed the experience, especially since he told the commissioner's office a couple of hours ago, he was done.

"I'll stay here. You know how I hate being in this damn thing, but you'll benefit from being on scene."

Paducah smiled, turned, and grabbed her jacket from a nearby chair. "I hear you, Chief, and thanks. I hate staying here too."

"Okay, get out there and be our eyes and ears and give me a report from the west end of the fire ASAP. I need all the vitals. We can't make decisions blind."

"Got it, Chief."

Paducah exited the coffin-like metal command post, the

door slamming shut behind her.

Chief Wilson stared down the row of chairs at the crew inside and sighed. His eyes drifted back to the exit, regret already gnawing at him for not following her out. But he'd made a deal with himself—stay at least fifteen minutes.

This could be his last fire, and the itch to feed his firefighting adrenaline one last time wouldn't let him walk away.

# Deft Precision

Final inning—bases loaded, two outs, down by one run. It was almost like Amelia Charlie Hall—everyone called her Mel—had scripted her own Hollywood ending. She stepped into the batter's box, eyes locked, nerves steady.

The runner on second was the fastest on the team, so a well-placed single would win the game. But Mel didn't play to hit a single. She played for moments that left no doubt. The back-breaking long ball was her goal. Always.

Mel thrived on pressure. She was built for it. Situations like this weren't luck; they were an expectation—a product of her success-filled nature. Somehow, she always found herself in hero-type scenarios, moments she couldn't help but manifest. And she loved every damn second of it.

Since childhood, when her father made bets on her abilities with anyone willing to risk losing a five-dollar bill, Mel learned success had its perks. She figured out early that if she focused on the outcome with clear intention, it almost always happened. Shooting baskets, throwing a football through a moving tire, sinking a golf ball on a tricky green, or dominating at ping-pong—Mel had a knack for being good at everything, and her father loved it.

Those five-dollar bets, along with lawn mowing, gifts from grandparents, and summers working odd jobs added up. By sixteen, she had enough cash to buy her first car outright. She often wondered what drove her more—the money or the grin on her father's face every time she came through. Sure, she loved making him proud—what little girl wouldn't? But deep down, she knew it was her own mind and relentless drive to succeed that pushed her.

When Mel got in the zone, everything else faded away. Distractions vanished. Sounds muffled to nothing. The world narrowed down to one simple goal: success. And she wouldn't quit until she reached it.

Like the predictability of the sun coming up every morning, her father, after her triumphs, always laughed. He'd pat the losing participant on the back, tell them, "Better luck next time," or "You realize she is eleven" or whatever age she happened to be. Her mother drew the line at fourteen when during one bet, a young man got so angry over losing to Mel in a ring-toss game at the county fair he threw a ring at the carney attendant and then tried to stare down Mel's father. Her parents argued the entire afternoon over the event.

After the fair incident and the obligatory family time, Mel ditched her parents and wandered the fairgrounds with her friends. But every time she crossed paths with her parents at the small county event, the tension hit like a gut punch. Her mother's face tightened with anger, while her father wore that familiar look—"WTF is it going to be like when we get home?"

The fallout lasted nearly a week before her father finally caved, apologized to her mother, and promised both he'd stop placing bets on Mel.

Part of her felt disappointed. Those little wagers built a special camaraderie between her and her dad over the years. But another part of her celebrated like a cymbal-banging monkey—finally free of the pressure to win and the looming fear of his disappointment if she failed.

Now in her early fifties, though most people guessed thirty-five, Mel couldn't remember a time when she hadn't achieved what she set out to do. If Angela Duckworth of TED Talk fame had asked, Mel's success would've landed squarely in the grit category.

Talent played its part—she knew that—but it was her inner drive, the unshakable force behind her determination, that

108

powered her accomplishments.

Mel wondered if her life would have turned out the same had her father not pushed her so hard toward success—treating it like one more bet to win. The thought made her chuckle. Futile, really. From a young age, life had been what she made of it—beyond grit, beyond inner drive.

Ease and flow, she reminded herself. Life should unfold in the present. Go with the stream.

Over the years, she'd watched so many people choose the uphill battle, convinced that working harder—not smarter—was the only respectable path. As if struggle was a badge of honor, a currency of meaning. But Mel had long believed otherwise. Unlike those who stood at the fork in the road and agonized over which path to take, she preferred to skip the drama altogether.

Frost's famous poem wasn't lost on her—but instead of roads, Mel liked to picture herself in a canoe, pushing off from the riverbank and letting the current guide her—less resistance and more peace.

Let the current carry you. Trust the flow. That, to her, was life less traveled.

A failed marriage—the one blip in her otherwise steady life. She reflected on the debacle once, then never again. It stood out as the single time she'd gone against the flow.

The mistake had taught her plenty—more about relationships than she ever wanted to know. From that point forward, she vowed never to force something that wasn't there. Going against the current never worked.

Life would provide, she believed, if you embraced the flow and rode the current.

Marrying another military pilot in her late twenties seemed like a good idea at the time. But months in, Mel realized the guy she married was more obsessed with her money, other

109

women, and everything he didn't have than anything he did. So, she ended the seven-month disaster.

She was grateful her father wasn't around to see the hiccup. Her mother, though, had plenty to say. Called it a mistake divorcing so soon and told her, "All men cheat at some point." The comment only made Mel more determined to end the sham of a marriage and left her wondering if her father had ridden his own wave of infidelity.

Mel filed for divorce, endured a short spell of harassment from her jilted ex-husband, then moved on. After twenty years in the military, she separated from service and headed west— to the Pacific Northwest. It was about as far as she could get from her Massachusetts roots while staying in the lower forty-eight. The place where she and her ex had grown up. The place they probably would've stayed if things had gone differently.

Sure, she missed Boston. The Red Sox. The endless Irish pubs. But the PNW had something Boston didn't—easy access to the wild. Nature had always been a part of her, something her soul needed. Being able to disappear into the woods with just a fifteen-minute drive beat any old bar, hands down.

The Mariners, though? They weren't the Red Sox. But they had heart. And hope. Their luck had to turn around eventually.

Edging a foot into the batter's box, her left foot twisted back and forth in dusty clay packed dirt for proper leverage. Mel held her left hand up to the umpire requesting time to prepare. She eased her right foot in the box, gathered her thoughts with a proper grip on the bat handle, and moved her head side-to-side, hoping for a popping noise and the relief that came with it. Mel lowered her hand, and the ump signaled the pitcher to go ahead. Mel focused on the hurler's delivery. As the pitcher's arm motion sped up, the softball left her hand below the knee. It looked like a large melon floating toward Mel. Focusing on a white floating sphere with red seams, Mel drove the barrel of her aluminum bat with power and memory muscle and watched as the ball smashed off her bat and sailed over the shortstops head slicing between two outfielders for the walk-off win.

Touching the bag on first base, happy for the win but disappointed in the single, Mel looked forward to a fun tournament weekend coming up soon in Portland now that the team won their qualifying game. Lifting her hand skyward, pointing with appreciation for her accomplishment, Mel noticed the darkening sky growing to the south.

Jogging across the field, Mel did the requisite teammate high fives, fist bumps, and hugs, then shook hands with the losing team. Looking at a smoke-infested sky, she rushed through the after-game process making her way to the dugout between teammates. Mel took her dusty duffle bag from under the bench then headed toward the parking lot.

Judging by the thick smoke pushing north, she wondered if her old flight crew was scrambling, gearing up to take off. Sitting on a dugout bench, unsure what to do with the rest of her day, Mel felt the frustration build—she *wanted* to be up there. Back in the VLAT, the Very Large Air Tanker. Specifically, the DC-10 she used to fly, retrofitted for firefighting, capable of dropping nearly 12,000 gallons of retardant in one run.

She missed gripping the yoke of that massive bird, missed the adrenaline of lining up a perfect drop, and giving the order to the flight engineer to release the load with precision—laying a fireline 250 feet below.

Mel contemplated the rest of her day, wondering what the hell to do. She'd already washed her pickup, scrubbed her house from top to bottom, and seen every movie worth watching at the cinema. Trail-running the Ashland watershed and scaling upper and lower Table Rocks had lost their thrill.

Maybe today called for a trip to Lake of the Woods and a

run on the High Lakes Trail. Nearly a mile high in elevation, it'd be cooler up there and far enough away from the smoke choking the valley.

Mel pulled out her cell phone, powered it on, and wondered if today was the day she finally caved and bought that mountain bike she'd been eyeing for the last three months at Flywheel— her favorite local bike shop. The High Lakes Trail would be the perfect proving ground for a new ride.

Retirement from aerial firefighting still felt premature, a nagging itch she couldn't scratch. Unaware of questions coming from passing teammates, she muttered, "Shit."

# Just Like Jimmy Ray

Kicking at random pieces of dirt and gravel, scattered, along with new ash, on the blacktop trail bordering Bear Creek, a disillusioned Sky let her thoughts drift—as if forced by a hot violent wind pushing through the woods.

*"Sky, please come here." Sky, daydreaming, moved her body away from the stream. She headed over to her waiting father near the campfire.*

*"Yes, Dad," she said with irritation and a sliver of childish disdain. The stick she held in her hand needed to be thrown into the creek, and she needed to chase it downstream. Whatever her father wanted to say to her couldn't be as important as her stick.*

*"Do you see how the coals are bright orange?"*

*Sky looked at him and nodded. She didn't feel like talking. At least not about stupid fire.*

"Okay, this is combustion. It's like a flame, just happening too slowly to ignite. So, be careful, alright?"

*Sky looked at her father, wondering why he told her. She didn't know what to say, didn't care why he said it, and didn't want to learn more. Fire—blah, blah, blah. So, she stared through him, thinking of the waiting stream and wishing a dog accompanied her. Dogs don't waste time talking about something she cared nothing about—like her father always did with fire.*

*"Are you listening to me, Sky? Fire can destroy everything in its path. It is merciless and greedy. It can kill. Don't play with fire, okay? Respect it."*

*Sky thought about the stick she held being the first to make it over the beaver dam to reach the Pacific. The countless other sticks over the past two days all got stuck. None of them ever would reach the salty water. Unless a massive flood happened, sending them all, along with her, to the ocean. This thought thrilled her. Way better than everything burning by fire.*

"Sky, take this bucket and go over to the spigot and fill it up. I am going to show you how to put out a campfire."

Sky reached out and felt the cold steel of the handle—her father always corrected her, calling it the bail. She knew it was the bail, even at eight years old. But out of pure stubbornness, knowing it would get under his skin, she still called it a handle. All the knowledge he had poured into her, she kept tucked away, locked in the back of her mind to use only when *she* wanted.

*She doesn't care an ounce about being a lame fireman. Why is it fireman anyway? Don't women fight fires? Shouldn't it be fireperson or firefighters? Her dad always said fireman. Sky struggled over her anger with her father in a way she did not understand. She thought it reflected her mother's disdain for the man.*

*Unwilling to dwell on her feelings about a man she knows loves her more than his own life, she turned away from her father and the smoldering campfire. Sky, reluctance running rampant in her mind, made her way to the camp toilets. She plopped the bucket down on the ground near the spigot post. The bucket fell on its side, kicking up a noticeable cloud of dust. Looking back at her campsite, she watched her busy father packing up their gear in anticipation of heading home.*

*So, Sky took the stick she refused to let go of and with a deliberate intent beyond her age, worked at righting the bucket. She wanted to position it under the spigot with the use of the stick she held in her hand.*

*She placed the end of the stick inside the metal bucket and worked to flop it over on its base. The metal bucket seemed too heavy for the stick, or at least too heavy for her fragile wrist.*

114

She tried again. The stick slipped out, and the bucket made a metal clanking noise as it fell against a rock. Sky pivoted her head toward camp and saw her father wrestling with the tent. Relief flooded through her since he hadn't heard the noise from the bucket. She did not want her effort to end so soon. If he heard, he'd come over and ruin it.

Another effort, and the same result. The darn bucket moved farther away from the spigot. How far would she have to push it for it to be positioned underneath the water? Another try, and another slip of the stick against the rigid metal.

A campy-looking youthful woman, whistling, strolled by on her way to the toilet.

"Do you need some help? Having a hard time with the bucket?"

Sky looked up and put on her distressed, angry face—the one she'd practiced in front of the mirror for hours until she could summon it on command. She shook her head. No words came out.

When she reached for the bucket to help, the woman lurched back, startled. Sky had lifted the stick too quickly, and for a second, it must've looked like she meant to strike.

The woman's smile vanished, replaced by a sharp frown as her hands instinctively pulled away.

"Fine then, are you retarded you little shit?"

The woman stormed away and slammed the toilet door behind her. Sky smiled and hoped that a snake would climb up out of the pee, poop, and toilet paper, and bite the intrusive woman on her butt.

Refocusing on her important self-created task, Sky wrapped both hands around the end of the stick and with determination, positioned the splintered end inside the bucket. She pushed upward, keeping her wrists stiff. She watched the sinewy muscles tighten underneath her skin. Thinking about *being a doctor—if she peeled back the layers of her skin, what would the muscles look like? Pulling her skin back though? She thought the pain might kill her.*

*The stick slipped, the bucket, almost upright, teetered, wobbled, and then came to a rest. She won.*

*"Sky, what's going on?"*

*Her father, from out of nowhere stood next to her. She kept her focus on her muscles and the bucket, angry at herself for not hearing him approach.*

*"I am trying to get your dumb water, Dad!"*

*It was the first time she had seen a hurt expression on her father's face—one she created. His eyes drooped. His mouth flexed down, and his head moved the slightest bit sideways. A pit formed in her stomach for an instant before retreating as quick as it had come.*

*She prepared for another boring life lesson and lecture. He always lectured her and always called them life lessons. At least for anything related to fire. Other than setting up a campsite and putting out fires, did her dad know anything else?*

*The Patagonia-clad woman came out of the toilet, smiled at her father, then frowned at Sky as she headed back to her campsite. Sky giggled knowing she got under the woman's skin.*

*Not wanting to listen to her father go on and on for the rest of the morning, Sky bent over, moved the bucket underneath the spigot with a free, stickless hand, and turned the water spigot on full blast.*

*"Sorry, Daddy. I was playing a game with the stick. Trying to make it fun. I wanted to fill the bucket without the use of my hands. I was trying to be resourceful like you always tell me."*

*Sky hated herself for capitulating. Up until last school year, she would've called it surrender. But then one of her teachers scolded little Jimmy Ray for "capitulating" all the time. The word sounded sophisticated, smart.*

After the teacher explained what it meant, Sky decided "surrender" would never find its way back into her vocabulary.

"Okay, well please hurry. I want to get home. We have a lot to do today." She watched her father as the hurt on his face transitioned into puzzlement. He walked away, back to the campsite, to finish packing everything in the pickup.

Sky wondered if a few select words from a woman, could manipulate all men with such ease. Her mother said as much before she walked out. A constant barrage of hurtful, and choice, words rained down on her father. He never responded, never raised a hand, or showed any resistance at all.

Reaching out and turning off the spigot as the water spilled over the side of the bucket, Sky shook her head. Frowning over the disappointment in her father, she feared her teacher might say her dad was just like Jimmy Ray.

# Capitulation

The wail of sirens echoed through the air, shoving Sky's thoughts to her father. Was he still letting women walk all over him? The thought sat heavy and unwelcome, like a bruise she couldn't stop pressing.

Up ahead, a flash of color caught her eye—she arrived at a pop-up library stand coated in thick barn-red paint, daring the elements to peel it away. Its door, a dingy, dirty glass panel smudged with fingerprints and streaked with years of trail dust, creaked as she pulled it open. The hinge groaned like it had never met oil.

Inside, books were crammed together, spines pressed tight like refugees seeking shelter. A couple of author names rang a bell, but most were unknown. Still, they looked decent. Mostly fiction. All in surprisingly good shape considering the kind of people who haunted this trail.

Beside the little library, another post jutted up with a notepad screwed to its top, pages fluttering like something trying to fly away. Names were scrawled across the sheets, jagged and impatient, most paired with faraway places she couldn't place. All out-of-staters.

She dropped the pen, the tattered cord swaying like a condemned man's noose. Who bothered leaving their name on a trail like this, littered with needles, trash, and tent cities huddled in the brambles? Sure, the concrete and asphalt path meant something to some—to her, it held a mess of teenage memories packed with what-ifs.

Returning her attention to the outdoor library, she looked around to see if anyone was watching. She thought of a book buried in her backpack. *The October Country* by Ray

Bradbury—a favorite author of her mother's. Somehow, the book had ended up in her pack when she fled home. She must have been reading it but didn't want to remember. Regardless of why it was there, it had become a symbol of Laura. A memory-laden piece of something she hung onto. Opening the book, she buried her nose in the pages and took a deep sniff.

*Sky's childhood memories of her mother were fading, but she did remember how much she loved to read. All the kids Sky knew treasured The Berenstain Bears, Dr. Doolittle, and Captain Underpants, among others. She saw the books when the kids brought them to school and became entranced by the big block words and colorful animations during class with a certain disappointing wonder and delight. When home, her mom made her read whatever books sat on their bookshelves. There wasn't a single children's book in their home. And her mother rotated the books out, save a few of her favorites, at least once a month after a trip to the used bookstore.*

*"Are you going to be a child, Sky, or an intelligent adult?" her mother asked every time.*

*Sky would pause, thinking about how the kids' books made her laugh out loud and feel light and happy. Knowing what her mother expected her to say, her robotic response went like this: "I want to be smart like you, Mommy." She hated feeling bad as a child for liking kids' things.*

*Sky couldn't remember her mother's eyes or the smell of her skin. However, she found familiarity in a well-read novel, and the smell of the pages brought a sense of time and space to her childhood. The paperback book returned a semblance of a mother's existence to her heart—filling a portion of misplaced longing.*

*Her mom used to grab books off their shelves, open them to a random page, and bury her nose in the inside crease, taking a big sniff. Pulling the book away, she'd turn to Sky and tell her, "I love the smell of books, Sky. It reminds me of my grandmother. Smell it, Sky? Here."*

*A dutiful child holding out a hand, Sky took the book from her mom and opened it up. She tried to open it to the same page as her mother, to experience the same smell, but her mom refused to tell her the page number, stating, "Half the fun is finding your own page with its own smell."*

*Perhaps that's why the books always smelled bad to Sky— she never opened one to the right page.*

*Her response to her mother—always a lie.*

*"It smells good, Mommy, for sure."*

*Her mom would take the book back, smile, and place it on the shelf. She'd turn and start talking in a tone that Sky always felt lacked authenticity.*

*"Smells are wonderful memories, Sky. They can transport you in an instant back to a memory."*

*Then her mother, without fail, quoted Ray Bradbury.*

*"If a book is new, it smells great. If a book is old, it smells even better... And it stays with you forever."*

*Sky, knowing better than to disappoint her mother, nodded in agreement even though she didn't understand. Every book she ever smelled returned nothing but disappointment. Like the inside of a wet canvas tent, set up for the first camping trip of the summer after being stored all winter in a damp barn.*

Retreating from memories, Sky removed the backpack from her shoulder and unzipped the main pocket. She grabbed *A Confederacy of Dunces*, thinking about swapping it for another book. Unable to come to terms with any book in the little outdoor library being worthy of a swap, Sky looked around again for any watchers. Seeing she remained alone, she dropped the Pulitzer Prize-winning novel back in her bag. Then she grabbed Margaret Atwood's *The Handmaid's Tale*. With a hurried sense of guilt, she dropped it in her bag, zipped it closed, and placed the pack on her shoulder as a reflective

120

thought came to her about her father and capitulation.

"Shit. Unbelievable!" Sky blurted out loud, staring at a rugged-looking scrub oak tree. Its roots, searching for relief from oppressive concrete over the years, had pushed up from below, cracking the path. Considering all the years she thought her dad acted like Jimmy Ray, for the first time, she realized she had behaved no differently in her response to her mother about smelling books.

Feeling a scratchy sting swell in her eyes, she closed the library door. Once again hearing a multitude of screeching sirens race by on the highway, she watched as more smoke billowed up behind her to the east. Contemplating her next move, thinking about capitulation and the way she thought about her father, she hurried her pace until she saw what she hoped to find: the well-beaten path off the trail that led toward her childhood town.

Her eyes flicked over the blackberry thickets crowding the edges, their leaves rustling with secrets. Ash drifted around her, stirring a restless urge to move—to get on with the inevitable.

Brushing her forehead with the back of her left hand, Sky surprised herself on a day already full of surprises: she wanted to go home more than she had imagined possible.

# Charbroiled

Chief Wilson's gaze locked on the back of a young woman at the far end of the narrow mobile command post. Her auburn red hair spilled over the padded chair, strands stretching downward like they were reaching for the floor.

The sight stopped him cold, breath hitching as his pulse stumbled.

It was his daughter's hair. It had to be.

The urge to rush over and tap her shoulder gnawed at him, his fingers twitching with the need to see her face. To find those dazzling green eyes that always seemed to glow, their brightness feeding off the world around them.

But he couldn't move. Not now. Not with the county's entire fire organization depending on him.

Grasping at scrambling thoughts, trying to remember his final interaction with Sky, the chief's mind drifted. A force or energy pulled, then propelled his thoughts to another place and time not so long ago with Sky.

*Standing in the family's kitchen, Sky sat at the counter, eyes fixed on him. It felt like she wasn't looking at him, but through him—as if he didn't exist. Her silence cut deeper than words, and the look he thought he saw in her eyes—disgust, maybe even hate—hurt more than he wanted to admit.*

*He'd never taken the time to heal a relationship he didn't know how—or when—it broke. Fear gripped him now, a cold truth settled in: if he pushed, if he confronted her, whatever fragile connection they had left might shatter. She might walk away, just like her mother did. And he couldn't bear to face that again.*

He felt stuck—trapped in a loop of doubt and silence—convinced his daughter despised him, too blind to see the fear behind her eyes was love, hidden and afraid.

He remembered watching her, mouth full of cereal—auburn hair tumbling over her shoulders. A bead of milk clung to the curve of her lower lip. Her green eyes, steady and unreadable, seemed to draw the color from her pale skin. She gave him that same blank stare—just like her mother.

Wanting to walk over and give her a hug, his feet froze. Unable to move the short distance to her, his shoes felt welded to the floor like a fly on a sticky trap. His ankles and toes flexed, trying to propel his body forward. The heavy leather in his work boots moved, that's it. Her mouth appeared open, efforting to speak. His imagination tricked him; his ears received nothing but dead air. There seemed to be a clear wall that kept him from going to her and blocked sound from traveling toward him.

He shook his head, attempting to wake himself from dismal memories, but failed.

Over the years, longing to see her grace the kitchen with her silence, his memories morphed into dreams. He had trouble distinguishing reality from fiction. Replaying countless interactions in his head, he struggled to remember times when he did what a loving parent was supposed to do out of parental reflex.

He never took personal time off, and he worked holidays, covered shifts for subordinates—anything and everything the county needed. He lived for work. Rock-solid, dependable, a firefighter's fireman—it would earn him a bloated pension and a broken family.

Why hadn't he listened to her? Listened with empathy and caring? He thought taking her to school, seeing most of her sporting events even if arriving late and leaving early, cooking for her, and keeping her clothed and fed met the requirements *of a dutiful parent. Work, dammit! His convenient baked-in excuse. Sky had called bullshit on him working so much, countless times. She'd chastised him for his lack of response to her when she questioned him. He'd stand, mouth agape, eyes glazed over as if he didn't have a tongue—his head hurt, like being squeezed in a vice. No words came out. He never knew what to say. Communication at work—easy peasy. But with his child, his brain sat idle, like a round cage full of bingo numbers waiting for someone to spin.*

*Not since their last camping trip, when his eleven-year-old princess belittled him while retrieving water, had he spent any loving, quality time with her—and then he had thought about work the entire three days and couldn't wait to get back to the familiar expectations at the station. After that, he started to tune her out, let her go, waiting for her to leave like her mother. There was a sad and secure safety in being alone. No one to make him feel less than—a singular goal of her mother, and all women in his personal life he dared to try and love.*

*Work puffed him up—soothed him. The harder he worked, the more time spent at the station, the more beloved he became throughout the county offices, city hall, and first responder community.*

*With no active parenting from his folks, he lacked any modeled understanding of how to be a parent, and his DNA provided no help either. Vacant of any adult teaching and guiding, his skills didn't transfer to the skills of a parent.*

*His parents worked six days a week. Sunday, other than weekday evenings when he lay in bed, was the one instance they were both home at the same time. And then, they spent their time cooking, cleaning, and taking care of the property. Anyhow, he had turned out decent—so Sky didn't need additional involvement from him. Distancing himself would toughen her up, he lied to himself.*

Someone in the command post interrupted his self-loathing thoughts.

"Chief."

Chief Wilson lumbered to the woman calling him. Seeing her face up close, relief flooded through him—and disappointed him; a new employee stared up at him.

"What do you have?"

"We received a radio call that the fire jumped I-5 at Exit 19. Several structures are on fire. Sounds like the fire jumped the Nauvoo Park Estates and crossed over South Valley View Road and is howling down Bear Creek."

"Turn that radio up."

The woman pressed the volume button on her laptop, and the speakers blared.

"Repeat, the fire jumped over South Valley View after the last bucket drop. The wind is wreaking havoc. We can't slow it down or get in front of it. Over."

The chief, impatient, waited for someone to respond. Grabbing the walkie, his seasoned mind paused. He needed to let the fire team work.

Silence hung long enough for the chief to put his hands together, cross his fingers, then turn his palms outward to stretch fingers and arms.

Paducah, after a lengthy pause, responded. "Standby Fifty-One."

"Chief, come in. Over. This is Paducah."

The chief couldn't get to the walkie button fast enough to soothe impatience.

"Go ahead, Paducah."

"Chief, the winds are driving the flames through Bear Creek faster than we can make any progress. It's heading west at an unfathomable clip. There are not enough crew on the ground to build any kind of line. Over."

"Where are you at right now, Paducah?"

A loud boom echoed through the command post and sent vibrations through the floor and walls, rattling everyone's bones.

"Shit," the chief lamented as he turned and stepped outside, letting the door swing shut behind him with a loud clank.

"Paducah, do what you can. Get the teams to protect structures. Forget the creek; there's too much trash and underbrush through there anyway. I know some of those mobile home parks are on the banks of Bear Creek, so prioritize those areas. If any of those homes catch fire, the likelihood of saving anything in the park is remote." The chief paused, thinking for a moment before finishing with, "Hang tight. We had an explosion outside the command post."

Standing on the top step, several feet off the ground, the chief looked skyward and watched as embers lifted and soared overhead moving westward. His eyes gazed at the command center flag rippling and snapping in the heavy winds. Across the road from the hotel parking lot, they had chosen for the command location, a fast-food restaurant and fuel depot burned with flames leaping into the sky. There were no fire trucks within sight as the structures burned with unimpeded ferocity.

"Paducah, Pacific Pride and Burger King are on fire. Not sure if you heard the explosion. Embers are exploding into the sky and pushing westward."

"What in the hell?" Paducah responded. "Is there any crew there?"

"No, and don't bother sending anyone. By the time anyone arrived, there will be nothing to save. I'll walk over there now and see what damage the damn thing's done so far. We must get ahead of this and build a defensible perimeter. If we don't, with the way the wind is blowing and the dry conditions..." The chief paused again, staring into the darkening northward sky.

"The fire won't stop burning until it hits the Rogue River north of Central Point. The whole damn valley will burn to the ground."

"Roger that, Chief. I'll continue to prioritize structures and pinpoint a defensible perimeter. Over."

The chief opened the command post door and looked inside, avoiding stepping all the way in.

"I am walking across the street for a quick analysis of the fire. I'll be right back."

A couple of heads nodded, but no one responded with any words. All were waist-deep in their own shit storms.

Closing the door, the chief contemplated walking the short distance across the road to examine the fire damage. Wanting to see if he needed to move the command post, then seeing the post's position was in no danger, he changed his mind and jumped in the county vehicle. The traffic was nuts with people fleeing the area, and he didn't want to risk walking across a busy road.

Flipping on the lights and sirens, the cars ceded, and he raced across the road, pulling in front of a burning building that used to serve charbroiled burgers. Ironic, he thought—charbroiled. The destruction he stared at made the restaurant's tagline pale in comparison.

# Back Up In The Air

Staring across the sports complex parking lot from a dugout laden with sunflower seeds, Mel walked toward her beloved Ford F-150 Raptor. She never wavered in admitting in conversation that her pickup truck was her adult toy. Twenty months into the purchase, she still found excitement in the thought of getting in the seat and gripping the steering wheel—the only thing better for her: the pilot's seat of an airplane.

Mel had learned long ago to value a reliable vehicle over any man—men, to her, were synonymous with untrustworthy. The choice was a no-brainer in her personal lexicon of adult priorities. A pickup truck and an airplane, unlike her marriage or that high school prom disaster, never let her down. A plane had taken her to places she loved—remote, beautiful corners of the world and across the U.S.—something no man had ever matched.

She couldn't imagine life without either. Men? They could be fun for a night, maybe a weekend. But a plane or a pickup, treated right, could stick with you for life—damn near to the grave.

Tossing her duffel in the passenger seat, she placed her phone in the windshield cradle, put on her seatbelt, and pressed the white back-lit button to start her rig. Turning the shifter dial to reverse, she checked her backup position on the monitor. Moving backward ten feet, she braked, stopped the pickup, and put it in drive. Lurching forward, chirping the tires, she eased off the accelerator and hurried out of the parking lot.

Mel looked at her phone in the windshield cradle. It lit up, vibrating with the word DISPATCH in block letters across the screen. Surprised—she hadn't received a call from this number since she left the department—she pressed the green answer button.

"Hello. Mel here."

"Hey, Mel. Swinson here." The voice paused. "Sorry to bother you now that you're retired and all, but I have someone who wants to talk with you."

"No worries. What's up? I'm guessing from the smoke and the fact you're calling me that there's a destructive fire in Ashland and you're all wishing I hadn't retired."

"Well, too soon to know the severity with certainty, but yes, near Ashland—and we're on standby. We're waiting on the official request from the ODF [Oregon Department of Forestry]. Hang on a second, I'm handing the phone over to someone."

Swinson stood, handed the phone to the individual standing opposite the counter, and exited the room, closing the door behind him.

Mel's mind swirled as exhilaration swept through her from a simple phone call. Adrenaline surged, chasing away the aches from softball. When the voice finally came on, curiosity gripped her.

"Hey there, sloth. Enjoying sitting around on your ass?"

"Hah! As much as I hate to admit it, Ed," Mel replied to her old boss, the head of the contracting air tanker company she had worked for the last decade. In that time, she'd dumped millions of gallons of retardant over massive chunks of forest throughout the United States. Fire season became a money-making machine, and Mel got plenty of exciting yoke time in aerial firefighting. Different from the military mission, but certainly not boring—and still very much edge-of-your-seat adrenaline inducing.

"Mel, I want to catch up, but I have an urgent matter I need to talk with you about."

Mel turned her pickup toward Central Point, where she had

called home since her military career ended. Her modest home faced east on a nice fifteen-acre spread, with views of picturesque Mt. McLoughlin and a sizeable swath of the Rogue Valley. She loved waking in the mornings and having coffee on her deck, taking in the Southern Oregon beauty. Late spring and fall. The last several years, smoke from forest fires filled the valley as early as July and could last through September depending on wind and weather. If smoke pushed into the Rogue Valley, she'd sit inside with her homemade iced latte and look forward to clearing skies. That is, if she wasn't somewhere across the United States—or abroad—fighting fires from the air.

"What, Ed, you need me to take one of the twins up?" Mel referred to the two DC-10 Air Tankers that the Air Tanker Unit (ATU) operated and that she, with deep admiration, had named the twins—Betsy and Bob. ATU owned and operated several planes for firefighting—DC-7s and MD-87s—but Mel flew the larger DC-10s.

"Listen, Mel. You know how much I respect you and think about your skills. I've got an untenable situation here in Medford. It's why I'm here and not at the tanker base in New Mexico."

Mel, drooling over the idea of something cold to drink, thought about a Dutch Bros blended Coco Mo with a couple of extra shots. She pulled off Highway 99 and into the blue and white windmill coffee stand parking lot. Parking out of the way of customers, she didn't want to hold up the entire drive-through lines, she'd reposition the pickup when she knew more about what Ed wanted.

"I'm listening, Ed," Mel said, curiosity tightening its grip.

"Confidential, Mel, okay?"

"Shit, you under investigation or some shit? What the hell is going on, Ed? You've got me bordering on beyond curious."

"It's Johnson." The name sent a touch of anger and a big

130

dose of frustration through Mel's body. Another pilot—one of her coworkers the last couple of years—Johnson happened to be one of the few people on the planet Mel couldn't figure out how to like. As hard as she tried, there was no redeemable quality in the man. An egotistical dick, by no stretch of anyone's imagination. No one she knew liked him—professionally or personally.

"ATU is done with him. I'm here to fire him—we're canceling his contract. I had Charlie Monthan flying here from Arizona to finish out Johnson's season in Medford, but his flight got delayed. Not sure when he'll arrive and, well, if you've looked out the window toward Ashland, you can see there's a little fire blazing. I can't cancel Johnson's contract until I have a replacement. I can't pull a pilot from the other tank because it's on the Obenchain fire. So, do you feel like flying?"

Mel stiffened. Her body reacted instantly—adrenaline surged, then mellowed into a warm wave of renewed purpose. Her mouth spoke before her mind caught up.

"Ha! Yes. I'll fly. How does this work though? Just for the day?"

"Excellent, Mel. No weeds right now. I need you down here ASAP, but we'll do a short-term thirty-day contract that we can renew depending on what's going on and if you want to keep flying. I know how torn you were to hang up your flight suit. The company needs you, and we don't want Johnson up in our planes anymore. Every time he goes up, all of us get a sinking feeling in our stomach that something bad will happen. The feeling is mutual throughout the executive team. With the Almeda Fire blowing up, I need a pilot—now."

Mel knew Ed referred to Johnson's penchant for taking too many risks in the cockpit. There was confidence, even a positive swagger—as a pilot, that was good. But Johnson embraced recklessness. Reckless abandon paired with arrogance didn't equal a healthy mix in an aerial firefighting pilot.

Looking at her watch, glancing at the duffel in the back seat, she replied, "I'll be at the airport in fifteen minutes, Ed. Will that do?"

"Damn, I love you, Mel. Don't tell my wife. And yes, that will do. Thank you. I already have the contract written up. You can sign it when you get here. Heads up: Johnson, as you can imagine, will be pissed. I don't know if he'll be gone before you arrive. Be alert when you enter the parking lot."

"Oh yeah, the parking lot." Mel thought about the keypad entrance and wondered if her code still worked.

"My gate code still good?" she asked.

"Hmmm, good question. Try it. If not, buzz in and we'll open it for you. Thanks again and see you soon."

"Last thing, Ed. Thanks."

"Roger that, Mel. See you soon."

Mel heard the line go dead. She looked again at the duffel holding her flight suit, socks, underwear, boots—all her necessary flight gear, packed neat and ready. She'd kept the bag in the truck out of habit. So many times, over the past couple of months, she'd almost taken it inside, but couldn't admit flying might be over. Keeping it in the pickup made it seem like she might not be done.

Of all the times she dreamed of getting back in the air, it had never occurred to her that her return flight wouldn't be to save trees—but to help save people, businesses, and entire communities.

# A Chaotic Scene

Chief Wilson sat behind the wheel of the county fire vehicle; its tires planted on scorched, ashy ground. Ahead, a building crumbled and melted into itself, consumed by the relentless blaze. Even from a hundred and fifty feet away, waves of heat seeped through the cab, prickling his skin. The radio crackled with frantic, overlapping voices, but their urgency faded into the background as his thoughts drifted backward, pulled once more into the past.

*"Sky, do you have practice tonight?"*

*"Yeah. Why?" Sky's voice echoed down the stairs from the hallway. The bathroom, Chief Wilson guessed.*

*"I'm trying to figure out what to make for dinner."*

*He stood at the bottom of the stairs, already dressed for work, coffee cup in hand. His foot tapped restlessly against the floor, nerves refusing to settle until he set foot in the fire station. Or maybe the nerves were about leaving the house, escaping the constant disapproval in his daughter's eyes. He knew the truth but wasn't about to admit it. Not now. Not for years.*

*"Don't worry about dinner. I'll find something when I get home."*

*The words, flung down the stairs, dripped with contempt and disappointment. He flinched. No matter what he did, it was never enough. Drive her to school, and she'd gripe about showing up in a fire vehicle. Don't, and she'd complain about the bus. Go to parent-teacher conferences, and she'd rage for a week about him embarrassing her in front of a teacher. Skip the conference, and he'd hear about how all the other parents showed up.*

*Since Sky's mother left, parenting had felt like fumbling*

133

*around in the dark, trying to assemble something without instructions. Work came easy. Managing personalities at the station, handling emergencies—that was second nature. Raising a young woman alone? That was a test he kept failing. And he had no one to turn to. His parents were dead, Sky's mother was gone, and the rest of his family wasn't worth a damn.*

*"Dad, we have this same conversation every morning. Go to work. That's what you want anyway."*

*Her voice cut through him like glass, sharp and precise. He took a sip of coffee, the bitterness coating his throat, a poor match for the ache in his chest. The sadness pressed down on him, heavy and relentless, squeezing his heart until it felt bruised.*

*He turned away, trying to shove the hurt aside. As he reached for the front door, Sky's music flared up, the bass thumping and Taylor Swift's voice blaring through the walls. Several images flashed through his mind—Sky sprinting barefoot through the pasture, laughing as she leapt the fence without breaking stride; dribbling a basketball with sharp, practiced rhythm; spiking a volleyball across the net with precision; swinging a tennis racquet with the same fierce focus she brought to everything. Her body moved with the effortless grace of an athlete.*

*She always left wet towels scattered on the floor, little islands of chaos in her otherwise tidy world. She never unplugged the hair dryer. He'd mutter to himself while picking up after her, grumbling at her carelessness even as a fond smile pulled at his lips. Cleaning up after her felt like the only way he knew how to care for her.*

*How did other single parents do it? How did they raise happy, well-adjusted kids without crumbling under the weight of failure?*

*He hesitated at the door, his hand resting on the knob. He wanted to turn back, to race up the stairs, hold Sky, and tell her he loved her. Instead, the dry air beyond the threshold tugged at him, the restlessness building. The high winds and parched conditions made him anxious. He needed to be at the station, ready for whatever might happen.*

*The hug would have to wait.*

*The door slammed behind him leaving Taylor Swift's wailing chorus to echo through the house as he headed toward the county vehicle.*

The chief, hearing faint sounds repeating "Chief" over and over on the walkie, shook his head from reminiscing and answered the call.

"Chief here. Go ahead."

Paducah replied in haste, "Chief. A mobile home park in Talent is burning out of control. At least a half dozen or more businesses are on fire. We're throwing everything we can at it, but to no avail. We don't have enough crew. I recommend pulling back and moving the line. Over."

The chief stared through the windshield at a building that fire had reduced to rubble in less than fifteen minutes.

"Move it, Paducah. I'll be back at the command post in two minutes to assess what reinforcements are coming in from the surrounding communities. Do what you can in the meantime. I need to meet up with you, but I have to hit the command post first."

The chief paused, waiting for a response. It didn't come. Knowing the demands placed on her, he waited longer than normal, not wanting to add unnecessary stress to her already fire-challenged day.

"Roger that, Chief, and thanks. Yes, we need you out here. It's going to be a long night, and what I'm trying to deal with skirts outside my expertise."

"Bullshit, Paducah. Trust yourself. You know the routine

better than anyone. Don't take crap from anyone, and don't second-guess yourself. A mistake made from your training, instincts, and gut is never truly wrong. Your job is to save lives and property. If something goes sideways because of a calculated decision, then learn from it and move on. You're smarter than you think, and you're sure as hell going to be better than me—and I'm damn good.

He couldn't see her, but he could picture the way his words steadied her. She always fed off his confidence.

"I'll get to the command post in about ten minutes. We'll regroup then."

With that, the chief cranked the wheel hard, tires screeching as the rig tore around the tight corner. The command post loomed ahead, a hub of frantic energy. He slammed the brakes, the vehicle jolting to a stop. In one fluid motion, he leaped out, boots pounding against the pavement as he charged up the short metal stairs. The door flew open, and he plunged into the chaos—voices clashing, radios blaring, stress thick in the air like smoke.

# Fathom the Destruction

Mel gripped the steering wheel, eyes flicking between the truck's side-view mirrors. Scenarios spun through her mind— shower at home, a change of clothes, maybe breakfast if time allowed. But her thoughts were already in the sky, flying the air tanker, scanning smoke-choked terrain for a place to drop slurry.

Lost in the clouds, she eased the truck out of the D Bros parking lot and pulled into the street. Too late, she registered the oncoming car's speed and distance. Tires screeched, and a horn blasted like an alarm.

"Fuck you!" The driver's shout tore through the air, sharp and furious. Mel's nervous laugh slipped out—a mix of embarrassment and relief. She couldn't blame them—it was the same knee-jerk reaction she'd hurled at clueless drivers more times than she cared to admit.

Mel told Google to call ATU dispatch. Swinson picked up after the first ring.

"Hey, Mel. This you?"

"It is, Swinson. Okay to talk?"

"Yes. Only me in dispatch right now. Ed left to go to the base manager's office to do—you know what."

"Okay, Swinson. Give me the skinny. Are we going up soon?"

"Standby right now. The state police are closing southbound Interstate 5. Highway 99 is closed in both directions, with the fire moving northwest through Bear Creek. There are Bambi buckets in the sky dropping water, but they're having little to no impact. I got a call less than five minutes ago asking if we were available. I said yes, but then Ed walked in and told me what's going on. So, we're in a holding pattern until approval comes down from ODF and we have another pilot. Tough to drop retardant without a pilot."

Mel laughed, then caught herself. She wanted to be condescending as hell—not being a fan of Johnson—but held her tongue. Swinson knew Johnson's reputation already—she didn't need to say a thing.

"I just finished winning a softball game, Swinson. Can I go home and shower, or should I come straight to the shop?"

Mel shook her head, her mouth pulling into a tight, frustrated line. Why had she even asked the question? Nervous chatter, probably. The dispatcher could make recommendations, sure, but in the end, it was the pilot's judgment that mattered. Her decision was already made, and it wasn't anyone else's call.

Still, something in her brain kept reaching out, like the question itself could somehow forge a stronger connection—build trust. Stupid. Pointless. Maybe even schmoozing. She had a bad habit of piling on words to keep a conversation alive, to dodge silence. And it pissed her off.

Mel had fallen prey to the time-wasting discussion more times than she cared to admit. She struggled to understand why her mind craved the need to lengthen conversations with certain people, as if a long discussion might provide clarity. "Shit," she muttered to herself as she thought about the tendency yet again. Childhood neglect, perhaps—add to the fodder list for counseling sessions. Mel made a mental note to bring it up if she ever took the time to find a therapist and make an appointment.

Tapping her left index finger on the door handle, waiting for a stoplight to turn green and signal for her to move on, Mel responded before Swinson answered.

"Disregard that question, Swinson. I'll be there in ten minutes." Mel guided her pickup onto the South Medford I-5 on-ramp and, moving around a slow-moving truck, floored the gas pedal.

Knowing the shower at the base office usually met her cleanliness standards, depending on the date the cleaning crew had last shown up, Mel contemplated: Did she even need to shower? She'd be a sweating mess inside fifteen minutes in the cockpit anyhow. Regardless, it made more sense to go straight to the flight-line shop than home. Time was crucial right now, and going home would add thirty minutes to her arrival.

Ending the call and navigating through lighter-than-normal I-5 traffic—thanks to the fire—Mel couldn't wait to get the plane in the sky. With a request to get the tanker airborne hinging on ODF approval, she eased off the accelerator and exited the interstate. The last thing she—or the citizens of the Rogue Valley—needed right now was her getting in an accident.

Mel wondered if she'd run into Johnson and how he'd reacted to being fired. Her gaze fell to the softball bat jutting from her athletic bag on the passenger-side floor. Johnson would be pissed and humiliated—a bad mix for someone with low self-esteem and a short fuse.

She'd grab her flight bag from the back seat, then pull the bat from the athletic bag up front. Just in case.

With several minutes of drive-time to the airport, Mel replayed her last at-bat over and over. What the hell happened with her swing? She should've connected clean, sent the big white, red-stitched ball sailing over the fence. Instead, her stat line read: single. It should have been a walk-off home run. Not a Gibson or Freeman shot, but one worth remembering. People remember walk-offs, not singles.

Had her back foot twisted too much in the worn-out dirt of the batter's box? Maybe she'd dropped her hands too low on the swing. Mel flipped the turn signal and aimed the truck toward the secure hangar parking lot. The feel of a perfect swing slipped further from reach with every mile, retreating to the darkest corners of her mind where it would stay buried for the long hours ahead.

Mel squinted at the smoke clawing its way across the sky, the wind shoving it southward. How close was the fire to the small towns hugging Interstate 5? The thought tightened her gut. She hoped the ground crews could hold the line, keep the flames from tearing through businesses and homes. But if the call for a VLAT from ATU came in to protect residential neighborhoods, everyone would know the blaze had blown past the point where trees and vegetation mattered.

Her post-military flying career had been all about soaring over America's forests, pouring bright red retardant over woods and hillsides—never towns. The untouched challenge drew her in. A hunger for the unpredictable, for the kind of day that demanded steady hands and sharp instincts. And today might be that day.

Stopping her vehicle at the entrance security gate, Mel entered her six-digit code, and the gate opened to her delight. Hurrying into the parking lot, she did a quick scan to see if Johnson's dark gray Tesla was in its usual spot.

It was. Shit, she thought.

"Oh well. Stop worrying about what you can't control," Mel muttered, her gaze fixed on the flight line beyond the chain-link security fence. The metal grid cut the scene into fragments—planes and crew split into pieces by the diamond-shaped links. She climbed out of her pickup, shaking off the negativity like dust from her boots.

Today had its own demands. Paperwork to sign. A pissed-off ex-pilot to dodge. A plane to get airborne. And a fire hellbent on devouring anything in its path.

Her thoughts drifted to the retardant. Its purpose wasn't to snuff out fires but to guide them, redirect them—force them to crawl instead of sprint. Years in the cockpit had drilled into her

140

the importance of precision. A split second too late, a hundred feet off course, and the drops were useless. But today, precision mattered more than ever. A stray drop in the woods was one thing. A missed line when flames threatened towns and homes was another situation entirely.

Mel wondered if people on the ground understood this as their businesses and homes burned. There would be no stopping the fire today if the wind continued its rage. Unable to fathom the destruction that lay ahead for so many people, Mel considered the devastation about to impact the Rogue Valley for years.

# Prom-moshun

Sky headed south, putting distance between herself and the fire, staying clear of anything burning. She picked her way along an unfamiliar path, weaving around smoldering trees, charred buildings, and cars melted down to twisted metal— almost everything scorched by the blaze.

Every sense stayed on high alert. The fire's relentless push northward felt personal, its destruction cruel and deliberate. Watching side-by-side structures—where one building stood untouched while its neighbor crumbled to ash, sent her father's old lectures zigzagging through her mind like tangled lightning bolts sketched across a dark sky.

During her youth, Sky had tried engaging her father countless times about how fire seemed to ravage what she saw as the less fortunate. He'd always shrugged her off: *"Fire has no friends or enemies, Sky. It takes what it wants."* Then he'd change the direction of the conversation with a lecture about fire and how to deal with it. His approach always left her unsatisfied, as if he were incapable of anything but surface conversation. She had wanted to dig into the why and how. He wanted to explain the facts.

Sky hesitated; her feet rooted to the ashy ground as doubt clawed at her. Should she keep moving toward her childhood home? Pulled like a magnet, it felt as if she had no choice. Flakes of ash floated down from the sky, drifting like lazy snowflakes on a windless winter morning. Her eyes dropped to the ground, where the delicate gray dust settled in uneven patches, clinging to her boots with every step.

The decision twisted in her chest, pulling her forward even as her legs resisted. She forced herself to move, each step stirring the fragile ash, making it swirl around her ankles in wispy, weightless curls. Her pace quickened, desperate urgency, as if fleeing some nightmare from her childhood.

But it wasn't flames or monsters chasing her—it was the memories, emotions, and everything she'd left behind clawing at her from the inside out.

Moving with cumbersome grace, her eyes swelled. Not from the smoke, but from the realization that for the first time, she couldn't recall an instance when her mother had cared for her with the unflinching love of a parent. The woman didn't know how to show affection or genuine love. Her father didn't know how to converse with her, but she had never doubted his love.

Stuffing the thoughts aside, Sky wondered if her bedroom remained intact or if her father had cleansed the memories of her.

Tired, alone, and scared, Sky reached her old driveway. The dented mailbox and clay-packed soil in the driveway brought conflicting memories. Realizing the family house, southwest of the fire, lay outside of harm's way, she eased up the driveway. The backpack strap pressed harder into her shoulder with each slow step toward the front door—scratchy eyes darting around the property, taking in everything surrounding the home.

The old green tractor sat where it always had, oil stains darkening the dirt beneath it. Weeds and blackberry vines tangled around the tires, pressing in from the edges but never quite overtaking the machine itself. The rust looked worse than she remembered, pitted and rough like scar tissue. Tired, but still holding on. Her father must still have been using it, pushing it to keep working through sheer stubbornness.

The wood fence sagged under its own weight, its faded gray boards patched here and there with newer planks that managed to keep it standing.

Sky's gaze shifted to the barn southwest of the house. Smaller than she remembered, but the fresh coat of paint gave it an unexpected vitality—like someone had tried to reclaim something from the decay.

Rounding the last corner of the driveway, she stopped. Her fingers traced the rough bark of a massive pine tree etched with her initials, scratched into its trunk over the years.

She stared at the house, its porch stretching the entire width of the building. But her eyes locked on the bench swing at the southern end, creaking softly as it swayed, the painted wood shifting like it was being tugged toward the fire.

Sky closed her eyes, moisture gathering at the edges. Voices from the past stirred in the wind, their words cutting through the years with a clarity edged in both purpose and regret.

*"Come on, Dad. Swing with Mom and me. Please..." Five-year-old Sky tugged at her father's hand, her eyes wide and pleading. He had stood there, tall and solid in his firefighter's uniform, the dark blue pants pressed sharp enough to cut. His belt buckle always sat perfectly centered, like it belonged there and nowhere else.*

*His shirt had matched the pants—neat and precise—the gold badge catching every bit of light as it gleamed from his chest. The shoulder patch declared his fire district, its texture rough and frayed—a sharp contrast to the badge's polished shine.*

*Sky had loved running her fingers over both—the smooth metal badge and the coarse, rugged patch. One sleek and untouchable, the other worn and real. Together, they made her think her dad was something bigger than life. Important.*

*Another Saturday morning—another day that her father wouldn't return until her bedtime. Swinging on the porch swing, holding on to her mother's reluctant arm, she had wanted her father to join them. He paused, stared at the fire vehicle in the driveway, then over at Sky, and smiled.*

*"Okay, but just for a bit. I can't be late to work." Sky's cheeks tightened, warmth spreading like a mushroom pushing through spring leaves, straining for light after the melt. Her father had crossed the porch to the swing in a few steps. His legs carried him so fast, she had thought. Would she ever move that quickly and effortlessly?*

*"Scoot over next to your mom, Sky. Make some room for me, please."*

*Sky squeezed in tight next to her mother and looked down at the smooth wood slats of the swing, pleading for the universe to make sure the swing held enough room for her father, so he'd sit.*

*"There, Daddy. Lots of room."*

*Her father smiled and plopped down, the swing's gentle rhythm jolting before finding its sway again under his weight. Sky had felt her mother tense; she always did when her father showed up. That tightness in her shoulders, the way her eyes drifted somewhere else, like she was already planning her escape.*

*Sky hadn't understood her mother's distance, but her father's tension made sense. It was her mom. Something about her presence set him on edge, his easygoing nature turning brittle and uncertain.*

*But when the three of them sat together and no one argued, relief had settled over Sky like warm sunlight. Even if her parents barely spoke, leaving her to fill the silence. It didn't matter. If they were all together, she could pretend, even for a moment, that everything might be okay.*

*"Are you going to fight fire today, Daddy?"*

*Sky, not wanting any distractions, tried not to listen to her mother humming. Something else she always seemed to do when Sky's daddy was around. Sky often thought her mother used humming as a way of escaping somewhere else.*

*"I don't know. Every day is different. Hopefully, everyone will stay safe and there won't be any fires."*

*"What about medical emergencies?" Sky looked up at her father, eyes wide with wonder, hoping to impress him with the word medical—a word her mom had explained yesterday. Her father's eyebrows lifted, surprise flashing across his face before he glanced at her mother and back down at Sky.*

*"Well, little lady. Impressive vocabulary."*

*Sky beamed, warmth rushing through her chest as her father kept talking.*

*"Probably, sweetie. It's normal to have at least one incident a day. You never know, though."*

*"Well, if you do, I hope you get to save a life. That must be so cool to help someone like that, Daddy."*

*Sky's mother squirmed on the swing, stopped humming, and sighed. She stood, her body rigid, and walked inside without a word. Her father's face tightened, anger flickering before it crumbled into sadness.*

*"I love you, Daddy."*

*The screen door thudded shut behind her mother. Sky turned to the window and watched her move through the kitchen.*

*Sky's gaze lingered on her mother's silhouette as questions swirled in her head. "Daddy," she asked softly, "why don't you talk to Mom more?" Her father froze mid-step. For a moment, he didn't move at all, like the question had knocked something loose inside him. He looked toward the kitchen window, then down at the ground.*

*"Grown-ups have... different ways of handling things, sweetheart," he said finally, his voice low and tight, lacking his normal confidence. Sky frowned. "But maybe if you talked more, she'd be happier."*

He ran a hand over his face, rough fingers dragging across his jaw as if trying to scrub away the thought.

"Perhaps," he said, but it sounded more like a breath than an answer.

He refused to look at her, afraid she might see the lie in his eyes. Sky waited, sensing something heavy behind his silence, but he offered nothing more.

Not wanting to lose her father's attention, unsatisfied with the explanation but knowing enough at a young age already to choose her battles, Sky wrapped her arms around him, pressing herself tight against the solid warmth of his chest. He felt like a board holding up a barn—firm, strong, but somehow comforting all the same.

They sat there in silence, Sky clinging to him, willing time to slow down. She felt him shift, his body preparing to leave. Desperation swelled in her chest, and she squeezed him as hard as her skinny arms could manage, hoping sheer willpower might keep him there.

Chuckling, her father said, right on cue, "Hey, little one, I have to go, or I'll be late."

"Can't you stay home today, Daddy? Let's go fishing. I bet the fish are biting at Applegate Lake. We can take the kayak out."

"Honey, I wish. That sounds wonderful. But I have a couple of meetings today I can't miss. I think I'm going to get a promotion."

Disappointment dug into her, but she pushed it down. If she kept him talking, maybe he'd stay longer.

"What's prom-moshun mean, Daddy?" Sky stumbled over the word.

"It's promotion, honey. It means my bosses think I'm doing a great job and want me to be in charge of the whole fire district."

"Wow! That's so cool. So, you get to tell everyone what to do?"

Her father tilted his head back and laughed, a real laugh that rumbled deep in his chest.

"Well, kind of, yes. But, sweetie, if I don't get to work and prepare, I might not get that promotion."

"Let's go in and tell Mom."

Standing, her father bent down and cupped her head in his big, rough hands. His touch was strong but gentle, his thumbs tracing soft lines along her temples. He kissed her forehead, lips pressing with perfect pressure, the warmth of him sinking into her skin.

"Your mom already knows. I told her last night."

Sky watched her mother's silhouette through the window, her shoulders tense as she moved about the kitchen. Why couldn't Mom be happy for her father? Didn't she understand how important he was now?

An idea sparked. Maybe if they surprised him, her mother would feel happy, too. They could make him a cake and take it to his work.

She leaped off the swing, her feet hitting the porch with a thud. She turned back to her father, who was already heading down the steps.

"I love you, Daddy. I can't wait to see you when you get home. Have a good day."

Sky bolted for the door, letting the creaky screen whine on its rusty hinge. She didn't care if he heard her. "Mom! Daddy's getting a prom-moshun today. Can we bake him a cake?"

# Sorry About That

Mel crossed the parking lot, duffel bag slung over one shoulder, her grip firm on the handle of her two-week-old Easton Ghost. She held the bat close to her side—all five hundred bucks of it. Cracks in the pavement, filled with black tar, snaked beneath her sneakers. She didn't want trouble, just wanted to crush softballs, not ribs. Especially not Johnson's. The bat could probably take the hit, but if it slipped and clattered onto the concrete? That'd be the real heartbreak.

Nearing the front door of ATU's base management office, Mel glanced through the chain-link fence and grinned at the sight of Betsy's tail number—orange and blue splendor gleaming under the sun. No sign of Bob, the second DC-10, on the tarmac. Either he was already slicing through the sky or dumping a load on some wildfire miles away.

Her gaze slid to the front of Betsy, where Ed Burgeon stood like a brick wall at the base of the ramp, arms folded tight. Blocking none other than Johnson, the pilot she was replacing from getting anywhere near the cockpit.

She wanted to stand and gawk, but the confrontation ahead played to her advantage. Let Johnson stew outside. She'd check in with the base manager, confirm her arrival, and get changed behind a locked door. After that, her bat and softball uniform would be stowed in a locker. Or should she carry the bat with her? Too obvious, she thought. Then why bring it at all? Her mind wrestled with the indecision. Once inside, the steady hum of activity and too many watchful eyes would keep Johnson's arrogance in check. She shouldn't need the bat.

If no bat? Well, she'd handle him. The little man carried his ego like a badge of honor, but Mel knew better. She stood only an inch or two shorter, but what she lacked in bulk she more than made up for in skill. He had muscle, sure—thick shoulders and a frame built for pushing people around. But Mel had speed. And she had twenty-plus years of Tae Kwon Do under her belt, a discipline she had picked up during her first Air Force base assignment in Korea and never let go of.

She had the trophies and bruises to prove it, racking up wins at local tournaments across southern Oregon. The crew had ragged on her for months after a write-up in a local paper— her name butchered in the headline, but her victories impossible to ignore. She wondered if that same article, yellowed and curling at the corners, still hung on the bulletin board in the flight office.

Within minutes, Mel was dressed and ready to go, snapping the lock tight on the locker. Normally, she wouldn't bother locking it, but with Johnson around, she took no chances. The bat cost too much to leave unprotected. She pulled her blonde hair back into a tight ponytail, wrapping a hair band around it until every stray hair was out of her eyes.

The moment she stepped out of the locker room, screaming echoed down the hall from the direction of the flight office. Sounded like Johnson was making a scene again. Mel started to turn back but shook her head. "Screw the bastard," she muttered.

She stepped into the hallway and immediately found herself face to face with the commotion. Johnson, red-faced and raging, stormed toward her, Ed Burgeon in his wake along with three flight crew guys—all of them bigger than Johnson— watching from ten feet away in the flight office.

Johnson's tirade stumbled to a halt when he saw her. His expression went blank, eyes wide, the angry crimson draining to an Irish-skinned shade of pale. Mel took a step back, instinctively settling into a stance drilled into her by years of Tae Kwon Do training.

Johnson knew better. Mel could see it in the strain around his eyes, the way his jaw clenched, fighting to keep his composure from shattering completely. She had been in enough tournaments and real-world encounters to recognize a man teetering on the edge of losing control.

"Are you fucking kidding me? You're retired, Hall." Johnson always called Mel by her last name. He called everyone by their last name. Near as anyone knew, Johnson used people's last names with deliberate disdain—like surnames were impersonal and smacked of a lack of care. Mel didn't flinch. Johnson could call her whatever he wanted; she'd give it no concern.

"How are you doing, Johnson? Rough day?" Mel couldn't help herself, her smile oozing passive-aggressive satisfaction.

Johnson's face twisted, his fists curling like he was one insult away from taking a swing. But the moment Mel shifted her stance—knees bent, body lowered into a slight crouch, her eyes locked on him with the intensity of a stalking tiger—he hesitated. He knew that stance. And he knew what she could do from it.

The anger in his eyes flickered, replaced by something else. Caution. Maybe even fear. His breathing steadied, and his posture relaxed—but not from confidence—from a survival instinct kicking in.

"Dream on, Mel. I'd snap you in two if I wanted. Get the fuck out of my way, dyke!"

"Dyke." The word rolled around Mel's head, more amusing than insulting. Really? That was the best he could come up with? As Johnson stormed past her, still radiating bubbling rage, Mel shifted to the edge of the hallway, keeping him in sight.

"I am suing your ass, Burgeon. You and the entire ATU fuck show. You have my word on it." His voice echoed down the corridor, his heavy steps retreating until a door slammed with a force that rattled the walls.

Mel stayed tense, her muscles coiled, but the adrenaline ebbed with each passing second. She straightened, rolling her shoulders, and made her way into the flight office. One by one, she extended her hand to Ed and the crew members, her smile more genuine now that the threat had stormed off.

"Sorry about that, Mel," Ed said, his expression weary but grateful. "And thanks for getting here so fast."

# What A Day

Teddy gripped the steering wheel, his knuckles aching as he navigated through the chaos. Cars crammed the roadways, a steady stream of metal surging northward, fleeing the smoke. Drivers darted from lane to lane, tires screeching and horns blaring, desperate to escape. The whole scene looked ripped from one of those end-of-the-world movies where panic turned highways into endless parking lots. It wasn't quite that bad yet, but the way things were going, it wouldn't be long.

He pulled his pickup into the manufactured home development and killed the engine. Gravel crunched beneath his boots as he strode over to the raised security gate, eyes locked on the faded control panel. With a frustrated grunt, he brought his right hand down hard on the panel.

The gate lurched, metal creaking as it shuddered and slowly began to lower. Teddy's eyes widened. "What the hell?" he muttered. Another hard slap of his fist, and the gate jerked back up, groaning like some rusty old demon dragged from its sleep.

"Shut the front door." Teddy couldn't help but say something aloud, letting his frustration show.

Thinking a broken wire—or at least a loose connection—had caused the issue, he felt a sense of relief.

"I see how it is. Well, guess what? I am done playing. I'm going to go get my tools and tear your ass apart until I find the problem."

Teddy talked to the control panel and gate as if the damned thing understood. Letting out a burp and wondering if his acid reflux would torment him for the next hour, he remembered how much he had enjoyed the burger and tater tots as he climbed back into his pickup. Any reflux issues that might arise were worth the pain.

Teddy twisted the ignition, and the sky-blue and white 1978 Silverado rumbled to life, its engine growling like a restless giant. He eased the vintage pickup forward, gravel crunching under the tires, and aimed it toward the shop. His gaze flicked to his wristwatch. Nearing 12:45. The smoke-choked sky painted everything in a dull, grayish hue, swallowing the sun's warmth and making it feel like dusk.

In the rearview mirror, he caught the security gate creaking and clanking as it descended. "You've gotta be kidding me," he muttered, words edged with frustration. The damn thing acted like it had a mind of its own. Maybe it did. Maybe the whole world was losing it.

His foot hovered over the brake. Part of him wanted to turn back, march over to the control panel, and bash the thing until it stayed open. But what good would that do without his tools? Just another headache to add to the already shitty day.

Another thirty seconds. That's all he needed to reach the shop. The cart and his tools waited—a sliver of control in a world unraveling at the seams. If anyone tried to pull up to that gate in the next minute, tough luck. They'd have to wait.

Parking, Teddy jumped out of the vehicle and moved quicker than normal toward his maintenance cart. When he reached it, he stared down at the seat. Stopping short before sliding in behind the steering wheel, his hand made a reflexive motion, sweeping away what looked to be ash. The oddity didn't register as Teddy started the cart and guided it back toward the gate.

Seconds later, he pulled up to the iron blockade, relieved no cars waited to exit or enter. Stepping out of the cart by the control panel, he grabbed his toolbox. With newfound determination and singularity of focus, Teddy grabbed a screwdriver and started dismantling the control box, piece by piece.

Humming as he began to disassemble the unit, Teddy, with newfound confidence, talked again to the control panel.

"Guess what, you little piece of shit. I'm fixing you today, even if it takes hours. I'll burn in hell before you get the best of me."

After his pledge, staring skyward at the ever-increasing smoke, he returned his gaze to the gate. Considering it was in the closed position; he wondered if he should leave it up rather than down before taking the panel apart. With one main entrance in and out of the park, having it closed at this time of day for any prolonged period presented a problem. An oncoming fire would, of course, amplify people's desire to race out of their little tin city.

There was a back way out of the park, but it confused most, and Teddy didn't want to take the time to set up signs and cones pointing the way. Nor did he have the desire to hack away all the blackberry bushes impeding the gate's path.

So, not concerning himself with up or down any longer—it was a waste of time—Teddy hunched over the control panel, sweat gathering at his temples despite the chill settling over everything. The temperature had dropped, the sun's warmth smothered by the thick ash hanging in the air. His fingers trembled, nerves buzzing with anxious adrenaline as he attacked the disassembly with rushed precision. A tiny screw slipped from his grip, clinking against the metal frame before plummeting toward the asphalt.

His eyes tracked its fall, but the damn thing bounced once and vanished. "Shit," he muttered, his voice tight, frustration sharpening the word. He'd worry about finding the needle in the haystack later. For now, he yanked three wires from the corroded green circuit board, the brittle plastic connectors snapping free with a reluctant crunch.

Midway through the chaotic teardown, it hit him, he should've taken a photo. Something to guide him when it was time to piece the mess back together. His phone. Where the hell was his phone? The shop? Hadn't he had it with him at lunch?

A car rumbled up to the gate, horn blaring like some angry metal titan demanding passage.

"Shit! What a day." Teddy glared at the control panel as if it were the source of all his problems, his pulse jittering like loose wiring.

# Bewildered

Chief Wilson stormed up the steps of the command post, his boots clanging against the metal as he pushed through the door. The roar of voices and radio chatter assaulted his ears, a frantic symphony of overlapping reports and shouted commands bouncing off the metal walls.

He let the door thud shut behind him, sealing out the outside chaos. For thirty seconds, he just stood there, eyes sweeping the room, ears sifting through the noise to find the thread he needed. Familiar faces blurred past, everyone glued to their tasks, oblivious to his arrival.

His gaze locked onto the dispatcher seated farthest from the door—exactly where he'd ordered the lead dispatcher's position to be years ago. *A change he'd implemented after watching too many command posts dissolve into chaos, confusion tearing through operations like wildfire.*

"Farthest from the door, fewest distractions," he'd drilled into their heads. Now, the system was second nature. He strode toward the dispatcher's station, his presence finally drawing a few glances but not slowing the relentless hum of work.

The chief, standing stoic and patient, waited for the woman to finish her current conversation before he spoke.

"Excuse me. It's Jaystone, correct?"

The woman, listening to both the voice on her headset and the chief, nodded.

"Please give me the latest update."

Jaystone commented into the phone, "Stand by, please. Chief Wilson is here, and I need a minute. I'll get right back with you."

"Well, Chief," the dispatcher said, her voice tight and ragged from too many hours on the radio. "The fire's tearing through everything in its path. Heavy winds are shoving it north up Bear Creek like it's got somewhere to be. And it's got plenty to burn—overgrown, bone-dry vegetation feeding it like a starving animal. Spot fires are springing up everywhere."

She glanced at her monitor, fingers twitching over the keyboard like she wanted to tear the data apart and force it to make sense. "Talent's burning along Highway 99 and to the north and west. At this point, it's all random wind-driven fires, no rhyme or reason. We've already lost structures, and dozens more are going up in flames. Housing communities, stick homes, mobile homes—it's all burning out of control."

She looked into his steady eyes, despite the chaos. "We don't have the resources. Ground crews are making split-second calls based on human life—what they think they can handle and how close they are when the shit hits the fan. Reinforcements are rolling in from across the state and NorCal, but they're an hour out. We're playing the long game here, Chief."

She let out a frustrated breath. "And the choppers? Their Bambi buckets are damn near useless right now. High winds are pushing the water drops everywhere but where they're supposed to go."

"Thank you. Any word on air tanker support yet?"

Jaystone redirected her attention back to her computer and looked back up at the chief.

The chief, impressed by the young woman's decisiveness and demeanor, made a mental note to talk to her supervisor. He loved her confidence and calm, no-nonsense attitude.

"Not yet, Chief. Waiting for approval from the Oregon Department of Forestry. They're telling us you need to make an official request."

"Okay, thank you. Apologies for taking you away from your

158

job."

The chief's voice boomed through the command post on his way out the door.

"Great work, everyone. Keep it up. It's going to be a long night."

Stepping outside and staring into the sky, bewildered by the thick plumes of smoke drifting northwest, the chief gathered his thoughts. Jumping back into his fire rig, he started the vehicle and headed out of the parking lot for Highway 99 and Talent, Oregon—several minutes from his location.

He took his right hand off the steering wheel, something he'd done thousands of times over the years, and, waiting for a break in the voice traffic, pressed a button on the mic sitting on his left shoulder.

"Paducah, come in. This is Chief Wilson."

Flipping on his vehicle's emergency roof lights, the chief watched traffic move aside without hesitation to let him pass. He guided the vehicle onto Highway 99 and floored the accelerator pedal when Paducah replied.

"Paducah here, Chief. Over."

"Where are you, Paducah? I'll head your way now."

"At the intersection of 99 and East Rapp Road, Chief. I planned on leaving and heading north."

Chief Wilson looked at his speedometer—70 mph. He eased back on the throttle until it showed 65, knowing he'd arrive at Paducah's location in less than two minutes.

As his vehicle tore down the road, his gaze swept between the driver's and passenger's windows. Smoke and flame blurred past, homes and businesses crumbling under the assault. His jaw tightened. He knew the fire crews were down in the creek gully, battling the blaze from below, but it wasn't enough. Not with this kind of destruction tearing through the town. They needed more boots on the ground, more hands, more everything.

"Don't leave. I'll be there in less than thirty seconds."

The chief's mind, a cyclone of competing thoughts that disturbed him for lack of focus, wandered back to his daughter. *He pushed the thoughts aside for a moment, reminding himself of the matter at hand.*

"This is Chief Wilson, command post. Respond, please."

Someone answered his call, and he thought the voice belonged to Johnstone.

"Go ahead, Chief. Over."

The chief's mind, from an extensive and thorough memory of the Rogue Valley, poured over roads and highways with the efficiency of a high-powered laptop.

"Call the police and request a shutdown of Highway 99 from South Valley View Boulevard north to South Stage Road. Close all off-ramps on I-5, both directions, from Valley View to South Medford. I repeat—Highway 99 from Valley View to South Stage, and all I-5 off-ramps in that stretch. They'll handle emergency traffic and evacuees—don't waste time worrying about that.

"The chief paused, searching for words to finish the train of thought, and cut the dispatcher's response off before she could speak.

"I'm pulling into a parking lot on East Rapp Road at Highway 99 to connect with Paducah. Call Paducah right away with any critical updates or requests."

"Roger that, Chief. Over."

Chief Wilson's truck rumbled through the intersection, tires spitting gravel as he aimed straight for Paducah's fire rig. She stood hunched over the hood, one hand flattening a large, wrinkled map while the other pressed her shoulder mic, lips moving with rapid-fire commands he couldn't make out over his truck's engine.

He didn't bother straining to hear her. In a few seconds,

160

he'd have her full report in person. Steering his truck within feet of her rig, he stomped on the brakes, the vehicle skidding a few more inches in the loose gravel before jolting to a stop. Turning the ignition off, he shoved the door open and jumped out, his gaze sweeping the valley.

Pockets of devastation flared across the landscape, thick smoke clawing at the sky while flames devoured anything unlucky enough to be in their path.

He hustled to Paducah.

"Glad you're here, Chief," she said without looking up, eyes locked on the map. "More crews are rolling in—Eagle Point, Central Point, Grants Pass. Klamath Falls teams should hit the valley throughout the next thirty minutes. Cal Fire's arriving in Ashland now."

"Okay, Paducah." He dragged a hand over his face, words tumbling out before he could temper them. "I'm sorry I left you hanging like this—out here alone. What a shitstorm."

"Unnecessary, Chief, but thanks. It's what you trained me on. If anyone owes someone an apology, it's me to you. I thought I'd be ready for this type of incident. 'Shitstorm' is an understatement."

"You're fine, Paducah, and more than ready and capable. And don't stress. We can divide and conquer. From all the radio chatter blasting through the lines, one person can't—and shouldn't—manage this alone. Not to mention the magnitude of the potential threat to human life. Damn, I had a strange feeling this morning when I woke up and looked out from the station in the mountains and felt the wind. Providential, some would say. As if the universe gave me a heads-up."

The chief stared at Paducah. Radio chatter blared over both their mics, and Paducah, unsure of what to say, looked back at the map. Growing tired of his unproductive reflective memories, Chief Wilson broke the silence.

"Any word from the other districts in Medford?"

Paducah's gaze snapped to the chief, her expression unreadable but confident, her posture radiating authority he couldn't help but appreciate. Her words cut off mid-sentence as she glanced down at her phone screen and pressed a button to answer another incoming call.

Even while her attention was divided, her hand hovered over her two-way mic, ready to relay orders at a moment's notice. The kind of efficiency he relied on. The kind of focus he wished he could maintain right now.

*But his thoughts drifted, his focus slipping from the present chaos to something far more personal. Lifetimes of memories crashed into him, a black hole of time devouring his attention in fractions of seconds. Sky's laughter as a child, the stubborn set of her jaw when she pushed back, the way her eyes searched his for something he was never sure he'd given her. The images struck harder than the roar of flames, his grip on the present fraying at the edges. Doubt coiled through him, whispering—if he couldn't control his own thoughts, how could he command the battle unfolding around him?*

*Sky. His daughter's name threaded itself through his mind like a stubborn weed, refusing to let go.*

*He pictured her from their last hike—just the two of them, a rare, too-short day on a narrow trail bordered by wildflowers and pine. Her voice echoing over the ridge, her eyes bright and carefree in a way they hadn't been for a long time. That look she got when she was away from the tension at home, her mother's unrealistic expectations and the strained silences.*

*In the deep lush green woods of Oregon, her guard was down, the quiet somehow filling her instead of leaving her empty. The memory hit him like a gut punch, sharper and crueler for the contrast against the chaos surrounding him now.*

*"Okay, Sky. Here's the deal. You know how to work the radio now, right?"*

*"Yes, Dad."*

*"What channel are we going to use?"*

*"Channel three. If you don't respond to me, I should try again. If you still don't respond, then I switch to channel four and try again. Each time, stay on a channel at least five minutes to give you a chance to hear."*

*"Perfect, Sky. Is there anything else?"*

*Sky stared up at him with innocent blue eyes. They were large and as clear as the greenish-blue water in Crater Lake. She spoke, then hesitated, before finishing her reasoned thought.*

*"Try to find a clear spot on a rise or hill if possible and try again if you don't respond right away. You said a clear line of sight would help, right?"*

*"Yes, Sky. Good."*

Not wanting to linger in the space of time his conscience couldn't afford, he let the memory drift away. Paducah's voice cut through the haze, crisp and direct, her call ending with a sharp click before she switched back to the radio.

"Yes, Chief. I've been talking with all the districts. We have the best coverage possible in terms of personnel and equipment. No issues with the water supply—yet," Paducah responded, as the chief pushed aside more thoughts of Sky and refocused on the map that lay on the hood of the county vehicle.

A request came in for Paducah, who wasted no time responding.

"Stand by. We are assessing the current situation. New directives are forthcoming in the next few minutes. Chief Wilson is on site. Repeat: Stand by."

"Okay, Paducah, and thanks."

The chief's gaze dropped back to the map, Paducah's eyes following as if tethered by the same urgent thread.

Brightly colored lines and scrawled notations crisscrossed the wrinkled paper, an incomplete picture of the chaos raging beyond them.

He jabbed a finger at the areas marked in red. "Alright, let's figure out what we need to protect first. Priorities. And if there's even a chance, where we can steer this damn thing."

His voice was hard, steady, but laced with a grim understanding. "Unless the wind dies down, we're not putting this fire out. But maybe—just maybe—we can guide it. Like Clint Eastwood breaking a wild horse."

A corner of Paducah's mouth twitched in something that might've been a grin if the day wasn't unraveling before them.

"Roger that, Chief," Paducah replied.

"Okay, there's enough intel to talk with the Oregon Department of Forestry about the air tanker. I'll call them. They're waiting to hear from us."

Paducah watched as Chief Wilson took his phone out of his pocket and slid his finger upward on the screen, scanning his contacts. Finding the name he searched for—Chuck Hobart, ODF—he pressed the call button and held the device up to his left ear, listening to the rings. Between the first and second ring, a voice so loud that Paducah, a few feet from the chief, heard it, came through the tiny speaker.

"What took you so long, dumbass?"

The chief smiled a tacit okay look toward Paducah and replied, "I've been trying for thirty minutes to call you, asshole."

The chief shook his head at Paducah, letting her know he bluffed, listening, knowing he'd accomplished what he wanted when the voice on the opposite end of the phone paused before returning a quiet and weak response.

"Sorry, Wilson. Like you, things are busy here. I should've reached out myself. This is an unusual situation, as you know."

The chief chuckled and cut his professional acquaintance off before he could continue apologizing—for no reason.

"Chuck, I'm messing with you. We're gathering intel, and now I'm ready to make the call. I've never requested a tanker drop over a residential fire before, and I needed time—and more intel—to assess what the hell is going on. Assistant Fire Chief Paducah agrees."

"Funny, Wilson. You son-of-a-bitch. Okay, I hear you, and you're right. You're a prick, and I know that. Bad on me for falling for your antics. Anyhow, the phone's been pasted to the side of my head for the last forty-five minutes with Salem trying to figure this out. With the increasing threat to human life, we have clear authority for whatever is necessary to stop this fire, okay?"

Chief Wilson, usually steady and straight-talking, felt off—disconnected from the moment. The resignation letter had shifted something in him, like a tether had snapped. He realized he needed to pull it together, rein in the jokes. Now wasn't the time for banter. Not with flames chewing through the valley. There was no room for screw-around energy in firefighting—especially not from the one still wearing the title of Chief.

Chief Wilson's voice came steady and measured over the radio. "My apologies, Chuck. I was out of line. No time to mess around. I resigned earlier today and I'm a bit spun up over it—off my game. I'll reel it in."

The chief didn't give time for a response.

"Anyhow, from our perspective at ground zero, this is about steering the fire now, if we can. We're not putting it out, at least not until the wind dies down. Retardant drops east of Phoenix along the 5 corridor should help with that."

He paused, eyes scanning the topo map spread across the hood of the rig beside Paducah. Years of experience filled in what the paper couldn't show. "I just came from the command post, but I know that terrain—Old Stage Road offers a real chance to hold the line. If we can anchor there and slow the fire's northward push, we might keep it from reaching Medford. If not…" He shook his head. "We're talking devastation. The kind that scars a valley for a generation."

He lowered his cell phone, his gaze lingering on the map spread across the hood of the rig. "I'm heading out to Old Stage Road in a minute to confirm. I need eyes on it. If I'm right, we've got a shot. If I'm wrong—" He left the words hanging, the unspoken truth heavy as he stared at Paducah.

The thought hit him hard and clear. He needed to let Paducah manage this incident. He'd stay active, sure, but from the background. His resignation—the constant pull of thoughts about Sky, thoughts he couldn't seem to shake ever since writing that damn letter—left him off-kilter. And off-kilter didn't cut it. Not with something as deadly as this fire.

He knew he could shove it all aside if he had to, grit through and bring this damn thing to heel. But for the first time in his life, the drive just wasn't there. And that scared him more than the fire itself.

Silence gripped the phone line for a beat. Chief Wilson glanced over at Paducah. Her expression had drained to something paler than her usual Ukrainian complexion, closer to ice. She'd heard the passivity in his voice and, for once, seemed to believe he meant it.

"Well shit, Wilson. That isn't ideal for the valley, but I hear you. No apologies necessary. I know you well enough. I should expect a smartass remark. Hell, if I hadn't gotten one, I'd wonder what's wrong with you. Dog balls on the resignation. Good for you. I wish I had the cajónes to retire. Two kids in college and a wife who loves the finer things in life will keep me working until seventy. You lucky asshole. Let's catch up after we get through this and grab a beer."

Paducah glanced at the chief, unable to hear the entire conversation. The chief guessed she wondered what words

166

he'd heard on the phone, knowing her potential position change would significantly impact how others treated her.

Chief Wilson nodded to Paducah and continued his conversation.

"Okay. Listen, Chuck, I'm handing the lead off to Assistant Fire Chief Kylee Paducah. I expect she'll replace me as fire chief moving forward, and I want her to use the full authority of the position from here on out. This fire is the perfect opportunity for a leadership transition. I'll be in the background and available if needed, but this is her fire now. Paducah's already in communication with the Air Tanker Unit. If anyone asks about her, this is my call. Mine alone. I'll text you her direct line once we hang up."

He hesitated, the weight of his decision sinking in. *The backlash would come, but that was his burden to carry—not hers.* "Chuck, just so you and everyone else understand, I'm not going offline. I'll be monitoring everything, at Paducah's beck and call. She's got this. Her hands are going to be more than full, so if you can't reach her, call me."

Satisfied, Chief Wilson lowered his phone, thumbed the red-end button, and looked down at Paducah. The bewilderment in her eyes spoke louder than words.

# Put Me To Sleep

Mel tore her gaze from the windows and yanked the door open, striding down the musty-smelling hallway toward dispatch. The silence felt wrong. The rest of the crew had to be on-site already, but she hoped the two she trusted most were waiting for her arrival.

She'd only worked with them for a few months before retiring, but that was enough. Ex-military jockeys, Air Force trained—both with the kind of cockiness that came from skill, not bravado. They knew exactly what to do in a plane when hellfire conditions hit. Just like her. Seasoned, sharp, and ready to push the limits if it meant getting the job done.

At the entrance, she paused and rubbed her right kneecap, wincing. Must've tweaked it during the game. She gave her head a slight shake, already imagining how it would feel crammed into the cockpit. Probably time to stop dodging that doctor's appointment—after this fire was wrapped.

Pushing through the door, she bit down against the bursitis ache flaring in her knee. Well, hell, she thought. No wonder she'd only managed a single in her final at-bat. The damn joint wouldn't let her rotate or drive with any real power.

Satisfied now that she had an answer for her weak finish at the plate, she called out toward dispatch, her voice echoing down the hall.

"Swinson, how the hell is it hanging?"

In his early sixties, another semi-retired ex-pilot, Swinson, laughed—a familiar sound—rolled his eyes, and responded.

"Awesome, like always, Meladonna. I am happy to show you anytime."

Mel chuckled. Swinson liked to give her shit over the years

and had nicknamed her Meladonna. The wannabe comedian's play on prima donna.

Laughing, pleased to be back in the building and facing purpose, Mel dropped her duffel, pulled up a chair next to Swinson, and plopped her ass in the seat. Her knee felt better, taking weight off it. Making a mental note, because the doctor would ask about her pain leaned forward in the chair toward Swinson.

"Okay, Swinson. Give me the rundown. On the drive here from the ball field, I noticed the smoke intensity picking up."

"Yes. Mother Nature's big-ass fan's pushing the fire hard, Mel. Wind's blowing nonstop out of the southeast at around forty to forty-five miles an hour, moving the fire faster than fire crews can move. Listening to radio traffic over the scanners—utter chaos. There aren't enough boots on the ground or engines in the valley. I can't tell you how many times in the last twenty minutes I've heard, *"I have no one to send you, do the best you can with what you've got."* It's worse than bad out there. Dozens of structures are already gone, and the fire is intensifying with the winds."

"Well, what's the word then? We going up?"

Mel's mind drifted to the cockpit of her Air Force C-17, one of her final missions in the military.

She'd received an alert call on her last day of active duty at two in the morning. A group of Air Force PJs, the equivalent of Navy SEALs or Army Green Berets, depending on which ego you talked to, had parachuted in to rescue a half dozen Army personnel trapped earlier in the day. Behind enemy lines in the rocky high desert mountains, several of them needed desperate medical attention. Mel, next in the rescue chain, would never forget her commanding officer calling right after the alert came in. He told her she didn't have to go—that a backup crew on standby could handle the mission since she was due to separate and out-process the next day.

Mel had smiled, thinking about her response, knowing she'd pushed it too far but not caring, it was after all, the last day of her Air Force career.

*"With due respect, sir. Go to hell! My crew has this. What good am I if I bail on my fellow airmen because I'm scheduled to go home? I wouldn't be able to look at myself in the mirror the rest of my life."*

*She'd waited for a dress-down from the colonel, but he laughed and responded, "Well, get the fucking bird in the sky then, you insubordinate piece of shit. Come see me when you get back. Remember, there is no backup—you and your crew are on your own. I can't send in a second team if you fuck this up. Understood?"*

*Smiling, she couldn't help but retort, "I know the routine, sir. Lucky for you and the United States, I'm so damn good at my job—which you know—that it won't matter. While you're sitting on your ass smoking those disgusting cigars and I'm out there being a hero, you might as well write up another medal of honor for my 'insubordinate ass,' okay?"*

Mel returned to the musty-smelling hangar office with a quick shout of her name from Swinson.

"Shit, Mel. I don't know what's worse: a pilot with condescending anger issues, or a daydreaming air-jockey wannabe who zones out from time to time?"

Mel laughed, watched the door open and, seeing the remaining aircrew walk through it, responded without hesitation to Swinson.

"Bite me. I heard everything you said, old man. If you could manage, just once, to answer my question in less than one hundred words, perhaps you wouldn't put me to sleep."

# Damp Cheeks

Sky trudged up the driveway, her legs heavy, each step a chore. When she reached the sidewalk, she pushed the home's small white gate forward. The springs let out their usual squeak, her leg brushing against splintered wood to keep it open just enough for her to slip through.

The concrete path stretched before her, its cracks overrun with weeds and fresh weather damage. Her father had hated weeds sprouting between the cement lines—always kept them sprayed down. But now, the jagged green tufts spilled from the crevices, the neglect as obvious as the wear on the sidewalk itself.

She stared at the first cut in the concrete, eyes locked on the narrow, weed-filled groove like it might give something back. Memories tugged at her, soft and slippery, like they belonged to someone else. A life she once knew—blurred at the edges, just out of reach.

*Sky looked up at her father, waiting for instructions.*

*"Okay, Sky. Nice job mixing the organic weed killer. Next time try not to put so much dish soap in there. The soap makes it foam up too much and it's harder to tell how much solution we have left in the bottle. This will still work, though. Pretty good for a first mix, little lady."*

*Sky studied the clear spray bottle in her hand, proud of the homemade concoction she'd mixed—vinegar, salt, and soap. Watching the blue dish soap slide down the inside of the bottle made her mind smile. It left slow streaks against the plastic before disappearing into the cloudy swirl. She'd shaken it hard, watched the foam bubble up and spill over the top before screwing on the spray nozzle. It reminded her of that Coke and*

171

mint video her friend's mom had shown her online—only gentler, less explosive. Still fun.

Her father's praise pulled her attention away from the bottle. Sky beamed, warmth rising in her chest. It felt good when he noticed. It didn't happen all the time, but when it did, it made her feel older—like she was getting something right.

"Now what, Daddy?" she asked, eyes bright.

"Let me see the bottle for a minute, please."

Sky placed it in his massive, outstretched hand.

"Follow me, Sky."

She watched him descend the short porch stairs, his steps light and smooth. For someone so big, he moved like he barely touched the ground; almost like floating. Sky tried to imagine herself doing the same, but she always felt heavy and awkward. Maybe it was something that happened with age—a secret grown-up trick. She hoped so.

Sky followed her father down the walk, stopping just before the little front gate. He dropped to one knee, resting an elbow across his leg.

"Okay, Sky. See this separation point in the cement?"

He pointed to a line between the sidewalk slabs. She'd counted eleven from the porch to the gate once, maybe twice— eleven being her favorite number ever since her aunt had said it was lucky.

"Yes, Dad."

"Good. Now take the bottle and spray the entire line twice. Once this way, and then again back this way."

His hand pulsed around the neck of the bottle, his forearm flexing as he sprayed. The stream soaked the crack, darkening the concrete, turning the weeds slick and shiny.

"Always start at one end and go line by line. That way you don't miss one. Got it?"

"Yes, Dad."

He handed her the bottle.

"Okay, now you give it a go."

Sky shuffled back toward the house, picked the next line in the sidewalk, and knelt. This one had a mess of weeds stretching like lazy green arms toward the sun. She squeezed the trigger—once. Nothing. Again. Still nothing.

"Nothing's coming out, Daddy. Sorry."

He smiled at her, the kind of smile that made her stomach feel light. His teeth were perfect—but not scary perfect like toothpaste commercials. Natural. Straight. Safe. Like they didn't belong to his body at all, just waited behind his lips like a lion behind bars at the zoo.

"That's okay, Sky. Your hands just aren't quite big enough yet. Try using both."

She wrapped her fingers around the neck of the bottle, stretching them out to reach the trigger. It felt like gripping a big stick just before she tossed it into a creek. She squeezed— harder this time—and the nozzle jerked sideways as spray shot out and splattered the middle of the sidewalk.

"Oops," she giggled.

Her father laughed. "There you go, Sky. Now you just have to work on your aim."

She took a breath, steadied her grip, and aimed down the line of weeds. This time, the spray hit half the target, the rest misting off to the side. Better.

"Much better. Keep going."

Sky leaned into the task. She took her time, dragging the spray across the crack and then back again. It wasn't as fast or clean as her dad's pass, but most of the weeds got hit.

"Excellent, Sky. Finish the rest of these lines, and when you're done, come out to the barn and get me. I'll show you what's next."

Sky watched her father move down the sidewalk and through the gate, his steps just as smooth as before. He still *reminded her of some Middle Earth elf, gliding over the grass like gravity didn't quite apply. For someone so solid, it didn't make sense—but it felt true. She wondered—hoped—he'd drive the tractor today.*

*Some of her best memories were sitting on his lap as he steered the tractor around the property, the rumble of the engine beneath them, his arm steadying her like nothing in the world could ever go wrong. Those rides only happened when her mother wasn't home—her dad always catching hell whenever she found out. Too dangerous, her mom would say.*

*But Sky couldn't understand. There wasn't a place on earth that felt safer than her father's lap.*

Releasing the memory, Sky stepped toward the front porch, her eyes brushing over the soft scatter of ash along the walkway. She noticed how it gathered in the cracks and corners like dust collecting around forgotten memories—but didn't linger on it. Not now. Her mind had become skilled at filtering out distractions, anything that might pull her away from the quiet work of reflection.

She wasn't stuck in the past, not anymore. It wasn't about reliving old pain, fear of rejection, or replaying regrets. It was about understanding. About finally asking why—not just what had happened. For once, her memories didn't feel like anchors. They felt like markers, points on a map that helped her trace her way back to who she'd always been and how it influenced who she had become.

The choices she'd made—some bold, some careless, some necessary—held meaning now. And in the stillness of recent years, that meaning had started to take shape. The pull to come home, to return to her roots, wasn't just nostalgia. It was clarity. A deep, quiet knowing that growth didn't always mean moving forward. Sometimes it meant looking back—and this time, seeing it differently.

Sky couldn't remember her father ever getting angry with

her. Not as a kid. Not even as a moody teen. Sure, he'd gotten frustrated now and then, but anger? That just wasn't him. And now, as an adult—by age, at least—memories ran through her mind like a flood-swollen river. The more she searched, the more obvious it became. Her father never seemed to get angry at anyone.

She stood frozen on the front step, her mind churning, desperate to dig up one moment of rage or fury from him. There had to be something. But the harder she searched, the emptier she felt. Every time she pried into her past, looking for something to justify her own anger, all she found was warmth and support.

Why the hell had she been so angry with him? Her mother left, not him.

Her knees hit the concrete, sharp edges of small stones pressing through her jeans. Her fingers reached out, trembling, to touch a weed growing from the first break line between cement sections. She ran her hand over the prickly roughness, her palm brushing the stubborn life sprouting from cracked cement.

Tears came hard and fast, her emerald eyes brimming before spilling over. Ash drifted down from the sky, clinging to her hair, mixing with the damp tracks on her cheeks.

# Before Now

Paperwork signed, Mel wriggled in the pilot's seat, her fingers drumming the armrest as she waited with her crew for the GO sign. The thought made her chest tighten, anticipation building with every second of forced idleness. This was the part of the job she despised—waiting.

Indecisiveness. Inaction. Two things she couldn't stand. Her whole life, she'd lived in perpetual motion, a constant drive to keep moving, keep doing. As a kid, a doctor had tried convincing her parents to put her on Ritalin. *Her father's response still made her smile.*

He'd torn into the doctor, calling him out for caring more about kickbacks than what was ethical and right. Told the man he should be ashamed for even suggesting it. Mel's parents never took her back to that "quack."

Years later, when she decided to join the military, she'd thanked her father for refusing the meds. He just grinned and said, "No kid of mine's going to use drugs as a crutch for mediocrity. You're too damn awesome for that."

The memory settled her nerves for a beat, but restlessness surged right back. She wanted the GO sign. She wanted it now.

Finishing her third trip through the pre-flight checklist, Mel took off her sunglasses, rubbed her eyes, then blinked, trying to get moisture to permeate her eyeballs. Unsatisfied, she unzipped her shoulder pocket on her flight suit and removed a small container of eye drops.

"Well, shit, Deuce. What's the word?" she asked her co-pilot, whose headphones sat at an angle on his head with one ear covered—a clear sign the wait frustrated him as well.

"Nothing new. Talent is in flames, and the fire is pushing

up Bear Creek toward Phoenix."

"Shit," the flight engineer replied.

"I know, right? Isn't your home in South Medford near Old Stage Road?"

"Yep."

"Your wife and kids evacuated?"

"Yes. Molly took the kids to her parents in Jacksonville. They're on alert as well, but if the fire reaches Jacksonville, shit has surpassed the fan. I can't even imagine that scenario."

"Me either, Deuce. But then again, I never thought Talent would be up in flames either."

Mel looked out the front of the plane, wondering where Johnson was. She smiled, knowing the cockpit epitomized security. He'd be apologetic, out of desperation for sure—his career now hung by a thread. Mel surmised the man's real anger today came not from the firing so much as from knowing *she* would be piloting his ride. Johnson never liked Mel because she didn't put up with any of his bullshit and called him out on his glaring mistakes. He despised her for her insolence toward him.

Johnson's recent antics were further proof of his lack of professionalism and reinforcement that he shouldn't be on the yoke of a $140 million plane.

"The look on Johnson's face, Mel, when Burgeon told him he was done—priceless," the flight engineer, sitting behind the co-pilot, Deuce, lamented.

"It's amazing, isn't it? Twenty bucks that in less than one minute I get a call from dispatch telling us that Johnson is back in the building and 'sorry,' and that he wants his job and seat back. Any takers?"

Mel unzipped a pocket on the thigh of her left-leg flight suit, stuck her hand in, pulled out some cash, found a twenty, and laid it on the console gauges next to her.

Laughter filled the cockpit. None of the crew took the bait.

"You may be right, Mel. The guy runs on a different brain than most of us," Deuce responded.

Less than a minute later, a voice echoed through Mel's headset.

"Hey, Mel. Swinson here. Johnson is back inside the base management office asking for you to relinquish the seat in Betsy. He's pleading with Burgeon for his job back."

Mel smiled and glanced at Deuce, who was laughing, shaking his head in disbelief. Her prediction had been spot-on, and he clearly hadn't expected it.

"I'm not surprised, Swinson," Mel retorted.

"Don't sweat it. I just got off the phone with the base manager, and security got Johnson back out of the building. Burgeon told him if he didn't leave and get off the property, he'd call the police and make this a legal matter as well."

Deuce, with a face-stretching grin, made Mel smile. Growing weary of Johnson's antics, Mel also smiled, though not with the same intensity.

Frustrated—beyond tired of Johnson's chronic lateness and total lack of professionalism and respect for his fellow crew—Mel took a deep breath. Intending to choose her words with care, she pictured a stream with cool water trickling over polished rocks.

"Amazing this is happening, Swinson. I dreamed of getting back up in the air a week after I retired, but I never imagined it'd be because southern Oregon's cities were burning."

"We're glad to have you back, Mel," Swinson said.

"Damn right," added Deuce.

"Hear, hear," the flight engineer chimed in.

Mel reached over, took the twenty-dollar bill off the console gauges, and stuffed it back into her pocket. Once she closed the zipper, she started flipping switches. The engines hummed and whined as Betsy roared to life. The cockpit crew—silent for a few seconds in the wake of everything that had just happened, and Mel knowing she'd ask for specifics later— burst into laughter. They were all eager to let go of the tension.

"He may be the single most narcissistic prick on the planet. You're my new hero, Mel," Deuce said, shaking his head, still laughing over the roar of the engines. "Man, am I glad you said yes to coming back."

Adrenaline-fueled anger subsiding, Mel grinned and replied, "New hero? What the hell? Who could it have been before now?"

# When or Where?

Frustrated, bordering on unapologetic anger, Teddy moved toward a horn-honking vehicle and motioned for the driver to roll the window down. As he rounded the front of the vehicle, he recognized the driver—Mr. Hinkle—who now looked like a pissed-off outdoorsman. Until today, the old guy—a forty-year retired railroad worker and a mountain of a man—had always exuded politeness and congeniality.

Teddy stopped short, standing farther from the door than usual, as Mr. Hinkle unleashed a barrage of frustration.

To Teddy's consternation, two more cars eased up behind Mr. Hinkle.

"Teddy, what in the hell is going on? You realize there's a fire in the valley, and it's headed this way, right?"

Teddy looked eastward, toward trees now shrouded in thickening smoke and a sky darkening like dusk had fallen five hours early.

"Well, Mr. Hinkle, I heard there's a fire, but it's to the south. Everything's fine here." The words spilled from Teddy's mouth, and even he knew they were pure bullshit.

"Teddy, where the hell have you been for the last hour? Good God, man. You know how dry it is, and the wind's blowing over forty miles an hour. If we get trapped, we could all die."

A wave of tension clenched Teddy's muscles and twisted his stomach, the sour burn of mustard and tater-tot bile creeping up his throat. He'd heard the stories—how manufactured home parks, when hit with fire, could erupt into blazing infernos within minutes.

"Well, your attitude seems a little extreme, Mr. Hinkle." Even as he said it, his own voice sounded thin and shaky, every word a betrayal of the fear crawling under his skin.

The second car in the growing line honked its horn. Mr. Hinkle looked like he was turning a deeper shade of pale, his cheeks flushed with blood.

Teddy gave a stiff nod to the driver behind Hinkle, the horn still blaring. He didn't know what to do—walk away, head back to the gate, or return to the shed to find the manual hand crank?

He turned toward the gate, trying to remember where in the shed he'd left it. His stomach churned harder now, bile clawing up his throat just as a sheriff's cruiser rolled in—lights flashing, siren silent—and came to a stop in front of the downed gate.

"What the heck now?" he muttered, the words slipping out before he could stop them. The day had officially crossed into strange territory.

The burn at the back of his throat flared again. Too much mustard, he decided. Probably that more than nerves. Though the beef might've played a part—his gut never liked cheap cuts. He made a mental note to ask if the restaurant had finally switched to grass-fed.

Under his breath, Teddy mumbled nonsense, nervous words strung together with no real meaning, just something to keep his mouth busy while his thoughts spun.

"Excuse me. What's that?" the deputy shouted from his car.

"Oh, sorry, officer. Stressful day. Talking to myself. You ever say something out loud thinking you were talking in your head?"

The young-looking lawman, who'd left his door open, approached Teddy and stopped just outside the gate, an arm's length away. He didn't answer the question. Judging by the look on his face, Teddy figured it must've sounded strange.

"The gate broken, sir?"

181

Teddy allowed himself a moment of offense at the "sir" comment but realized, before making an ass of himself, that the deputy was just being polite and respectful.

"Yes, officer. The darn thing keeps giving me fits. Hasn't worked right for months. Come hell or high water, I decided to fix it today." He cursed under his breath, still bitter the landlords hadn't called a repair company like he'd requested multiple times.

"It's deputy."

"Oh—sorry, deputy. You look like an officer to me. I never gave police rank much thought, but I suppose, like the military, there's a difference."

The deputy nodded and stood stoic, his left hand hanging near his sidearm. Teddy hoped it was just a habit.

"Yes, there's a definite difference. How about fire?"

"What?" Teddy blinked, confused.

"You said, 'come hell or high water.' I'm saying—how about fire? Is that a good enough reason to open the gate?"

Teddy froze, his fingers tightening around the plastic handle of the screwdriver in his left hand.

"Um... I suppose. Why?"

"Everyone near Bear Creek is under evacuation. The Almeda Fire is tearing through Talent, and this development is directly in its path."

Bile surged up Teddy's throat, a small amount searing the back of his tongue. The beer, burger, and tots didn't taste nearly as good on the way back up. Not today.

"What's that mean?" he asked quickly, desperate for clarity.

"It means everyone in this development has to get out. The fire is burning north, up Bear Creek. These homes will likely burn to the ground. There's no time to waste."

Teddy turned and looked at the cars, now six deep. The only reason they weren't leaning on their horns was because of the sheriff's cruiser parked out front with its lights flashing.

"Um, the whole park?"

"Yep. Everybody. Can you raise this gate? Manually lift it?"

Teddy hesitated, frozen in place. His arms dropped to his sides. The screwdriver slipped from his hand, landed with a muted thud on the asphalt, and rolled to a stop beside his left shoe. He stared at the handle—dirty yellow, the color of old Jell-O, smudged with grease and grime. His gaze lifted slowly back to the deputy, thoughts racing toward his family's safety.

"Shit. Can I make sure my daughter and granddaughter are, okay?"

"Excuse me?" the deputy asked.

"My granddaughter, Emma. She goes to school in Phoenix. I just want to make sure she's okay."

The deputy looked around, checked his wristwatch, then glanced back through the gate.

"How old is she?"

"Nine," Teddy replied, unsure if he'd gotten it right. "Why?"

The deputy, visibly agitated with the conversation's direction and the growing line of cars behind Teddy, didn't waste time responding.

"The elementary schools under evacuation. Her emergency contact will pick her up. I presume that's her mother or father, correct?"

Teddy bent over and picked up the screwdriver. He thought of his daughter and how long it would take her to drive from work to Emma's school in Phoenix.

"Yes, her mother. But she works in Medford. I should go to the school and get her."

"Listen, unless you're an emergency contact, the school won't release her to you. Your priority has to be this gate. Do you understand?"

Teddy nodded, the truth of the deputy's words sinking in.

Arguing would get him nowhere.

"The damn gate's been a problem for ages. And today, of all days, I decided I'd finally fix it, no matter what. Now, unless I reconnect everything and pray it works, the only way to raise it is with a hand crank I've got back at the shop."

He winced, frustration bubbling under the surface. The hand crank should've been loaded in his cart already. Why he'd taken it out in the first place was beyond him. Rookie mistake. And now, of all days, it could end up costing lives.

"Shit," he mumbled to himself.

"How long to put it back together?"

"Fifteen minutes. Give or take," Teddy responded while he stared at dangling electrical connectors in the control panel.

"Look." The deputy glanced past Teddy, eyes counting cars. "Ten cars in line trying to get out of here. There'll be more in minutes. If you say fifteen minutes and mean it, I can hold the fort for that long. Any longer, and these people will probably ram the gate and drive over it."

"Shit!" Teddy blurted, wondering where in the hell the crank was. He couldn't remember the last time he saw it.

"Please open the pedestrian gate, and I'll talk to each of the cars waiting so they know what's going on until you get back," the deputy ordered.

Teddy liked this deputy—confident and cool under pressure. Something Teddy realized he lacked when it really counted.

"Okay." Teddy opened the pedestrian gate and let the deputy inside. The sharp kid in uniform walked toward the first car in line before stopping and turning back toward Teddy, who stood motionless.

"Hey, go find that crank and hurry back here so we can let these people out."

"Um, oh, okay. Right."

Teddy hustled to the maintenance cart and threw himself

into the seat, his foot slamming the accelerator so hard the pedal nearly scraped metal. The cart shot forward, tires squealing against the pavement, the sudden jolt rattling his teeth.

Sweat trickled down his temple, his breathing shallow and ragged. His eyes darted over his shoulder and around the cluttered cart bed as if the crank might magically appear. His fingers twitched against the wheel; his grip so tight his knuckles bleached white.

Where the hell was that damn crank? His memory was a fogged-out mess, every corner of his mind turning up nothing but frustration and panic. How long had it been since he'd seen it? Days? Weeks? His stomach twisted at the thought of where it might be, the sinking realization that he'd been careless enough to lose it when he needed it most.

# A Monsoon of Memories

Sky reached for the screen door, her fingers trembling slightly, half-expecting iron bars to crash down and lock her out for good. Instead, the door gave a soft squeak, its worn hinges groaning like an old friend greeting her after years apart.

The cool metal handle sparked something in her chest. *Summers with the inner door wide open, only the screen between her and the world. Southern Oregon breezes laced with pine and lavender drifting through the house, making everything feel safe and endless.*

She shook off the memory and wedged herself between the screen and main door, her backpack pressing awkwardly against the frame. She twisted the knob. It turned—but didn't open.

Her pulse quickened. Had her dad moved the spare key? Did he lock her out on purpose? Her eyes darted left, then right, searching for something, anything, to prove she still belonged.

She stepped back and let the screen door slap shut behind her, the sound sharp in the stillness. Then she moved down the porch steps and paused at the edge of the flower bed, scanning the ground.

The mulch caught her eye first—flattened, dull, tired. Usually, her father kept it fresh and crisp, the fire-resistant kind he always said was worth the extra money. But now, a thin layer of ash dulled the contrast, softening the edges.

Maybe it wasn't neglect. Maybe the ash just made everything seem worse.

But the longer she looked, the more the details added up. The grass was too long, the edges ragged with weeds. The rhododendrons sagged, brittle and colorless. More than ash littered the walk—twigs, leaves, broken bits of random mulch. None of this would've happened when she lived here. Her father had always taken pride in keeping things just so.

She stepped slowly along the wide porch, each foot dragging more than the last, until she stopped beside the flower bed. The weeds were thick, stubborn. In the middle, a rhododendron drooped as if it had given up.

Something behind it caught her eye—a weathered rock, softball-sized, wedged deep into the soil. She crouched, brushed aside the overgrowth, and pried it loose. Beneath it, nestled like a secret, sat a smaller fake stone.

She picked it up. Grit clung to her palm. The plastic was lighter than she remembered. She flipped it over, slid open the little white door. Inside, dusted in dirt, lay the key. Familiar. Worn. The metal still caught the light, still held the weight of old habits.

Sky stared at it, a dozen memories pressing forward—fingers fumbling with this very key, sneaking in late, covering for a mistake, wondering if her dad would notice—or hoping he would.

Back then, things felt simpler. Even when she screwed up, the stakes didn't seem so high. Holding the key now, she realized it had never just been about access. It was about understanding. About being understood.

*Memories sent her back thinking about her fingers holding the plastic rock countless times.*

*"Dad, I can't get in the house," she said, not bothering to hide the edge in her voice. Almost shouting into the phone, a familiar frustration flaring.*

*"Where's your key?" her semi-attentive father asked.*

*She paused. Sky wanted to be mad—but anger was hard to fake when she knew the truth: she'd left her key in her bedroom that morning. Again. A semi-regular occurrence.*

*Deflecting, she threw back a louder response, frustration tinged with just enough*
*drama to mask guilt.*

*"The plastic rock isn't in the flower bed, Dad. I checked. It's gone. You must've moved it."*

*There was a pause on the other end. She could hear muffled voices—her father responding to someone else. Probably a meeting. Guilt nipped at her. He always picked up for her, no matter where he was, no matter what he was doing. That should have softened her.*

*But it didn't.*

*Not completely.*

*She didn't care how important the meeting was. She should be more important. The world—his world—should revolve around her.*

*"Sorry, honey. I'm in a meeting," he said. "I don't use the key, you know that. And no, I didn't move it. Did you put it back the last time you used it?"*

*The question lit a fuse. Not because it accused her—but because she knew it was*
*her fault. She just didn't want to admit it.*

*Her mind raced. Friday. Volleyball game tonight. She needed to shower, then get back to school. At least she had something to do. Something to watch from the bench. She never played. The coach blamed her "attitude." Whatever. Every girl on the squad knew she was the best spiker—even as a ninth grader. Adults always needed a reason to keep you in your place.*

*Monday. Practice ran late. Her dad was off at some city council thing. She'd forgotten her keys, had to use the spare. She remembered digging through the flower bed, the grit under her nails, the familiar clink of metal against plastic. She'd slipped the key in the lock and ducked inside.*

*Routine.*

*She always put it back. Well almost always.*

*The memory sharpened. She was bouncing on her toes. Had to pee. Bad. The door barely closed behind her before she was racing to the bathroom. She saw it—clearly now. She'd slipped the plastic rock into her jacket pocket with the key still inside.*

"Shit," she muttered, pulling the phone slightly away from her mouth. Hopefully he hadn't heard that. He hated cussing.

She pictured the moment again—key, plastic rock, jacket pocket.

"Got it, Dad. Thanks. Sorry. I gotta run—I've got a game tonight," she said, already turning back toward the door.

"You don't have to come," she added quickly. She knew she wouldn't play. But she also knew he'd be there. He always was. The only game he'd ever missed was tee-ball—and that was because of a firefighting convention in Vegas.

"Seven o'clock, like always?" he asked. "Think you'll get on the court tonight?"

Sky sighed and dropped her backpack beside the porch railing, leaning against the post with the phone pressed tight to her ear.

"Maybe. Coach says my attitude's better this week." She tapped her fingernail against the peeling paint, eyes on the overgrown yard. "We're playing South Medford."

"They're monsters. We're gonna get wrecked," she said. "Coach says tougher competition makes us better. She's half right. The other half's just her talking big, trying to pump us up with the usual bullshit."

A quiet beat passed. Through the speaker, she could hear the faint buzz of her dad's radio—someone talking in the background.

"I'll be there," he said. "Tell them not to hold the start if I'm a few minutes late."

*Sky knew he was smiling. He always was. A joker to the core, constantly fishing for a laugh—even when it didn't land. Most of the time, she appreciated it. All her friends adored him, which only made her feelings more tangled. She was grateful, sure, but also jealous. Why couldn't he be like the other parents—distant, distracted, invisible? Why did he have to care so damn much?*

*Then came another one-liner. Classic Dad.*

*"Ha ha.. Papa makes a funny," she replied on cue, voice flat.*

But something twisted inside her. His attempt to make her laugh irritated her—and she didn't know why. Maybe because it worked. Maybe because it didn't. Maybe because he still tried. The warmth in his voice made her chest ache, and all she wanted in that moment was to push it away. She wanted to hate him for it. Hate was easier than love. Love took effort, consideration, empathy—and she didn't have the time.

*"Gotta go, Dad. I have to shower and then ride my bike back to school."*

*She pulled the phone from her ear and hit END, heavy thumb on the screen like it could quiet the noise inside her, too.*

*She looked up the side of the house, tucked her phone into the back pocket of her skin-tight jeans, and grabbed the lowest slat of lattice that led to her second-story bedroom window. She hoped it would be unlocked. Her dad hated when she climbed up, said it was dangerous, said she'd fall. But sometimes it was easier than asking for help. Her mind drifted—game day, frustration, feeling benched again. She started the climb anyway.*

Easing out of the memory, Sky found herself back at the front door. She wiped a smear of gritty ash from her cheek. The texture flashed an image—her dad's stacks of sandpaper in the shop, all grit and order, coarse and unavoidable.

Annoyed at how easily her thoughts hijacked her, she

pulled the screen open. It creaked again—this time, the sound felt like an old friend.

She slid the orange-and-black SF Giants key into the lock and twisted. The metallic click—the clean, satisfying sound of success—settled in her chest like breath after holding it too long. She pocketed the moment, then slipped the key back into the fake rock. From the porch, she lobbed it into the flower bed. It landed just shy of the Rhody. Close enough. I'll fix it later, she thought. Probably won't, and the grin surprised her.

Sky hesitated at the threshold, hand resting on the doorknob. The house looked the same—but it didn't feel the same. It wasn't hers anymore. It was her father's now—his dust, his space, his solitude.

She walked out. Just like her mother had. And the thought hollowed her chest.

Still, her body ached for the familiar comfort inside. The creak of floorboards. The scent of roasted coffee and southern Oregon pine pushing through open windows. The quiet hum of being safe.

She stepped over the threshold and paused. The door clicked shut behind her.

The hush of the house wrapped around her—part blanket, part warning.

Then it hit her: a faint scent. Warm. Familiar. Like her father's sweat after a long day—clean, human, edged with the sharp bite of the soap he always used. Not cologne. Not smoke or turnout gear. Just *him.* It clung to the walls, settled in the floorboards. It anchored her in place.

What struck her more, though, was the absence. No trace of the floral perfume her mother used to wear. No echo of her presence at all. Not even the sour tang of a half-drained wineglass was left behind. As if the house had long since exhaled her—and only her father remained.

Her throat tightened.

Then, without permission, the tears came again. Moist. Heavy. Another dam, broken.

And behind them surged memory—fast and full—catching her in its current.

# Causation

Chief Wilson dragged a finger across the map spread over the hood of his pickup, eyes locked on the Bear Creek Greenway. "Okay, let's get on the phone with the Air Tanker base. Make a formal request for support."

The paper crinkled beneath his finger as he tapped it, firm enough to send a soft vibration through the engine-warmed metal. Paducah stood across from him, focused, tracking every word.

"The freeway's closed right now, correct?"

"Yes, Chief."

"Good. With this wind, it'll be impossible for the pilots not to dust the freeway. We'll need constant communication with them. Call and coordinate. I want you managing that channel. Understood?"

"Got it, Chief. I know a few folks on the dispatch team. I think Chet Swinson's on today."

That raised his brow. Swinson was the real deal—sharp, fast, blunt. He didn't waste time on people who didn't know what they were doing. The fact Paducah knew him—and sounded so sure—told Wilson everything he needed to know. She was ready. She just hadn't fully stepped into it yet.

"Good. Let me know what you find out and how soon they're airborne. I'm heading into Phoenix to get eyes on the ground and gather intel."

He caught the slight shift in her stance, the way she held back—not uncertain, but still waiting for the right moment. That moment had already passed. What she didn't see—or maybe didn't believe yet—was that she had the authority now. Not because someone handed it to her. Because she'd earned it.

"We're drawing the line at Old Stage Road," he said, voice calm but firm. "That's our best shot to hold the edge between Phoenix and Medford. If the fire jumps that road, we're in a different fight entirely."

And if it did, we'd all be running out of moves.

"Shit." The chief didn't lose sight of the direness of the situation. Years of experience let him picture Old Stage Road and the farmland—an excellent point to defend southern Oregon's most populated city.

"Okay, hold tight here for now. I like the spot you picked." The chief stopped talking as a fire truck and police car roared by on the highway. The unmistakable sounds of horns and sirens drowned out whatever else he meant to say.

"That looked like Cal Fire, didn't it?" he said, more statement than question.

"Looked like it, Chief."

"Okay, anyway, stay here for now. If you need to change your position to help, then do it. Keep me posted on what they say and where they'll drop. Chances are, you'll need to reposition closer to the drop zones. For this to work, you and I need to stay in constant communication."

"Roger that, Chief."

Chief Wilson headed back to his vehicle as Paducah chattered on her radio, connecting with the Air Tanker base. The last thing the chief heard before his mind drifted: Paducah yelling, "Swinson, don't give me any shit right now. We need tankers in the air."

Guiding his chief's rig away from Paducah, Chief Wilson smiled at the sound of her voice crackling through the radio as his mind drifted—into memories, into hopes, into the quiet longing that maybe, just maybe, he could bring his daughter back to him, if only for a moment.

*Cresting a small knoll dotted with scrub oak, he spotted his mysterious little Sky sitting on a large, downed Douglas fir tree, picking at tufts of bright green moss and crumbling bark. Her radio rested beside her. He stayed back for a while, watching.*

*She looked happy. Content. Legs swinging, humming to herself, the picture of calm. Not a care in the world.*

*He watched her for thirty minutes, never losing sight. Every few minutes, she fumbled with the radio—pressing the mic, speaking, then twisting the dial. He tracked her through binoculars, noting the way her fingers rotated the channel selector every five minutes, just like he'd taught her. She was humming. Maybe even singing. It struck him—how unbothered she seemed. Out here in the woods, alone, most kids would be panicking by now.*

*When he got lost hunting at her age, he remembered, fear gnawed at him until he followed a creek back to camp. His mom wept and wrapped him in a blanket. Dad just nodded and let him lie about chasing a buck. He knew it was bullshit—but smiled anyway. Mom didn't let him out of her sight the rest of the night.*

*Adoration welled up in him as he watched Sky's feet swing from the fallen tree. Her calm gave him pause—how was she not afraid? At her age, he would've been pacing, flipping through channels in a frenzy, yelling into the handset like it was his lifeline.*

*He checked his own radio to confirm the channel, then made more noise than usual as he approached. If she was startled, she didn't show it.*

*Sky hopped down from the old snag, leaving the two-way perched on the rotting wood. "Hey, Dad. Good to see you. I'm glad you're okay. Ready to go home?"*

*He tried to mask his incredulity behind a chuckle. "Excuse me, young lady? Did you even try the radio?"*

*"Of course, Father. I started on Channel 4, waited five minutes, then switched to 5, then 3. You didn't say which one*

*to start on, so I rotated."*

*He blinked. "Why Channel 4 first? We talked about 3."*

*"You never said to start on 3. You just mentioned 3 and the other channels. I figured if I began on 4 and cycled through, we'd eventually overlap. If I started on 3 and you started on 5, we might miss each other."*

*She said it plainly, as if working out the theory in real time. Her brow furrowed slightly, thoughtful, focused.*

*Wilson processed her logic. It made sense. Still, part of him suspected she knew 3 was the default—they'd used it that morning. Maybe she just wanted to be clever. Or different.*

*"You little knucklehead. You knew we started on Channel 3."*

*Sky shrugged. "Well, since your goal was to teach me communication in the wild, I assumed you'd test me. And mix things up."*

*Leaning against a nearby stump now, she looked up at him with bright, confident eyes and just enough smugness to make him laugh.*

*"Well," he said, "once again, you've taught me something. I should've told you where to start."*

*"Exactly," she said, holding up the radio. She pointed to the channel dial. "Also, there's an auto-channel search. See?" She pressed a button until the display read A. "Why don't we use that?"*

*He laughed, chest rumbling as he reached out and patted her head. "First time using a radio, and you already know about auto-scan?"*

*Sky grinned. "Just exploring my options."*

*"Well," he said, still smiling, "yes, I was trying to teach you the basics. But what if you're out somewhere with a different radio—no auto-scan?"*

*She didn't miss a beat. "Then I'd make sure to tell the other person exactly what channel we're using. Like you should've*

196

*done."*

*She paused, then added, "Can we go now? I want to clean my room before The Voice. You won't let me watch Gwen's team if my room's a mess."*

*Wilson shook his head, beaming with pride. His daughter—smart, calm, stubborn as hell. Just like her mom, without bitter anger and resentment.*

Come in, Chief Wilson. Paducah, over. Come in, Chief Wilson, this is Paducah, over!

Paducah's voice blared over the speaker in the cab of the county vehicle. Chief Wilson, on autopilot as he drove toward Old Stage Road, blinked out of his memory stupor. He flipped on his turn signal and grabbed the mic to respond.

"Chief Wilson here. Go ahead, Paducah."

"Chief, the air tankers are waiting on the tarmac. Their spotter plane is already airborne, and I'll be in direct contact with them. We'll give feedback and recommendations from the ground. Choppers are still up in the air with buckets as well."

"Excellent, Paducah. Where are you?"

"I repositioned to Blue Heron Park in Phoenix to get my bearings on the area in relation to the fire. I'll head up into the Phoenix Hill area in five minutes. I think there's a better view from there."

Chief Wilson used his decades-long memory of the terrain to paint a mental picture of her location before responding. "Good call. Try heading up to the end of Bloom Street. That should give you the access you're looking for."

"Roger that, Chief," Paducah replied, appreciation in her voice.

"Okay, Paducah. I'm on Old Stage Road now. I want to plan a control line here. This is going to be our best defense of Medford. If this fire gets by us, it'll go from a disaster to a catastrophe. Let's tie off in another ten minutes."

"Roger, Chief. That should give me enough time to get into position. Over."

With that, Chief Wilson guided his vehicle along Old Stage Road. Looking down at the sun-decayed, cracked blacktop toward the west, he pressed the gas pedal, increasing the fire rig's speed. He wanted to head out a couple of miles and then backtrack toward the fire to better understand the options for a containment line—and how best to deploy the tankers.

He couldn't help but consider the fierce winds that propelled the fire with reckless abandon—they'd wreak havoc on the tankers' retardant drops. He and his team had to ensure they relayed their needs quickly and clearly. Retardant was limited. A misplaced drop wasn't just a waste, it was a setback. And timing was everything.

Satisfied with the ground he'd covered heading west, Wilson whipped the rig around and barreled back toward the heart of the fire. Radio chatter crackled through the cab—urgent voices overlapping, each pleading for more support as crews dug in against the wind-driven inferno.

A flicker of a smile tugged at the corners of his mouth—he couldn't help it, thinking

about his feisty daughter.

"Then I'd make sure to tell the other person exactly what channel we're using."

But the warmth soured fast. The smile faded, replaced by a weight pressing into

his chest. Was she okay? Where the hell was she?

He gripped the wheel tighter, jaw clenched. What was it about him that drove women away? His wife. Sky. Was there some invisible flaw stitched into his wiring—something in the way he loved, or didn't?

# Comfortable

Several hours into another routine shift, patient after patient offered up a new version of the same old story. Kaley let her mind drift. The melodic voice from that morning's podcast still lingered in her head, stirring fleeting images of a life that had felt light, meaningful—maybe even fun. She held on to them, trying not to slip back into the familiar weight she carried. That quiet, persistent darkness had gripped her for as long as she could remember. *Even as a kid, she often felt like the world was on the verge of collapsing.*

The sadness never stopped. Every day brought more of it—grief, anger, confusion, depression. It all ran together. Patient faces blurred. Their voices melted into one indistinct tone, like a swirl of crayon colors left too long in the sun.

She went through the motions. Clock in. Check boxes. Sign forms. Eat whatever passed for lunch. Exchange hollow words with Mia. Bite back the urge to snap. Then go home. Take off her legs. Pour a drink. Sink into the quiet. Wake up and do it all again.

Today, every patient had something to say about the fire. Or the price of healthcare. Or both. Kaley had no energy left to feign interest in either.

Under normal circumstances, talk of fire sent Kaley spiraling into a volatile borderland of PTSD—a mental terrain no one, including herself, wanted her crossing into. Her usual passive, depressive shell would crack wide open, replaced by belligerence, sharp edges, and the threat of violence if someone looked at her wrong, said the wrong thing, or—God forbid—touched her. But today, the wildfire talk slid right past her, barely registering. It was as if her mind had decided not to let it in.

Her latest patient arrived with a pair of loud, unruly twins in tow. The woman was heavyset, her legs thick as tree trunks, layered with rippling skin beneath overtaxed spandex. The synthetic fabric clung for dear life, stretched so tight Kaley imagined if a single thread snapped, flesh would flood the cubicle like water escaping a broken dam. The woman reeked of cheap cigarette smoke, the stench conjuring *memories of overflowing ashtrays—and her mother, likely still buried under blankets at home.*

"Please have a seat," Kaley said, then added silently, *or three,* eyeing the width of the woman's backside.

The woman yanked one of the twins by the arm, jerking him like a rag doll. Kaley blinked. That took strength. She noted the woman's thick, swollen arms, her sausage fingers clamped around the boy's wrist. The kid's smallish body trembled from the force.

"I told you both—we'll get ice cream after, if you behave. Momma has to get her blood tested. Now be nice or so help me."

Kaley tilted her head. So, help me what? Half a scoop instead of a full one?

The three of them barely fit in the cramped exam room. Ice cream, however, worked like a charm. The promise settled the kids enough to get them into their chairs, their noisy energy simmering to a low buzz. Watching their fidgety movements, Kaley guessed they were six or seven, though their size suggested closer to twelve. She wanted to ask—but didn't. No good would come from starting a deeper conversation with this woman.

Kaley had always struggled with overweight patients—a bias she knew she carried, even if she hated herself for it. That morning's podcast, all sunshine and self-worth, had planted a seed of guilt. It sprouted now, curling through her mind as she watched the children—too big, too fidgety, too loud—struggling to behave.

She forced her attention away, eyes landing on the computer screen. Time to check the chart, read the numbers, avoid the emotion.

"Okay, Mrs. Hairston, it looks like you're here for bloodwork today. Correct?"

"It's Ms. Hairston. I'm single."

"That's hard to believe," Kaley said—before she could stop herself.

The patient blinked. "Excuse me?"

Kaley scrambled. "Sorry, I just meant... with the kids..." Her voice trailed off, the unfinished sentence dangling in the air like a bad joke. She had no idea how to reel it back in.

The woman narrowed her eyes but let it go. "Yes. Bloodwork for my diabetes."

"Thank you. Please spell your last name and give me your date of birth."

The kids were already unraveling. Ice cream had lost its power. One had an index finger shoved halfway up his nose. The other turned around, dropped to his knees, gripped the back of his stained cloth chair, and raised his rear like a flag. Then came the fart.

The cubicle went still for a beat. The boys froze, sensing they might have crossed a line. Then they burst into laughter—pure, unfiltered chaos.

Kaley flinched. She prayed the stink wouldn't slip through the holes in the plexiglass barrier. Judging by the kid's body type and general condition, *she suspected he ate roadkill for breakfast.*

Their mother turned and whacked the gassy one on top of the head.

"Sit down. That's it. I mean it. Behave, or we go straight

home after shopping. You hear me?"

Kaley blinked at the woman's threat—*go straight home after shopping.* The logic twisted in her brain. *Shouldn't it be straight home after the hospital?* She caught herself caring, then got annoyed that she cared at all.

It didn't matter. None of it did.

Across the plexiglass, the woman began reciting her information, pausing between syllables to suck in shallow breaths. Each word came wrapped in a strained gasp, like speaking alone required all the air she could manage. Kaley tried not to wince as she listened—one labored exhale at a time.

"H-A-I-R-S-T-O-N. July 16, 1985."

"Thank you," Kaley said, nose twitching as the stench from the kid's butt music somehow made it through the half-inch plastic barrier. She turned her head as far back as it would go, hoping to catch a breath of cleaner air behind her. No luck. *That fart had stamina.* Defeated, she slid her surgical mask up over her nose and mouth. *Thank God for COVID,* she thought, as the woman across the barrier lowered her eyes, clearly catching Kaley's reaction.

Kaley rushed through the rest of the check-in, abandoning her usual instinct to connect with patients. Today, there would be no idle chatter to escape the gray drag of her own life. She wanted the three ghastly humans gone—waddling off into the hospital and, hopefully, never returning.

She yanked the shade down over the plexiglass and pressed the button that flipped her sign to CLOSED. Pushing herself upright, she steadied on her rigid carbon legs. As she passed Mia's open door, she kept her gaze forward, avoiding eye contact, and made a beeline for the break room.

Outside the door, three nurses clustered, peering in. Odd. The break room was normally a sterile, soulless little kitchen— quiet except during official breaks. Curious, Kaley muttered a soft "excuse me" and wedged herself through, finding a small stretch of wall just inside. She felt the stares as she hobbled in, her gait uneven, legs clicking. *Normally, she'd care—feel that familiar twinge of freakishness bubble up inside.* But today? Not so much. She only cared about what was on the TV and why the room was so packed. She leaned her back against the painted sheetrock, letting it catch her weight. The ache in her lower spine eased just enough to remind her how much it hurt.

The break room was over capacity—clearly a fire code violation—but no one said a word. The only sounds were the low hum of the wall-mounted TV and hushed crosstalk from hospital staff, each wearing their color-coded scrubs like a living Pantone chart. Kaley caught herself counting the blues, grays, and teals, then stopped. It didn't matter.

"What's going on?" she asked the room, launching the question without aim, assuming someone would bite.

A woman beside her—Kaley pegged her as a nurse based on the scrubs—answered without looking up. Her voice was soft, as if volume might tip the room's fragile balance.

"The Almeda Fire. It's not slowing down. Talent has been hit hard. It's moving toward Phoenix. Wind and dry fuel... it's bad."

"It has a name?" Kaley asked, instinct kicking in. In the military, weather or fire events mentioned by name typically meant one thing: it was real, and it was bad.

"Almeda?" She repeated the word aloud, mostly to herself, the syllables sticking to her tongue like ash.

The nurse finally responded. "They say it started near Almeda Drive in Ashland. That's how it got the name. I wondered too."

A doctor in dark blue scrubs lifted a remote and, without looking away from the screen, said, "Quiet, please," then turned up the volume. *Fucking prima donna,* Kaley thought, as the room fell obediently silent.

The newscaster's voice filled the space.

"We repeat: Highway 99 is closed from Ashland to South Medford as fire crews battle the blaze. Evacuations are underway in Talent and Phoenix. South Medford residents are on standby. First responders have full access. We're working to get updates from Talent-Phoenix Fire District."

Then, without warning, the screen cut to a commercial pushing the importance of shopping local.

In an instant, the room emptied. Nurses, doctors, greeters, janitors—all filed out in a wave of anxious purpose, chairs askew in their wake. Kaley stood frozen for a second, then stepped forward, grabbed the remote, and straightened a chair to face the screen. She dropped into it with a thud, her carbon legs clicking against the tile.

She lowered the volume, glanced around the now-empty room, then muted the TV completely. An aging actor peddled a reverse mortgage with practiced sincerity. Kaley rolled her eyes.

Did Mom take her heart meds? The question surfaced without warning. The pills made her drowsy. Add that to an old, manufactured home in the path of a fire, and the thought came uninvited: Would anyone hear her scream?

She didn't feel guilty. That bothered her more than the thought itself.

Staring at the screen, she let the commercial play. Then unmuted it. Leaning back in the chair, she adjusted her weight, trying to find some level of comfort, even if it wasn't real.

# Now He Knew

Teddy slammed the cart to a stop in front of the shop, the vehicle coated in gray ash that clung to everything like death. The metal-sided building, streaked with rust and grime, had long been his escape from the world. Concrete floors, fiberglass panels, oil stains—it wasn't pretty, but it felt safe.

His usual calm demeanor had vanished, swallowed by fear for his granddaughter. He jumped out before the cart fully stopped, eyes locking on the roof. The place should hold against fire. At least, it *used* to feel that way. *In his mind, the building had always been a last resort, a bunker.* But with fire now real and closing in, he wasn't so sure. How much heat could old sheet metal and rusted bolts really take? And shit, what about the fiberglass panels?

A part of him, one he rarely acknowledged, had always imagined surviving some catastrophe. *Something to prove he could outlast it, grit it out, live when others couldn't.* Now, facing the real thing, he saw that idea for what it was: bluster.

Smoke thickened fast. He rushed inside, breath ragged, scanning the cluttered shop. Every tool passed through a filter in his mind. Could he use it? A push broom? Wrenches? Yard tools? None of it mattered if he couldn't find the one thing he needed.

"Fuckin' hell!" he shouted, tossing tools aside, shoving old gear and clutter out of the way. The wall hangings, the overflowing workbench—he looked at it all and admitted what he'd refused to before: *he was a hoarder. His grandfather had warned him, told him that your home and your shop reflected your life.* Both were a mess.

Dropping to his knees, Teddy yanked back boxes of

plumbing odds and ends. He popped open a drawer and, finally—under cobwebs, rat droppings, and a rusted pipe wrench—found it: the manual crank arm. He grabbed it and turned toward the door, promising himself he'd clean all of this up *if he survived.*

Outside, smoke hung like a curtain, almost begging for the final act. He floored the cart toward the front gate. A dozen cars were already lined up, horns blaring, drivers shouting. He didn't care. His plan was simple: open the gate, get the hell out, and find his family.

But he was too late.

A massive county water truck sat parked near the gate. Chains were hooked to the iron frame. Teddy stared. A deputy raised his hand, gave a whistle, then stepped back. The truck lurched forward. Metal groaned. Bolts popped. The gate tore free from its base. The truck kept moving, dragging the wreckage into a nearby field.

Cheers erupted from the drivers behind him. Teddy stood frozen, crank arm in hand, stunned. "What did you do?" he shouted toward the deputy, though the words were all but lost in the noise of honking and cheering.

The deputy gave a head nod and climbed into his cruiser. A moment later, his voice boomed from the loudspeaker.

"Residents, proceed with caution. Turn right and head north on Highway 99. Southbound lanes are closed."

Cars started rolling out. Teddy caught every glare, every insult. He avoided eye contact with residents who grew to trust him over the years, guilt rising in his throat.

The deputy pulled alongside him.

"Sorry about the gate," he said through the open window. "But people had to leave. There's an imminent threat to the whole development. I waited longer than I should have."

Teddy nodded, still trying to catch up.

"What now? You couldn't wait?" he asked.

"You were gone almost thirty minutes. I didn't know if you were coming back, and it took time to find a truck with chains."

Teddy blinked. "I didn't think it had been that long."

"It was. And now I need help. We still have people inside. I can't knock on every door by myself."

Teddy looked toward the black sky, then at the homes scattered across the park like fragile dominos. His daughter and granddaughter filled his thoughts. *Were they okay? Had they made it to his house?*

He reached for his phone—nothing. Not in the pouch, not in his pockets.

"Shit," he muttered.

The deputy gave him a look. "You helping me or not?"

Teddy hesitated. He wanted to find his family. *But his daughter was smart. She knew what to do.* And others still needed help.

"I need to call my daughter first. I just can't find my phone."

"Didn't we already go over this? She's in Phoenix, right? Schools are evacuated. She's not there."

Teddy nodded slowly, his thoughts racing.

"Help me clear the park," the deputy said. "There are residents in the back who don't have vehicles. They can ride the bus."

Teddy glanced toward the rear of the park, where smoke drifted around rooftops. The deputy slid back into the cruiser and opened the passenger door.

Teddy didn't answer. He just climbed in, the door shutting behind him with a solid, final thud.

Years ago, he'd ridden in the back of a police car as a dumb teenager. The front seat felt different. Still confined. Still foreign. But now, somehow, it felt earned.

# Trapped

Sky couldn't recall ever seeing her mother grease a pan, stir batter with a wooden spoon, or dice vegetables with practiced hands. She closed her eyes, searching her memory like sifting flour through a sieve—but nothing came up. No clatter of pots, no scent of onions in butter. Just silence. Except for coffee.

Every morning, the ritual was the same. Her mother pressed a single cup of jet-black coffee, poured it into a ceramic mug, and added a swirl of warmed heavy cream with just enough sugar to hold any bitterness at bay. Then she drifted to the living room, settling into the same chair tucked beside the tall bookshelves. A book always in her lap, always half-read. Her eyes, sharp and narrow, moved across the page, lips mumbling a line here or there—never loud enough to understand, just enough to let the room know she was in it.

Sky used to think that was the point. To be noticed without engaging. Her mother rarely spoke but always made sure her presence hummed like background noise.

She never folded laundry. Never stood over a stove. Never packed a lunch.

Sky remembered her friends arriving at school in fresh-pressed clothes, trading stories about chicken casseroles and packed sandwiches with handwritten notes. None of them spoke of a mother rooted in a chair, whispering lines from yellowed paperbacks like spells no one else could decipher.

Her dad did the laundry, cooked dinner, and packed her school lunches—when he had the time. Balancing all that with a firefighter's schedule wasn't easy, but he carved out every spare minute for her. On mornings when he left early, the house felt colder. *If her mother was even out of bed,* she sat in her usual chair, murmuring lines from a book, coffee steaming in her lap, while Sky rifled through the pantry looking for sandwich fixings. Most days, it was peanut butter and honey on whatever bread she could find—sometimes a heel, sometimes a cracked, shriveled slice pulled from the back of the freezer, buried under mystery items with no hope of ever seeing a kitchen again.

Groceries were Dad's job too, though even then, the fridge was often a sparse landscape. Some days, her lunch was just carrot and celery sticks, dipped in peanut butter if she was lucky. At other times, mayonnaise was the only option, and she didn't bother packing anything at all.

By eight, she started making her own shopping lists—blocky handwriting on lined paper, tucked into the pockets of her dad's work jackets in the mudroom. If he found one before his shift, there was a better chance she'd open the fridge to more than condiments and takeout packets. Most days he noticed. But sometimes, she guessed the wrong jacket.

After days of light lunches and missed chances, Sky started duplicating her grocery lists—one for each of her dad's two jackets. Eventually, she forgot to remove the extras. A few times, they ended up with double the carrots and celery. When the veggies went bad, Sky made sure the deer behind their property had snacks. Her father never scolded her for forgetting.

*One afternoon, he came home early and found her tossing wilted celery to a small herd near the fence. Stepping out of his county vehicle, he smiled.*

*"Some veggies going bad, Sky?"*

*She froze, guilt nipping at her heels. "Yes, Dad. Sorry."*

*He only nodded, calm as ever. "Be careful, little one. A deer can hurt you if it feels cornered."*

*Little one.* The words always sparked something in her chest. The way he said it—warm, gentle, sincere—made her feel the way she imagined every daughter wanted to feel. Like she mattered more than anything. Like she was safe.

So why did she push him away? Why at times did she mimic her mother's coldness, snapping at him with sharp words or silence? The guilt pulled at her, sticky and stretched thin like taffy. If she kept pulling, it might break. But staying close to him felt like betrayal. *Any kindness toward her father brought tension. Her mother's eyes, even when not present, loomed in her mind.*

Affection had consequences. So, Sky rationed it, giving her father the softer parts of herself only when her mother wasn't around. She tried to be nicer then—just not *too* nice. Not enough to forget how she was expected to behave when the three of them shared a room.

But something was changing.

For what felt like the first time in her life, Sky looked at her father through new eyes—older, worn by more experience, sharpened by loss. The man she once walked away from, just like her mother had, now lived in a different space in her mind. *Something had shifted.* The memories no longer came wrapped in confusion and disappointment.

Months of hard ground and harder nights—sleeping on concrete, keeping watch, running from strangers in the dark—had stripped away the illusions. What she once thought was weakness in her father now looked like strength. What she thought was indifference from her mother now looked like a cage.

A vision flickered in her mind, half-dream, half-truth:

*Her father stood outside the iron bars of a prison cell. Inside, her mother screamed at the walls, fists clenched, voice ragged. The door hung open just a few feet away, but she couldn't—or wouldn't—step through. He reached out, hand trembling, tears streaking his cheeks. But her mother didn't see him—or refused to. She only screamed louder and backed into the shadows, choosing the bars over freedom. Over him.*

Sky blinked, trying to hold on to the image. She didn't understand everything yet, but something in her continued its long path of waking up—a truth forming in the silence.

# Camping

Chief Wilson parked the county rig along Old Stage Road, facing east. Radio chatter spilled through the cab, fast and frantic. Voices blurred, overlapping requests for more engines, more people, more water. Ambulances. Evacuations. Help. The fire had torn through the town of Talent without mercy, flattening homes and businesses. In untouched pockets, the contrast was surreal. One house stood, another beside it reduced to ash. *Just like those tornado scenes on the news from the Midwest.* Fire danced with the wind. Unpredictable. Unforgiving.

His entire district—every firefighter under his command—along with hundreds from nearby cities, were out there. Fighting. But the fire didn't care. Dug lines failed. Embers leapt thousands of yards ahead.

The crews had become rescue units, dragging people from homes and rushing ahead of the flames. If they had any shot at saving Phoenix—and keeping the fire from ripping through Medford, a city of over 250,000—the air tanker had to drop retardant with precision. In this wind, it would take a miracle. Weather reports promised no relief until well into the night.

Wilson grabbed the two-way.

"Paducah, come in. This is Chief Wilson."

Silence.

He waited, frowned. "Paducah, do you copy?"

Before he could call again, she crackled through. "Paducah here, Chief. Apologies. I was on with Air Tanker dispatch. You should see them overhead any minute."

"Roger that. What's the plan?"

"They're focused on the defensive line you

recommended—Old Stage to the north, I-5 to the east. Wind's dictating the rest."

"Who's in the scout plane?"

"Dennison."

Wilson allowed himself to breathe. "Good. He's solid. Knows fire. Any word on the wind?"

"Not yet. I was just about to check with command."

Wilson leaned back, thoughts drifting to the resignation letter he'd handed in that morning. For once, he didn't second-guess it. No twisting gut. No guilt. Personally, he felt torn. Professionally? That was harder. He'd given this department everything—years of sacrifice, sleepless nights, political headaches—and joy. But the job had taken its toll. Somewhere along the way, he'd traded closeness with his daughter for duty to the badge. *Now, with Sky grown and gone, he wondered if stepping away had come years too late.* Still, he was done.

Paducah was why he could leave. Not because he hoped she'd rise to the occasion—but because he *knew* she would. He'd trained her. She had the mind, the instinct, the grit. Everyone saw it the day she walked in the door, and he'd known it within a week. She was sharp, tenacious, and didn't let the job harden her heart. She defined grit—and had a soul.

Over the years, she'd become like a daughter to him. The kind of relationship he'd once dreamed of having with his own.

"I hate you!"

Sky's voice echoed in his memory, slamming into him as hard as the door she'd run behind that day. She was fourteen. They'd argued about a camping trip—one he didn't feel good about.

It started in the kitchen.

*"Are the parents going, Sky?"*

*Her pause told him everything.*

*"They're driving us up and setting up camp. They said we'll*

*be near the host site. Jodi's sister and her boyfriend will be there too..."*

*"Davey Johnstone?" he asked, brow raised.*

*Another pause. "I think so. Why?"*

*"You know how I feel about that kid. Trouble follows him."*

*Sky didn't miss a beat. "Cooper David is going too. You like him."*

*"I do. From what I know."*

*"It's just two nights, Dad. Her parents will be there most of the first day and night. That really just leaves one night."*

*He almost smiled. She was smart—quick with her angles. "What did your mother say?"*

*They both glanced toward the living room. His wife sat frozen, eyes locked on her book, as if the world around her didn't exist.*

*"She says it's up to you. Like always."*

*Wilson swallowed his frustration. His wife had made disengagement an art form. She'd appear just long enough to claim credit when Sky shined—but never stepped in when things were hard.*

*"Listen, Sky. Davey's not responsible. I don't feel good about this trip. How about we go fishing this weekend instead? Camp overnight—just us?"*

*He'd make it work somehow. He always did for Sky.*

*She shouted. Ran. Slammed the door. Pictures rattled off the wall.*

*Moments later, questioning his parenting, he grabbed his jacket to head to work, and he found a note. A grocery list: carrots (the small ones), radishes, celery, apples (no bruises), Eggos, butter, milk. He smiled. His daughter was growing up. And he'd just crushed her desires.*

*Heading back upstairs, he tapped on her door.*

*Sky pulled the door open a crack. "What?" she sniffed.*

*"Are there any boys your age going?"*

*"No."*

*"What campground?"*

*"Kangaroo Lake."*

*The door opened more with each question. Her room was a warzone, clothes scattered everywhere, bed unmade—but he saw the hope in her eyes. She knew where this was headed.*

*"I love Kangaroo Lake."*

*They stared at each other.*

*"Okay," he finally said. "But here's the deal—"*

*Sky tackled him with a hug before he could finish. "Thanks, Dad! I love you!"*

*He hugged her tight, laying out the rules: life jacket on the lake, gear ready by the shop, parents must call me before leaving. If they didn't, he'd drive up and get her. Period.*

*"Got it," she said, texting furiously.*

*"Give them my number," he added. "And clean your room."*

*"Yes, Dad," she said, barely listening.*

*He stood at the door. "Sky?"*

*"What?"*

*"I love you. I trust you. Be smart."*

"I love you, Dad. Thanks! Have a great day at work! See you Sunday night!"

She didn't look up.

He thought she'd leave a vague note—that much was typical. But the call from her friend's parents? That wasn't optional. He expected it. Demanded it. It was the condition for letting her go, the one line he wouldn't bend on. Sky was mature beyond her years, smarter than most kids her age—but trust still had rules, and this one mattered.

Still, less than forty-eight hours later, he regretted letting her go.

"Chief," Paducah said over the radio, "just got off the line with Dennison. Fire's worse than we thought. The tanker's airborne now. First drops in ten, winds permitting."

"Copy that. I'm on Old Stage, watching the chaos. Keep it coming, Paducah. You're doing great."

He paused, then added without warning, "By the way, I was serious about handing in my resignation today."

There was a beat before Paducah replied. "Yeah, yeah. We've heard that before, Chief. Don't get my hopes up, we've got a fire to fight. Believe it when I see it."

He chuckled, stepped out of the rig, and leaned against the hood. A police cruiser passed, the officer inside giving a wave. In the distance, he heard the familiar low rumble—whales in the sky, roaring. Looking north, he spotted the slow climb of a fire-dousing aluminum bird, banking east through columns of smoke.

His eyes welled as he thought of Sky.

And all he wanted, at that moment, was to walk away from all of it. To find his daughter. To take her to Crater Lake. To look through the coin-operated binoculars and see if they could find the Old Man of the Lake.

# That's What I Said

Mel stared down the runway, eyes flicking across gauges as Betsy rumbled beneath her. Everything checked out. She glanced at her co-pilot, gave a curt nod, and waited for his nod. The moment he returned it, she eased the throttle forward. The engines leapt from a purr to a full-throated roar. Betsy—loaded with nearly 9,500 pounds of retardant—charged down the strip, steel and rivets straining against gravity until the plane finally surrendered to flight.

Smoke swallowed Southern Oregon in every direction.

*In her mind, Johnson's smug face reappeared.* She'd half expected a brawl with the guy in the hallway—probably not the best pre-flight mindset. She shoved the image aside. There was no space for him in the cockpit. Not today. Not on a mission like this.

The lead pilot's voice crackled over the headset, calling out terrain and target. Mel banked right. The plane groaned under the weight, wings flexing as the fuselage adjusted. Her arms, sore from that morning's softball game, stayed steady on the controls. Then she saw flames crawling toward Payne Creek Estates.

Her mother's neighborhood.

A pulse of something sharp and tight—not panic, but not far from it—rushed through her. She forced herself to study the scene. Orange walls of fire surged north. Smoke boiled upward and drifted like a tide. The drop needed to be precise. Visualizing the retardant hitting the fire line, Mel focused on terrain—trees, brush, bare ground—not houses or cars. Her chest vibrated with the engine's growl, the sensation traveling through her core, down her legs. They were close.

Her mother had sent photos from Italy the day before.

Tuscany, she thought. Mel pictured the cats, alone in the new house, hiding in closets or under beds. Please don't be inside, she thought.

She hit the switch.

Four and a half tons of bright red slurry poured from Betsy's belly, blanketing the lead pilot's mark.

If they were lucky, it would hold.

As they climbed, Mel tried not to think about the cats. She'd text her mom from the ground, maybe ask about a neighbor who could help. But they'd only lived there for a short while, and her mom wasn't exactly the neighborhood socialite. *Kaley crossed her mind—her old friend who also lived in her mother's development—but they hadn't talked in months. Not since things fell apart between them.* Not ideal timing for a favor.

After a feather-soft landing, Mel taxied toward the refill station. The lead pilot stayed airborne with eyes on the fire. Mel listened as he confirmed the first dump was effective—momentary guidance in steering the fire at least.

Urban fire was different. They weren't saving forests; they were saving people. Homes. Businesses. Lives. There was no buffer zone of wilderness to buy time. The stakes felt heavier, faster.

Her mother's home had only just started to feel like home. It had been less than a year since she moved in—eighteen months after Mel's father died unexpectedly. A lifetime together, gone in a breath. Europe was going to be her mother's reset.

Engines idling, Mel rolled Betsy to a stop. On the tarmac, the ground crew rushed like ants swarming a dropped crumb. She pulled her phone from her flight suit and took it off silent. Notifications stacked like falling dominos. She ignored the dating apps and scanned her mom's texts—six in total, the first one timestamped twenty minutes ago.

The last read:

*"You must be playing softball, or I'd have heard from you. Please call when you can. Love, Mom. BTW, Europe is wonderful. I wish your dad were here with me. :-("*

"Trouble in paradise?" her co-pilot asked, glancing over.

Mel didn't answer right away. She stared out the window at the crew, motionless now as the retardant surged into Betsy's belly.

"No. It's my mom. She's in Italy, first trip without my dad. I think she's wondering about her house in Phoenix."

"Better she's not here to see it firsthand."

Mel nodded slowly. "Yeah. If she were, I wouldn't be here, I'd be trying to get to her house instead. She's probably worried about the cats."

"Did you see the neighborhood on our pass?"

"I did, but not sure I saw her home. I'll try again on the next run. The neighborhood looked okay—for now."

"My dad lives in Phoenix. He'd love an excuse to throw on his fire gear and play hero. Want me to call him?"

Mel smiled. "Thanks. That's sweet. I hate talking to my mom on the phone. She never stops."

"Well, you've got eight minutes," he said, pointing to the load timer. "Perfect excuse to hang up."

Mel pressed dial. One ring.

"Hi, Charlie." Her mom's voice chirped. "Calling about the fire? Too bad you hung up your flight suit. You'd be flying that tanker."

Mel sighed. "Yeah, about that..."

"Don't tell me—you finagled your way back into a cockpit."

"It's a long story. But yes."

"I knew it. No one flies better than you, Charlie. Good for you."

"Thanks, Mom. Retardant's loading now. I've only got a few minutes. You asked me to call?"

"Oh, right. Lucy picked up the cats. Took them to her place in Jacksonville."

Mel exhaled. "Seriously? She made it through all this?"

"She knew someone in Ashland who called her. Word traveled fast. And Lucy's always first at everything. Lucky for our cats, she called me first."

Mel noticed the slip— "our cats." Her mother still talked like Dad was alive. After sixty years together, Mel felt a tinge of sadness for her mother.

"You, okay?" Mel asked.

"I'm fine. Sitting on the balcony, sipping wine, watching the stars. I miss your father, but I'm learning I can do things alone."

The city noise buzzed faintly through the call. Mel imagined the streets below, the warmth of the Italian evening, and her mother—peaceful.

"You worried about the house?" Mel asked.

"No, Charlie. It's just stuff. Important things are still in storage. I'm okay. Now go save lives. And just know, if your dad were here, I wouldn't be watching a rom com in bed. we'd be making our own."

"MOM. TMI. Seriously."

"Oh, get over yourself. It's only sex. Love you, sweetheart. Be safe."

Silence.

Mel stared at the screen.

"Everything good?" her co-pilot asked.

"My mom is sipping wine, reminiscing about sex with my dad when he was still alive. And she hung up first. I don't think that's ever happened."

"And the cats?"

"Safe with a friend."

"Well… good. Except for the sex part."

"Yeah," Mel groaned. "Definitely could've lived without that visual."

# Shame

From the outside, Sky's childhood home looked unchanged. But inside, something felt off. The air hung heavy, like the house had been left behind—steeped in loneliness.

As a child, the house had wrapped itself around her like armor—solid, familiar, a shell that shut out the world. It felt safe, but it was a brittle kind of safety, the kind that cracks when pressed too hard. Inside, the silence could scream. The walls had absorbed every unspoken resentment, every slammed cupboard, every quiet retreat behind closed doors.

Still, it was home. And home, to a child, is sacred—even when it hurts.

The illusion had held until the day her mother walked out the front door with a stranger and didn't look back. *Sky remembered the silence more than the argument that came before it.* The door didn't slam. It didn't even click shut. *It stayed open—just swung there, half-ajar, like an unfinished sentence.* Her mother never left doors open. *That, more than anything, made it feel permanent.*

Now, as she crossed the threshold years later, the tears that had trailed down her cheeks slowed. In their place came an eerie stillness, something not quite peace, not quite pain. It drifted through her chest like smoke. She wanted it to waft away.

Her body moved forward, slow and detached, like she was observing herself from somewhere above—a ghost inside her own skin. She drifted into the main room, heart tightening as her eyes landed on the bookcase.

Most of the books were gone. In their place, from a distance, stood a row of framed photographs.

Sky blinked. That didn't make sense.

Her mother hated clutter, sure—but she hated photographs more. Memories, sentimentality, the messiness of a past she didn't want to be a part of. She'd never even put up Sky's school pictures, let alone frame moments to be remembered.

Sky took a step closer, unsettled. It felt like finding someone else's fingerprints in a locked room. The absence of the chair, the one molded to her mother's form by years of silent reading and long sips of wine—only deepened the dissonance. She searched the corners for it, expecting to see its slouched outline waiting in a patch of filtered light. Nothing.

Maybe her father had hauled it off to the secondhand store. Or maybe, in one of his winter purges, he'd fed it to the fire like kindling. Another erasure.

The photos, though—they stayed fixed, watching.

*"Doesn't it make you feel better to clean up the property and burn old twigs and limbs and some of our worthless trash, Sky?"*

*She didn't answer. He wasn't really asking—just sharing the lesson, like always.*

*"I love the feeling of looking around and seeing it clean. Everything in its place. Aren't the trees beautiful, the way they stand so tall, so stoic and strong. Like guardians of our property? What's your favorite thing outside, Sky?"*

*She looked up at him, caught off guard by the thought of trees as protectors and the warmth in his voice. It felt like an invitation. Eager to meet it, she said, "I love to watch the squirrels and the birds, Dad."*

*"They are fun, yes. Bursting with joyful energy."*

*Sky tilted her head back, her eyes catching on the cotton-ball clouds drifting through a blue so vivid it made her squint. An idea struck. "Oooh, Dad. Can I change my mind?"*

*He grinned. "Well, of course. What do you have?"*

Still watching the pine and fir tops sway like dancers leaning into the wind, she said, "I love the way the tops of the big trees move back and forth in the wind. The sound makes me think of the ocean. That's my favorite."

Her father dropped a broken limb into the fire, then walked to her side. Together, they looked up.

"Nice choice, Sky. My grandma used to say the wind sounded like 'the ocean in the trees.'"

Sky smiled, eyes fluttering closed as she pictured the swaying tops—tree after tree bending in rhythm to something ancient and unseen. They danced, she imagined, not because they had to, but because the wind sang to them. And when the song stopped, they stilled.

The Oregon forest had never let her down. Not like people could.

When she opened her eyes, her father was watching her, a wide smile stretching across his face. Warmth bloomed in her chest.

Then she asked, "How come Mom won't come out and help us? This would go quicker. We never really do stuff all together."

His smile vanished. He turned away without a word and began tossing limbs onto the fire again. The only sounds were the snap of pine needles and the low roar of flame.

After a while, he spoke with a demanding reluctance. "She doesn't enjoy being outside, I guess. Says it's my job, not hers."

Sky hesitated. "All she does is read. Shouldn't she get outside sometimes? I mean, you shop, cook, do the laundry, clean the bathrooms, work..."

Her voice trailed off. She glanced at him, then looked back at the fire. "Do you ever talk to her when I'm not around?"

Not expecting a reply from her father, immersed in tossing more and more limbs onto a fire that could never offer answers, *she drifted back into present thoughts.*

Thinking about the missing chair, Sky moved toward the bookcase, her mind tugged back to the long hours her mother used to disappear—not minutes, but whole afternoons. *And yet, to this day, she still didn't know where her mother went.*

As a child, she hated being left alone. Even if the house felt safe, comfort only came when someone else was nearby. She clung to the sounds of life around her. Her father, though often busy, always made space. Once a year, she'd spend a whole day at work with him, and every month, she'd tag along for an hour or two, he always seemed to want her around.

Her mother was different. Distant, but not unloving. Sky believed her mother cared as best she could. But love from someone who struggled to find joy felt more like a flicker than a flame.

Sky searched for memories of her mother, trying to unearth something lighter. There was the reading, the endless hours in front of her computer. And then there were the drives—silent departures without explanation. Her mother would vanish for hours, no note left behind, just the hum of the engine fading down the road.

Sky always asked to come along. Only once did she get a yes.

They drove to the market. Her mother bought a large bottle of wine and a box of crackers. Sky had reached for a Coke. Her mother looked at her—smiling, but not kindly. More like amusement edged with something sharp. Her eyes said, *"You're joking, right? You stupid little girl."*

That's how it felt, anyway.

Her mother paid, and they returned home in silence. Less than twenty minutes. *Sky never asked to go again.*

Standing in front of the bookcase—now stripped of books, Sky stared at a collection of photo-framed memories. Thirteen in total, each one a different size, each one of her and her dad.

Warm moments carefully preserved. Smiles that still felt real.

All except one.

Tucked behind a dusty candle sat the only photo of all three of them—her, her father, and her mother. She pulled it out, her fingers brushing the edge like it might sting. The image hit her like it always did. That day was etched into her mind with painful clarity.

She carried a copy of this photo with her every day, folded and worn soft from years in her pocket. This one was different—fresh, uncreased, untouched. Somehow, that made it worse. Sharper. Sadder.

Sky was seven or eight when they took a day trip to Crater Lake. One of the only times she could remember the three of them going anywhere together.

*The two-hour drive felt like ten. Her mother spent nearly every mile talking in that sharp, mocking tone she reserved for Sky's father—lecturing, belittling, jabbing at him as if he was a child who couldn't do anything right. Her father kept both hands clenched on the steering wheel, knuckles white, eyes forward. He barely spoke. Just the occasional grunt or huh, like he wasn't there at all.*

*Sky was, though. She heard every word. Each one a stone dropped in her gut. She wondered if any of it was true. Her father didn't seem like an idiot. How could someone so dumb be a good firefighter? And small-minded—what did that even mean? His head seemed fine. She made a mental note to ask her teacher when school started.*

*When they arrived, her mother all but sprinted to the lodge, saying she needed the restroom. Sky stood beside her father, watching the birds swoop and circle for scraps in the parking lot. Her mother was gone so long, Sky wondered if the lodge sold wine. She returned eventually, smelling like a cork left too long in the sun. But her mood had changed. Softer. Like—for* just a little while—she could stand being near them.

They walked over to the trail near the lodge and gazed down at the water. The lake shimmered blue and endless.

Sky turned to her dad, excited. "Can we go for a hike? My friend Jimmie said there's a building with a machine you can look through and maybe see the Old Man of the Lake. Can we, Dad?"

"I'd love to, Sky," he said gently. "But it's up to your mother."

Those were the words she dreaded. It's up to your mother always meant no.

A young couple walked by. The woman smiled and asked, "Would you like me to take a photo of you three? It's such a beautiful day."

Sky wondered why she asked. Neither of her parents had their phones out. But her dad—quick and confident, like when he was working a fire line—slipped his phone from his pocket, handed it over, and pulled Sky close. His arm reached around her mother's shoulders, trying to draw her in.

Sky and her father looked like they belonged in the photo. Her mother looked like she'd wandered into the wrong frame. There was actual space between her and her father, and through that gap, the lake's blue gleamed—a perfect divide. Her father's long arm stretched across, awkward and uncertain, the only thing linking them.

The woman who took the photo handed the phone back quickly, her smile gone. She sensed it—the heaviness, the tension. Like someone was held captive.

"Have a nice day," she said softly, like she didn't want to wake something sleeping.

Her mother shrugged off her father's arm and started walking toward the car.

Sky stared up at her dad. He looked like he might cry.

"I'll tell you what, Sky. Mom's not feeling well. We'll come *back another time, just the two of us, and go find that building your friend told you about. Sound good?"*

*Sky nodded, but the thought of getting back in the car filled her with dread. Another two hours of sharp words and silence. As they walked toward the lot, she glanced at the lodge and imagined running inside. It looked like a magical school— something out of Harry Potter. Surely there were secret rooms to hide in. Maybe she could live there, sneaking food from the kitchen at night, turning hikers' forgotten clothes into blankets and pillows. It'd be hard in the winter—she'd seen pictures of Crater Lake buried in snow—but her dad always said she was a survivor. And she believed she could be.*

*Still, she got into the car. Back into her place of silence in the backseat. Wishing Hogwarts was real. Wishing there was anywhere else to go. And wondering what it would take to make her mother happy.*

*Sky set the photo back on the shelf behind the candle. The air around her felt heavier. She blinked against tears as one more memory returned—her own words, bitter and childish, rising again from that day as they walked back to the car:*

*"I hate you, Dad! You always do what Mom wants—never what we want."*

Knees aching in front of the tattered, dust-covered bookcase full of frozen memories, Sky wiped the tears from her cheeks and drew in slow, steady breaths. She needed to pull herself together.

But the words echoed—*I hate you, Dad*—and now, for the first time, she understood the weight of them.

She saw him clearly in her mind: the quiet strength, the way he looked at her like she was the center of his world. The man who showed up, day after day, even when no one showed up for him.

And still, like her mother, she'd left.

The memory of his expression that day—just a flicker of pain he tried to hide—gnawed at her. That moment had probably cut deeper than all her mother's cruelty. Her mother's barbs were expected. But hers? Hers came from the one person he loved without question.

Sky pressed her palm flat against the shelf, grounding herself.

She needed to talk to him—really talk—about why she left. About the silence she left in her wake. About the words she couldn't take back, and the ones she never had the courage to say.

It wouldn't erase the pain. But maybe, when the time came, it could start to wash some of it away—regret, guilt, distance, misunderstood anger.

Maybe there was still room for recovery. For forgiveness. To let go of shame.

# Burned to the Ground

Tired of fielding questions from every staff member wandering into the breakroom for a fire update, Kaley left without a word, the guilt about her mother gnawing at her. She tried to shove it down—tried to stay focused—but it swirled in her chest like smoke.

She pivoted in the corridor and nearly collided with a child in a wheelchair. Catching herself, she muttered an apology and kept moving, heading toward her boss's office with no real plan other than *go.*

Minutes later, after weaving through the hospital's maze of halls in her steady, deliberate, carbon-limbed rhythm, she reached the office. Relief hit her at the sight of Jim—the man she'd always said looked more suited to mopping floors than running a customer service department.

"Jim, I have to get my mom out of her house. It's in the fire's path," she said, without preamble.

She didn't wait for his answer. Didn't care. She spun on her carbon and ambled out just as fast as she'd ambled in.

As the door clicked shut behind her, she thought she heard him shout, *"I thought you already left!"*

Back at her workstation, she spotted Mia helping a patient. Kaley opened the door without hesitation. Mia turned, her expression flashing immediate annoyance. Kaley knew better—interrupting during registration was a HIPAA landmine—but she didn't give a shit. Not now.

"Sorry, Mia. I'm leaving. I have to get my mom out. The fire's coming for her place."

The patient, clearly irritated by the disruption, softened—her scowl shifting into something closer to shock.

Mia nodded, her voice steady. "Okay, Kaley. I'll tell Jani what's going on."

Kaley smirked at the nickname—*Jani,* her private theory that Jim was a janitor in disguise. "Thanks, but no need. I already told him."

She turned to go, but Mia called out, "Let me know if you need anything!"

At her desk, Kaley logged out, threw her blue nylon pack over her shoulder, and started toward the parking lot. Her gait, practiced and strong, moved with the rhythm of a seasoned lumberjack.

Still, somewhere deep in the back of her mind, the guilt-soaked corners she didn't like to acknowledge—*she found herself hoping the manufactured home community where she and her mother lived was already gone.*

Burned to the ground.

# Nightmare

Teddy sat nervously in the deputy's car, words spilling out faster than his brain could filter them.

"There's a rear exit not many people know about. It dumps out onto Bear Creek Greenway. The gate's a pain in the ass to open—blackberry bushes I can't seem to kill off or control."

The deputy shot him a look. "What is it with this development and the gates? You should get them fixed."

Teddy bristled, his nerves flaring, bordering on anger. "You think? If the owners of this goddamned park gave me the budget I've been asking for, you wouldn't have needed a truck to yank the damn gate out of the ground. I've been fighting with that piece-of-shit gate for years."

He caught himself, exhaled, and added, "Sorry. Bit of a sore spot. Turn left up here."

The deputy gave a small shake of his head and turned the wheel.

"I didn't mean to give you crap," he said. "This fire has everyone on edge. It's bad—and getting worse. Your park's directly in the path. Fire crews are doing everything they can to steer it, but it's not working. Not yet."

Teddy went quiet, mind spinning back to his family. *Where the hell is my phone?*

"What's your name, officer?" he asked after a moment.

"Deputy Morrow. Jason Morrow. Call me Jason, if you want."

"I'm Theodore Daley. But everyone calls me Teddy."

"Alright, Teddy. Here's what we'll do—I'll take one side of the street, you take the other. Knock on every door. If someone answers, tell them they have to evacuate. Lives are at risk.

Understood?"

"Got it. What if no one answers?"

"Good question. Knock harder. Yell. If there's still no response, move on. We have to assume the place is empty. There's no time to go inside and check. It sucks, but that's the reality right now."

Morrow pulled off a smooth three-point turn and stopped the car, now facing the entrance of the community.

"I'm leaving the car here while we knock. I'll move it every five or six houses. I don't want it too far away. I may need it to transport someone to the bus."

Teddy unbuckled and jumped out, slamming the door behind him.

"There's one resident with mobility issues," he said. "Retired. Lives with their kid. I don't think she's bedridden, but she might need help."

"Which house?"

"Elderberry Street. First street inside the gate, but the last one we'll reach."

"Alright. Point it out when we get there—we'll handle it together. Speed's everything. And if you think someone's home but not answering, come find me."

Teddy gave a dry, half-laugh. "Hah. Most of these folks hit the road already. The rest are probably asleep or glued to their TVs, totally unaware. I wonder if local news or radio is even getting through."

"There are alerts," Morrow replied. "But they're not foolproof. Too many variables."

"You're telling me," Teddy muttered. "A good old-fashioned air-raid siren through the valley could solve a lot of this."

Morrow left his car door open and stepped across the street toward the first house. He turned back with one last instruction.

"Don't forget—if people don't drive, tell them to get to the bus at the entrance. If they can't walk, I'll drive them. And keep count—bus holds about forty. If it fills up, I'll request another."

"Got it, Deputy." Teddy's voice stiffened slightly. *Jason* felt too casual. *Deputy* carried authority—something these residents would listen to.

As he walked up the sidewalk toward another cookie-cutter home, Teddy's mind flicked back again to his missing phone. Where the hell did I leave it?

# Takeoff

Mel steered Betsy toward their second landing of the day after releasing another well-placed load of retardant in the destructor's path. The fire, driven wild by unrelenting winds, continued to rage—but at least it was trending in the direction fire crews wanted, thanks in part to the strategic drops from Mel and the rest of the ATU pilots.

John Dennison, lead pilot for the Oregon Department of Forestry and someone Mel deeply respected, was calling perfect shots from the sky, directing the tankers with calm precision.

Bringing the aircraft to a stop for refueling and reloading, Mel unbuckled and rose from her seat.

"I'm stretching my legs this stop, Deuce. Mind staying put for the next one?"

"Aye aye, captain." Deuce gave a lazy salute as Mel exited the cockpit and made her way into the cargo bay.

She paced the bay, rolling her shoulders and shaking out her arms, the stiffness in her lower back nagging with each step. She paused near the bulkhead, planted a foot on a crate, and leaned into a deep hamstring stretch. The tightness flared—a familiar burn from years of softball and a body that didn't bounce back like it used to, though she refused to give age any credit for it.

She listened to the murmur of the ground crew outside, using their rhythm as her clock. She stretched, hands to feet. Her thoughts drifted—to the fire, to the playoff game in Portland she might miss, to the Medford field complex directly in the fire's path. She hoped the blaze wouldn't touch it, though *nothing felt certain anymore.*

Mel tried to stay present, but it was hard today. She wouldn't be flying forever. Her mother was traveling alone. And she... *she wasn't sure she wanted to be alone forever either.*

She moved to the cargo wall, planted her palms against the metal, and stepped back into a deep stretch. Her calves burned—comfortably. Until—

"Mel, you're gonna want to see this."

She straightened, muttered a curse, and moved toward the cockpit. The navigator stood aside, and she slid into the pilot's seat, eyeing Deuce.

"What's up? We've still got about ten minutes."

Deuce pointed out the window, chin raised.

"In the parking lot. Isn't that your pickup?"

Mel followed his gaze past the busy tarmac to the fenced employee lot. She tilted her head, squinting. Across her truck's hood and side, huge letters had been scrawled in red spray paint. *Bitch* stood out clearly. The rest was harder to make out from the distance.

"That motherfucker," she muttered, shaking her head. "Unbelievable."

"Looks like Johnson didn't take the firing too well," Deuce offered cautiously.

"You think?"

Mel dropped back into the seat, calm but seething, and placed her headset on with exaggerated care.

"Swinson, this is Mel. Come in."

"Hey, Mel. Just a few more minutes and we'll have you back in the air."

"Copy that. Where's Johnson?"

A pause. Mel arched an eyebrow at Deuce as the silence dragged.

"You're not gonna believe this," Swinson finally said. "He made a couple calls after you went up, went ballistic when he

235

didn't like what he heard. Screamed at management, trashed the upstairs pilot's office, and stormed out."

Mel laughed—short, sharp, disbelieving.

"Figures. Do me a favor, Swinson. Look at the parking lot. You know my truck—the Raptor."

"Yeah, I know it. Why?"

"Take a peek and then call the police. I need to report some property damage."

Another pause. She imagined Swinson walking to the second-story window.

"Holy shit, Mel."

"Yep. Call it in."

"I'm sorry. I'll take care of it."

"Don't worry about it. Trucks can be fixed. I've been wanting to check out the new RAM 1500 anyway. Guess I've got a reason now."

She smiled, gave a nod to Deuce, and cinched her harness tight. As she gripped the yoke with the fire of a twenty-year-old plebe, she started humming *Ain't Gonna Drown* by Elle King.

"Tower, this is ATU 2 requesting permission for takeoff. Over."

# You Only Get One Life

"Come in, Paducah. This is Chief."

"Paducah here—go ahead, Chief."

"Still on Old Stage Road. First couple of drops from the tanker were spot-on."

A pause. Paducah was likely managing chaos from all sides.

"Roger that. From my vantage, too. Dennison's going to keep the tanker hitting this line, depending on the wind. Goal is to steer it toward Old Stage Road."

"Tell him I already resigned—he doesn't need to chase me off by pushing the fire my way."

Chief Wilson winced. Another joke that didn't land. His timing had gone to hell lately. He thought, maybe I really do need to disappear into the woods for a while.

Fridays used to mean something—relaxation, laughter, and plans. Not anymore. The only place where he felt any real comfort was at the station or anywhere outdoors.

Staring at the smoke but not seeing it, his mind drifted to more regret. Life at the station on Fridays had its own rhythm. Lighter, more relaxed—unless the engines were out nonstop. The crew made weekend plans: fishing, camping, rafting the Rogue, skiing Mt. Ashland, or just getting lost on a trail. This valley never ran out of ways to breathe.

Wilson often imagined his perfect day—hiking until the legs ached, then a glass of red at one of the Rogue Valley's vineyards, a charcuterie board, good company. A laugh that wasn't forced. A partner who didn't hate him, trusted him, wanted to be with him. But all that lived in dreams now. His wife had no use for the outdoors—or for him. Just her books, her wine, and her distance.

*This particular Friday had him restless. He was already looking forward to seeing Sky on Sunday evening. She gave him a reason not to burn out and fade away. That morning, he kept checking his phone, hoping for a message from her. Nothing. By three, he got a call from the parents of her friend Jodi—explaining their weekend camping trip to Kangaroo Lake. He'd asked a dozen questions before giving the okay, then hung up wondering if he should head there himself. Knowing she'd be furious if he showed up there, he wrestled with letting go. She was growing up. But this soon?*

*The station buzzed with activity. Warm weather meant open bays, clean rigs, loud voices bouncing off concrete. A distraction. Not enough. He couldn't shake the unease.*

*He checked his phone again. No message. Maybe she left a note at home. She was supposed to.*

*At 1530, he gathered the paperwork on his desk, made a few neat stacks, stood, and pushed his chair in. On his way out, he reminded the crew to stay safe, stay sharp, and enjoy the weekend.*

*Fifteen minutes later, he pulled into the driveway. Sky's paddleboard and gear were gone. Good sign. He parked, stepped inside—and there she was. His wife. Sitting in her chair with a book in one hand, a nearly empty glass of wine in the other. He said hi. She barely looked up. That was fine. Silence was better than contempt.*

*He checked the kitchen for a note. Nothing. His stomach tightened. Upstairs, Sky's room looked like she'd attempted a clean—but no note on the desk, nightstand, or dresser. The knots grew tighter.*

*Dreading the confrontation, he went back downstairs.*

*"Laura, excuse me, is there a note from Sky about camping? I told her she needed to leave one with specifics."*

*She sipped her wine, nose buried in the book.*

"Laura, I told Sky she needed to leave a note. Did she give it to you?"

She drained the glass, stood, and brushed past him, whispering, "You're a fraud."

Bordering on anger he responded, "excuse me?"

She ignored him, filled the glass to the brim with the rest of the bottle, slammed the empty bottle on the counter, and returned to her chair. Sat. Read.

"Is there a note from Sky?" he asked again, forcing calm into his voice. But the storm was building. Nothing.

He snapped. "Listen, Laura, keep pretending I don't exist—fine. But do it after you answer my question. Did Sky leave a note?"

She looked up. "I'm sorry, did you say something?"

He gritted his teeth. "I told her she could go with Jodi, but she needed to text me or leave a note. She didn't text, so I'm asking—did she leave a note? She always follows through with me."

"Why didn't you ask me before you told her she could go?"

A laugh escaped him, bitter and sharp. "You're joking, right? Passive aggression isn't usually your style, that's my department. WHERE IS THE NOTE, LAURA?"

She lifted her glass, took a sip. Laughed that nervous, fragile laugh she gave when cornered, nervous, afraid. Said nothing.

"I didn't ask you," he continued, "because you never give two shits about what she does. If she'd asked, you would've guilted her into staying. You'd have lectured her about unreliable people, men who only want one thing. Then you'd tell her to fetch your wine—or spike your coffee, assuming you made it out of bed this morning before she left. Which you probably didn't."

He stopped. Not because he was done—but because he

*wasn't going to waste another word on someone who'd already checked out of their own life.*

*He paused, breathing through the anger. "Let's cut the shit. This is about Sky. Just give me the note."*

*"There is no note, you goddamned Neanderthal. Like me, she doesn't care what you say. Now leave me the fuck alone. Unless you're here to suck up and cook me dinner. Maybe do that little baton-twirling routine—you know, the one where you pretend you're too dumb to keep the baton in your hands. That might make me laugh."*

*The anger surged through him. But for once during an argument with her his mind stayed clear. He stepped closer. She tensed. He saw it in her posture—unmistakable fear. Not of him hurting her, but his sudden calm.*

*"Go ahead," she sneered. "Hit me, Chief Wilson. You'll regret it."*

*He shook his head. "I don't know what I did to make your world so miserable. And I don't care anymore. Let a therapist sort you out."*

*She stared at him, silent.*

*Almost grinning, moving his head back and forth in a slow deliberate motion of disbelief, he responded. "You know that little note you wrote on the fridge, 'You Only Get One Life.' You're right. You do. So, take yours and leave. I am begging you. Leave So Sky and I can try and salvage what's left of ours."*

He glanced at the clock. If he was going to make it to the lake before dark, he had to move. He turned toward the stairs, resisting the urge to look back at her one last time. Laura no longer deserved a second glance. One way or another, he was through.

*Upstairs, he changed clothes, feeling the weight lift off his chest—an internal tectonic shift. For the first time in years, he felt free.*

His phone buzzed. Paducah.

He picked up. "Hello?"

"Chief? You, okay? You sound… different."

He smiled, then sighed. "Yeah. Just tired. This fire. My daughter. Retirement. I picked the worst day in history to resign."

"You're serious?"

"As soon as the commissioners and the board accept the letter, yeah."

"Can they refuse?"

"They can. But they won't. My contract's up in two weeks. I've got five months of vacation stored. And if a chief quits publicly, it makes things look bad. They'll try to talk me out of it. Not this time."

"Damn," Paducah said. "Okay. Well, if you hear me screw anything up, call me. I want your job, but if I don't handle this fire correctly, the board won't approve me."

"You're doing everything right, Paducah. You've got this. And you'll get the job."

He ended the call and slid the phone into his pocket.

Outside, the glow of the fire painted the valley like a war zone. The night would be long. Destructive. Unforgiving.

But his thoughts were with Sky. And for once, only Sky.

# Belonged

With raw emotions still pressing at the edges of her composure, Sky decided to put off going upstairs. She wasn't ready to face her old bedroom—not yet. The idea of finding it untouched felt impossible, and the thought of it gutted or stripped bare like her mother's chair was worse. She wasn't ready for that kind of confirmation. Not today.

Instead, she turned toward the laundry room. Something easy. Practical. A task she could wrap her hands around. She told herself it would be simple—grab supplies, clean what needed cleaning, keep moving.

But the moment she opened the cabinet beneath the sink, the past surged forward.

There it sat—the red plastic bucket. Scuffed, sun-faded in places, but instantly recognizable. Her mother had packed it with industrial precision: sprays, brushes, gloves, a sponge still warped from its last use. Everything except rags. *Rags belonged in their own drawer, neatly folded.*

Sky's stomach clenched. She hadn't expected to find it. She hadn't expected the sudden rush of memory.

*She was eleven when her mother handed it to her. No explanation. No smile. Just the weight of it, heavy and unwelcome. You're old enough now. Start pulling your weight.*

*Sky touched the edge of the bucket, then drew her hand back, as if it burned. So much for simple. So much for easy. Even here, even in the most ordinary corners of the house, the past waited. And it hurt.*

*"It's time you started pulling your weight around here, Sky. You're cleaning the bathrooms. When you're done, dust and vacuum the living room."*

*Sky remembered gripping the red plastic bucket, her arms aching beneath its weight—unopened bottles of soap and disinfectant sloshing inside. She'd never cleaned a bathroom before. Her mom never showed her how. The only things Sky had seen her do were rinse her own wine glass or put away a dish or two. The house stayed neat, but not because of her.*

*Sky remembered her dad—the vacuum hum on weekends, the long-handled brush and rags disappearing into the bathroom, the steady rhythm of someone who cleaned with care.*

*Her first attempt ended in tears. She cried until her body gave up. Water pooled around the base of the tub, soaking every towel she could find. The mop was missing—or maybe there never was one—so she wrapped disposable cleaning sheets around a plastic broom and shoved them across the floor, again and again. The trash filled quickly with paper towels and rags.*

*Thirty minutes in, red-eyed and exhausted, Sky stood in the doorway, proud of her effort. The knobs sparkled. The air stung with chemicals.*

*She called down to her mother.*

*"All done! Want to see?"*

*No answer.*

*"Mom! I finished!"*

*Still nothing.*

*Resentment pressed on her shoulders like a heavy blanket. She trudged downstairs and found her mother in her chair, wine in hand, a book in her lap.*

*"Mom, I'm finished with the bathroom. Should I vacuum now?"*

*Her mother set her glass and book down with a smirk.*

*"I guarantee, young lady, that the bathroom isn't even close to finished. Follow me."*

*Sky trailed behind her upstairs.*

*"You think you're done?" her mother scoffed, not waiting for an answer. "I see grime in the tub."*

*She lifted the toilet seat. "Hair. Dirt. A ring. Wet floor behind the toilet." Her voice sliced, each critique a blade.*

*Then the sink. "The sink's a joke. Don't say you're done until the bathroom is spotless."*

*She swept past Sky, back into the hallway.*

*"But I don't know how…" Sky whispered. "I did my best. Dad would show me."*

*Her mother stopped, turned sharp and fast.*

*"No one taught me either. Use that brain of yours and figure it out. Your father's an idiot for always trying to teach you. You'll forget his words. But you won't forget this."*

*Sky stood alone, the sour sting of chemicals in her nose, blinking back tears—not from the harsh words, but from hearing her dad dragged through the mud again. He would've shown her. He would've helped.*

*She looked around. The bathroom was cleaner than it had been in months. She knew—she used it every day. But if she had to redo it, she'd do it her way.*

*She returned to her room, unplugged her clock radio, and carried it to the bathroom. She set it on the counter, plugged it in, and adjusted the dial until her favorite station played. Keith Urban filled the air.*

*Smiling for the first time all day, she snapped on rubber gloves, opened the medicine cabinet, and pulled out her mother's pink toothbrush.*

*Forty-one songs later—she counted—Keith Urban played again. Sky ran the hot water until steam curled from the drain. She dipped the toothbrush briefly, waved it dry, and slid it back into its slot.*

*She unplugged the radio and carried it back to her room.*

*Returning, she cleared the trash, the rags, the bottles. She*

244

stood in the doorway, admiring the bathroom. It sparkled. She almost took a picture.

Downstairs, her mother was asleep in her chair, book on her lap, wineglass empty on the table.

"Mom," Sky whispered. No response. She hated waking her, hated how sharp things got when she was startled.

"Laura," she said louder.

Her mother stirred, wiped the corner of her mouth, then straightened.

"What, Sky? Jesus! Can't you stop bugging me?"

Sky flinched—but stood her ground.

"I finished the bathroom, Laura. It's ready for inspection. I'd like you to see it before I do my homework."

The use of her first name landed like a dropped plate. Her mother blinked, caught off guard. She smiled—but not kindly.

"I already checked it."

"It's been over two hours."

Her mother's eyes narrowed. Then she stood.

"All right, Sky. Let's see how big of a disappointment you still are."

"I'm confident, Laura, that you'll find it spotless. Not sure who cleaned it last—but mine's better."

Sky hated the potential dig at her dad. But saying "spotless," her mother's own word, made it worth it.

She stood outside the door as Laura inspected. Finger across the tub. Sink. Toilet. The soap dish. She checked the trash, even the liner.

Finally, she brushed past Sky and muttered, "This is sufficient. Now leave me alone."

"Yes, Laura. Enjoy your alone time. I'm going to my room to do schoolwork."

"I don't care what you do, as long as you don't bother me."

Sky didn't flinch. She'd expected it. But it still hurt.

*She climbed the stairs, closed her bedroom door behind her, and whispered thanks to whatever force had made her mother forget about vacuuming and dusting. As she sat on her bed, Sky wondered what time Laura would brush her teeth tonight.*
*And if she'd notice that her toothbrush didn't taste quite the same.*

Despite her effort to hold onto the memory of becoming more independent, Sky felt it slip away as quickly as it came. She turned from the weight of upstairs—of her childhood bedroom—and moved back into the living room. Something about the shelves bothered her. They needed order.

She began removing the photos and a couple of candles—laying each item out in neat rows across the hardwood floor, precisely where they'd return.

She grabbed a bright lime-green microfiber cloth from a stack of three folded on the shelf beside the cleaning bucket. First pass: dry dust. She moved methodically, shelf by shelf. When finished, she swapped for the pale blue cloth, sprayed her father's homemade Dawn-vinegar-water mix, and wiped the wood clean.

The scent hit her—sharp, familiar. A thousand childhood memories stirred. She blinked them away. Not now.

Satisfied with the result, she returned each item to its place—except one.

The photo from Crater Lake. It remained on the floor.

It didn't belong. Not anymore. The image, half-hidden behind a candle, looked out of place in a house already purged of Laura's chair and presence. Sky stared at it, unsure why her father had left it. She'd ask him—eventually.

She thought back to something she'd once overheard while homeless in a park in San Francisco. *A woman had said to her friend, "I think of happy things, surround myself with people who make me feel good, and get rid of what makes me sad. Yes, I'm selfish. But that's the point—when I'm happy, those around me feel better too."*

Sky hadn't understood it then—how selfishness could equal happiness. But now, years later, it made a strange kind of sense. Being with her dad had always made her feel safe, like she mattered, like his smile existed because she was in the room. Maybe choosing what stayed in her life—and what didn't—was the first step to healing.

She picked up the photo, carried it into the kitchen, and stepped on the trash can pedal. The lid popped open. She dropped it in—image side up—and whispered, "Bye, Laura. I hope you find a bit of happiness in your life."

The lid clanked shut. Something loosened inside her chest. A heaviness, dislodged. A quiet calm settled into the space it left behind.

Sky returned to the bookcase, adjusted a few of the remaining items. They fit better now. She moved to the coffee table, then the end tables, before grabbing the vacuum from the laundry room.

She made quick work of the hardwood floors, then crossed into the small dining area and finally the kitchen. Everything she touched felt a bit better, cleaner, loved—like someone had taken care of it. Her father's touch lingered in every corner. Even if the yard had been left to weeds and dust, the inside still had soul.

She smiled at a toothbrush nestled in the cleaning bucket. Pulling it out, she sprayed around the faucet knobs with the familiar solution and scrubbed them clean. The rhythm calmed her.

When finished, she draped the used rags over the laundry hamper and headed back to the kitchen. As she pulled out the trash bag, she caught sight of the photo again—cracked glass slicing down the middle, right between her mother and father, separating her from the rest of the family.

Sky didn't remember the glass breaking when she tossed it in, but the symbolism wasn't lost on her. She chuckled. Seemed about right.

She passed through the laundry room, carried the bag outside, and tossed it in the can. Ash flecked the lid. She looked up—toward the northwest, toward Talent—and read the wind. Still blowing away from them. A small relief.

Back inside, she slid a new bag into the bin and gave the downstairs a final once-over. It looked... peaceful.

Still avoiding the stairs, she wandered again into the laundry room, searching for something else to clean—but found nothing. Then, something caught her eye. A wooden box, oak-colored and unfamiliar, tucked beside the coat pegs on a shelf above. About the size of a recipe tin.

She lifted it with curiosity, cracked open the lid—and froze.

Inside were sticky notes. Dozens of them. It looked like it was every note she had ever written her dad, from the time she could barely scribble letters, all carefully saved.

A smile crept across her face, stretching wider and wider before it broke into fresh tears.

Sky held the box close, her breath catching in her throat. She didn't know he kept them. All this time. Every little message, every "I love you, Daddy," every silly drawing or reminder for school supplies and groceries.

She leaned against the wall, clutching the box, and let the tears come—not out of pain, but from something softer. Something healing.

For the first time since coming home, she felt like she belonged.

# Dark

Kaley guided her car into the Dutch Bros drive-thru, tapping her fingers on the steering wheel and bouncing her left carbon limb like a drumstick. Patience wasn't her strength—especially not today. A teenage broista zigzagged between cars, tablet in hand, taking orders like she ran the place. The girl didn't look a day over fourteen.

Kaley smirked. *Do they still call them broistas? Or has the Woke Agenda hit Dutch Bros too? Perista? NonBinista?* She chuckled, amused by her own nonsense. "God, I must be getting old," she muttered.

She glanced out the windshield at the sky. Smoke billowed thick and ominous, darkening the afternoon. Part of her felt guilty for sitting in line for a coffee. The other part—deep in the recesses of her scarred brain—felt something like hope.

Hope that her mother won't survive.

It wasn't something she could ever admit out loud, but the thought of being free from obligation, from the chains of that house and that woman, stirred something close to relief. *Would that make me a bad person? Or just free?*

She thought of insurance. *Does the old bat even have coverage?* Maybe the fire would wipe the slate clean. No more filth. No more chain-smoking. No more bitterness to inhale every day she walked in the door.

Her father had died in a whiskey-fueled accident with a hay baler when she was nine. Her mother spiraled after that—booze, pills, useless men. Kaley survived thanks to the Boys & Girls Club and a few good teachers. And eventually, the military. Now, she lived on carbon legs because of the very country she tried to serve—because someone, somewhere, decided oil was worth more than soldiers.

A voice pierced her thoughts.

"How's your day, ma'am?"

The broista's cheerfulness was like a slap to the face. Kaley winced. *Damn, I need to get laid.* She shook her head, unsure if the girl noticed.

"I'll take a small blended Cocomo—half sweet, two extra shots."

Kaley had spent weeks perfecting her drink. Too sweet at first, but the half-sweet tweak and two shots of espresso mellowed it out. She considered asking for a quarter sweet. *Would they even do that?*

"This fire is sure scary, huh?"

Kaley stared at the girl's bright smile, her mind still on sugar ratios. "Yeah... hey, listen. I usually get half-sweet, but it's still too much. Could you do a quarter?"

"Of course!" The girl tapped her tablet. "Paying with the app today?"

Kaley lifted her phone, payment screen ready to be scanned. "Yep."

As the scanner beeped, she glanced at the two cars ahead, smoke curling through the sky like a warning.

"So, do you live around here?"

"No," Kaley lied. She didn't recognize the girl and didn't want to be recognized.

"Me neither. I live in Central Point."

Kaley's brain begged for the cars to move. "Isn't there a Dutch closer to home?"

"There is, but I'm waiting for an opening. I don't mind—it's only a fifteen-minute drive."

Kaley nodded and prayed for silence. Her morning had started with a podcast on manifesting—some nonsense about *vibrational vortexes.* She clung to the idea anyway. *Why not? At this point, I'll take any hope, woo-woo or not.*

The car ahead moved. The broista beamed. "Have a good day! Stay safe!"

Kaley exhaled hard as the girl skipped to the next vehicle. She pulled forward, finally able to relax into the anticipation of her quarter-sweet coffee.

Most of the traffic headed north—away from the fire. Kaley drove south *into* it. Cars flowed endlessly in the other direction, like salmon swimming upstream to survive.

She kept her eyes on the road. The smoke was disorienting, and her PTSD flared with it. Every instinct screamed: *run, hide, get out.* Her darkness whispered that someone else—*anyone* else—could get her mother out.

That maintenance guy. What's his name again? Always too helpful. Too nice. That's a red flag.

She laughed bitterly. Nice people always want something. Usually flesh. Another lesson from Mom.

Kaley hit the turn signal and waited in the center lane. Her mind drifted.

She thought of the bullying. The tattered clothes. The smell. The pity. Her drunk dad. Her broken mom. Her runny nose and stolen lunches. *White trash,* they called her. The school handed her a diploma out of mercy. An Army recruiter saw her pain, saw her potential, and offered structure. A way out.

And here she was. *Going back in.*

She crossed the road into Payne Creek Estates. The gate had been torn off, tossed aside like one of Godzilla's toys. A rusted city bus sat idling near the entrance. A few people sat inside—faces pale, scared. Kaley turned onto Elderberry Street.

Please be gone. Please be gone.

The home still stood. Ash fell in thick, quiet flurries. Everything was coated in gray. Still, for a split second, Kaley thought it looked beautiful. Like snow.

She parked. Hesitated with the key. *Leave it in for a quick escape?* No. She pocketed it, got out, and hobbled toward the house.

The screen door stuck, like always. She jiggled it free, unlocked the door, and stepped inside.

A different kind of smoke hit her—thick and stale. Cigarette smoke. Somehow worse than outside. The TV blared. She hoped her mom had made it to the bus.

No such luck.

"Mom? You in your room?"

Kaley headed down the hallway. Curtains drawn. Air thick. Cigarette stubs everywhere. Ashtrays overflowing.

"Mom, I'm home. They sent me back because of the fire."

From the bedroom: "What?"

Kaley stepped in. Her mother sat reclined, cigarette in her mouth, coffee mug in hand. Whiskey-scented steam rose off it.

"The Almeda fire, Mom. Talent's burning. Phoenix is next. The fire's coming. We need to leave."

Her mother snorted. "I haven't seen flames. You're just trying to steal my money. Just like your drunk-ass father."

Kaley clenched her fists. How can someone be this cruel?

"Mom, this house is going to burn to the ground. Do you want to be in it?"

"I'd rather burn than let you steal from me."

Kaley laughed. "Money? You're broke. *I* pay for everything."

"You goddamned liar. I paid for this house. I paid for your car. Your education. Everything. You haven't done a damn thing—just like your father."

Life insurance paid for the house. The car's in your name, yeah—but I pay for the fuel, the upkeep, the meds, the groceries... everything.

Kaley stared at her, unsure whether to scream or leave the

ungrateful, pathetic bitch.

She walked over and turned the TV off.

The remote slammed into the back of her head.

Kaley turned slowly. "Get up, Mom. I might be on carbon legs, but I can still kick your ass."

"Don't touch me. You're not getting my treasures."

"What are you even talking about?"

Kaley stepped closer. "You don't want to die in a fire, Mom. It's pain you can't imagine."

Her mother didn't reply. Kaley's mind flared with memory—heat, pressure, the moment her legs disappeared in a blaze of white light.

Then, in a flash, her mother lunged.

A shoulder slammed into Kaley's chest. Her chin cracked against something hard. Balance gone. Her prosthetics wobbled—then gave way to gravity.

She fell.

The back of her head hit something sharp and merciless.

Everything went dark.

# Say No More

Radio chatter filled the rig—constant, frantic, and rising like heat. Every frequency was overrun with urgent calls for more: more fire crews, more cops, more hands, more help. Chief Wilson leaned against the side of his rig and looked skyward; the horizon blurred in smoke. He turned the volume down on his two-way, just enough to still catch the cadence of Paducah's voice rising through the chaos—steady and sure.

She was holding it down. Hell, she was running it. Barking orders with the kind of confidence you couldn't teach.

He smiled, warmth crashing around inside his chest. He'd prepped her for this. All those years. And now, she stood in the middle of the worst disaster they'd seen in a decade, perhaps ever, leading like she was born for it.

It made him think of Sky. Everything did today.

*The Waze app on his phone, perched in the dash cradle, showed under two hours to Kangaroo Lake. He pushed the speed up to eighty while the freeway lasted. Once he hit the county roads, he'd have to slow way down—tight curves, blind corners. He wanted time to pass faster than his tires could spin.*

*He turned the radio on. The Stones. Of course. He laughed out loud and shut it off before the first chorus. Never understood the obsession. Jagger sounded like a jackrabbit caught in high beams. His mind wasn't interested in noise anyway. Not today.*

*He pressed SEND again on Sky's number. Straight to voicemail. Same as the last six tries. No reception up at Kangaroo. He knew that. Still, he kept trying.*

*They'd been to the lake a dozen times—fishing, paddleboarding, camping. Just the two of them. And then one day, everything changed. Laura accused him of being too close to their daughter. It wasn't just hurtful. It was dangerous. He couldn't even look at Sky the same way after that, afraid someone else might misinterpret it. Afraid, Laura might take it to the police. She knew exactly what to say to ruin him.*

*Sky never understood why the trips stopped. Why he retreated even further into his work. She only knew that he did.*

*So, she found her own escapes. Friends. Freedom. The open world. And now this trip.*

*He regretted not divorcing Laura the second she made the accusation. Maybe short-term damage would've succumbed to the long haul. Maybe Sky would still trust him. Maybe she wouldn't have walked out like her mother.*

*The interstate exit to Kangaroo was ten minutes out.*

*His thoughts drifted. Back to that backyard BBQ. Three years into the job, still new to the fire service. The chief invited everyone, hoping to climb the ladder—sixty people, easy. He remembered Laura standing near the grill, beer in hand, ballcap on, looking like she didn't give a damn what anyone thought. Natural beauty. Milk-bottle skin. No makeup. Just effortless.*

*He'd always envied the guys who could move through a crowd like sharks—confident, charming, always closing the deal. He was more like a catfish, stuck in the mud, hoping someone would fall in front of him, unable to resist.*

*But that night, Laura swam right to him. And for the life of him, he never understood why.*

*The marriage came quick. Vegas. A long weekend and a short memory. The ballcap charm? Just a mask. The real Laura obsessed over her appearance, buried herself in mirrors and self-loathing. His reassurances only made it worse.*

*At home, he became invisible. Or worse—wrong. Always wrong. Nothing he said or did ever hit the mark. So, he buried himself in work, in service, in Sky. Anything to stay away from Laura.*

*He thought love was supposed to be a refuge. A place to drop your armor. Instead, it was a war zone. Years of it. Until numbness replaced the pain.*

*If it weren't for Sky, he would've gone out in flames. Literally. He'd taken risks—stupid ones—on the job. Always hoping one of them would end him. A quick death wrapped in heroism. That's the only way he ever saw himself escaping.*

*But Sky kept him tethered. She always had.*

A loud voice shattered his memory quicksand.

"Chief, Paducah here. Over."

The voice pulled him out of spiraling thoughts. He smelled the smoke—acrid, complex, thick with melted plastic and scorched wood. Years of work gave his nose the same precision as a sommelier's.

He keyed the mic. "Go ahead, Paducah. I'm here."

"Thanks, Chief. I need a huge favor. I know you'll say no if you have to, but… I haven't been able to reach my sister. She's got a place in Phoenix—Payne Creek Estates. It's right in the fire's path."

Wilson didn't hesitate. He cut in with his best attempt at a Monty Python voice: "Say no more! Send me the address. I'm heading there now."

# Yes, Please!

Airborne again, Mel noticed her hands on the yoke. Muscle memory took over. The plane moved with her, like an extension of breath and bone. Her mind drifted as chatter filled the headset—background noise at this point. The calls blurred together. She let her body do what it knew, the movements burned so deep into her brain they required no thought. Like riding a bike. Except the current bike weighed two hundred tons and dropped fire retardant from the sky.

She was one of the best—no question. And for a moment, instead of feeling pride, she felt a strange emptiness. *Why did I walk away? Why did I retire?* The question echoed where joy should've been.

Her eyes scanned the valley below. The subdivision came into view—her mother's home sat somewhere in that neat little grid, square in the fire's path. The flames didn't care about roads or property lines. They carved their own route, pushed by wind barreling down from the Siskiyous and funneled hard by the surrounding ridges. The retardant helped steer it, but not enough. Not today.

Roaring flames devoured everything: homes, trailers, fences, barns. Tires exploded. Aluminum wheels turned into puddles of gleaming metal. Chaos with an unrelenting pulse.

She flipped the release switch and felt the shudder of the load dropping from the belly of the plane. Somewhere below, a line of red cut through smoke and flame—at least, she hoped it did. The tank was empty.

So was she.

Darkness crept over the valley. Not night—just smoke swallowing light. She guided Betsy back to base, aching everywhere. Her joints, her back, her thoughts. She caught a glimpse of the sunset's last stand through the haze. Red turned gray, then black.

Touching down smooth, she taxied in and shut Betsy down. The ground crew swarmed. She handed over controls and climbed out to a few high fives and relieved looks.

Mel wasn't sure she'd fly tomorrow. Part of her wanted to. Part of her wanted to disappear. Another fire—burning hard northeast—had already claimed more property and was spreading faster than containment could keep up. They might need her again. Might not. Rest-time rules would decide. So would her gut.

She walked toward the flight office, every step heavier than the last. "Shit," she muttered.

"You good, Mel?" someone called out.

"Yeah, just thinking about that last drop," she lied.

She regretted signing the thirty-day contract so quickly. But maybe the time would fly by. *Maybe it's what I need to know if the clouds still call to me louder than the quiet of retirement.* She could always bail. ATU owed her that much.

It appeared they'd saved Medford. At least for now. Talent and Phoenix weren't so lucky. Two towns, all but gone in a single afternoon. Flattened. Scorched. Only pockets of homes and businesses stood—like teeth after a bar fight. No small town had looked this bad since Paradise, CA.

Inside, she thought again about her spray-painted pickup. And the end-of-season bonus. Maybe she'd stay longer if the money looked good. *New truck. Fresh start.*

Or maybe not. She had no clue how long body-shop waitlists were—probably weeks. And with the pickup stuck there getting de-graffitied, she'd need a rental. Which meant getting to the airport. And since she wouldn't have a vehicle, she'd have to hitch a ride.

*Her mom's still overseas. That's out.* The thought of asking

258

someone for a lift—one of the crew, or one of the softball women she kept brushing off—made her jaw tighten.

This is exactly why I don't do friends. No favors. No guilt. No sitting in someone's passenger seat pretending everything's fine while my truck sits behind a shop looking like it lost a fight with a pissed-off spray can.

The whole mess made her think of Kaley.

She hadn't reached out in months—not since retirement. Not even a text. She kept meaning to but always found an excuse. Too busy. Too tired. *Not in the mood to deal with someone else's mess when she was finally enjoying everyday life.*

But this? This was the perfect excuse. Kaley wouldn't care about the graffiti or the truck. Hell, she'd probably have a dark joke lined up before Mel even finished the story. And yeah, Kaley could be a lot—sharp-edged, heavy to mentally carry—but she was real. Honest. A rare thing these days.

Mel sighed. Maybe it's time.

Inside the office, she scanned for Burgeon. No sign.

"Swinson," she said, heading to the front counter, "I'm in a rush. You know if I'm flying tomorrow?"

Swinson held a phone to his ear. "He's across the way with security. Told me to let you know the police got photos of your truck. You're good to take it. Call in tomorrow and he'll give you the rundown on your next twenty-nine days."

Mel wanted to throw him a smart-ass quip but saw he was deep into the call. She nodded, winked, and left.

Out in the lot, she spotted her truck immediately. The driver's side looked untouched. She walked around the front—and stopped.

**Lying Bitch** in big silver block letters scrawled across the hood.

She kept walking. The passenger side shouted:

259

**Honk if you want a Blow! I Am Kinky**

Mel laughed. Deep. Belly. Unfiltered. It rolled through her like a spring flood.

She climbed in, hit the start button, and cranked the radio. She had about thirteen minutes to Phoenix and Kaley's place at Payne Creek Estates.

One of her crewmates drove by, honking, and yelled out their window, "Yes, please!"

Mel let loose.

For the first time in a long time, it felt good to laugh.

# Cathartic

Ash clung to Teddy's boots like guilt. Every step up another sun-warped staircase groaned under his weight, the wood long tortured by southern Oregon summers. He wiped his brow with the back of his sleeve and coughed into his arm. The last window he passed caught his reflection—grimy, gray, and half-suffocating. He'd thought about running back to the shop for a mask, but figured the deputy might give him hell. Instead, he tugged a filthy handkerchief from his back pocket and tied it over his face.

Better than nothing.

He knocked on the glass part of the door. Number thirty-something. So far, two retirees had thanked him. One woman walked straight to the bus without a word. One old man—someone's father, Teddy couldn't remember whose—stood silently until the deputy pulled up and drove him out.

This door didn't open. He knocked again, already turning to leave when it swung open and banged hard against the siding.

A kid stood there barefoot, glazed, and baked out of his mind. "Stay off my porch," he slurred.

Teddy stared. "You mean your *parents'* porch?"

He was tired. Covered in sweat and ash and trying to help. And this stoned little shit was worried about his *porch?* Teddy fought the flash of anger that lit in his chest. For half a second, he considered walking away and letting the flames do the convincing. But his conscience pulled tight.

"Whatever, dude. I'll be fine," the kid mumbled, squinting past Teddy at the smoke-dark sky and the gray film coating the lawn.

Teddy saw the hesitation flicker behind his bloodshot eyes.

"I don't care what you do," Teddy said flatly, "but that deputy over there does. I'm assisting him. Want me to get him over here to explain things?"

Across the street, Deputy Jason waved, mid-stride between houses.

"So?" Teddy asked. "What'll it be?"

The kid blinked. "C'mon, bro. No need for that. I'll grab wallet and phone. Just a second."

Teddy exhaled. The kid darted inside and returned in under thirty seconds.

"What's your name? Anyone else in the house?"

"Tim. Sorry for being a dick. I was mid-Fortnite in a match and didn't want to stop. It's just me—Mom's at work."

Teddy shook his hand, then lifted the handkerchief back into place.

"Alright, Tim. There's a bus at the front of the park. It'll take you to a shelter. Got your phone?"

Tim patted his pocket. "Right here. The cop driving?"

"Nope. Neither of us are. The deputy's got other things to worry about than whether you're high, Tim. Just get on the bus."

Tim chuckled. "Fair enough, bro. I'll text my mom. Let her know I'm okay. Where's the shelter?"

Teddy hadn't asked. He looked across the street. "Hey, Deputy Jason! Where's the bus going?"

Jason, halfway up another porch, turned and called out, "Jackson County Expo!"

Teddy relayed the info. "You hear that, okay?"

"Yep. Thanks, bro. I owe you. When this shit's over, come by. Mom will make dinner, and we can play some Fortnite."

Teddy managed a nod. He had no clue what Fortnite was. A game, obviously. He didn't care. The idea of spending hours in a make-believe world drove him nuts—*waste of time and*

262

*money.* Still, a home-cooked meal didn't sound half bad.

As Tim shuffled off, hoodie pulled over his head, Teddy watched him disappear into the curtain of ash. He glanced across the street—Jason was helping another man off a porch, pointing down the block toward the bus. Always talking. Always explaining.

Teddy scanned the road, trying to count how many had made it on the bus. Maybe a dozen. He had only helped three people so far, or was it four?

He debated running back to the shop—grabbing his pickup, looking for his phone, calling his daughter, his granddaughter. But guilt pinned him in place.

He stopped under the street sign: *Elderberry Street.* Only a few homes left. He looked down and stomped the ash off the toe of his boot.

It didn't help much.

But it felt cathartic.

So, he did it again.

# Call Me Anytime

Sky didn't know where to begin.

She sat at the kitchen counter, elbows on the scratched granite, the same spot where she'd eaten cereal alone more mornings than she could count. She started counting—thirty-three, thirty-four—but stopped. Hundreds, maybe. The number didn't matter. What mattered was it appeared that her dad had kept every single one.

Her throat tightened.

Shuddering at the thought of fleeing home without so much as a simple bye, Sky sobbed—again—losing track of how many times she'd cried since walking back into the house.

Trying to breathe, she moved to the sink and grabbed a glass from the cupboard. The faucet sputtered before spilling clean, cold well water. She drank deep and grateful. Water meant something different now. After sleeping on the street, hustling for clean taps and free café refills in Fog City, she understood water. It meant life.

As a child, she'd spent countless hours playing in it—chasing sticks down creeks, splashing barefoot through irrigation ditches—never once thinking about where it came from or what it meant. Back then, water was just fun. Now, she understood.

She set the empty glass in the sink and stared out the window. The yard was quiet. The sky still dumped ash like the world was burning to the ground—because it was. Her dad wouldn't be back soon. Not with the fire still raging.

Sky opened the fridge. She spotted the white bread—the soft, bad-for-you kind she and her dad always took camping. A loaf of memories. She grabbed the yellow mustard and pulled open the meat drawer. Bologna. Her favorite. Their favorite. Quick, salty, satisfying.

She smiled.

Behind it sat a four-pack of kombucha. Lonely, tucked in the back. Her dad hated kombucha. Too sour, he always said. Sky plucked one out and checked the date—expired by two years. She held it anyway. It must have been hers. Her dad never threw it out.

She shut the fridge and thought about the cans of beer—cold ones her dad saved for hot days after yard work. Sometimes he'd crack a second, take a sip, and mutter, *"Why do I always open a second?"* He drank because he liked the taste, not to forget.

Unlike her mom.

She lined everything up on the counter—bread, mustard, bologna, the expired kombucha—then turned and bolted up the stairs. No hesitation.

She pushed open her bedroom door.

And stopped.

The room looked... new. Like a magazine spread. Too clean. Too perfect. Not like hers. And yet—exactly hers. The *Sweet Dreams* paint she'd picked out at Farmers Building Supply still fresh on the walls. They'd bought it together. Planned a weekend to paint.

Then she left.

The smell of paint hit her, and something caught in her chest. She crossed the room, brushing her fingers over the sharp corners of picture frames and book spines. A new Patriots blanket covered the bed. Tom Brady. Her dad couldn't stand him—Niners fan through and through—but here it was anyway.

She laughed, surprised, and opened the closet door.

Everything hung in perfect order, shirts and jackets on

matching hangers, even color-coded. Her shoes, once scattered like breadcrumbs, now lined up on new shelves. Her hats hung neatly in rows on cloth straps. She reached for her favorite gray PNW trail cap and placed it on her head.

Her only regret when she left: not taking a ballcap. Dumb.

She adjusted her hair under the hat, shut the door, and stared at the room.

"Alexa, play music I like."

To her surprise, the device answered—and music filled the space.

She opened dresser drawers, each one perfectly folded. Except the top. Underwear and bras, jumbled in a messy knot, untouched. Dad drew a line there. She smiled.

The next song kicked in. "Feel It Still."

Sky danced. Like a dork. Like she was fourteen again.

Portugal The Man. She remembered every lyric. She'd begged for those Britt Festival tickets for weeks. He wouldn't say yes. Until one day, she opened her lunch and found them— four tickets tucked inside a sandwich bag.

He even chaperoned. One ticket for him, three for her friends.

*"You won't sit with us, right?" she'd asked.*

*"Nope. I'll help you set up your blankets and then give you space. But I'm not missing the show. Your mom wouldn't go. This one's for me, too."*

She knew it was his gentle way of keeping an eye on her and her friends. Making sure they were okay. Safe. So, he pretended to like a band she couldn't imagine him enjoying— though he did have a broad taste in music, for an adult.

She'd hugged him hard that night.

The song faded into another. She stopped dancing and walked to the window.

From the second floor, the flames looked like a wall of molten orange on the northern horizon. Unreal. And yet she

266

knew. Her father had taught her the reality—this fire would gut everything in its path. And tomorrow, daylight would expose the truth.

She didn't know what she'd say to him, when he came home. If she stayed long enough to see him.

Her fingers played with the fringe of the blanket. A part of her wanted to collapse into his arms and cry until she ran out of tears. The rest wanted to run—again. Farther this time.

Because strangers couldn't break you. But your father could.

"Alexa, stop."

Silence returned.

She turned off the lamp and went downstairs, pacing in the kitchen, chewing on her sandwich, sipping expired kombucha that still tasted okay. The mustard burned her tongue.

Or maybe it was everything else.

Why did she leave? What was she running from? What scared her so much she'd become her mother? Only shame, or much more?

She rinsed her plate and set it in the sink. *Dishwasher later.*

Then, slowly, like peeling back a layer of skin, she pulled the wrinkled square of paper from her pocket. Flattened it on the counter. The ink had faded, but she knew what it said.

Nice knowing you, Sky.

Call me anytime.

On or off the lam. :)

Billy Johnstone

555-797-6589

# Holding it Back

Chief Wilson slid behind the wheel of his county rig, the seat worn in all the right places, familiar under his weight. His thoughts drifted to his vintage pickup parked in the barn, its faded paint and stubborn engine waiting like a loyal dog. For over a decade, the fire chief's rig had been his only ride—no need for a personal commuter when duty was constant.

But everything had changed. His resignation made things real and he'd need his own set of car keys now.

Should he sink money into the old pickup, make it roadworthy again? Or give in, finally, and buy something new? The thought of a brand-new truck sparked a flicker of excitement. No more relying on Sandi and her SUV for those rare trips out of town—fishing, cycling, whatever escape he'd allow himself.

His mind drifted toward the Painted Hills again, the red earth and open sky. *God, I could use a ride through that kind of quiet.* Then his phone rang.

He glanced down. Sandi's name lit up the screen, a picture of her holding up a fat smallmouth bass she landed last spring on a kayak trip to Applegate Lake. She was in Idaho, visiting family, and had already called a few times today. He hadn't answered. The chaos of the fire had swallowed the day.

"Hi, Sandi. How are you and the family?"

The silence on the line stretched a little too long.

"Hello?"

"Seriously, Murph. What the hell? Why haven't you been answering your phone?"

"Kind of busy. Southern Oregon's on fire."

He winced. Not at her tone—at himself. For the first time,

he hadn't wanted to talk to her. The fire, the resignation, everything about today forced him into a place he didn't like—focused and detached. If the call dragged on, he knew he'd blurt out the truth. That he'd stepped down. *Again.*

And he wasn't sure she'd believe him this time.

Twice before, he'd handed in his resignation, and twice she'd dared to hope—planning trips, imagining time together—only for some emergency to pull him right back in. Each time, he'd let her down.

As if there were no other people who could handle it, she always reminded him.

"I figured," she said, her voice softer. "But damn, Murph—you've got to understand, I've been worried."

He didn't answer. His thoughts were spinning too fast.

"Well, I'm relieved to hear your voice. I won't keep you. How's the house? Coverage is spotty, and no one's answering their phones."

He pictured the place—his home, his past, the only constant he'd ever known. He'd seen the footage earlier at the command post. The flames had come close. Too close.

"I'm sorry, Sandi. It's a complete shit show here. I haven't been home, but I saw aerial footage. Fire got within half a mile, but it's pushing north. If the wind doesn't shift—and we're not expecting it to—it should be okay."

"Thank God." A breath, audible through the line. "Okay. I'll let you go. I was thinking of heading home tomorrow. What do you think?"

He hesitated. "As much as I'd love to see you, hold off another day. Roads are closed, and it's a mess. I'm going to be swamped."

That part was true—even with his resignation. Resigning didn't mean stepping away. There'd still be paperwork, transition, questions, second-guessing, gaps to fill. He'd be backing Paducah from behind the scenes, helping hold it all together while giving her the space to lead. She needed that. And the board needed to see she could handle it.

Regardless of the letter, he was still in charge until it became official—and he would act as such.

"Okay. Please be safe and take care of yourself."

He hesitated again. Then: "Sandi... thanks for calling. I just—" He swallowed. "I love you. And... do you think I'll ever see Sky again?"

Silence. A long beat.

"Murphy Wilson, I love you too. And yes, I do. I feel it. Funny you mention her—I dreamed about Sky last night. A happy dream. I can't remember most of it, but I saw you two together again."

She paused. "I'll call you late tomorrow—give you time to rest. You can tell me when it's okay to come home."

"Okay. Sounds good, Sandi. Talk soon—and thanks."

He ended the call, her dream still echoing in his mind—Sky, smiling, the two of them together again. The image lingered like smoke that refused to clear.

As he turned into Payne Creek Estates, his vision blurred. His eyes burned, the road ahead shimmering through the swell of emotion he could no longer keep buried. Just minutes ago, Paducah had asked about her sister. And now, the weight of everything—Sandi's words, Sky's absence, the years of silence—rose up in him, pushing against the wall he'd built long ago.

It buckled.

Grief, guilt, longing, they all surged at once, raw and unfiltered. He blinked hard, trying to stay focused, but the pain, carved by her absence, hit him like a wave—fast, heavy, and drowning. The nights Sky slammed the door. The mornings she left without goodbye. The way her handwriting changed in middle school. The time she reached for his hand after a nightmare and he almost cried from the softness of it.

He hadn't let himself feel this deeply in years—maybe ever. But now, there was no holding it back.

# Sharp and Brief

Mel turned into Payne Creek Estates and blinked hard at the sight of the community gate lying twisted and mangled on the asphalt, like a giant had ripped it from the earth. Her eyes flicked to a bus parked crooked near the community lot—lights on, engine idling. It looked empty except for the driver, but the tinted windows made it hard to tell for sure.

Most roads had been closed off by fire crews, and traffic signs warned people to flee. Mel had used her knack for slipping through barricaded backstreets and forgotten alleys to make it this far. Everyone else was heading in the opposite direction.

She should've gone home. Called Kaley. Waited like a rational person. But something—maybe instinct, maybe stubbornness—pulled her toward this place. Toward the development where Kaley lived. Toward the streets where smoke now hugged the rooftops and fire crews battled like hell just to hold a line.

From the air, destruction always looked abstract. Swaths of gray. Scorch marks. Impressive columns of smoke. But on the ground, driving past homes with melted siding and scorched lawns, past panicked faces and the heat pressing through her windshield—it became real. Personal.

Mel turned left onto Elderberry Street. Kaley's mom's place sat near the end. Her gut tightened. She'd been here only once to pick Kaley up. Kaley always insisted on meeting at Clyde's—smoke-free, with decent pizza and a good selection of beer.

She parked behind a familiar car and exhaled. *Kaley's.* So, she had to be here—*unless she and her mother were the ones on the bus.*

Mel climbed out, coughed through the rising haze, and approached the porch. The house looked quiet. Lifeless. She rapped on the screen door. No answer.

She glanced up the street. A uniformed officer was walking door to door. Across the way, some guy in jeans and a dark T-shirt knocked with less urgency, probably a volunteer, maybe a neighbor. He looked like a criminal with a bandana across his face.

Mel turned back and knocked again, louder this time.

"Kaley? You home? It's Mel."

No answer. The pit in her stomach twisted tighter. She yanked open the creaky screen door and hooked it to the little eye screwed into the siding, locking it in place so it couldn't swing closed. Then she pounded harder on the main door, her fist landing with a sharp urgency she couldn't hold back.

Bang bang bang. "Kaley, it's Mel! You in there?"

Still nothing. Her heart thudded harder. She grabbed the handle and twisted. Locked.

A quick glance over her shoulder—cop getting closer. If she was going to bust in, it had to be now. She hovered there for a second, hand on the knob, adrenaline buzzing in her fingertips. But she waited.

Seconds later, the officer stepped up beside her.

"Hi, ma'am. It's time to evacuate. The fire is imminent."

Mel offered a quick smile, appreciating the deputy's calm confidence, and extended a hand.

"Hi, Deputy. I'm Mel Hall—one of the air tanker pilots."

The young man nodded but didn't take her hand. Mel didn't hold it against him. Given the circumstances, staying focused made sense.

"Deputy Jason Morrow," he said. "Nice job on the drops today. That's what they're called, right? Drops? Why aren't you flying?"

"Yeah, that's right," she replied. "We exhausted our retardant supply, and we don't fly at night."

They stood facing each other, the conversation hanging awkwardly between them. Ten seconds of silence. Maybe more.

Finally, the deputy broke it. "Do you live here?"

"No. A friend and her mother do. I haven't been able to reach them, and I'm worried."

"You knock?"

Mel nodded. "Pounded on it. Tried the handle too." She demonstrated, giving the knob another twist. Still locked.

"What makes you think someone's inside?"

Mel hesitated, then spoke. "My friend—Kaley—is a double amputee, combat vet. She doesn't get around easily. Her mom's older, mostly stays planted in a chair, chain-smokes in front of the TV. If Kaley's car is here, odds are she is too. Trust me."

Deputy Morrow checked his watch, then glanced down the smoke-hazed street. He looked tired. Frazzled around the edges.

"I can handle this, Jason," Mel offered.

"I don't doubt it," he said. "But this is on me. Can you step aside and let me knock?"

She moved down the steps, giving him space on the narrow porch. He stepped up and knocked with sharp, deliberate authority.

"This is Jackson County Sheriff's Deputy Jason Morrow," he called out. "Evacuation is mandatory. Fire threat is imminent. Please unlock the door—we're here to help."

Across the street, someone called out. "Everything okay, Deputy Morrow?"

Mel turned to see the bandana man standing near the last home in the park.

"Fine, Teddy. How about you?"

"One left. After I check it, mind if I head out?"

"Do it. Go see that daughter and granddaughter of yours. But before you go, come say goodbye—I'll give you a get-out-of-jail-free card."

Teddy gave a wave and started down the block.

Deputy Morrow turned back and knocked again—louder. "Jackson County Sheriff's Deputy. Please respond. You need to evacuate."

Still nothing. He looked at Mel. "How well do you know them?"

"Well enough. Why?"

"You think they're inside?"

Mel nodded slowly. "I won't bet my life on it, but if they're not, I'll buy you a beer and a shot."

That got a smile. Morrow tried the knob himself, then squared his shoulders and slammed into the door. It gave, but not enough.

"Damn. Stronger than it looks."

He stepped back, adjusted his stance, then drove his shoulder into the door again. This time, it gave way with a crack of splintered wood and a shriek of twisted metal.

Mel felt something stir unexpectedly in her gut—a flush of arousal she hadn't felt in longer than she cared to admit. *Jesus,* she thought. *How old is he?* And *did I remember to plug in my vibrator this morning?*

As Morrow stepped inside, his hand hovered near his sidearm—a practiced motion born of training and instinct.

"Stay here," he said. "But listen. If I call, come in."

"Okay," she managed, her pulse now shifting from distracted heat to something far colder. The tight coil in her chest reminded her this was real—dangerous. Not some fantasy.

She watched him start to enter the house; her eyes drawn

to the way his uniform clung to his frame. His hand hovered over his gun but nothing more. She wondered if he should take the gun out.

Then—an all-too-familiar Concussive Snap!

A gunshot shattered the day's eerie silence.

Deputy Morrow's body hit the jamb, then crumpled to the porch with a brutal thud.

Mel flinched—just for a fraction of a second—but her training kicked in. She dropped low, pivoted off the porch steps, and pressed herself against the side of the house, scanning for cover and the source of the shot. Her pulse slammed in her ears, but her mind stayed clear. Focused.

Disbelief flashed through her, sharp and brief.

# Payne Creek Estates, Pt. 1 – DOZENS

Anxious and relieved, Teddy knocked on his final door. He waited a good thirty seconds—no movement, no voice. One more knock, harder this time. Still nothing. Satisfied the place was empty, he turned and headed across the street to say goodbye to Deputy Jason Morrow.

He still wasn't sure what a get-out-of-jail-free card meant—maybe getting out of a parking ticket? He grinned at the thought, but then a sharp, violent *crack* split the ash-choked air.

It reminded him of the pop his acetylene torch made when he lit it too fast—only louder. Angrier. Hard to tell where it came from, with all the smoke, sirens, and that low roar the fire made when it chewed through dry timber and rooftops.

He froze.

Across the street, the woman he'd seen talking to the deputy earlier suddenly jumped from the steps and slammed herself into the porch lattice, using it like a shield. She waved her arms at him, wild and urgent.

He picked up his pace, eyes drifting to the porch where she'd been. Something was there—a dark shape. A lump. As he jogged closer, the woman shouted.

"Get down, you idiot! Get down!"

*Down to what?* he thought. The ground? That felt a little dramatic. He crouched—halfway between standing and not—and kept moving forward. He wanted to see what was going on. He wanted his free card.

The lump was clearer now.

Not a lump at all. A body.

"Fucking ash—what a day," he muttered.

"Get down, you fool! *There's a shooter!*"

He looked around, half expecting her to be yelling at someone else. But no—those eyes were locked on him, fierce and frantic.

The woman suddenly shot to her feet, bumped into the porch, then sprinted toward him and dove behind a black Ford pickup. She waved him over with a quick flick of her arm.

Teddy didn't hesitate. He ducked low and ran to join her behind the truck, skidding on the pavement as he dropped next to her. She looked scared and angry.

That gave him pause.

And then he saw it—crudely spray-painted on the side of the truck:

*If you want a blow...?*

His brain stuttered trying to process everything. Her flushed skin. Her short, controlled breaths. Her eyes—sharp and alert.

"Who are you?" she asked, voice steady despite the chaos.

Teddy blinked. "Who are you?"

She turned to him, not breaking eye contact. "I'm the one asking the questions and have no time to fuck around. Want to try again?"

He almost laughed, but her calm sent a chill through him.

"Teddy. I'm the maintenance guy for this place. Deputy Morrow and I were clearing houses, getting folks to the bus down there." He pointed down the street. She nodded.

"Hi, Teddy. I'm Mel. Officer Morrow's dead. Half his face is gone."

Teddy's breath caught. He started to rise, needing to see for himself, but she grabbed his arm and yanked him down.

"Trust me—he's dead. I was right next to him on the stairs when he got shot trying to enter the house." She paused; jaw clenched. "The woman who shot him…"

278

"Yeah?"

Mel blew out a breath, her voice clipped. "Shit."

Teddy stared at her. "The woman *what*?"

He'd seen someone in that house before. A woman with two strange-looking legs—moved like she was walking on stilts. He'd always wanted to ask but never figured out how without sounding like an asshole. So, he kept his curiosity quiet.

"The woman who lives here," Mel said finally, eyes still locked on the house, "she's ex-Green Beret. Dozens of military weapon certifications."

She paused. "She doesn't miss."

Teddy's brain snagged on the phrasing.

"*Dozens?*" he echoed, eyebrows raised.

Mel didn't answer. She was too busy watching the house, eyes narrowing like she could see through walls.

# Got a Pen

With a mix of newfound confidence and old doubts, Sky pressed the numbers on her phone. The dial tone buzzed once—twice—and panic surged. She hit end before it could connect.

Pacing, she wondered if her dad kept whiskey in the house. He used to.

She made her way to the back of the main floor and slid open the pocket door to his office.

The room looked untouched. Two plaques hung on the wall—one for county Firefighter of the Year, the other for the state of Oregon. That was it. No clutter, no desk trinkets. Just quiet, restrained pride.

She smiled. As a teenager, that kind of attention used to make her squirm. People would stop them in town, compliment him, shake his hand. She'd shrink into her hoodie, wishing she were invisible. The truth? She never felt like she measured up.

Crossing the threshold into his sanctuary, she remembered sitting behind that very desk as a kid, sorting through her football cards, obsessing over Tom Brady's stats. Rodgers too. How Rodgers only had one ring still bugged her. Eli had two. Pure luck. Who catches a football with their helmet?

Behind the desk, she reached for a panel and slid open the shelf she hoped was still there.

Jackpot.

Bottles lined the hidden compartment like old friends waiting to be chosen. One stood out—Dead Rabbit.

She tilted her head. *Who the hell names a whiskey after roadkill?*

She turned the bottle in her hand, scanning the label. Irish whiskey. Figures. Leave it to the Irish to make something sound both poetic and vaguely threatening.

She grabbed a crystal glass from beside the old ice bucket and poured a generous shot, mimicking her dad's old trick—finger parallel to the whiskey line. She corked the bottle, swirled the liquid, then raised the glass and took a deep breath. The smell punched her in the face.

Still, she downed it. Her throat lit up like fire. Her eyes watered. It was disgusting but oh so warm.

"Damn," she coughed, blinking through the burn. "No wonder the homeless drink this stuff."

She poured another—two fingers this time. Sat down in his leather chair. Watched the bronze swirl in the glass. Sipped. Hated it. Tossed it back anyway.

Leaning back, she thought about putting her feet on the desk. Instead, she sat in silence, willing the liquid to do its job. A warmth settled in her stomach. She didn't feel better, but in less than ten minutes she felt braver.

She grabbed her phone, found the number, and pressed the digits on the screen.

"Hello?"

"Billy?" Her voice caught.

"This is Billy. Who's this?"

"This is… On-The-Lam, Sky." She held her breath.

A pause.

"Sky? What's up? How are things in Talent? Isn't that town on fire?"

"It is. But my dad's place is in the southern foothills. Just ash so far—no fire damage."

"Wow, that's… sad, but good to hear. Is he happy to see you?"

"I haven't seen him yet. He's probably managing the fire.

281

That's why I called."

"Oh. Okay. What's up?"

She hesitated. Words tangled somewhere between her chest and throat.

"You gave me your number, so…"

"Yeah?"

"Billy, I'm not good at this. You seemed nice when you picked me up. My dad's going to be home soon, and… I could use someone here. I don't think I can face him alone."

The silence that followed made her stomach twist.

"Would you mind coming over and just… hanging out until he gets home?" She inhaled sharply. "I know it's weird, we harldy know each other—I need someone here with me when I face my dad."

Still silence. Did he hang up?

"I mean… sure, I guess. But is it even safe for me to get there? The fire's all over the news—roads are shut down, evacuation orders popping up everywhere. Is your neighborhood's in the evacuation zone?"

Sky moved to the window, watching the dim sky, smoke-blurred but calm. "It's okay. My neighbor told me less than an hour ago we're in the 'be prepared to evacuate' zone. The fire's pushing north. We should be safe."

"Should be." Billy let out a short laugh

Sky let out a breath she didn't realize she'd been holding.

"I figured we could get to know each other, keep tabs on the fire, maybe have a drink on the porch. I don't know when my dad's coming back… you might want to pack a bag—" She winced. "I'll make up the guest room."

Another pause. Her nerves unraveled fast. "Never mind. Dumb idea."

"No, no—it's okay. I get it. Give me a second…"

A pause.

"I can come over, but I'll need to leave by 6 tomorrow

282

morning for work. That okay?"

Relief flushed through her chest. "Yes. Totally. If my dad isn't back then, I'll deal with it. Thank you."

"Cool," he said, a small hint of something hopeful in his voice.

"Got a pen? Here's my dad's address."

# Payne Creek Estates, Pt. 2 - COOPER KUPP

Butt pressed against bumpy asphalt dusted with ash, back braced against the tire of her tagged pickup, Mel eyed Deputy Morrow's gun—still cradled in its holster, probably a lock or button needing pressed to release it. Not an easy grab.

Instinct told her to move. Crawl forward, snatch it up, secure it—if only to keep someone else from doing the same. But she held back. Not yet.

The gun wasn't going anywhere, and the porch felt like a stage with a sniper's scope trained on it. She wasn't about to walk into that trap.

So, she stayed put.

The middle-aged man crouched next to her. Teddy, she thought muttered something. Low, nervy. Maybe a question, maybe just rambling. She didn't bother to listen.

Her breath stayed steady, but her mind raced. She needed a plan. One that didn't get anyone else killed.

Mel kept her eyes on the porch, focus sharp, thoughts circling like aircraft waiting to land.

She turned to Teddy. He sat awkwardly, physically capable, but radiating hesitation. Not good. Not now.

She knew that feeling in her bones. Military training left no room for freeze-ups. If in doubt, get the hell out. You didn't survive in a cockpit—or a combat zone—by hesitating. You acted. Or you died. And someone else usually did too.

With a dead deputy on the porch and a shooter inside, she didn't need deadweight.

She turned to him. "Listen, Teddy, right? I'm Mel Hall. One of the tanker pilots dropping Phos-Chek all over this fire. I came to check on a friend. The deputy showed up to evacuate, and now he's dead. Shot trying to do his job. The woman in that house—I think she's the shooter. She's also my friend. And if I were you, I'd get to your car and get the hell out of Dodge."

Teddy blinked. "What about the deputy? Shouldn't we call an ambulance?"

Mel stared at him. His voice sounded like Mr. Rogers questioning how mail works.

"You ever seen someone get shot, Teddy?"

He shook his head. "No, but I watch a lot of TV—"

"TV." She let out a sharp laugh. "Solid source."

"You okay, ma'am?" Teddy asked gently.

"No. I'm pissed off. And I'm about to storm that house and try to get a gun away from my friend before someone else dies."

Teddy squirmed. Something in her seemed to have softened. He wasn't built for this. He needed to feel like the world still made sense.

"You got your phone?" she asked.

"Shit." He paused, then lied. "No. It's back at the shop."

Perfect. She didn't want him here anyway.

"Good. Go call 911. Tell them that Deputy Morrow is gone. Half his head's gone. He died before he hit the porch. Tell them where we are. Say you were helping him evacuate. Say it turned into a possible hostage situation."

He nodded, pale.

"Tell them Mel Hall is on scene. Ex-military. Air tanker pilot. They'll check me out. Tell them I know the people inside. And tell them this—" She leaned in, voice dropping. "I'm going in."

Teddy's mouth opened slightly. "You are?"

"Yes." She didn't blink. "If Kaley's having a PTSD break, this could spiral. They'll tell you to stay put and wait for backup. But good news—you'll already be gone."

Teddy pushed up to one knee, scanning the street like he wasn't sure which way was out. Mel figured the shop had to be close if he said a minute or less.

"Anything else?" he asked.

"Yeah. Hurry."

Teddy turned to go, then paused. "What about the fire?"

Mel looked south. Heat pressed against her skin. The low roar was louder now.

"Shit," she muttered. "Yeah. Another reason to move your ass. That fire's coming for all of us."

Teddy hesitated, then smiled for some strange reason—nerves or maybe relief. He remembered his phone was still sitting in the cradle in his truck.

"Leave as soon as you call," Mel barked. "There's nothing more you can do. Don't Linger."

He nodded and took off—faster than she expected, quick, precise, surprisingly nimble.

*Damn,* Mel thought, watching him go. *Teddy has a little Cooper Kupp in him.*

# I Like That Name

A knock at the door. Then the doorbell. Someone was outside. Billy? Already?

Her chest tightened. *Shit. Did he stalk me? Wait outside like some Dateline villain?*

No—that didn't track. She hadn't given him the address yet.

Her thoughts pinballed as she made her way downstairs, distracted by too many questions and not enough answers. She opened the front door, expecting Billy.

"Sky? Oh my God… Sky?"

Standing on the porch was Sarah, the next-door neighbor. Babysitter turned family friend. The woman who used to step in when her dad was on shift and her mom was halfway through a bottle of red with a paperback in hand.

Sarah's smile was as luminous as ever. Her gray hair might've said *grandmother*, but her skin and eyes still clung to youth like it owed her something.

"Hi, Sarah," Sky said, unsure if it came out warm or wary.

"When did you get home?"

Sarah looked stunned—like she was seeing a ghost.

"A few hours ago," Sky said, watching the woman sift through memories like puzzle pieces.

"Well… it's good to see you," Sarah said finally. "I saw the lights on. It surprised me. I knew Sandi was out of town, and I figured your dad would be knee-deep in this damn fire."

Sky's eyebrows rose. "Sandi?"

Sarah flinched. Her expression shifted from surprise to instant regret.

"Um… yes. Your dad's friend," she said quickly, eyes

flicking away.

Sky gave a tired smile. *Sandi.* The name sounded lovely. Maybe her dad had someone. Maybe someone good.

"I'm not sure I'm staying," Sky said. "Just needed somewhere to shower. Grab a change of clothes."

She wanted to say more. But didn't.

Sarah nodded. "Okay. Well, just so you know—the fire's heading north. We're in the 'be prepared to evacuate' zone. If that changes, I'll come by."

"Thanks."

"It's good to see you, Sky. I hope you stay. Your father mentions you often."

Sky gave a small nod, then gently closed the door—maybe a little too fast for how kind Sarah had always been.

She paused. She should've said more. *I'm sorry I was short. I'm just... tired.*

But the words stayed locked inside.

She leaned back against the door, letting her head rest with a soft thud.

"Sandi," she whispered.

A hint of a smile touched her lips.

"I like that name."

# Payne Creek Estates, Pt. 3 – IN HELL

Kaley had no idea how long she'd been out. Her head throbbed, but the sharp *pop* that cut through the fog snapped her awake. The ringing in her ears receded just enough to confirm what she already knew.

She took a knock on her head that made her black out. How? Who—her mother?

She shoved the haze aside. Pain could wait. Training took over. *Survive. Assess. Protect. Heal when the dust settles.*

Dragging her aching, uncooperative body across the floor, every bump and scrape against the warped laminate screamed like a damn siren. Stealth? Out the window. The house was too small, too cluttered. She pressed her back against the dresser, breathing hard. The room spun. She forced it to settle.

A shattered vase lay among socks and dirty laundry, pieces glinting in the low light. She reached for the biggest shard, fingers closing around its cool edge.

Not ideal. But it would have to do.

*What the hell just happened?* Her mother—angry, cruel, drunk—sure. But homicidal? She'd never seen that coming.

She raised a shaky hand to the back of her head. Wet. Sticky. She hissed through her teeth. Blood. The knot swelling under her fingertips pulsed with each beat of her heart.

*Breathe. Focus. Count.*

Her eyes flicked to her carbon limbs. *Damn my life.* Movement was clumsy. Predictable. She couldn't crawl fast. Couldn't run. Couldn't even roll without knocking into something.

She considered crawling under the bed. Or checking the drawers for anything useful. But her gut said *don't move.*

*The voice in her head—memories of the soldier's voice—shouted, Stay low. Stay sharp. Threat assessment first.*

She blinked hard. Trying to will the tears away.

Not now. Not here.

But one slipped out. Then another.

She gritted her teeth, clawing for rage—anything to shove the panic back down. But then came the voice. Not from inside her head. From the doorway.

Sharp. Cold. Familiar.

"Quit crying, you goddamned pansy. I thought I raised you better. You fought in the Middle East, for God's sake."

Her mother's silhouette darkened the frame. Gun in hand.

She stepped forward and—casually, like she was checking a bruise on a child—touched the back of Kaley's head.

"It's a small bump," she muttered. "You'll live. Man up."

Kaley wiped a tear with the back of her hand and straightened up. Her whole body tensed. Her mother was moving better than she had in years. Too smooth, too reactive. Kaley didn't trust it. She'd have to play along. Stay small. Stay sharp.

"Mom... why'd you hit me?"

The TV blared behind them. Kaley thought she heard shouting outside, but the noise inside swallowed everything else.

"I hit you because I don't trust you," her mother said, voice flat. "You want to abscond with my riches. And this fire—it's the perfect cover. I know what you're up to. It's what I'd do."

"Abscond? Riches? What the hell, Mom?" Kaley muttered.

Her mother started pacing, agitated, peeking through the curtains, muttering.

"To protect myself," she snapped, answering a question Kaley hadn't asked. "There's some woman out there hiding behind a truck. Looks familiar. Bet she won't try anything now. God, that felt good."

Kaley's stomach turned to ice. "What felt good, Mom?"

"Blowing that motherfucking cop away," she said, grinning. "Dumbass walked into my house uninvited. I got him right in the head."

Kaley's breath caught. Her whole chest locked tight.

She turned—instinct, taking over, eyes toward the door. Maybe he's alive. Maybe I can help...

Her mother shoved her hard, and Kaley hit the floor. The gun was in an instant, inches from her face.

"You stay the fuck down," her mother hissed. "I'll put a goddamn bullet in your head if I have to. Your little inheritance scam ends today."

Kaley's rage flared, hot and clear. She never imagined she'd have to disarm her own mother—but here she was. Her eyes locked on the pistol. Every ounce of training screamed: act now. Disarm. Control. End it.

Her mother laughed. Low. Unhinged. It crawled under Kaley's skin.

"You were always the reason your father drank," she sneered. "Sit tight, Kaley. The fire's coming. And we've got one last visit to make—together. It's almost time to go visit you father—In Hell."

# I'll Be Right Back

Sky stepped into the garage and opened the refrigerator door. Cool air spilled out, but the shelves inside felt empty. No beer. Just rows of kombucha bottles and seltzer cans in cheerful colors.

She stared for a moment, hoping she'd missed something tucked behind the ginger-lemon brew. Nothing.

*There used to be beer.* Always a few kinds, none with names she recognized from TV. Her dad didn't touch that stuff—*"factory-made garbage,"* he'd say with a grunt. He liked the local brews, the ones with pine trees, mountain ranges, or sasquatch on the label. After a long day in the yard, he'd lean on the shovel or the rake and ask her to fetch him one.

She used to love that. Picking the right can, a different type each time to surprise him. The small weight of responsibility. The way his eyes softened when she handed him the bottle. She'd grab something for herself, too—sparkling water or kombucha—and stand beside him, back against the garage wall, barn, or fence, mimicking his posture.

For a few minutes, they'd sip in silence. Just the two of them. *Her pretending the world made as much sense to her as it seemed to make to him.*

The contents of the fridge made her feel like she'd opened a stranger's door, not her father's. Kombucha. Seltzer. Not a single beer in sight.

This Sandi—whoever she is, doesn't she drink beer? Or has Dad given up alcohol for some inexplicable reason?

The dust-covered whiskey bottles in his den didn't exactly scream enthusiasm. Their condition made Sky question whether he still had any real taste for alcohol at all.

Does whiskey go bad, she wondered. I hope not—not after those shots of Dead Rabbit.

Maybe a little more liquid courage would help steady her nerves before her dad came home. Or maybe it'd numb her too much. She thought about Billy—wondered if he smoked. Would he bring anything with him? She'd ask soon enough.

For now, she told herself no more whiskey. The buzz lingered anyway. Better to be sober when Billy showed up—and especially when her father walked through the door.

Billy doesn't need to know about the bar in Dad's office. That was a detail she'd keep to herself. For now.

Sky closed the fridge and headed back inside, grabbing the kombucha she'd left on the counter, leaned against the kitchen island, and took a swig. The carbonation bit the back of her throat.

Footsteps sounded on the porch.

She froze, can still in hand. Was it Sarah again? Or had Billy made it through the maze of detours she knew there would be due to the fire? Shit, can he even get here?

She tightened her grip on the can and moved to the front door. When she opened it, there he stood—Billy. Taller than she expected. Funny how you couldn't tell when someone was behind the wheel. She got a sense, thinking he might be tall, but didn't know until now.

She realized she'd never seen him outside of his truck—easy on the eyes. Real easy on the eyes. *Damn*, she thought.

He had that effortless kind of build—tall, muscular, with the sort of athletic swagger that didn't try too hard. Confidence radiated off him, grounded and unshaken, like he belonged wherever he stood. The antithesis of Steele, She giggled to herself.

A sudden, unexpected flush of excitement washed over her. When she asked Billy to come over, she hadn't anticipated feeling *this*—at least not in any way she was willing to admit to herself.

"Damn, Sky. I don't know how I made it here. Roads are shut down everywhere, and there's fire all over the place. It looks like a warzone in the distance. WAZE helped, but barely. I wasn't even sure this place would still be standing."

Her thoughts twisted, emotions all over the place. Sky stared at the ash falling outside, wondering if they really *were* safe.

"Back to not talking, huh?" Billy said, grinning. "You know I risked my life to get here?"

"Oh—shit. I'm sorry, Billy. Yeah, I'm a spaz." She stepped aside quickly. "This whole homecoming has me completely out of sorts, and with this heinous fire... my heads everywhere. Come in. And thank you. I didn't know who else to call. I felt safe with you, so…"

As soon as she said it, she wondered if she'd said too much.

She held the door open. Billy stepped inside, his arm brushing against hers as he passed. The contact sparked something—an electric tension that caught her off guard.

Then, it hit her. She hadn't showered. Hadn't changed. Hadn't done anything to clean up in any way since arriving at her dad's house.

"Shit."

Billy stopped mid-step. "What's that?" His voice edged with concern.

"I need to shower. I must smell awful," she said, flustered. "My nerves have been pegged since I got here and I... I literally forgot to clean myself up."

She closed the door behind him, set her kombucha on the counter, and started for the stairs.

"Billy, give me fifteen minutes, please? There's kombucha and seltzer in the garage—right through that door. And more in the kitchen fridge, too. Help yourself. I won't be long."

Billy smiled. "It's okay. You can relax. I'll be fine. Go clean yourself up."

Sky offered a grateful smile and turned for the stairs. She'd only made it up three steps when he called out behind her.

"You know, it's been a while since you had a real shower, right?"

She froze. *God, do I smell that bad?*

"Too long," she replied cautiously. "Why?"

"Well... do you need any help? You know, in the shower? I'm happy to show you how to use the soap."

Sky stopped cold. A flicker of fear crawled across her skin. *What kind of signal did I send him?*

"Um... are you serious?" The words came out small, uncertain, hesitant.

Billy burst out laughing. "I'm fuckin' with you. You should see your face. You look like I just told you I was gonna kill you."

Sky didn't laugh.

"Go get cleaned up," he said, waving her off with a grin. "Can't wait to see what a clean Sky looks like."

He turned and disappeared into the garage, leaving her alone at the foot of the stairs.

She stood there, heart hammering, trying to steady herself. Fear—fleeting but sharp—passed through her like a cold draft, followed too quickly by a warm flush she hated to admit felt like excitement.

*Get it together,* she told herself and climbed the stairs two at a time.

In the bedroom, she tore open her backpack. The clothes inside were damp, crumpled, and no better than what she was wearing, perhaps worse. She crossed to the dresser. Top drawer—underwear and socks. Third drawer—jeans. She grabbed the top pair of Levi's. In the closet, she found an old gray Oregon State Beavers sweatshirt.

Holding it close, she tried to remember the last time hot water touched her skin. Really touched her. Not a quick rinse or cold splash—but a long, quiet, cleansing moment.

She needed it now. Wanted it now. Something to help wash the shame.

Easing down the hall, Sky slipped into the bathroom and locked the door behind her. She turned the water on full blast and stared at the wire basket hanging from the showerhead pipe.

Her favorite shampoo sat in the tray—bright blue bottle, slightly dusty but still there. She tilted her head, wondering if it had been touched in the two-plus years she'd been wandering Fog City. Probably not. Her dad had his own bathroom off the master, and if Sandi stayed over, Sky figured she'd use that one too.

She peeled off her clothes. The T-shirt clung to the damp mat of hair under her arms, making her wrestle it over her head. The fabric stuck, the movement awkward and irritating. She winced at her reflection, then opened the medicine cabinet.

Inside, a sealed bag of pink razors made her smile—like finding a gift from a past life. Shaving cream resting beside it, unopened.

She pulled out a razor, set it with the cream on the shower tray, then stepped in.

The hot water hit her back like a hug she hadn't known she needed. She closed her eyes, feeling months of San Francisco grime swirl down the drain. Her hands worked through her hair, sticky and tangled. Looking down at her legs, she sighed.

"Nope," she muttered. Tackling them now would take forever.

Then she glanced a little higher.

Shit.

The briar patch between her legs would need some wine

296

and a dedicated afternoon, maybe a Keith Urban song or five, and industrial-grade wax. *Another time.* She focused on the hair under her arms instead, letting the steam and hot water soften her skin. One step at a time. The Neanderthal makeover could happen in phases.

Fourteen minutes later, she stepped out, wrapped in a towel, skin pink from the heat. Back in her room, she dressed in clothes from her past, gathered the filthy clothes from her backpack and the floor, then headed downstairs.

The living room was empty.

No Billy.

Her gaze fell on the front door, it stood slightly ajar.

That sight, in this house, carried bad memories.

Her breath hitched. She crossed the room, peered outside, then turned away and made her way to the laundry room.

She tossed everything into the washer, Deep Cycle, Extra Hot, full scoop of detergent. Slammed the lid. Hit start.

Then she exhaled.

Satisfied the machine would churn her clothes into a different level of dirty, Sky walked back toward the front door. She eased it open and peeked outside.

Billy sat in the porch swing, a joint pinched between his fingers. The scent floated on the air—pungent, unmistakable—and, surprisingly, it won a brief battle against the smoke curling in from the fire burning through Southern Oregon. For a moment, the sharp, earthy smell pushed back the acrid reminder of everything still burning.

"Now, see," he said, grinning as she stepped out and let the screen door ease shut behind her, "I knew you'd look good all cleaned up."

The compliment landed, but Sky let it slide past. She wasn't going there. Not now. Romantic thoughts stirred aches she wasn't ready to feel.

Instead, she redirected her focus, grounding herself in the heavier question that simmered since she arrived: *What am I going to say when I see my father?* How was she supposed to act? Smile? Cry? Pretend nothing was broken between them?

The porch swing creaked. The idea of possible relaxation from the joint called her. Sky stood still, letting the cool air brush against her damp hair, trying not to flinch at the weight of everything waiting inside—and everything still unsaid.

"Make yourself at home, Billy."

She sauntered toward him, eyes drifting to the swing. She'd spent years curled up in that exact spot beside her dad. Quiet evenings, the creak of wood, the hum of crickets. No other man—outside of a Wilson—had ever sat there. Until now.

Billy looked comfortable. Too comfortable. His hair matched her father's—same deep brown—and damn if his eyes weren't cut from the same mold. Same color. Same quiet steadiness.

"Didn't mean to overstep," he said, voice easy, joint balanced between his fingers. "Not a regular smoker—maybe once every couple weeks. But something about this place… felt like the swing asked me to sit. Strange, huh? It feels like it's carrying something. Sadness, maybe."

Sky smiled—both knowing and uncertain—as if a question she'd never had the guts to face drifted just out of reach: *Why the hell did I leave home in the first place?*

"Yes, it is," she said, responding to Billy's comment. "Now scoot over and give me some of that. I'm the one who needs to relax."

She plopped down at the far end of the porch swing, leaving a couple of feet between them. Billy handed her the joint. She took a long drag—the smoke catching in her throat—then passed it back.

"Thanks," she murmured. "I hope this helps when my dad

gets home. Honestly? I think I'd rather spend another night on the street than face him."

The swing creaked in rhythm as silence settled between them. Then Billy spoke.

"Well, what gives? Why in the hell did you ever leave a home like this? Your dad, being a fire chief and all, can't be that big of a douchebag. Why's it so hard to face him? What happened?"

Sky stiffened. The shame hit fast—a sharp wave crashing through her chest. Her heart sank. Her body bristled. Something inside her curled up, small and aching. The weight pressed against her ribs, too much, too fast.

She forced herself to breathe—deep, slow, steady. In. Out. Her body listened. The tension began to ebb.

"Give me a minute," she said, standing. "I'm going to grab my kombucha. You want anything?"

Billy winced. "Sorry, Sky. I didn't mean to fuck up the mood. I'm just... curious, that's all."

"No, it's okay," she said, softer now. "I'm glad you're here—honest. I've been avoiding my shit for too long." She paused, with a hand on the screen door. "You sure you don't want anything from the kitchen?"

Billy looked down, then reached for the seltzer can at his feet. He rolled it back and forth slowly before taking a sip. "Nah, I'm good. Thanks, though."

"Okay," she said. "I'll be right back."

Sky stepped inside, leaving Billy on the porch.

"You can do this," she whispered. "It's the past. Move on."

The kombucha sat on the counter where she'd left it. She grabbed it, then paused in the doorway.

Billy. The porch. The swing. Her father's house. It all looked like a snapshot from a life she'd walked away from—and wasn't sure she deserved to remain in.

She lingered, studying the scene—Billy's profile against the falling ash, the empty spot beside him, the faint creak of the swing swaying in the breeze. She considered the railing across from him. That had been her favorite spot as a kid— legs dangling, back against the post. But not tonight. Too much distance in that angle. Too much room to hide.

She walked to the swing and lowered herself onto the other end. Not close. Not far. Just enough space to feel both separate and tethered.

Sky eased back, her gaze drifting into the darkness where ash floated like snow, softening the outline of towering pines. The porch creaked beneath their weight, the swing swayed in a gentle back and forth motion.

Neither of them spoke.

For the first time since she'd gotten back, the quiet didn't feel empty. Just still.

And for now, that was enough.

# Payne Creek Estates - Part IV – DISBELIEF

Chief Wilson wiped his damp cheeks with the back of his hand as he pulled into Payne Creek Estates. A pickup nearly clipped him, barreling out of the development like the world was on fire—which, in truth, it was. He glanced in the rearview, out of habit, catching no plate and not caring, then turned his eyes back to the road.

The gate lay twisted on the asphalt, torn clean off its hinges. Southeast, smoke loomed. The radio chatter over the past fifteen minutes all pointed to one thing: this place didn't have long.

A Talent PD cruiser idled near a bus. A few yards away sat two sheriff's vehicles and a state patrol car. The bus was rolling out, waved along by a deputy. Not one of the cruisers had a cop inside. That many law enforcement rigs without bodies made his gut prickle.

He parked the fire rig where the bus had been and climbed out. No helmet this time—just his fire-resistant chief's jacket. Heavy, awkward, but necessary.

"What can I do for you, Chief?" asked a young deputy walking toward the knot of parked units.

"Looking for someone—sister of a coworker. Just want to make sure she got out."

"Every house is cleared," the deputy said. "A deputy went door-to-door. Everyone's out, unless someone's hiding. One home left."

"Which one?" Wilson asked, praying it wasn't the address Paducah had texted him.

"End of Elderberry," the deputy said, pointing.

Wilson exhaled. Paducah's sister lived on a street named after a local mountain—he'd have remembered a berry.

"Where is everyone else? You need backup?"

"Dispatch told me to escort the bus out and block entry. We've got a shooter. One of ours is down. Got hit while evacuating homes."

Wilson's gut dropped. He hadn't caught a word of that over comms. Too much noise. Too much chaos. But when a cop goes down, the whole network locks in—as it should.

"Shit."

"Yeah. He was my buddy. Grants Pass High. Police academy in Salem. We came up together."

The deputy's voice thinned. Wilson saw it—the glassy eyes, the twitch at the cheek, the way his shoulders stiffened to keep from folding.

"Listen," Wilson said. "You two talked about this, right? Back in the academy? About getting shot. About making the call. You both knew the risk. And your friend—he saved lives today. That bus? It's full. He did his job."

The deputy nodded; eyes locked on the horizon.

"What's his name?"

"Jason. Jason Morrow. I have to tell his parents. Fuck."

"And you?"

"Ricky. Ricky Eberflow."

"Deputy Eberflow," Wilson said, careful not to reach out. The young man needed space. Not sympathy. Not yet.

"You honor him by keeping your shit together. You fall apart now; it won't help anyone. Would you want Jason to crack if it were you lying there?"

Eberflow swallowed, jaw tight.

"I hear you, Chief. This is fucked, though."

"It is. But you keep doing your job. That's what matters right now."

Eberflow turned to walk away, then stopped.

"If you're heading in, go down Elderberry. You'll see a Ford pickup and a bunch of people behind it. Stay low. And thanks, Chief. For the talk."

Wilson gave a nod and watched him drive to the gate, lights flashing as the cruiser slid into position, blocking entry.

The chief returned to his rig, repositioned it to face out—just in case—then started down Elderberry on foot. The air thickened with ash, his boots trudging through it with every step. Darkness crawled in from all sides, and the smoke made the sky unreadable.

This wasn't a fire scene anymore. It was a war zone.

He crouched as he moved toward a police car and pickup where several figures hunkered down. Someone raised a weapon on instinct—then lowered it once they spotted the fire chief's coat.

"Chief. What can we do for you?"

"Nothing," he said. "Except leave. This fire's marching straight for us."

A trooper in a blue-gray uniform stepped forward and offered his hand.

"Davies. State Police. We've got a sheriff's deputy down on the porch. Shot in the head. Shooter's still inside."

Wilson shook his hand. "What's the plan? Because this place will be cinders in under an hour."

Before Davies could respond, Wilson noticed a woman in an olive-green flight suit rocking back and forth, muttering to herself. Something about her movements clicked—a pre-mission ritual, maybe. Then she jolted upright, crossed herself like any good Catholic, and sprinted forward.

She leapt over the body on the porch and vanished into the open door.

Wilson turned to the officers.

They just stared.

"Who the hell is that?" he asked.

Nobody answered.

Everyone just watched the door.

And the fire kept coming.

# Off Guard

Billy sat calm and stoic and hummed next to Sky on the swing. After a few more bars of his tune, then a beat of silence, he spoke.

"No life is perfect, Sky. Families can be both great and difficult. I didn't have a perfect upbringing." He dropped his chin and shook his head, the movement slow, weighted. "Parenting's tough. There's no handbook, no prep course. By the time parents figure it out, the kids are heading out the door."

Sky reached over, took the joint from Billy, and inhaled. The tension in her limbs melted, her body easing into the familiar slats of the swing. She passed the joint back, eyes locked on him.

"Home life sucked, Billy. I spent too much time trying to keep the peace. Trying to make her happy." Her voice dimmed, lost in the swirl of thought. "I had a lot of time to think on the streets of San Fran. Long nights. Too many of them."

Billy kept his eyes on her, nodding—solid, quiet, present.

"I guess the early years were okay. Mom was around more when I was little. She cooked sometimes. Dad never asked much of her. He encouraged her to chase whatever passion she had—teaching, painting, going back to school. We must've been fine financially, because I don't remember her ever working. No money fights, at least not then. Dad just wanted us to be happy."

"Shit," Billy said. "My parents were always at each other's throats over money. Dad spent it. Mom hoarded it. You can guess how that played out."

Sky glanced at him, eyebrows raised—*You wanted honesty, right?*

Billy caught it. "Sorry, didn't mean to interrupt. Felt like I should say something."

She reached across her chest and plucked the joint from his hand again. "I'll let you know when it's your turn." She smirked, took a hit, then held it. "Now, mister, this weed is mine. You can sit and listen to my sob story or hit the road."

Billy smirked, shifted, and leaned back—arms crossed and smiling.

There was something about him—grounded, self-assured without swagger. Sky felt it. Noticed it. Couldn't place what the it was yet. She flicked the roach into the yard, where it disappeared into the blanket of ash. Not something she'd usually do, but nothing else would burn out there tonight.

"I won't say my dad worshipped me, but he loved me. Really loved me. Did all the right things. He was supportive, present when he could be—but he lived to work. And Mom... she let herself drown. She had every chance at happiness and chose not to take it."

Sky paused, the swing creaking beneath them.

"She didn't want to be happy. Or maybe didn't know how. Or maybe she just liked the attention she got for being miserable. She'd drop her tragedies on strangers if they let her."

The porch swing moved with a steady rhythm. Whether it was the weed or the motion, her pulse settled. She let out a breath, then smiled.

"Am I a lightweight, or is this strong weed?"

Billy laughed, head tilting back, the sound easy and full.

"If you didn't hog it, maybe you wouldn't be reeling."

"I'm not reeling," she said, laughing. "Okay, maybe a little."

"It's strong, yeah. But mostly, you're small. And not a regular smoker. Right?"

She scooted closer, telling herself it was just to avoid the swing's chain digging into her side. "Nope. Second time I've

306

ever smoked."

Billy choked on a laugh. "Seriously?"

"Yep. Not really into the drug scene. I'm paranoid. But tonight... I needed something."

She rubbed her eyes, rolled her neck.

"Okay, so why did you leave, Sky? You make it sound like things weren't that bad."

Sky studied him. There was something familiar in his posture, in his tone—echoes of her father. She hadn't felt this kind of pull in... ever, really. Childhood crushes, teen infatuations—sure. But this? This scared her. And it brought guilt with it.

She thought about grabbing her backpack, filling it with clean clothes, slipping out before anything could get complicated.

But she stayed.

It was time. Time to stop running. Time to say it.

Living on the street hadn't worked. This house—*her* dad's house—still felt like home. If her father would have her.

But that depended on what she had to say.

And what he'd do when he heard it.

The man responsible was gone. At least she hoped. Unless he came back.

"Shit," she mumbled.

"What?"

"Nothing, Billy."

She liked his name. *Billy*. Not Bill. *Bill* sounded like someone with taxes and a lawn to mow. *Billy* sounded like someone who might stay and play.

She stood and walked into the yard. Ash drifted around her, soft and silent. Billy followed, stepping beside her, both staring into the trees. The moon hung like a ghost behind the smoke. She stared at it, as gray as the ash settling in Billy's hair, dusting it lightly. She imagined him as an old man—and liked the thought.

Sky exhaled slowly. The air burned a little. Her arms were freckled with soot. She stared at them, remembering campfires—how the smell used to mean warmth and safety. Now it just meant ruin.

She pressed her lips together, drew a breath through her teeth, trying to filter the grit.

Her mind spun.

She stood there, uncertain of what to say. How to move forward.

Billy's voice, gentle but insistent, cut through the haze.

"You still haven't said why you left, Sky."

She slid her foot across the sidewalk, scattering a layer of ash into the air. Then she turned and climbed the porch steps. Billy followed but stopped at the bottom one.

There was something in his eyes—an honest, open kind of care that caught her off guard.

*Who the hell is this guy?*

She moved toward the porch swing, chewing on the words that never seemed ready. For so long, the memory of that camping trip, the one that fractured so many lives—lived only inside her, heavy and unspoken.

But she wanted to speak. Needed to.

She paced, trying to summon courage. Willing the words to form.

Finally, she stopped in front of Billy and looked up into his eyes. So damn beautiful. There was something in him she needed—something steady and secure. And whether she believed in fate or not, she couldn't ignore the odds of meeting him outside that diner, just as she'd fled the white van.

"I'm trying to find the courage, Billy," she said, her voice shaking. "I've been holding this for a long time."

Billy lifted his hands, palms open, offering them to her.

Without hesitation—like some Svengali pulling her into his calm—she placed her hands in his.

"Please don't tell anyone," she whispered. "Okay?"

Her chest heaved. Her heart felt like it might burst out of her rib cage in an *Alien*-style eruption—or shrivel and stop altogether.

Billy gave a weak, nervous laugh. "What did you do—kill someone?"

He saw the look on her face and immediately shook his head. "Sorry, Sky. That was a terrible joke."

He took a breath, steadying himself.

"Listen… whatever it is, it can't be so awful that you can't overcome it. I mean, look at you. You're smart, strong, beautiful. You survived on your own in the fucking streets of San Francisco. You came back. You're here. Whatever you need to say, I won't judge you. I like you, and I promise—no matter what happens between us—we'll always be friends. Okay?"

Sky watched his mouth move but didn't register the words. Not yet. Maybe later, if he stuck around, she'd ask him to repeat them.

She tightened her grip on his hands—harder than she meant to—then asked her heart to be kind.

*Let the truth out,* she begged, *even if it comes ragged and broken.*

"My best friend's dad raped me," she said. The words tumbled out in a rush. "My best friend's dad raped me. My dad relied on me to be responsible. My dad trusted me, and I let a man rape me."

Sky dropped Billy's hands and bolted—into the house, through the door, toward the kitchen. Away from any judgement.

Her breath caught in her throat; panic chased every step.

And in that desperate silence, she hoped—*begged*—that Billy would follow her inside and somehow make everything seem okay.

# Payne Creek Estates Part V - Now or Never

Leaping over the deputy's lifeless body sprawled across the blood-streaked porch, Mel knew—almost instantly—it was a dumb decision. One she'd later catalog as idiotic. Doubt ricocheted inside her skull like a super ball in a racquetball court. The young deputy's head looked like someone had erased half of it with an Etch-a-Sketch. Sour bile rose in her throat, burning as a heavy pit of regret settled in her gut like wet clay.

She wasn't afraid of risk—never had been—but this?

This bordered on reckless stupidity.

She landed hard in the front room. Her left shoulder slammed the cheap linoleum, skidding her across the entryway until she crashed against the side of a couch. Scrambling for cover, her face mashed into cigarette-stained upholstery. Her nose crinkled. Her mouth flattened. She jerked back with a quiet gag and focused on steadying her breath.

*God, please don't let the shooter start firing into this couch.*

A voice—no, voices—echoed behind her. Relief flickered. Whoever they were, they weren't in her line of fire, and it didn't sound like they'd seen her dive into the house. She stilled her body. Tuned her ears. Words remained garbled, lost in a surge of rage—or maybe just a blaring television.

The stench of cigarettes, gunpowder, and death thickened the air.

Her mind, unbidden, lurched backward—toward another time. Another place.

Another hell.

The cot creaked beneath her. Fabric, stale with sweat and dust, clung to her fatigues. Mel focused on her breathing. Even in combat, sleep—when it came—was sacred. Missions hit without warning, often at the worst possible moment. Preparation meant everything. Years of training had drilled one truth into her bones: sleep when you can.

Her body sank into the cot like wet cement. Third day on standby, filling in for a flu-ridden buddy. Her thoughts drifted stateside—green grass, mountains, cool, clear water. No sand.

But the dream never came.

Pulled back before REM could claim her, she snapped upright, grabbing her officer's hat. Within thirty minutes, she and her crew were airborne, piloting a C-130 toward a hot zone.

She throttled the aircraft hard. Ninety minutes in the air. No complications. They lit up the ground with a strafing run— precision fire chewing through the terrain, leveling everything in their path. Radio chatter confirmed: no second pass needed.

She landed in the zone. PJs leapt out with clean efficiency. Aside from a few rogue rounds punching holes in the plane's side, it was textbook. Almost.

The evac went fast. The wounded piled in. Up they went— engines roaring, wheels up, gone in minutes.

Back at base, news trickled in over headsets. Most of the Berets were intact—physically. One comms guy, bleeding and barely coherent, mumbled about his wife and kids. Another—a weapons sergeant, a woman—had saved the entire detachment.

Pulled two soldiers to safety. Took a position. Opened fire. Got caught by a landmine. Her legs were shredded.

There was no time to thank her. No comfort to offer. No mercy in the silence that followed. Only speed. Only survival.

*Team first.*

*Mission focused.*

*No hesitation.*

*No regret.*

*That came later.*

*Always later.*

A voice snapped Mel back.

"I know you're stealing from me; you paralyzed little thief."

Voice sounds crashed down the hall—sharp, human, angry. Not Kaley's voice. That left one possibility: the mother.

Mel's memory offered an image—decrepit, bitter, buried in a chair, chain-smoking her days away.

Could she be the shooter?

Doubt crept in.

Mel scanned the room.

Stayed low. Stayed on her ass—for now.

Leaning out from behind the couch, slow and deliberate, she let her left eye clear the filthy edge of the furniture.

The front door lay ahead.

Outside, police stirred. Ready to move.

Clock ticking.

She measured the distance. If everything went right, she could reach the door, surprise the shooter, and end it.

No weapon. No bat—she'd left that behind.

Stupid. No, that bat was five-hundred bucks and was meant to hit leather, not flesh and bone.

She scanned again.

Nothing worth grabbing. No lamp. No bottle. No blunt object. Just filth and furniture.

It had to be now.

Or never.

# By The Way

Sky sat at the kitchen table, staring across at Billy. Her eyes drifted to her hands—young, but not really. They trembled; the skin roughened by years spent in unforgiving places. Hands that looked older than they should.

She tried to stay focused on the cribbage game between them, the one her father had taught her on camping trips. But the memories pressed in—too fast, too heavy. Without warning, tears came again.

She started bawling.

The walls around her, the very roof that now shielded her from the falling ash outside, held too many ghosts. For a second, she thought about bolting—racing upstairs, slamming her door, drowning out the world with music like she used to during the worst of her teen years.

But she didn't. She couldn't. No more running. No more hiding.

Exhausted from sleepless nights and sick of avoiding everything that hurt, Sky stayed where she was. She buried her face in her hands and let the sobs shake through her.

She let the tears come. For once, she didn't try and hold them back.

She knew Billy was still there. That made it harder somehow—being witnessed. She wanted to say something, anything, but no words came. Just strangled sounds, broken syllables tumbling out of her like bingo balls clattering inside a metal cage.

Then came a sound—soft, familiar. The scrape of a chair on tile.

A moment later, Billy's warm, steady hand settled on her

shoulder.

She didn't look up.

His touch didn't ask anything of her. It was quiet. Solid. Comforting.

But even that kindness triggered a fresh wave of regret—memories of her father's hand, his presence, the long silence between them now. Her sobs deepened, her chest fighting for breath.

"It's okay, Sky," Billy said, his voice low and calm. "You're safe. You're home."

Minutes passed, silent and full.

She slowly worked to steady herself. Her breath hitched, but her body began to calm. Billy didn't move. His hand remained where it was—grounding her. Guarding her.

She hadn't known someone could care like this, especially someone she barely knew. But in his quiet way, Billy stood beside her like a sentinel, unwavering. And somehow, through the tears and the wreckage, that simple act offered her something she hadn't felt in a long, long time.

*Hope. Care. Love.*

Sky wiped her eyes with the backs of her fingers, then used her palms to clear the rest of the tears. Her breathing, still shaky, began to settle.

Billy stepped away, easing to the sink. She watched him open a cupboard, grab a glass, and fill it with water. When he turned back, there was calm in his expression—genuine, grounded, unforgettable.

He held the glass out to her.

"Drink this," he said gently. "Then I want you to take three deep breaths. Take another drink, then close your eyes and count to ten. And repeat to yourself: Today is a good day. I am where I need to be. The universe has my back, and I am open to whatever is in store for my life."

When she finished, she handed him the empty glass. Still seated, still reeling, but quieter inside.

"I don't know where you learned that" she said, her voice softer now. "But it helped. Thank you."

Billy set the glass in the sink and leaned back against the counter; arms loosely crossed.

"My mom," he said. "She's spiritual. Believes we're all connected, part of the universe—part of something bigger. When I was a teenager, I thought she was full of it. Used to get so embarrassed when she'd talk like that in front of my friends' parents."

"Really?" Sky asked, surprised.

He turned toward the window, watching ash drift against the glass like gray snow.

"Yeah. But now? I get it. She's different, sure—but the kind of different that matters. She's kind. Intuitive. Wants people to be happy. She just wants to live with intention and love and grace. And honestly? She's one of the wisest people I know."

Billy turned back to her, meeting her gaze.

"She sounds amazing," Sky said. "I'd like to meet her. I could use someone like that in my life—a strong, healthy adult woman who has her shit together."

She looked up at Billy and found the strength to smile. It wasn't much, but it made her feel lighter—like maybe, just maybe, things would be okay.

Billy, still gazing out the kitchen window, spoke without turning.

"Well, Sky, we'll have to see if we can arrange that sometime soon."

A pause.

"By the way… someone's walking up the sidewalk. Judging by their outfit, I'd say it's your dad."

# Grit and Disbelief

Creeping along at fifteen miles per hour on a road posted for fifty, the chief gripped the wheel with steady hands, his thoughts far from the empty street ahead. Over the years, he'd seen devastation in every form—twisted metal, scorched earth, lives changed in an instant. But this fire…

This one was different.

This one was personal.

The Rogue Valley burned—entire neighborhoods reduced to rubble. Hundreds of homes and businesses were gone. Thousands of lives changed forever. Ash swirled, twisted and fell, smoke hung heavy in the air, and flames still danced in the distance, devouring anything left to consume. Charred cars sat in driveways, the heat so intense their aluminum wheels had melted into silver puddles before solidifying like spilled mercury.

The fire had shown mercy in strange, selective ways—skipping over some homes entirely, as if by divine decision. It reminded the chief of those Midwest tornado photos: entire blocks flattened, yet one house left untouched, pristine in the middle of chaos. If there was a higher power, maybe those spared homes had earned favor in some cosmic lottery.

Earlier that day, the fire had roared past his neighborhood, driven by wind and fury. Now, as he made the final turn toward home, his thoughts shifted from destruction to what could be salvaged. The full extent of the damage wouldn't be known for weeks, maybe longer.

Not tonight.

Not in the dark.

He shook his head as he passed a familiar corner. The

bike shop—one he drove by every day—was gone. Nothing remained but a smoldering skeleton of charred steel, molten aluminum, and carbon strands from once-high-end bicycle frames.

At least he picked up Sandi's bike yesterday.

One small grace in a day with far too few.

Slowing the county rig, he eased up the driveway toward home. A wave of relief rolled through him at the sight of the house still standing—the house his grandfather built. It had survived. But for a shift in the wind, it could've been reduced to an ash stain on Southern Oregon's scorched soil, like so many others.

He skipped the mailbox. Mail probably hadn't run today—not with the chaos consuming the valley.

As he stared at the house, something caught him off guard: lights. Several of them. Inside and out.

He blinked, surprised. Could Sandi have made it home? No—impossible. They'd spoken just hours ago. She was still at her parents' place in Central Oregon. No way she could've gotten back that fast—not with all the road closures and fire detours.

Maybe Sarah, the neighbor? It'd be just like her—thoughtful and practical. She'd dropped by countless times over the years to shut windows before a storm, lock a door left ajar, turn off forgotten irrigation, or open the upstairs windows to cool the place in August heat. A good neighbor. One of the best.

He thought of the other neighbors, those lucky enough to still have homes. A twinge of guilt stirred in his chest, knowing hundreds of others weren't so fortunate.

But the lights…

They didn't feel like Sarah.

Something about them—too many, too warm, too lived-in.

A flicker of unease tightened in his gut.

Then, memory surged.

*The worst day of his life—the day he came home to a house empty of his daughter.*

Losing a child to death was one thing—unimaginable, but final. But losing a child by choice... having them walk away, disappear without a trace, not knowing if they were okay—that pain didn't end. It just kept chewing.

At least death, as brutal as it was, came with closure.

His throat was constricted. The muscles in the back of his neck pulled tight, like a rubber band stretched to its limit.

And inside, the lights kept flickering.

Staring through the windshield, he searched for any movement inside the house. His body, stiff from hours in the rig, had finally sunk into the leather seat—unwilling to move, whether from the ache or the reluctance of what he might not find.

Fear gripped him, unexpected and uninvited. *It reminded him of his first fire, decades ago—frozen outside a burning home, feet locked in figurative mud, paralyzed until his captain clapped a heavy hand on his shoulder and barked, "Get moving, Wilson. This isn't a fucking parade. You've got a job to do."*

That was the moment everything changed. He'd learned to shift fear into function, to treat fire like a job, not a monster. Since then, fear hadn't touched him.

Until now.

He stared at the second-story window. Light spilled through the curtains—Sky's bedroom.

His chest tightened. Breath shallow. His heart shriveled like an orange left too long in the sun. One hand gripped the steering wheel, trying to steady the shaking in his fingers. His mind raced—he wanted to call Sandi, to hear her voice, to make sense of what he was seeing.

*Maybe Sarah was up there.*

That would make sense. She'd check for open windows, trying to keep the ash out. She wouldn't know there weren't any left open. She might turn on lights.

*Yeah. That had to be it.*

He forced his fingers to unclench, pulled the key from the ignition, and stepped out into the smoky dusk. He paused beside the truck, eyes drifting toward the barn. Gratitude rose again—at least the land, the home, the history—they had survived.

*Maybe Sarah would invite him over later. Dinner. Distraction. Something simple and human to cut through the day's madness.*

Neighbors would have questions, and he welcomed that. Anything to keep his mind from spinning, from diving deeper into thoughts of Sky.

It happened every time—during long, stressful days.

Regret. Memory.

The aching question of whether he'd ever see her again.

Tonight was no different.

Fear and longing swirled in his chest, thick as the smoke above the trees.

Gathering forward momentum, his tired legs carried him up the sidewalk toward the porch. Each step felt heavier than the last. Ash coated the concrete like gray powder.

And then he noticed something strange—multiple sets of footprints.

*Is John with Sarah?*

That would be unusual. The man was a hermit. In the past twenty years, the chief could count on one hand the number of times he'd seen him outside their yard.

If both were here, maybe that meant dinner.

Sarah might even suggest they stay and eat—she'd cook, of course, and he and John would devour whatever she made.

320

But he knew the odds were slim.

Still, he let the thought carry him forward.

At the base of the steps, he stopped.

Something tugged at soul.

He turned, glancing down the driveway, across the road toward Sarah and John's house, as if the answers crowding his mind might be hiding in the shadows.

Then—

A sound. Faint. From the porch.

He turned.

Expecting Sarah. Maybe John.

But what he saw hit him like a punch to the chest.

His heart skipped, then lurched into overdrive—racing like a Formula 1 engine around the Monaco circuit. For a moment, reality stuttered. Smoke, ash, exhaustion—maybe they were playing tricks on him. He blinked, trying to make sense of it.

But the figure on the porch didn't fade.

Adrenaline surged. Emotion slammed into him like a pack of wolves tearing through his composure. His muscles locked. Legs trembled. Knees threatened to give. A tear slipped from the corner of his eye, tracing a path down his ash-smudged cheek before stopping—caught in the grit and disbelief.

# Sky

She heard her name—just one word, cracked and breathless. It stopped her cold.

"Sky."

Her father hadn't moved. He stood at the base of the steps, as if time had folded in on itself. Smoke curled around him, ash clinging to his coat, his face lined with exhaustion and disbelief.

She wanted to run to him, but her feet stayed planted. She couldn't read his eyes—not yet. Couldn't tell whether they held forgiveness… or something else entirely.

"Hi, Dad," she said, steadying her voice, even as her heart pounded.

He didn't respond. Just stared, as though looking at a ghost.

She stepped forward, into the glow of the porch light. Ash clung to her hair, and for a moment, it shimmered, sparkling like stars. She saw it then, in his eyes: a flicker of something soft breaking through the shock.

And just like that, the past stepped into the present.

She stood still, unsure of what came next.

But in that fragile space between the girl who left and the woman who returned, she saw it—reflected in his eyes, and felt it echo in her chest:

Memories of an Ash Covered Sky.

# A Southern Oregon Denouement

## Teddy

Teddy walked through the ruins of Payne Creek Estates against the advice of the police. The only reason they let him in was because of the deputies he'd met during the fire—and the fact that he wore hazmat coveralls and a mask. The area remained off-limits to the public, deemed hazardous and unstable. They gave him strict instructions: go to the maintenance shed, take whatever photos he needed, and leave.

As he moved down ash-covered streets, the scale of the destruction struck him harder than expected. He'd seen the photos. Watched the news. But standing in it—inhaling the scorched silence—was something else entirely.

Nothing remained but skeletal frames and smoldering piles. Asphalt and concrete marked where homes once stood. Trees thicker than a few inches were now blackened matchsticks. Everything else is gone. Just ash, lawnmowers, bicycles, wheelbarrows... warped metal and melted plastic, barely recognizable.

Teddy couldn't begin to fathom the financial loss. He wondered if it would ever be rebuilt. *Could* anyone start over in a place like this?

As he neared what used to be the maintenance shop, the question that haunted him since the fire was answered—no, he wouldn't have survived.

The shed was gone. Incinerated. A twisted shell of corrugated metal sagged inward, warped and blackened. The fiberglass panels that once alternated with the metal had vanished entirely, burned to a scatter of brittle fibers. If they rebuilt it, he'd tell them—*use all metal next time.*

He turned in a slow circle, taking it all in. Then, something caught his eye. On the ground, just a few feet away, lay his baseball cap. Covered in ash, but somehow untouched by flame.

He picked it up, shook it clean, and held it for a long moment.

Would he ever work here again?

A wave of depression rolled through him. Seeing it now—what was left—he realized: his job was gone. Gone for good he couldn't say but he couldn't imagine it returning any time soon.

*Shit.*

He hadn't looked for work in almost two decades. Panic tugged at the edges of his thoughts.

And then came another weight—heavier, quieter.

Deputy Morrow.

Teddy had worked side by side with him, helping to evacuate residents. The young man had been calm, focused, exactly the kind of cop you wanted in a crisis. And now he was gone. Shot while doing his job. No warning. No chance.

Teddy swallowed hard, eyes stinging. That kind of loss... it didn't make sense.

He forced a breath, then glanced back one last time at the place that had been his second home for nearly twenty years.

Turning, he made his way to the front of the development, back to where he'd parked.

Passing the damn gate, the one that had felt like a bad omen less than forty-eight hours ago—he gave it a half-hearted kick. Not out of anger. Just frustration. Disbelief. Loss.

He climbed into his pickup, started the engine, and turned toward the road.

Toward his daughter's home.

Spending the rest of the day with Emma was the only thing that made sense now. A small comfort in the aftermath of devastation.

A much-needed salve after witnessing what remained of Payne Creek Estates—and after remembering those who didn't make it out.

## Mel & Kaley

Mel tapped the espresso machine's filter against the small stainless-steel compost bin on her kitchen counter. After rinsing it, she glanced at the two nearly perfect lattes and smiled. She picked them up and carried them through the kitchen, across the dining room, and out the sliding glass door to the deck.

"Here you go, Kaley. Hope you'll like it," Mel said, setting the latte on the side table beside her.

Kaley looked up and smiled. "Someone made something for me. I'll love it. Food always tastes better when someone else makes it."

She took a careful sip. Foam settled on her upper lip like a caterpillar taking a nap. "Why is that?"

Mel chuckled but didn't answer. Some questions didn't need one.

She dropped into a deck chair beside Kaley, the two of them surrounded by open sky and the distant, smoke-streaked sweep of the Rogue Valley.

"What a view, Mel. Fuck, this is nice," Kaley said, exhaling. "I'd be out here all the time. Jesus—yeah, that's Mt. McLoughlin, right?"

Mel nodded.

Kaley tried to focus on the beauty of Southern Oregon surrounding her, but the last forty-eight hours had frayed her nerves. Her home, her car, her mother—everything gone, consumed by tragedy. And now? She had no idea what came next.

"I'm out here a lot," Mel said. "Even when it's cold. I wrap myself in a blanket and sit. It's the late-summer smoke that sometimes keeps me inside. Otherwise... this deck is my favorite place."

They settled into a quiet moment.

Mel found herself staring—not meaning to—at Kaley's carbon-fiber legs. The way she moved, how naturally she adjusted, fascinated her. *Did it hurt?*

Kaley noticed. She always noticed.

"I make do," she said casually. "I've had them long enough that I don't think about it much. They're a part of me now. Except two days ago, when I was stuck—trapped with my wicked fucking mother. Otherwise, I can do just about anything anyone else can."

Mel smiled. "Busted. We've talked so little over the years about anything with depth, I forget sometimes. I've probably already asked this, but... do your legs hurt?"

Kaley grinned. "Um, no—I don't have legs, asshole."

Mel blinked. Kaley laughed softly.

"I'm fuckin' with you."

She took another sip, then continued, more serious now.

"Sometimes, yeah. The ends ache or throb. Especially in the cold. And I still get phantom sensations—like my toes are curling, or my calves are cramping. It's weird how your brain refuses to believe they're gone. It's like part of me is still reaching for something that isn't there."

She tapped one of the carbon limbs with a knuckle, producing a dull thunk.

"But mostly, I've adjusted. They're just...part of me now."

326

Silence stretched. Mt. McLoughlin, Table Rocks, and a see of southern Oregon timber listened.

Mel nodded. "I think about that day a lot. I wish there was more I could've done."

Kaley's tone sharpened. "What—besides saving my life?"

"You know what I mean."

"I do," Kaley said. "Look, I owe you my life—again. My guardian angel named Mel. An angel named Mel... that's fucking weird. I don't think George Bailey would believe me if I told him. But really—what the hell? We haven't talked in a year, and you decide to show up today?"

Mel laughed, taking a long sip of her latte, staring out toward the valley thinking about walking up Roxy Anne and if Kaley could do the hike.

"Something pulled me here," she said. "No idea why. Just this... feeling. Like a magnet. Probably didn't hurt that I flew over your place a dozen times today."

"Thank the heavens you did. I would've burned alive. I couldn't get upright—too close quarters, too much smoke. My mother—God. I still can't believe she went out like that. I wonder if the autopsy will show anything..."

Mel shook her head. "I'm sorry, Kaley. I don't have the right words."

"I'd wanted to move out for months, perhaps a year. I felt... stuck. I even wished her dead sometimes."

"What?" Mel asked, startled.

"You heard me. She was awful. Not that I wanted her to die that way—hell, not at your hands—but it could've been worse. She could've gone in the fire."

They both took another drink, the silence growing heavy again.

Kaley broke it, her voice lighter.

"That stunt you pulled—taking her down like that—holy

shit. I keep replaying it. Watching you go airborne and slam her into that cheap-ass floor."

"I didn't know what else to do. The cops seemed stuck with options. The fire was coming fast. And honestly? I was hungry. I wanted to get home."

"You and your fuckin' appetite Mel, Jesus!"

Mel's laughed out loud then her smile faded as she stared back out over the valley.

"I thought you'd lost it. I was sure I'd have to confront you. I didn't even know your mother knew how to handle a gun. I thought... I thought it was you."

"You thought I shot a cop?" Kaley's voice tightened.

Mel winced but didn't retreat.

"From my perspective... I knew you were trained. I knew you weren't in a great place after leaving the military. It wasn't hard to imagine the worst. I just hoped like hell it wasn't you."

She paused, choosing her words with care.

"Based off everything you shared with me over the years, I was not a fan of your mother... but I'm still sorry she's gone."

Kaley's eyes brimmed. Swollen and glossy, ready to burst. Mel noticed and shifted gears.

"Like I said, Kaley, you can stay here as long as you need. The whole downstairs is yours. I mean it. Payne Creek's not getting rebuilt anytime soon—not in months. Probably years."

Kaley smiled through the emotion, grateful for the pivot.

"Thanks, Mel. I don't know what to say. I promise it won't be long.

By the way... what size pants and shirts do you wear?"

They both burst out laughing, the tension finally breaking.

Mel wiped her eyes.

"Ah, hell no, girl. I don't think so."

# Sky

Easing out of her seat in Literature class at Southern Oregon University, Sky smiled. Tonight, she'd get to see Cake at the Britt Festival, her dad's favorite band. He used to go on and on about that old Outdoor Research video set to *"Short Skirt/Long Jacket."* Sky hadn't been much of a fan, but the band was growing on her. She liked *Comfort Eagle*—had even written a paper on the lyrics for her Lit class. The professor—fifty-something and kind, someone who reminded her of what her mother might have been like, if she still walked the earth—praised it. Sky wasn't sure she was any closer to unlocking the song's meaning, but it earned her an A.

Maybe she'd ask the band herself. Post-show meet and greet? Stranger things happened.

With her last class of the day behind her, she strolled toward the student union, knowing he'd be there—iced latte and peanut butter cookie in hand. Their new Thursday ritual.

She loved the SOU campus. Something about it reminded her of Fog City, minus the filth. It wasn't the buildings or the trees, it was the energy. Still, old instincts tugged at her. Her eyes scanned the usual places: behind shrubs, stairwells, loading docks—places she used to look for a safe place to sleep.

She giggled to herself. *I have a bed now. I have a home.*

But survival habits weren't easy to rinse from the brain.

At the entrance to the union, she nodded at a few familiar faces, then scanned the room. There, in their usual spot, sat Billy—dusty, tired, and completely hers.

She still couldn't believe they were a couple and giggled at the thought. Her first real relationship. Maybe her only. Maybe her last. She'd tell someone eventually, maybe her dad during their planned camping trip. Maybe not.

She reached the table. Billy stood and gave her the hug she loved most—firm but not overpowering. Just enough to let her know she mattered.

"Hey there, filthy man. How was your day?"

"Lousy," Billy said as they sat. Sky picked up her latte, took a long drink—extra shot, splash of coconut milk. Perfect. She needed caffeine tonight. No way she was falling asleep on the Britt lawn again—not like when she was a kid under the stars, listening to classical music. Her mother had smiled in public, but once the car door closed, the anger poured out in sharp, whispered screams over Sky falling asleep. That was their last Britt Festival together.

"I'm sorry," Sky said. "Uncle getting mouthy again?"

"No. He was fine. It's just the heat. And the damn roofs. I'm wiped. I keep trying to stay positive, but I've got to find something else."

Sky wrapped the peanut butter cookie and tucked it in her backpack—a treat for this weekend's camping trip.

"Thank you for my goodies," she said. "I'm so glad you're here. You're going to find something. I know it. I'm impressed with your grit. I'd have quit and hoped for the best."

Billy smiled, leaned back, and adjusted the brim of his SOU Raiders hat—faded, sweat-stained, and well-loved. An impromptu gift from Sky.

"If it weren't for you—and needing survival money—I'd be gone. But lately, I'm starting to wonder if there's anything here for me at all."

"You can always move in with me and Dad... and Sandi," she added, slightly delayed. She liked Sandi. But the house was hers and her father's first. Still, the thought of her dad being in love—or at least not alone—was something she planned to ponder under the stars.

"Did you bring your stuff so you can get ready at my place?"

"Yep. Remembered everything. I'm just glad I get tomorrow off—even if I have to say goodbye to you for a few days."

Sky had lain awake last night, thinking about school, the weekend trip, and Billy. She realized they hadn't spent a day apart since the night she stood covered in ash, staring at her father as he stared at her in disbelief.

"Good," she said. "You can shower with me, Mr.—after all, water conservation, you know."

She grinned as Billy flushed red and ducked his head.

"Um... won't your dad be home?"

"Probably. You think he'd kick us out?"

Billy blushed deeper and slurped the last of his Rebel—something he never did. Sky laughed.

*That monkey brain of his is picturing it right now.*

"I love how simple men are," she teased. "Keep them happy in the shower or bed—cough, cough—and they'll take a bullet for you. It's amazing there are so many divorces."

Sky stood, picked up the empty cups, and tossed them in the recycling bin. Then she turned and held out a hand.

"Come on, my dirty knight. Let's get you cleaned up so we can go lie under the stars. Cake better put on a good show, or I swear I'll give my dad shit for the rest of his life."


# Chief

Fully retired and still adjusting to the rhythm of civilian life, Chief Murphy Wilson pulled the now-finished Mercedes Sprinter van out of the barn and parked it in the shade out front, beneath the tall pines. Sitting in the driver's seat, he chuckled, looking back over his shoulder at what was once just an empty shell—now transformed into a road-tripping dream on wheels.

A small kitchen, fridge-freezer combo, enclosed shower with a composting toilet, fresh and gray-water storage, queen-sized bed, a slide-out shelf for two mountain bikes, camping gear, even a portable shower. Most of it unnecessary. All of it awesome. He couldn't wait to hit the road with Sandi.

But, as fate would have it, Sandi would be the first to take it out—solo. Heading to Bend to see her parents.

He laughed, shaking his head at the memory of her pitch.

"Well, hey," she'd said, "if you and Sky are going to go tent camping like old times, why don't I take the Sprinter to Bend? It might be best if one of us tests it out solo first before our first trip together. Don't you think?"

She'd laughed, expecting the old Murphy's reflexive no.

Instead, he kissed her forehead and said,

"I think that's a great idea. I'd love for you to take it and tell me how it handles."

Her eyebrows had raised with a noticeable flare.

"Haha, very funny. Who am I even talking to?"

"I'm serious," he said. "Call it the new me. You should take it. That way if something isn't quite right, you've got a house to retreat to. Beats being out in the woods together with a broken water pump and a bad attitude."

"You're serious?" she'd asked again.

"Dead."

Sandi had grinned and nodded.

"I liked the old Murphy, but this new version, he gets me hot all over."

They both laughed.

"I really am happy you and Sky are getting this time," she added. "Where are you going again?"

"Fish Lake. Outside of Tiller. Middle of nowhere. Took her there once when she was nine or ten—just the two of us. First time we did an overnight alone. It's got great hiking, mountain lakes, and trout begging to be pan-fried. Paddleboarding too, if we're crazy enough to haul them up there."

Sandi scrunched her nose.

"Three days in the woods? Can you even fish that long?"

"We'll fish. But there's hiking, hammocks, books, lake photography, walkie-talkie tests, cribbage... all of the best camping shit."

"Glad you're taking her and not me," Sandi said. "As you know, my idea of roughing it is pulling into the parking lot of a five-star resort. I'll use the Sprinter van for bike storage and a backup bathroom."

Murphy laughed.

"So, your 'I love camping' we were first getting to know each other was just bait?"

"Pretty much," she smirked. "I'll camp if I have to. But not in a tent."

"Fair enough."

He started down the porch steps, then stopped.

"Babe, I'm heading to the barn to get Sky's and my gear ready for tomorrow."

"Why is Billy going again?"

"He's not. He's just driving us. I don't want to leave the pickup eight miles from camp. Feels like an invitation for hooligans."

"Hooligans? Does anyone say that word anymore?"

"Only wise, intelligent people."

He exaggerated the word—*hoo-li-gans*—until Sandi chuckled.

"Okay, okay, wiseass. You can stop now."

Murphy turned toward the barn.

"Love you. Be in soon."

"Don't take too long. We're seeing Cake at Britt,

333

remember?"

He paused.

"No, I didn't remember. Why are we seeing Cake the night before a 5 a.m. departure for camping? Whose brilliant idea was that?"

Sandi laughed.

"Not mine. You're the one who bought four tickets and told Sky and Billy we were taking them to see 'one of the best bands around.' Cake, really?"

Murphy tilted his head back and let out a deep laugh, whistling *"Short Skirt/Long Jacket"* as he walked. Thinking about strong women in the wild, he felt a twist of nerves. He hadn't had much time with Sky since retiring. Since the fire.

He'd pulled away when she was young, burying himself in the safety and structure of work. It wasn't noble, and it certainly wasn't brave. He'd tell her this weekend; he'd been scared. That he hadn't known how to be a good father, so he hid in the one place he felt competent.

*Dumbass,* he muttered.

At the barn, he took a deep breath and pushed open the doors. The gear was stacked neatly—some of it untouched in years. He'd need to inspect everything, watch for moth holes and signs of rats.

*Little bastards better not have chewed through the tent.*

He popped open the first storage bin.

Inside, a pair of pristine walkie-talkies lay on top.

And just like that, a grin stretched across his face—wide and honest.

The kind he hadn't worn in years.

A smile the size of a Southern Oregon crescent moon.

# Author's Final Thoughts

## On Writing *Memories of an Ash Covered Sky*

I grew up in Southern Oregon, surrounded by towering pines, winding rivers, and the kind of natural beauty that settles into your bones. The landscape shaped me—fishing local streams, camping in the mountains with friends and high school love, watching sunsets from places that haven't changed much, though I have. What once felt ordinary now feels special. I see it all with more presence—because of where I've been, what I've lost, and what I've learned to appreciate. In my youth I loved the outdoors, the quiet in it, the adventure. And I still do. More than ever.

In September 2020, I—like so many others—watched the Almeda Fire tear through my hometown region. It wasn't just homes and businesses that burned. It was history. It was memory. It was pieces of ourselves. The fire moved so fast, so violently, that even now it feels surreal. Entire neighborhoods were turned to ash in hours. Generations of life—gone.

Writing *Memories of an Ash Covered Sky* was my attempt to make sense of that loss. To capture the emotional truths that don't always make it into headlines. The characters in this story, while fictional, are rooted in real feelings—grief, guilt, survival, and the complicated bond between parents and children.

For me, this story isn't just about fire. It's about the fires we carry inside—the slow-burning regrets, the sudden flare-ups of anger or love, the sparks of hope we fight to keep alive. It's about the quiet, internal reckonings we all go through. Learning when to fight and when to forgive—others, and ourselves.

As a father, as a son, and as someone who has sometimes gotten it wrong in the name of good intentions, I felt compelled to explore how parent-child relationships can bend, break, and—with care—begin again.

One thing I've learned—and something many of the characters in this story come to understand—is that sometimes, forgetting is healthier than remembering. That might sound strange, maybe even wrong to some. But some memories burn hotter than they teach. There's a difference between honoring the past and living in it. And it's okay to let some things turn to ash. To not carry every regret like a badge. To move forward. It almost always makes more sense to paddle with the current.

So, if you've read this story and saw pieces of yourself in Sky, or Mel, or Kaley, or Teddy—or even in Chief Wilson—I hope you also see the possibility of healing. The beauty in second chances. And the strength it takes not just to survive, but to begin again.

Keep going. Keep moving forward. Remember to enjoy the Journey. And never forget; some of the most beautiful skies are the ones that come after the smoke clears.

—Mike Walters

# Memories of an Ash Covered Sky

Thank you for reading *Memories of an Ash Covered Sky*. It means the world to me that you chose to spend your time with Chief and Sky, walking alongside them through their struggles, their fears, and their hopes. Writing this story was both a challenge and a gift, and I'm grateful that you trusted me with a few hours of your life to share in their journey.

If the story resonated with you, I'd love to hear your thoughts. Leaving a review—whether on Amazon, Powell's, Barnes & Noble, IngramSpark, or wherever you purchased your copy—helps more than you might imagine. Reviews not only help other readers discover my work, but they also inspire me to keep writing stories that matter.

I'd love to stay connected. You can subscribe to my newsletter at mikewaltersnovels.com for updates, behind-the-scenes insights, and early news on upcoming books. And if you'd like to drop me a note, I'd love to hear from you.

Thank you again for being part of this journey. Keep an eye out—my next novel is coming later this year.


With gratitude,


Mike Walters

Made in United States
Troutdale, OR
05/17/2025

31289937R00204